Battlefield U

MW00875825

Book One of the Red Storm Series

By James Rosone and Miranda Watson

Disclaimer

This is a fictional story. All characters in this book are imagined, and any opinions that they express are simply that, fictional thoughts of literary characters. Although policies mentioned in the book may be similar to reality, they are by no means a factual representation of the news. Please enjoy this work as it is, a story to escape the part of life that can sometimes weigh us down in mundaneness or busyness.

Copyright Information

©2017, James Rosone and Miranda Watson, in conjunction with Front Line Publishing, Inc. Except as provided by the Copyright Act, no part of this publication may be reproduced, stored in a retrieval system or transmitted in any form or by any means without the prior written permission of the publisher.

Table of Contents

Chapter 1

The Shot Heard Round the World

July 2017

Kharkiv, Ukraine

Freedom Square

Petro Kolomoisky was tired after working his eight-hour shift at the steel mill. His father and grandfather had been steelworkers, and it had seemed only natural to follow in their footsteps, but it had become a difficult path. This was one of the first months that business had been good enough for the mill to run a full forty-hour workweek. Petro meandered toward Freedom Square, where tonight's political rally was taking place, and he suddenly felt incredibly hungry. As he sniffed the air, he could smell the charbroiling of some chicken kebabs from one of the vendor trucks parked nearby. His stomach began to grumble, and he knew he would need to stop and grab something to eat.

"Hey, there you are, Petro…"

Petro turned around and smiled broadly as he recognized his friend, Andriy. The two of them had known each other since childhood, when they used to play in the same sandbox near their homes.

"I had just about given up on you," said Andriy jokingly.

"We had a full shift today at the mill. I just got off work," Petro replied. He waved his friend over to where he was waiting in line to get some dinner from the food truck.

"The crowds have really come out tonight. Look at all these people," Andriy said, motioning toward the developing assembly.

"Yeah, I'm surprised so many people have shown up after everything that went on last night," Petro replied. He paid for his kebab and started to walk toward the edge of the square. He took a deep breath of the steam that was drifting from the meat, letting the spices fill his nostrils before he took a giant bite. The juices ran down the side of his mouth, and he dabbed at it with a napkin.

"Those police officers got what they deserved," his friend retorted angrily. Andriy had gotten hit by one of the riot police truncheons two days ago, losing a tooth in the process. He was still fuming about it.

Petro sighed. "Andriy, I am really sorry you were punched. It was wrong of the riot police to have attacked us like that, especially when our protests have been peaceful and completely legal. But no one deserves to lose their life over this, even the police."

He looked across the growing throng of people. The crowds had been protesting in Kharkiv a lot this summer because of the breakdown in diplomatic talks in Kiev; folks were angry that no real progress was being made. The political leaders in the capitol were pushing for policies that would integrate Ukraine into the EU, which many feared would strip away the country's wealth and pass it off to France, Germany, and Britain, just like what they had seen in Greece. This was despite popular support; more than half of the citizens of Ukraine wanted to join the Russian trade union with several of the other former Soviet states, believing that this would keep more of people's money out of the hands of fat-cat politicians.

Kicking a small stone as they walked toward the large mass of people, Andriy grumbled, "I know. I feel bad for those officers' families. I do. But they had no right to just come in like they did and ambush us. Something must change, my friend. This constant bickering in Kiev is tearing our country apart."

****

As the protesters continued to pour into Freedom Square, Colonel Petr Croski was ready. The central government in Kiev had ordered his Anti-Terrorism Unit or

ATU to Kharkiv to put down this protest movement before it grew any larger or spread any further. After several police officers had been killed the other day, it had been determined that an ATU had to be sent in to deal with this mess. President Groysman was not going to allow the city of Kharkiv and the surrounding region to erupt into civil war like the rest of Eastern Ukraine had. The time for negotiating was over; now it was time to restore order and bring the country back together, even if that meant the use of force.

Major Dimitri Dremov walked up to his commander, who was standing near the armored vehicle that was acting as their command vehicle. "Sir, I have a company of soldiers at the east end of the city, ready to move in and close off the eastern exit of Freedom Square. I also have another company opposite the zoo. They are prepared to move in when you give the order," he said with a smile on his face.

They had been planning this operation for nearly a day. Their goal was to apprehend as many of the protesters as they could and charge them with crimes against the state. Then, they would identify the ringleaders and charge them with treason and fomenting insurrection against the government.

Pleased with the news, Colonel Croski handed his deputy his flask to join him in a little sip before the operation began. "The snipers are in place, right?" He wanted to be prepared in case things turned violent.

Major Dremov nodded as he took a swig of vodka and handed the flask back, "Yes. I have the three sniper positions set up. I've personally seen their positions and they have a good overwatch of where our troops will be."

"Excellent. Then all we need to do now is sit back and wait for the main speakers at the rally to show up and let the police begin to box them in. Once they herd the crowd into the target area, then send the men in," ordered Colonel Croski.

****

Oleksandr Prasolov looked out at the eager faces of the crowd. Their energy fed him, filling him with an adrenaline that overcame the fear of publicly contradicting the central government. Now that he had children, the legacy that he left behind was so much more important to him than any potential suffering he might have to endure in this life.

Oleksandr was from Kharkiv. He had met his wife in high school and married her before leaving to attend undergraduate university and graduate school in London. After completing his master's degree in economics from the London School of Economics in the mid-1990s, he had gone on to work for a well-known global management consulting firm. He had led a team for his firm in Russia as the government worked to privatize much of the economy, which had been state-owned during the era of the Soviet Union. Despite his busy schedule, Oleksandr and his wife managed to have two sons during this time. He'd then directed many other major projects for his firm, traveling to a number of former Soviet republics. Being fluent in English, Russian, and Ukrainian had given him an edge in being able to handle the complex privatization projects these former Soviet republics were undertaking.

After Oleksandr had made partner with the firm, his wife gave birth to their twin daughters. At that point, he had four children, all under the age of seven. One Christmas, as his kids were running around him playing with their new presents, he suddenly realized his children were growing up right before him, but he hadn't been there for them as much as he should have. One of his young sons crawled into his lap, and as he kissed the little head before him, he wondered how much of their young lives he'd already missed because of his job. His wife and children might have been living a posh lifestyle in London, but he'd been spending most of his time away from them, traveling from one country to another.

If he didn't change something in his life soon, he realized that he'd never be the father his children deserved.

After the holiday, he reached out to some of his contacts back in Kharkiv and was offered a job in the governor's office, helping him with growing the economy in the region. Within a year of taking that position, he was offered a position as a deputy minister in the Yanukovych administration. The President was in the process of negotiating the Ukraine-European Union Association Agreement, which would help to integrate Ukraine slowly into the European Union. While Oleksandr had been a supporter of the EU as an expatriate living in London, the more he delved into the details of this agreement, the more he saw this was not as great a deal for Ukraine as the government had been led to believe.

He'd known Ukraine was struggling financially, but he saw that the proposed agreement wasn't going to help the situation. In order for his country to receive any of the EU subsidies, or a bailout from the European Commission or the International Monetary Fund, they would have to undergo a series of austerity measures just like Greece, Spain, and Portugal. This would cripple Ukraine, taking their short-term issue and making it a long-term economic problem.

He brought these concerns up to others in his committee and to the president; however, most of them were willing to go along with the austerity if it meant Ukraine could get the bailout money they needed and move politically further away from Russia. Oleksandr was frustrated that no one listened to him.

Then, one day, President Yanukovych asked him to start talks with Russia about joining the Eurasian Customs Union, which was led by Russia and included the countries of Armenia, Belarus, Kazakhstan, and Kyrgyzstan. Having led a number of privatization projects in many of these countries, Oleksandr was familiar with this customs union and the benefit it could provide Ukraine. The Russians had also offered to infuse Ukraine with a lump sum of cash without imposing austerity upon them. They'd even offered a heavily reduced price on natural gas, which would further help the Ukrainian economy.

Unfortunately, the Euromaidan uprising had taken place and then spun out of control. Before he knew it, President Yanukovych had been removed from his role within the government and forced to leave Kiev. Yanukovych fled to Russia, and the Ukrainian government was taken over by a pro-fascist EU-dominated element. However, Oleksandr hadn't been willing to let his country fall into the hands of these rogue fascists who were trying to bring his nation back into civil war. By working with Russia and other separatist groups, he gained enough support to rally others around his cause. Together, they called for Eastern Ukraine to become independent from the central government and join the other separatist regions.

Oleksandr began to hold rallies all across the region. With each passing event, he felt more and more confident that he was gaining the support of the people there. This was now his third evening speaking in Kharkiv, and by far the largest crowd; nearly ten thousand people gathered to hear him deliver his message.

One of the community organizers worked the crowd up into a frenzy. The people roared with excitement as the lead organizer of the event introduced him, waving for him to come to the center stage. Oleksandr smiled as he walked toward his friend, shaking his hand as he took the microphone from him. The crowd slowly calmed themselves, enough so he could speak and be heard.

"My fellow citizens, I want to thank you for your support and for coming here tonight to hear me speak. Our nation has been torn apart by those wanting to impose the will of the German-dominated EU on us. Let us not forget that it was the fascist Germans who occupied our nation once. Now they want to occupy us again—this time, through their dominance and control of the EU."

The crowd roared. The people were really eating this rhetoric up. People saw what was happening in Greece, Spain, and Portugal and didn't want that same fate of austerity to be imposed upon them as well.

Oleksandr raised his hands to calm the people. "Look at the southern EU members," he continued. "Greece has been reduced to a beggar nation. They have over fifty percent unemployment…and this has everything to do with the German-imposed austerity they had to agree to in order to receive a bailout from the European Central Bank. Look at what has happened to their country—not just from the austerity, but from the migrant crisis that once again has been created by the fascist German government."

"They welcome these Muslims into their country by the hundreds of thousands. Now, millions of Muslim refugees are flooding across the Greek, Italian, Macedonian, Bulgarian, and Hungarian borders." The crowd booed.

"These Muslims do not represent our European Christian values, yet the Germans, in their effort to divide and control Europe, have imported them by the millions to sow chaos and anarchy. If the fascist jackals in Kiev get their way, Ukraine will become a part of the EU, and then we will have to accept the German austerity plans and take in hundreds of thousands of Muslim refugees, just like every other EU member."

"I say enough! It is time for the people of Kharkiv to rise up and form our own republic, independent of the fascist-led government in Kiev!"

Now the gathering cheered wildly. Oleksandr let the roar of the crowd wash over him as he stood there, basking in the energy of it all. Thousands upon thousands of supporters chanted his name and demanded that they separate from the central government.

Within minutes of the end of Oleksandr's speech, police dressed in riot gear began to show up at several entrances to Freedom Square. They pulled out their loud speakers and ordered the crowd, "Disperse! Leave the square! If you refuse, you will be arrested!"

Oleksandr grabbed the microphone he had just relinquished to the next speaker and yelled to the crowd, "See?! The fascist government doesn't want your voices to be heard! They want you to submit to their iron will and that of Germany! Will we submit?"

The crowd angrily shouted a collective, "No! We will not submit!"

Seeing that the situation was only escalating, the police tossed dozens of tear gas canisters into the crowd. As the people began to wail, screaming from the pain of the chemicals attacking their eyes and lungs, the officers stormed in, yelling with a unified roar to create the maximum psychological impact.

Several armed security personnel rushed the stage to protect Oleksandr and the other speakers as the riot police made their way toward the stage. Then, without warning, a single shot rang out and hit Oleksandr in the head. The side of his face exploded, splattering skull fragments, brain matter and blood on one of the community organizers standing next to him. His body collapsed to the ground.

Several more shots rang out. More speakers on the stage began to drop. Some had been instantly killed like Oleksandr, while others howled from the pain of their injuries.

A number of the armed security guards began to fire wildly at where they thought the snipers were. At first, the riot police were unsure if the shots were being fired at them, but when one of the police captains saw the armed guards on the stage start to shoot at something in their general direction, he ordered the officers around him, "Use your rubber bullets on the crowd!"

The crowd began to drop like flies. Some were seriously injured by the impact of the fast-flying projectiles. Others were simply stunned with the shock of being shot.

****

Petro had just turned to tell Andriy that they should try to get out of the square when he saw dozens of military vehicles blocking their avenues of escape. The shooting intensified, and the teargas cloud continued to rise and move closer to them.

"Andriy, we need to find a way out of here!" Petro yelled.

"I know," said his friend, scanning the scene for any possible mode of escape. "Over there, look. If we can get to that store, we can see if they have a back entrance we can use to get away."

Petro nodded. They both bolted toward the store, almost running straight into several other protesters. The people were all screaming and running in different directions. It was sheer chaos. They couldn't believe what was happening. Someone had just assassinated Oleksandr Prasolov right in front of thousands of his supporters. If they survived the evening, there was going to be hell to pay.

Andriy made it to the entrance of the store. He pulled on the doorknob, only to find the owner had locked it. He turned around to tell Petro when suddenly he was hit hard by something in the left shoulder. He grabbed at his shoulder and pulled his hand back. Blood oozed through his fingers.

"Andriy! You've been shot! Are you OK?" Petro yelled over the screams of everyone around him.

His friend looked dazed. Andriy didn't respond to his question, but instead stared down at his hand as if he were confused by the red liquid pulsing through his fingers.

"I feel so cold…" he mumbled, which was a strange statement considering that it was the middle of July.

Andriy leaned his head against the doorsill to rest his head and closed his eyes for a second…he drifted off and his body slumped to the ground.

By the time Petro got to his friend, he could see that Andriy was dead. *"The bullet must've hit something important,"* he thought as he helplessly grabbed at his friend's hand in grief.

Just then, a soldier ran up to Petro and whacked him in the side of the head with something heavy. His world went black.

Chapter 2
Escalation

August 2017
Kiev, Ukraine
US Embassy, Chancellery

Ambassador Duncan Rice sat at his mahogany desk, reviewing several proposals for bringing eastern Ukraine back into the fold as he sipped on his morning coffee and nibbled on his everything bagel smothered with cream cheese. He wanted to go over the options again before his meeting with the Ukrainian prime minister tomorrow. The PM had pressed the Secretary of State for a review of the current options being pursued and asked if new political and military options could be drawn up. Ambassador Rice and his staff had worked around the clock for almost a month before the Secretary of State had finally given his blessing on the proposals.

The embassy staff's proposal was for continuing sanctions against Russia, maybe even strengthening them. This policy had been implemented by the previous president's administration, with mixed results. The goal of the sanctions was to make the Russian government hurt enough that they would stop their support of the rebels in Eastern Ukraine. So far, all it had done was antagonize Russia into a tit-for-tat response. They had been sticking their nose into the affairs in the Middle East and vetoing additional sanctions against North Korea, despite that country's continued violation of previous UN sanctions. However, as the sanctions stayed in place, they were starting to have an effect on a number of influential Russian businesspersons. The hope was that strengthening this approach would provide more expedient results.

The second proposal had been put together by the nondiplomatic side of the embassy, the CIA's Chief of Station and the Defense Attaché's Office. The plan involved sending US Special Forces soldiers as advisors to direct the Ukrainians on how best to defeat the rebels. The Department of Defense's Office for Defense Cooperation had helped to make this plan possible through a massive increase in foreign military aid since the start of the Gates administration in January.

As he read the proposal, Ambassador Rice had to admit that it looked like it would work, though he still had a lot of concerns that it might provoke an excessively negative response from the Russians.

Unlike most diplomats, Ambassador Rice had a good sense of how the military worked. He had served as an officer in the Marines before leaving to pursue a career in the diplomatic service of his country. He knew the enemy would respond in ways that could not yet be calculated, as in any military operation. Chances were, this plan, as good as it was, would not survive first contact with the enemy. His goal was to solve conflicts through diplomacy whenever possible. Military force should only be used as a last resort, not a first option.

Rice had been a career diplomat with the Department of State for nearly eighteen years. As a diplomat, his purpose was to represent the interests of the United States and to help defuse tensions and conflicts in whichever country he was assigned. He still felt a peaceful solution could be found in Ukraine, though it was becoming increasingly difficult as tensions between Washington and Moscow continued to mount. Duncan sat back in his leather office chair and placed the papers down on the desk in front of him. He closed his eyes, thinking back to how he had become the ambassador to Ukraine just four months earlier.

When it became clear that the former Secretary of State was not going to become the 45th President of the United States, he had seen a unique opportunity to help distinguish himself from his peers. Rice quietly began jockeying to be reassigned to Ukraine. Having served ten years at the US embassy in Russia and in other Eastern European countries throughout his career, Duncan felt he understood the Russians and could help to defuse the conflict that had been going on in Ukraine for the past four years.

He wanted to spearhead the efforts to establish a workable peace deal in the country, something that basically none of his other colleagues wanted any part of, especially under what many thought to be a novice president. Many of his peers held great disdain for the incoming president, and several had even resigned in protest. While Duncan hadn't agreed with or voted for the President, he had recognized that Gates had been duly elected by the people and felt that it was now his job to help implement his country's foreign policies.

*****

Prime Minister Volodymyr Groysman was a young man to hold a position of such great power in Ukraine. He had been helped in part by his family's connections within the unspoken oligarchy of the nation, but he was also an incredibly charismatic speaker in his own right. His message had resonated with the people of Ukraine, who were mostly enticed by the idea of a modern European existence. It hadn't been long before he had risen to the top of the opposition party that had ousted Yanukovych.

When he had originally taken power, PM Groysman had hoped to approach Eastern Ukraine calmly and bring them back into the fold through diplomatic means. He had certainly heard often enough from his EU partners that they wanted him to handle the issue peacefully. At first, he'd agreed with their reasoning, but after a while, he had begun to feel bitter that he was constantly being told how to run the country, as if the heads of state in the European Union thought he were a child.

After four long years of conflict, Groysman was losing patience. The constant protests undermined his legitimacy as the true leader of Ukraine. He took great offense to this and began to work with his Public Information Officer to make sure that stories favorable to his administration were dominant in the public information sphere.

When President Gates was sworn into office in the United States in January of 2017, Groysman was initially unsure of the new leader's intentions toward Russia. He worried that he would have another man in office who would try to convince him that he should win over the separatists with simple kindness. However, within a matter of months, Gates had changed the US policy toward Ukraine and had started providing the country with military aid.

"Perhaps I have misjudged this man," thought Volodymyr. Gates seemed like he might be someone who was not afraid to stand up to the Russian dictator.

The prime minister was very pleased with the assistance that began to pour in from the US. In addition to equipment and manpower, Special Forces soldiers began to train Ukrainian military fighters, introducing a lot of new tactics.

****

Unbeknownst to Groysman, Ambassador Duncan Rice was behind the scenes, trying to slow things down. On more than one occasion, the ambassador had picked up the phone and tried to talk some sense into his direct superior, Secretary of State Travis Johnson.

"Sir, I serve at the pleasure of the President, but this place is a giant powder keg waiting to explode," Rice had asserted. "We need to cool things down here, not send additional weapons to the area. Why don't we defuse the situation by providing substantial economic aid to the affected areas? We could try to get people focused on rebuilding the economy here and healing the wounds of conflict," he'd pleaded.

The ambassador's appeals had fallen on deaf ears. "Rice, while I respect your opinion, I recently spoke to your new Senior Defense Officer, George Luka, and he has a different assessment. He views this Ukrainian conflict as a counterinsurgency fight, and feels confident that with the right training, military advisors and equipment, we can win."

"Mr. Secretary, I value my colleague, but George was just promoted to brigadier general very recently. He hasn't been on the ground here that long. I feel that his experiences in the Special Forces in Iraq and Afghanistan may have impacted how he sees things here," Ambassador Rice had explained.

"Well, Ambassador, you may have a point," Secretary Johnson had agreed. "However, the Secretary of Defense also shares the same views. He wants to take a hard line against Russia, and he feels that Ukraine is the perfect place to do it."

"Sir, I agree that something needs to be done to counter the separatists, but I feel strongly that applying economic pressure on the Russian government is a better approach. If we make the sanctions arduous enough, the

Kremlin will stop supporting the rebels in Eastern Ukraine," Ambassador Duncan claimed.

The Secretary of State didn't budge. "I think we are going to have to agree to disagree on this one, Rice," he countered.

Duncan was frustrated. The Secretary of State and his SDO were not the only people to disagree with him. The CIA Station Chief, a man by the name of John Williams, also sided with General Luka. He despised the Russians and blamed them for meddling in the American election. Agent Williams hadn't wasted any time. Soon he had convinced the President's National Security Advisor to allow "the Agency" to deploy a Special Activities Division or SAD unit to help counter the separatist movement.

Once Ambassador Rice learned of this plan, he definitely had reservations. *"Nothing good can come of a SAD team operating here—they're killers, nothing more,"* he thought. Still, despite the challenges and divergent agendas and personalities, Duncan began to feel that real progress was taking place in Ukraine.

****

Several months went by. Prime Minister Groysman knew that Ambassador Rice preferred a diplomatic solution, but the support from the United States continued to ramp up, which he appreciated more and more as the situation in Eastern Ukraine continued to escalate.

One day, Marko Tereshchenko, one of the Prime Minister's senior military advisors, showed up at Groysman's office unexpectedly, sweating as if he had just run a mile to get there as quickly as possible.

"Prime Minister," he began, "I apologize for my unannounced visit, but I must speak with you very urgently."

Groysman waved him in. "What is it, Marko?"

"Sir, Oleksandr Prasolov is going to be speaking at the protests in Kharkiv," he announced, out of breath.

"The former deputy minister from the Yanukovych administration?" Groysman asked.

"Yes, Prime Minister," Marko responded. "Prasolov has been a problem. He will try to rally the people of Eastern Ukraine to join the other separatist regions, and our intelligence on the ground shows that he is a very effective voice for the opposition."

"Enough is enough," asserted Groysman. He stood up and paced the room. "I'm so tired of these constant protests and attacks against our government. The soft touchy-feely European approach isn't working anymore. We have to get serious about shutting this down! I want you to give me some options for how we can use the military to support the local police there." He smacked the desk. "I want to see the proposals here by the end of the day, do you understand?"

"Yes, Sir," Marko replied. He dashed off to get the plans in order.

Volodymyr had a tendency to be rash. He didn't have the patience that many men develop with age and life experience. However, even though he'd ordered 1,500 soldiers to Kharkiv to put down the insurrection, he hadn't intended for things to go sideways the way they had.

Things had been going smoothly until one of the soldiers, a sniper, had shot Oleksandr in the head, killing him instantly. Once Oleksandr was dead, the security guards surrounding the other speakers had begun to shoot at the soldiers and police officers, who in turn had fired into the crowd of protestors. By the time the sun had risen the following day, twenty-eight protestors had been killed and another 112 had been taken to the hospital. Nearly two hundred others had been arrested, along with several protest leaders who had survived the bloody evening. The separatist provinces had begun calling the tragedy the Freedom Square Massacre and had taken to the airways to proclaim, "This is proof that the fascist government in Kiev is never going to negotiate with us in good faith about the reforms that they promised. The time to act is now!"

Groysman read every report that came in regarding the activities in Kharkiv. His partners in the EU and the US kept calling him and telling him how poorly this was all being received in the West. He stopped answering his phone.

"They don't know what they are talking about," he thought. Although he could concede that things looked different from the outside, he felt satisfied that his men had ultimately been successful in stabilizing the city. The multi-day protest had finally ended and those who were loyal to the government would no longer feel that they had been left to fend for themselves behind enemy lines.

As much as the prime minister wanted to end the separatist movement and evict the Russians once and for all, he didn't realize that the Freedom Square Massacre had ignited new passion in the separatist movement in Eastern Ukraine. Russian propaganda and fake news began to pour across social media throughout Ukraine, hyping up the government's use of soldiers against peaceful civilians. Footage of the head shot that killed Oleksandr Prasolov had been caught on someone's smartphone and was instantly turned into a powerful propaganda image against the central government in Kiev.

Though Ambassador Rice had no proof, he suspected that Oleksandr Prasolov had been killed by the SAD team, or that they had at least influenced the Ukrainian soldiers at Freedom Square. Regardless, after the massacre, the new head of the Russian separatist movement, Alexander Zakharchenko, organized a series of violent protests against the central government in a number of major cities across eastern Ukraine.

The situation continued to become more volatile. The US had been providing training to the Ukrainian military leaders for around six months, and those leaders began to become more and more confident in recommending a military solution to the separatist problem. General Luka worked with his partners at US Special Operations Command in Europe, and they were on board with providing additional US military advisors if needed.

After everything that had happened, Ambassador Rice sat at his desk, staring at two different paths. One option would lead them to further the diplomatic route, and the other would steer them into a swift military conflict to crush the separatist movement without mercy. Ambassador Rice wasn't sure which one Prime Minister Groysman would choose.

******

The morning of Saturday, August 5th was a beautiful day. The sun was out, the birds were chirping, and most people were enjoying a lazy Saturday morning at the numerous outdoor cafes and restaurants around the prime minister's office. Like many of the buildings constructed during the Soviet Union days, the PM's office was a grand and majestic edifice, created to impose a feeling of power on all those who entered it.

General Luka opened the enormous iron front door and held it open for Duncan and Colonel Avery to enter. Every time the three of them walked into that building, they could not help but feel small as they looked up at the high ceilings and large paintings of government officials.

As Ambassador Rice entered the PM's office, he saw the head of the Ukrainian military and the Defense Minister seated on the couch in the parlor section of the room, casually talking with each other and smiling. He shook the prime minister's hand and greeted him warmly in his native tongue.

Once the pleasantries had been completed, he walked over to the couch, where the other men were currently sitting. Duncan sat down and graciously accepted the cup of coffee offered to him by the prime minister. As the ambassador surveyed the leader's face, he could tell that the job had aged him. He had substantially more grey hairs than the average man in his late thirties, and the creases around his eyes seemed deeper than the last time they had met in person.

Many of the leaders who had come to power in the decades following the fall of communism had a history of going out of their way to enrich themselves rather than focusing on lifting up the people of their countries. Prime Minister Groysman was an exception to this rule. Ambassador Duncan saw in the man an intelligent visionary who truly wanted what was best for his people; he hoped he would stay in power for several more years.

As Duncan lifted his mug to his mouth, he took a deep breath through his nose to inhale the aromatic steam before taking a sip. He was a bit of a coffee connoisseur—his friends occasionally joked that he was a java snob—and for some reason the prime minister seemed to have a lock on the best coffee he had ever tasted. He had tried on numerous occasions to find out who his supplier was, but Groysman held onto that information like a closely guarded state secret.

"Mr. Ambassador, thank you for meeting with us this Saturday. As you know, it has been a trying time in Ukraine these past several weeks." His face was solemn. "I assume you've reviewed the military plans to end the conflict in the east?" he asked.

"I have, Mr. Prime Minister. As a diplomat, I still recommend caution. Although the window may be closing, I do believe a peaceful solution to this conflict is possible. A military operation could result in hundreds of thousands of people being displaced as refugees, not to mention the civilian casualties that would surely be suffered," Ambassador Rice warned. Duncan wanted to make sure the PM fully understand the consequences of moving forward with a military operation.

Groysman stiffened. He nodded in acceptance of what Ambassador Rice had said. "We are in a tough situation, Ambassador Rice. This conflict has been going on for several years. It has ruined our economy and divided our country. The separatist regions are governed by a small group of leaders, and they are controlled by a group of militias that number roughly ten to twelve thousand members. Unfortunately, the Russians continue to arm and train them. There are even unofficial Russian combat units operating in the East. If we do not act soon, they will become too strong and the divide in our nation will become permanent."

The PM continued, "We've spent the last four months getting ready to conduct this operation. With the Russians putting forth a renewed effort to go after ISIS in Syria, they are currently sufficiently distracted from intervening here any further. Your own CIA does not believe the Russians will intervene militarily. Therefore, with the military advisors and training your country has provided, and the substantial amount of weapons, food, fuel and vehicles your country has given us these past months, we now feel we are ready to move forward with the operation." Groysman paused to take a sip of his coffee, as if the group were discussing their weekend plans and not a war.

He placed his coffee cup down and looked Ambassador Rice in the eye. "In forty-eight hours, we will begin the operation. Our forces will begin to move into the Kharkiv Oblast, Dnipropetrovsk Oblast and the Donetsk regional state administrations."

This made it official. Duncan sat there for a moment, not sure what to say. *"This is a dangerous move,"* he thought. It would certainly result in a military confrontation between separatist fighters and the Ukrainian military, but it could also result in a direct confrontation between the 'unofficial' Russian forces that are not officially in Ukraine and central Ukraine loyalists; plus, any American advisors on the ground would certainly be caught in the crossfire. This was the exact situation Rice had desperately wanted to avoid.

Duncan put his own coffee down. He leaned forward, returning Groysman's unrelenting eye contact. "Mr. Prime Minister, I implore you one last time to reconsider this action. We are starting to make headway with the Russians. Through the sanctions, we can get them to end their support for the separatist movement on their own. Then the movement will die and lose support." He could see by the expression on his face that the PM didn't want to wait any longer. "I ask for you to give diplomacy more time," he pleaded, placing his hand over his heart. Duncan hoped that he might somehow be able to sway the man before him from making this potentially disastrous decision.

As Groysman sat there listening to the American ambassador, he couldn't help but marvel at how determined Ambassador Rice was to see a diplomatic solution to what everyone could see was a military problem. He sighed before speaking. "Ambassador Rice, I greatly appreciate the efforts of yourself and others to help solve the problems in Ukraine via diplomacy, but you must see that this has now moved to a problem that must be solved militarily. There are limits."

The prime minister then leaned forward. "General Luka and my senior military advisors assure me that our military is now up to speed and ready to handle this. We've received hundreds of Javelin antitank missile systems, fuel, food and other needed equipment and supplies to sustain a military operation such as this." Groysman could see the diplomat was saddened by this information. "The Russians are now involved in the Syrian conflict. They are finally too busy to get heavily involved in our conflict. This is not 2014, and America has a new president, one who will not back down in the face of threats made by President Petrov."

Duncan could see the PM was not going to change his mind, so he changed tack. "If I can't talk you out of this military operation, then how can we support you to ensure its success?" Duncan hated the idea of offering military aid, but the Secretary of State and the President had told him in no uncertain terms that if he couldn't persuade the Ukrainian prime minister to avoid a military operation, then he was to offer whatever support would be necessary to guarantee its success.

PM Groysman leaned back in his chair. He held all the cards now, he realized. After all, the new American president didn't want to lose face with the Russians. With all the allegations of him being a Russian puppet after their meddling in the American election, he needed to look strong. *"They are eating out of my hands now,"* the PM thought.

"Ambassador Rice, thank you for your offer. I truly do wish we could have found a diplomatic solution, and I will rely on your help once the time comes to pursue a diplomatic end to the conflict. Right now, I must do what the people who elected me are demanding—I must unite our country and put down this separatist movement."

Groysman paused for a moment, calculating what he could ask for. "What I *will* need American help with is intelligence. We also need help with surveillance, supplies, and logistical support while my ground forces carry out the actual fighting."

Sighing, Duncan replied, "Well, you know that I wanted to try and talk you out of this confrontation. However, seeing that I cannot, I want to make sure it succeeds. I'll hand over the rest of this discussion to General Luka and Colonel Avery, the US Air Force liaison officer to the embassy," the ambassador said, nodding toward his two military counterparts for them to speak up.

He had to give them both credit; they were true professionals. Not once had they tried to interrupt or add anything to the discussion. They had sat there passively and waited for their turn to talk, knowing that it would come. They knew the Ukrainians were not interested in further peace talks, but they also knew every effort had to be made before they moved forward with the military option.

General Luka cleared his throat. "Mr. Prime Minister and General Popko, as you know, the US has leased the former military air base at Pryluky, roughly seventy miles from the Boryspil International Airport in Kiev. We've spent the last two and a half months rebuilding it, transforming it into a training facility and forward operating base for the US and NATO to support your operations. Now that military action is going to move forward, you should go ahead and assign those ten liaison officers we previously talked about, along with additional interpreters."

General Popko had been expecting the request. He smiled and nodded in agreement.

The Pryluky airfield had been Ukraine's primary Tupolev Tu-160 "Blackjack" bomber base until it had been decommissioned at the end of 2012 due to budget cuts. When the US and NATO had wanted to lease the base and build it back up, it had been seen as a huge economic boon to the cash-strapped central government. It had brought thousands of high-paying jobs to the local area and imported thousands of NATO servicemen who would spend hard currency in the surrounding area. It was estimated the base would bring in several hundred million euros a year in economic activity alone.

Much to the angst of the Russians, the Ukrainian government had leased the facility to the US three and a half months earlier. The base had been in a bad state of repair, but a fleet of contractors and military engineers had shown up and the base had begun to transform overnight. Living quarters and offices had been rebuilt and the runway and other aircraft facilities upgraded. The US and NATO had poured roughly $80 million into the facility, transforming it into a modern military facility.

The Air Force LNO spoke next. "We have eight Predator drones, two Reapers, and two Global Hawks that are ready to provide 24/7 surveillance of the battlefield as your forces move forward. We also have several electronic surveillance tools that will be made available. Starting tomorrow, we are going to close off the air base to all nonessential personnel. We want to minimize the chance of any separatist forces gaining access to the base," he said as he showed some of the plans they had for securing the air base.

"When your forces head into the disputed territory on Monday, they will have constant drone surveillance and signals intelligence. We'll help you root these separatists out in short order," the Air Force colonel said, confident that this military operation would be wrapped up before the end of the year.

While Ambassador Duncan sat there listening to the military members talk, he had a sick feeling in his stomach that things were not going to work out quite as well as everyone thought it would. *"I hope I'm wrong,"* he thought, *"but military operations seldom turn out how they are supposed to."* There was an adage he'd heard that he'd found to be true—the enemy always gets a vote in the matter, too.

The group continued to talk for a while longer, going over details about the logistical support that would be needed. There was some debate as to what would be provided by the Americans versus NATO, but at the end of the day, a complete plan had been formalized.

Chapter 3

Donetsk

06 August 2017

Donetsk, Ukraine

The air was musty and humid as a group of well-muscled men and women sat in an old Soviet underground bunker in Donetsk. During the Cold War, this hideaway had been used as a command center to help coordinate the air defense of the Motherland. Now it served as a secretive meeting room for the various leaders and rebel commanders of the Russian separatist movement.

Alexander Zakharchenko, the self-appointed prime minister of Donetsk People's Republic, pulled his lighter out of his cargo pocket and proceeded to ignite another cigarette. He took a long pull, letting the smoke fill his lungs as his body absorbed the nicotine. As he slowly let the smoke out through his nostrils, he turned to Anton Antyufeyev. "If what Strelkov says is true, then we have a serious problem."

Anton took a puff from his own cigarette and nodded. "We need to mobilize our militias and get ready to meet the government forces when they start to move into the cities and surrounding villages."

Alexander continued smoking as he replied, "We backed down in Kharkiv, and they killed Oleksandr Prasolov. They believe that they succeeded in crushing our movement in Kharkiv, but they did not. Now the government thinks they can replicate the success that we gave them there and throughout our area of control. What they fail to realize is that we allowed them a victory in Kharkiv—we chose not to use our soldiers in retaliation for killing Prasolov. We won't make that same choice here."

Strelkov leaned forward and looked Alexander in the eyes. "This will be different, Alex. They are not sending a small contingent of soldiers to help augment the police like they did in Kharkiv. They are sending a much larger military force with the intent of engaging our soldiers and forcing us to either surrender or flee across the border—"

Pavel interrupted to add, "—We must mobilize our militias and tell the Russians to be ready to help us."

Strelkov cut Pavel off before he could say anything else. "Pavel, sit down and speak when spoken to. I am not done yet," he grunted, annoyed at being interrupted before he could speak his piece. He had valuable information, and these guys were not letting him have a chance to spit it out.

Pavel looked startled, but he sat down obediently.

Strelkov continued, "Look, my contact in the Ukrainian military said the Americans have spent the last four months getting them ready to come root us out. They have provided them with Stingers, vehicles, antitank missiles, and other heavy weapons. They are also going to offer them several hundred military advisors and surveillance drone support. The advisors are almost exclusively American Special Forces and infantry soldiers. They mean business, and these are soldiers who know what they are doing."

He wanted to make sure they fully understood that these weren't going to be the same ragtag government soldiers they had been fighting against up to this point. This was going to be a newly trained and well-equipped military force, advised by American combat veterans.

Those around him nodded resolutely. They were preparing themselves for a true battle.

Strelkov surveyed the faces before him. Satisfied that they were adequately concerned, he went on, "They are going to deploy the 30th Mechanized Brigade and the 1st Tank Brigade to lead the assault. These units will be supported by roughly 9,000 light infantry soldiers. My source in the 30th said they are also going to have nearly 100

American Special Forces advisors and another 300 NATO advisors with them on a daily basis."

He showed them images on his tablet of the new equipment the units had received, including images of the venerable American Javelin antitank missile system, which would all but negate any advantage they had enjoyed up to this point.

Strelkov waited a moment for the images to sink in before he resumed. "Judging by the number of advisors, it looks like each platoon-level element will have either an American advisor or a NATO advisor with them. They will be coordinating surveillance drones, artillery, and air support for them, just like they do for the Iraqis and Afghans in the Middle East."

Alexander whistled softly. "I still can't believe the Americans supplied them with what looks like 45 Strykers and 80 MRAP vehicles," he said in disbelief and anger.

Strelkov just nodded. "They can still be destroyed; the Americans learned that in Iraq. However, the Strykers and MRAPs are going to make it a lot harder for us to engage them," he explained in disgust.

Changing topics, Strelkov pulled up a new set of photos on his tablet. "As you know, PM Groysman leased the old Pryluky Air Base to NATO several months ago. As you can see from these photos, NATO and the Americans have been busy. The Germans moved a squadron of Eurofighters to the base, and the US has established a Patriot missile battery there as well." On the screen flashed images of American soldiers setting up the Patriot system and unloading various types of military equipment.

"You can see they've also moved a number of drones to the base. We can assume the Americans will be providing the government forces with a lot of intelligence-gathering support. Most of these drones can be armed, but we do not believe the Americans are going to be providing the government with armed drones."

There was a collective sigh of relief by everyone in the room. The last thing any of them wanted was for the central government to be armed with American drones, carrying out assassination missions like they did in the Middle East and elsewhere in the world.

The group sat back in their chairs then, quietly digesting the information Strelkov had just shared. They were not quite sure what to say or do just yet. Strelkov's sources were good; if they had passed this information to him, then chances were, it was accurate. This was going to happen. Strelkov was a colonel in the Russian military intelligence agency, the GRU, and he had developed an effective method of collecting intelligence throughout the Ukrainian military over the years. Mostly, he just bribed them with American dollars, and they told him whatever he wanted to know. He was also the primary point of contact between the separatist forces and the GRU, which routinely provided their group with as much accurate and up-to-date intelligence as possible.

Igor Bezler hadn't said anything up to this point. He cleared his throat to get the attention of everyone at the table before speaking. "Now that everyone has heard the information Strelkov has to share, we must formalize a plan for what we are going to do. The Russian Army can deliver thousands of additional RPG-7s and other heavy weapons to help us turn the surrounding villages approaching Donetsk into a fortress. However, we know that this battle will have to be fought by the separatist forces. Russian paramilitary forces are and will continue to act as active advisors, but the army will not send uniformed forces into the Ukraine."

Igor was the paramilitary representative to the separatists. Igor had a Spetsnaz background himself and had spent over two decades in the Russian Special Forces. He had nearly 200 fellow Spetsnaz operating in the Ukraine, mostly to carry out specialized missions against Ukrainian military units when they strayed into separatist-held territory. They also helped to run several of the training camps, teaching specialized courses in sniper operations, explosives, kidnappings, and other advanced activities.

The next man to speak was Taras Kolomoisky. He ran what was arguably one of the most stable separatist regions. He maintained an uneasy peace between the separatist movement and the central government by trying to play both sides. In the past, he had often strived to be an honest broker between the two groups. However, his son had been killed by central government soldiers nine months ago. He had been trapped at a checkpoint, trying to re-enter the separatist region, and when he refused to pay the bribe that they demanded, they shot him.

While the death of his son had torn him apart, what had really caused him to throw his lot fully behind the rebel cause was the rape of his daughter two months later. The sons of two prominent law makers in the central government had attacked his daughter while she attended a university in Switzerland. Whatever restraint Taras had been trying to maintain in the hopes of achieving a peaceful end to the conflict had been evaporated by these two events.

Now he was doing what he could to help support the separatist movement and undermine the central government. Being the governor of the Dnipropetrovsk region meant his district was a buffer zone between the separatists and the central government zones of control. Now that he had turned on the central government, he had begun to provide them with as little support and cooperation as possible. His region had stopped sending taxes to Kiev, and then a week ago, he had essentially cut off all communications with the central government.

Taras leaned forward to address the group. "Before we break up our meeting and head our separate ways to prepare, I'd like to offer a suggestion. In Iraq, the Americans owned the night, they owned the skies, and they won every direct engagement. However, this didn't stop the insurgents from attacking the Americans or inflicting a terrible cost on them. We must do the same. If the Americans are now actively backing the central government, then we need to find a new strategy."

Taras continued, "I agree that turning the cities into fortresses will help, but what we also need to do is make the roads nearly impossible for them to use. We need to have teams constantly placing improvised explosive devices and carrying out hit-and-run RPG attacks. If we can make the roads treacherous to use, we will limit their ability to move freely within our regions. We will grind them into the dirt until they eventually leave," he said confidently, as if he had just laid out the most comprehensive battle plan they had ever heard.

Smiles could be seen on the faces of the men around them. They had already planned on doing exactly this, but they were happy to finally have Taras come to the same conclusion.

After another hour of discussions, the group broke up and the leaders dispersed to begin getting their various groups ready to meet the government forces.

Chapter 4

It Begins

Pryluky Air Base

92 Miles East of Kiev

Several birds were chirping in the nearby tree as a summer breeze moved the leaves in a hypnotic way. Technical Sergeant Jason "JP" Parker turned away from his view of the nearby trees to put his cigarette out with his boot. Then he began to walk back to the drone trailer where he had spent most of his day.

They had finally gotten things up and running about a week ago, just as the Ukrainian military operations started. It had been a very busy and frustrating week for many of the drone operators. On several occasions, they had spotted a cluster of enemy soldiers preparing to launch an ambush against the government forces. He had spotted individuals placing IEDs along the roads, but he was unable to directly engage the targets. Under the "normal" conditions he had become accustomed to in Afghanistan, Syria, and Iraq, they would have engaged them with their hellfire missiles, but these were not normal conditions and they were not authorized to carry out direct kinetic strikes.

1st Lieutenant Michelle Shay looked up as the door to their drone trailer opened and saw Jason walking back in. "JP, we have another convoy getting ready to move. Can you do a quick scan of that village over there before they approach it?" she said, drawing circles with her cursor around the appropriate place on the map being projected on the wall. "Intelligence says that's one of the separatist strongholds."

She hoped this mission would go better than the last few had. The patrol they'd provided overwatch for on their last shift yesterday had been hit by several IEDs. Several people had been killed, and all they could do was watch.

JP sat down and got to work. As he began to analyze the various approaches to the village, he spotted several people crouched behind a small wall in front of a house that overlooked the main road. He zoomed in to get a better idea of what they were doing.

"Lieutenant, take a look at this. It appears that one of those individuals there has an RPG. I'll bet they have an IED planted somewhere down there as well."

She squinted for a moment as she focused on the image. She saw it too. One of the individuals definitely had an RPG; it looked like they were setting up an ambush. She grabbed her radio to warn the command element, located a few buildings away.

"Archangel, this is Angel One. We have a couple of individuals lying in ambush of convoy 017. We are sending you the images and coordinates. Please advise the convoy that they are heading toward a trap."

"Angel One, acknowledged. We will relay your intelligence," came the reply.

They quickly contacted the MRAP that had the American advisors in it. "Echo Five, this is Archangel One. We have probable ambush at grid...sending images of tangos."

Sergeant First Class Trey Perkins looked at the image of the attackers. He could see two men, and one clearly had an RPG. "*I don't like this at all,*" he thought. "*Where are the IEDs?*"

Sergeant Perkins signaled to the Ukrainian convoy commander for the group of vehicles to stop. Once they did, he showed the images and video to the Ukrainian captain. "How should we proceed?" he asked.

Sergeant Perkins had deployed several times to Afghanistan and Iraq. Speaking from his previous experience, he advised, "I think we should approach the position with caution. We need to have everyone look for possible IEDs. Once we get in range of the .50-cals, have your gunner engage that insurgent hiding behind this wall." He pointed to the location as he spoke. "Once that hostile is taken out, we should dismount your troops and have them fan out as we approach the village with the gun trucks."

The convoy moved cautiously toward the village. As they reached the range of their heavy machine gun, one of the soldiers fired a short burst from the weapon, exploding the wall and killing the two attackers. The sixty soldiers traveling in the convoy dismounted from their vehicles and began to approach the village from several different angles. As the vehicles continued to move into the village, all hell broke loose. Despite the drones providing overwatch, they didn't spot the series of IEDs that had been placed in the drainage system along the side of the road.

A total of four 152mm artillery rounds had been placed in the storm drains. As the Strykers and MRAP vehicles moved into the kill box, the separatists sprang the trap, remotely detonating the IEDs. The shockwave from the blasts threw several of the vehicles on their side, severely injuring the occupants inside. Shrapnel flew through the air, hitting the men who had been patrolling on foot next to the vehicles.

While the soldiers were still in a state of shock and trying to assess who all had been hit, the separatists opened fire. Many of the Ukrainian soldiers ducked for cover, while others began to provide medical attention to the wounded. Dozens of attackers suddenly emerged from buildings not far from the main road and opened fire on the remaining government forces with RPGs and heavy weapons. Their ultimate goal was to wipe out the government troops and steal whatever equipment they could before they dashed out of there.

The two American LNOs were a bit shaken from the explosion that rocked their MRAP, but otherwise unhurt. As soon as the shooting started, the two Special Forces soldiers grabbed their weapons and assisted the Ukrainians in repulsing the attack. The two Special Forces soldiers killed several of the separatists, rallying their Ukrainian partners until one attacker came around the corner of a building a block away and fired an RPG at the vehicle they were using for cover. The explosion killed them both instantly.

The ambush lasted nearly an hour, until additional government reinforcements arrived to help evacuate the wounded and secure the village. Many on both sides had lost their lives or been injured; however, the real tragedy of the day was the innocent civilians who had been caught in the crossfire. In all, eighteen townspeople had been killed and another fourteen were wounded.

****

US Embassy, Defense Attaché Office

Brigadier General George Luka was not a happy camper as he sat in his office reviewing the latest after-action report from one of the US advisor teams. The recent attack had resulted in two MRAPs and two Stryker vehicles being completely destroyed, and the ambush had killed nearly two dozen Ukrainian soldiers. Though he was upset about the loss of those men and women, Luka was probably more disturbed by the loss of the American Special Forces captain and sergeant first class who had been killed in the ambush. In all, the US had already lost thirteen advisors since the beginning of the military operations nine days ago.

From the very beginning, the Ukrainian forces had hit heavy resistance once they crossed the demarcation zone. In the first week, they had encountered stiff fighting in the city of Dnipro while securing the critical bridges crossing the Dnieper River. However, once the Ukrainians had secured the city and the bridges, they'd established Dnipro as their forward operating base for the rest of the operation.

It was not until government forces had started to approach the outskirts of Donetsk that the fighting intensified to the point of forcing a stalemate. The rebel forces had begun to make heavy use of conventional and rocket artillery to hammer the government forces. This had forced the Ukrainians to introduce attack helicopters and ground attack aircraft.

Unfortunately, the Russians had supplied the rebels with several 2K22 Tunguska anti-aircraft self-propelled vehicles, also called SA-19 "Grisons." These were the Russians' newest anti-aircraft vehicles, which had a mix of 30mm guns and surface-to-air missiles. The introduction of the SA-19 had been a rude surprise to the Ukrainians, who had quickly lost four Mi-24 "Hind" helicopters and five Sukhoi Su-25 "Frogfoot" ground attack aircraft. The stalemate and loss of critical aircraft and helicopters was causing some concern among the NATO advisors, especially since they were less than two weeks into the operation.

As General Luka was reading over the latest reports, he heard a knock on his door and looked up to see Chief of Station John Williams. He waved him in and indicated for him to take a seat at one of the chairs in front of his desk. Then he asked, "What are your thoughts on yesterday's attack?"

Luka looked at the Chief of Station, hoping he had better news than what this latest report indicated. "It looks like the Ukrainians got stomped…again," he grumbled, disappointed in the ability of their proxy to execute a battle plan and root out these attackers. The CIA and DoD had spent a lot of money and man hours training their counterparts. They had hoped things would have gone better up to this point.

"I don't think the prime minister can continue to sustain these losses without some sort of victory," John said, stating the obvious. The civilian populace was growing concerned with the number of soldiers and civilians being killed, and so was the international community.

"I spoke with some folks from SOCEUR. They told me if the enemy air defense weapons could be neutralized, air support could start to make a difference and would turn the tide," General Luka explained, hinting that he would like to use the Special Forces assets in Ukraine a bit more aggressively and liberally than just as advisors.

John thought about this for a minute. The challenge in using SF units in direct action was that if they get caught or killed, it would be a political win for the enemy. "If I could, perhaps we can use some SAD units…plausible deniability and all. We know where the vehicles are at. It's just a matter of getting close enough to destroy them."

General Luka didn't like using CIA direct action teams for what was obviously a SF mission, but he also knew he was under strict orders not to widen the conflict beyond the use of providing military advisors. The fact that several military advisors had already been killed, some in direct combat, was becoming a problem.

"I'm not comfortable with having your teams carrying out this type of mission on your own. What if we could get the Ukrainian Special Forces unit to accompany your men? This way, your guys are still in an 'advisor' role," the general offered.

"Hmm…I think we could work with that," John replied.

Chapter 5

Prisoners of War

US Embassy – Chancellery
Kiev, Ukraine

Ambassador Rice felt like the situation in Ukraine was starting to spiral out of control as he read the latest intelligence summaries provided to him by US European Command and the State Department's own intelligence group. After a rough first couple of weeks of this new military operation, the CIA decided that they wanted to get more involved in helping the Ukrainians eliminate some of the separatist air defense vehicles. "The Agency" had been monitoring the enemy air defense units since the start of the Ukrainian operation, so once they received the go-ahead to work directly with Ukrainian Special Forces to take them out, they executed a mission with one of their Special Operations Group teams.

The covert operation had taken place the night before. It had not gone well. Two CIA SOG units, in cooperation with a Ukrainian Special Forces team, attempted to destroy four of the separatist SA-17 Buk air defense vehicles and three of the SA-19 Grisons. The first team succeeded in destroying two of the vehicles without losing a single SOG member. The second SOG team, however, hadn't been so lucky. They were ambushed in what the CIA believed was a well-coordinated and pre-planned trap. Two of the four CIA men had been killed, and the other two had been captured. The entire Ukrainian Special Forces team had been killed in the ambush.

Now, two Americans were being held captive by the separatist group, who was demanding the withdrawal of American military advisors from Ukraine. The Russians had also taken to the airwaves, announcing, "If NATO and the Americans are no longer going to remain neutral, then neither are we."

After finishing reading the report, Ambassador Rice looked up at General Luka and John Williams, his Chief of Station. "Well, you gentlemen pushed for a military operation several months ago. So, what are your recommendations now that two Americans have been captured?" The left side of his lip curled up in disgust.

General Luka sighed, but he remained determined that it was the right decision to move forward with a military option. "Ambassador, there are always going to be miscues and setbacks in any military operation. The Ukrainians have strengthened their hold and position on the separatist territory since the start of this operation. They have also seriously degraded their ability to continue to hold onto the cities. Despite the losses, they are accomplishing the stated goals. At this current rate of engagement, the separatists are nearly broken as a fighting force. They have sustained heavy casualty rates and equipment losses, far more than the Ukrainian army has. We need to continue to stay the course."

John Williams added, "Putting the military objectives aside, we have people being held captive right now and we need to get them back. Our surveillance has identified the safehouse they're holding our guys in."

"What? How?" asked Ambassador Rice, incredulous.

"They keep moving our men every couple of hours, but we placed an isotope tracker in all of our personnel operating in Ukraine, in case they were ever kidnapped. We can track them fairly easily," explained John.

Duncan's eyebrows revealed his surprise.

Stopping only to take a drink from his water bottle, Williams continued, "Before coming over here, we intercepted two messages. One communiqué was between the Russian paramilitary units and the separatists, ordering them to bring the Americans to a specific compound immediately. This was about two hours ago. The second communiqué we intercepted was between Russian military headquarters in Moscow and a Spetsnaz unit operating near the Ukrainian-Russian border. They're going to escort the Americans across the Russian border in two days to be brought back to Moscow for further questioning." The CIA man clenched his fists at the thought of his men being held in a gulag.

Looking at General Luka and then back to the ambassador, John continued, "I've spoken with Major General Lansing from JSOC, and we have a Delta team that just arrived in country that can execute their recovery."

General Luka nodded in agreement. "We need to move fast on this then, Ambassador. We need to get our guys back before they are moved across the border. Once that happens, I have no idea what will happen to them."

Ambassador Rice looked at them incredulously. "You realize they are being guarded by Spetsnaz, right? How do you propose getting them back?"

John explained, "We get them back by sending a Delta team in to kill everyone there and recover our people. We don't just leave them to rot or be tortured by the Russians." There was a hint of sarcasm to his tone; he was surprised that the ambassador would be so daft as not to know how this was going to turn out.

"You understand that you will be facing *actual* Russian soldiers. This could spiral things out of control quickly is all I'm saying. We need to proceed with caution," Rice responded, hoping to get these two hotheads to realize how quickly things could become worse.

General Luka saw the ambassador was not comfortable with this option, and he suddenly pictured the ambassador going above their heads and fouling up the entire mission as he tried to "negotiate" for their release. "Ambassador Rice, I know you are nervous about the situation getting out of control, and that is a valid concern. However, we can't allow two of our men to remain captive. They know too much and are too valuable for us to leave them. It also sets a bad precedent that if we aren't willing to come for them, we might not come for others. That is not something we can allow to happen."

The ambassador sighed.

Luka continued, "We're coordinating this with SOCEUR and JSOC. We have additional assets being moved into the area as we speak. Everything is already underway. We're bringing you into the loop now, but the decision has already been made by the National Security Advisor, SOCEUR, and JSOC to get our people back. We've lost fifteen guys…we are going to show these separatists what happens when they test the might of the American military. I assure you, this will not turn out like past operations with the Ukrainians. This will be an American operation all the way through."

The ambassador sat back in his chair, feeling defeated and blindsided. The military had been pushing for confrontation from the beginning, but at least they had been keeping him informed of what was going on. Now it seemed like they were maneuvering behind his back.

"Don't they realize these actions are going to have long-term consequences?" he thought.

Chapter 6

Rescue Operation

East Ukraine near the Russian Border

Spetsnaz Training Camp

Colonel Vadim Lebed, the Commander of the 45th Guard's Detached Spetsnaz Brigade, had just arrived at the training camp several hours ago to inspect the prisoners and take charge of them. He had left his base at Kubinka, outside of Moscow, to personally take charge of the American prisoners once it had been discovered that these men were responsible for carrying out the attacks against the various air defense vehicles the Russian military had provided to the separatist militias. Those air defense vehicles had been preventing the Ukrainian army from being able to use their air force or helicopters, and Colonel Lebed harbored some desire for revenge.

As he opened the door to the SUV that drove him to the camp, he was greeted by Major Anatoly Pankov, the camp commander, who smiled as he extended his hand. "It's good to see you, Colonel. Do you want to see the prisoners now, or would you like a brief tour of our facility?"

Major Pankov was an outstanding soldier, a real mover and shaker in the Spetsnaz world. If he kept his nose clean, one day he could command the regiment. Colonel Lebed had selected him to run this camp because he knew that no one would be able to turn these separatist militias into a viable fighting force like he could.

"Major Pankov, it's good to see you too, my friend. Congratulations on the capture of these two Americans. I believe I'd like to see what you've done here at the camp first, then we can discuss the prisoners...Please, lead the way." He gestured for him to proceed with the tour. His aide shadowed them, giving them space to talk freely but remaining available in case the colonel needed him.

The two men walked toward one of the buildings that was being used for classroom instruction. "We use this building to go over the construction of improvised explosive devices," Pankov said as they walked into the room. There was a class going on, with eight separatists being shown how to attach the control wires to a 152mm artillery projectile. In time, they would learn how to properly use other explosive objects, like mortars, 122mm rockets, blocks of Semtex, and C-4.

"We run this course weekly, teaching as many people as possible how to construct IEDs. Since the start of the Kiev offensive, the separatists have been using them multiple times a day. In fact, the separatists we've been advising and training are placing nearly a dozen IEDs a day."

Colonel Lebed nodded in approval. The only way to win a war when heavily outgunned and outnumbered was through asymmetric warfare. The enormous use of IEDs since the start of Kiev's most recent operation was having the desired effect. They had stopped the fascist forces from crushing the separatists and demoralized their army.

The People's Republic of Donetsk and Luhansk was still in its infancy. Their ability to defend themselves from the fascist government in Kiev largely depended on their militia forces. It was the responsibility of the 45th Guard's Spetsnaz Brigade to turn this militia force into a viable standing army and force that could protect the new republic's national borders.

The two men left the classroom building and made their way toward the main building in the compound. It was a three-story building, which functioned as their operations center. "We have a number of ranges nearby, where we teach them a myriad of different weapons systems and how to emplace the IEDs and detonate them. We train a hundred soldiers every two weeks at this camp and have been doing so for nearly two years. To help build up their officer and sergeant corps, we provide a separate four-week course. We train a total of eight officers and sixteen sergeants per training group," Major Pankov explained proudly.

"Anatoly, you've done a marvelous job turning these unorganized militias into a real military fighting force," Lebed commented, impressed with how well his protégé had been doing.

The two of them walked through the rest of the building before ending on the third floor, where the two Americans were being held. The Americans were bound and had a few bruises and cuts that they probably obtained during their capture, but otherwise, they looked to be in good health.

"Do you want to talk with them?" Anatoly asked, wanting to make sure his commander had the opportunity if he wanted it.

"No," Lebed replied. "I just wanted to see them. Come, let's go to your office and talk further. We need to review how we are going to handle the American drones and the NATO base at Pryluky."

The two men talked for several more hours about the new NATO base and whether they should or shouldn't attack it. It was bad enough that NATO had accepted Latvia, Lithuania and Estonia as members, now they had positioned a base in Ukraine. They had crossed a red line; something needed to be done.

****

Twenty-four hours later, Major Brian Runyon stood in the team room at the Pryluky Air Base, loading his last thirty-round magazine of 5.56mm ammunition for his M4. He placed the loaded magazine into one of the front ammunition pouches on his tactical vest. The men around him were mostly quiet, carefully doing last-minute checks of their equipment, weapons and ammunition. Thirty minutes ago, they had been given the final go-ahead by Joint Special Operations Command or JSOC to proceed with the recovery of the captured CIA members. Once they had run through the mission brief, they would quickly move out to the aircraft that would fly them to the target.

As Brian looked around the room, he could see the intense look on everyone's faces. These men were killers— professionals, but killers just the same. This mission, unlike many others they had conducted over the last decade, was against an actual army, not Islamic extremists. They would be battling against what would most likely be a Russian Spetsnaz team, one that knew how to handle themselves in a gunfight.

Colonel Richards, who had been the Commander of 1st Special Forces Detachment Delta for nearly two years, walked into the room with General Luka and John Williams, along with several other military members. The table at the center of the room was covered in weapons, and the briefers were loading up their presentations to project on the big screen at the end of the room. As Richards and his cohorts walked in, all activity and chatter stopped, and the men's eyes turned to their leader. They all had tremendous respect for this man, who had been in Special Forces and floated around between various groups, in and out of Delta, for most of his career.

Looking at Major Runyon, Colonel Richards said, "I won't sugarcoat it; this is going to be a tough mission, Brian. However, I have complete faith in your team to get this done and bring our guys home." His voice was filled with sincerity and confidence.

Major Brian Runyon just nodded in acknowledgment. Like Colonel Richards, he had spent most of his military time in Special Forces. He had joined Delta as a captain after serving a number of years in the Army Rangers, with whom he had completed a whole series of combat deployments. Now a major, Brian was aware that this was by far the most dangerous mission of his life.

The briefers indicated they were ready to begin. Everyone in the room moved to the chairs and took out their notebooks. The first briefer began, "All right, men—here is our target. We are going to be assaulting an unofficial Spetsnaz base camp, located deep inside rebel territory, near the Russian border. As you can see, the compound consists of one three-story building, two smaller outbuildings, and a four-car garage. It also has a six-foot-tall cinderblock wall surrounding the buildings. There are two personnel entrances, here and here, and one vehicle entrance, here."

Everyone was paying careful attention as the images on the screen continued to update. "Surrounding the compound is a wooded area. About 500 meters to the south, behind the compound, there's a small creek that snakes toward the highway. This is where they've parked an air defense vehicle. In front of the compound is an open field that leads to the main road and runs through several fields." He picked up a ruler and pointed to this area for emphasis. "This is where the exfiltration will take place," announced the briefer.

The men nodded, and the briefer continued. "On the base, you can expect to find a Spetsnaz detachment, which consists of roughly twenty operators. Perimeter security for the compound is provided by a company of Russian soldiers in addition to the SA-17 and SA-19 air defense vehicles I previously pointed out. This location has been used as a logistics, training, and operational hub by the Russians for the past three years. Since they've set up operations here, they've trained hundreds, if not thousands, of separatist fighters here."

An Air Force master sergeant stood up to present his briefing next. He brought up a 3-D animation of the structure, showing various guards at different locations and began to describe the images. "This is the building where the prisoners are being held. Surveillance indicates the prisoners are being held on the top floor of this three-story building, in this room here." He used his laser pointer to identify the specific room they believed the prisoners were being held in.

"As you can see, the building has an entrance to the roof here. We've identified three guards on the roof. One of them appears to be holding a MANPAD, while the others are carrying assault rifles. There's one guard outside the prisoner's doors, also armed with an assault rifle. The guards are clearly on alert for a potential raid—they anticipate we might try to rescue our people—so you need to neutralize them."

Half of the men seemed concerned that the soldiers were going to be prepared for their mission, and the other half were excited about the orders that had just been given; they would not have to hold back.

The master sergeant continued, "The second floor appears to be their sleeping quarters. We estimate the various rooms can house roughly twenty personnel. From our observation, roughly six to ten people appear to be sleeping in there at any given time. The first floor is where their operations appear to be run out of. This room is the communications room," the briefer said, pointing with his laser pen, then moving to identify the other rooms on the first floor as well. "Here is the weapons room, the kitchen, and two storage rooms. We are not sure what they're using the basement for or what's down there. The outbuildings appear to be training rooms; they will be empty this time of day."

He switched to some new images of the exterior of the compound. "This is what concerns us. The Russians have deployed one of their SA-17s, which is near the tree line here." The briefer pulled up several satellite images of the unit in relationship to the structures around it.

Pulling up a different image, he continued, "About a quarter mile away, in this area here, is a SA-19 Grison air defense system. These two systems provide both short and medium air defense capabilities against aircraft and helicopters. Therefore, you will be inserted via a high-altitude, low-opening jump and land in this area here." Several additional images were shown of an empty farm field maybe a quarter mile away from the compound.

The briefer then brought up some live feed surveillance videos being taken by a Global Hawk operating not too far away. The briefer talked to the drone operator, and they walked through the terrain of the landing zone and the various approaches to the Russian compound. They clearly saw guards on various roving patrols. Everything they had been shown on the previous slides matched up to the real-time video they were watching.

Colonel Richards spoke up. "As you can see, there are the roving patrols that are going to need to be dealt with."

The JSOC briefer then resumed talking to the group. "There are the three guards on the roof. Then there are two groups of three roving guards that walk the perimeter." Images shifted to show the vehicle locations, and various guard positions that would need to be neutralized.

Several of the members of A Squadron looked around at each other, a little apprehensive about what they were hearing and seeing. This was clearly going to be a tough and complex raid. It was not every time they got to see live video surveillance of a target they would be hitting in less than six hours.

The master sergeant carried on. "Upon landing, Alpha team will immediately move to the north side of the perimeter to neutralize the guards at the air defense systems and place the explosives on the truck. It's imperative that you take out that SA-19 first, then move to the next unit. If those vehicles are not taken out, it's going to be a long walk for you guys back to friendly territory."

"Bravo team will move to the south side of the perimeter, taking out the guards here and here, and the three guards near the vehicles on this side of the compound. There are six armored personnel carriers, which are a mix of BTRs and BMPs. You will also need to get your explosives placed on those vehicles. Charlie and Delta teams will enter the compound here, at this entrance. Once inside, there are two guards here, at the entrance to the compound. They will need to be eliminated quickly. Once they are cleared, you will have to move down the hallway past one door, which should just be a closet."

He coughed once, then took a swig of water from his canteen. "The stairs leading to the other floors will be on the right. The stairwell continues all the way to the roof. I'll leave it to your discretion as to how you want to clear the building and recover the prisoners."

Major Runyon interrupted to ask, "—Assuming this all goes according to plan, how are we going to get out? I suspect the Russians probably have other air defense assets in the area." He wasn't sure he was going to like the response he was about to be given.

An Air Force LNO replied, "They may have additional air defense units in the area. We are going to have a couple of jamming aircraft loitering over friendly skies to assist in your recovery. When the time comes, they'll turn their jammers on and blanket the area. This should neutralize any additional air defense systems."

A member of the Night Stalkers picked up where the Air Force LNO left off. "Once you've secured the prisoners, you will send the coded message, letting us know you are ready for extraction. The exfil aircraft will be loitering at this location here, roughly five minutes from your location. We'll be using three of our new and experimental V-280 'Valor' tilt-rotor wing helicopters for the exfil. They'll be escorted by a pair of Apaches."

Several of the men let out a soft whistle as they looked at the image of the V-280. "I wasn't aware that the Night Stalkers had a new helicopter," General Luka said in admiration.

"This will actually be our first mission using them," explained a Chief Warrant Officer 4 or CW4 from the Night Stalkers. "We started training on them about three months ago. We didn't plan on using them in an operation for at least another year, but because of the air defense threat of this mission, it was felt they should be used. They are not stealth per se, but they have a significantly reduced radar signature and are extremely quiet for a helicopter."

"As long as we don't end up with a scenario where one crashes, like what happened on the bin Laden raid back in 2012," Colonel Richards said. He was unsure if this was a good idea, but he had been overruled on the decision.

The CW4 added, "This is why we're bringing a third one with us. They can carry eleven soldiers and their gear, more than enough room for this mission."

Major Runyon asked, "What air support do we have? Also, what will be the contingency plan if things go downhill fast?" No one wanted to think about the worst-case scenario, but Runyon's personal philosophy was that if you plan for it, then you have a better chance of survival.

The JSOC briefer piped up, "This is why the rest of your Delta group and the Ranger Company are here in Ukraine. They are your quick reaction force if you need to be bailed out. The Night Stalkers have four Blackhawks and three Chinooks, along with another two Apache helicopters on standby. They will lift off once you guys start your insertion, so they'll be loitering over friendly skies, ready to move if given the order. As for air support, the Air Force will have one of their electronic jamming aircraft initiate a full-spectrum jamming across the targeted area. They'll take the Russian communications system down immediately once you are in place; they will also make sure their radars are down when it comes time to exfil. If things really go south, there are also two F-35s loitering at high altitude, ready to provide direct air support if needed."

The Air Force LNO jumped back in to add, "We know that if the strikes are needed, they will pose a threat to our own forces by proximity, so the F-35s will each be carrying four 250 lbs. Joint Direct Attack Munitions and two 500 lbs. JDAMs, which are small enough and precise enough to carry out a surgical hit. Beyond that, we have a Spector gunship that will be on standby on the runway here at the airport, along with four additional F-16s carrying more JDAMs." The LNO's tone implied that this was probably overkill.

General Luka then spoke up. "Listen, we're hoping this operation will go off smoothly. We understand you're going to hit some resistance, but we do not want to escalate the situation any further than it already has been. You guys are the best special operators we have. Just get in, neutralize the guards, and get our people out of there."

John Williams, the CIA man, sensed the apprehension in the room as the gravity of the mission began to sink in. He decided to try and rally the crew. "Look, it's an awful situation we find ourselves in, but we have two operators being held captive, and we do not leave a man behind. You guys are going to go in there and get our guys back. Plain and simple."

The briefing ended after a few more questions. The operators who had been assigned to the mission began to discuss the plans amongst themselves. They went over who would be responsible for taking out each guard, their sectors of fire, and how they would proceed. The men spent the better part of two hours deliberating every aspect of the mission with the briefers before they felt they had a firm grasp on exactly how things were going to go down. When they were done talking it through, it was 2300 hours, and they were set to board the C-17 that would take them to their jump points at 0130. The real festivities were scheduled to begin around 0300, roughly an hour before the next shift change for the guards.

****

It was relatively dark in the back of the C-17 as the Delta team got ready for perhaps their most dangerous mission in decades. The aircraft had reached its cruising altitude for the jump, and the pilot had already dimmed the cargo lights and switched them over to a soft red tone. The two crew chiefs walked toward the back of the aircraft and lowered the ramp at the rear of the plane. Their eyes slowly adjusted to the darkness, until they could see everything without additional lighting. The men mentally prepared themselves to make this dangerous night insertion into separatist territory.

As the cool night air circulated through the back of the aircraft, Major Runyon wiped a bead of sweat from his forehead. He stood up and moved toward the ramp with the rest of his team. The men began the ritual of checking and double-checking their equipment, and the aircraft tilted to one side as it made one final correction. As the aircraft leveled out again, the jump light turned red, indicating it was time for them to get ready. The crew chiefs lowered the ramp the rest of the way, opening the back of the aircraft to the black abyss below. Then the light turned from red to green, and the eighteen operators disgorged from the aircraft to attempt a high-stakes rescue.

As the wind whipped past his face, Brian couldn't help but think how insane this mission was...they were jumping into what was essentially a Russian Special Forces base. This was a far cry from the previous assignments they had undertaken, going after Islamic extremists and the occasional drug lord. This was a mission against a legitimate army, one that trained tirelessly to fight America.

****

In the operations room at the airfield, the JSOC team, along with the CIA and SDO, watched the various helmet cams and drone feeds of the mission on large 50-inch screens, anxious as the team members began their approaches to the target. The first team was just coming into weapons range and would engage the guards soon.

The four team members of Alpha broke off from the group and headed stealthily through the woods in the direction of the SA-19. They wound their way through the brush and undergrowth silently, like only trained operators could do. Once they arrived at their checkpoint, they would neutralize the guard force and prepare to blow up the missile system remotely.

Two of Bravo team's six-man group assembled their sniper rifles and moved quickly to their over-watch positions. As soon as they got settled into their spot 400 yards away from the compound, they would engage the guards on the roof. It was a good evening for them to get off clear shots—there was barely any wind, and it was just overcast enough to block some of the moonlight, so the Russians would be less likely to see them coming. Once the roof guards had been taken out, they would shift their fire to the rest of the guard force, allowing time for the rest of the Bravo, Charlie and Delta teams to move into the compound.

At the airfield, everyone held their collective breath for a minute as Charlie and Delta teams continued to move toward their targets. The Bravo team snipers cleared a path for them as they moved quietly through the woods. They stopped every so often to peer around the tree trunks and make sure that the enemy hadn't spotted them yet.

As they got closer to one of the air defense vehicles, one of the Charlie members spied two men manning the system and three more guards. He silently exchanged hand signals to explain how many men he had seen and where they were positioned. Within moments, they had neutralized all five men with surgical precision, barely making any sounds at all. Their rifles had silencers, and they had all been taken down with two shots to the chest and one to the head, so none of them were making any noises either.

A couple of the Charlie team members verified that the five men were indeed dead. Then they all walked around the bodies so that they could begin to place C-4 bricks on the control panel and directly on the missile pods, which were wired to remote-control detonators. Then they quickly moved on to the next task, continuing to clear the perimeter around the compound.

Delta team approached the entrance on the south side of the perimeter wall. As they moved toward the parked enemy vehicles, they shot three of the guards with their suppressed rifles. They all dropped instantly, with hardly a sound.

At that moment, a Spetsnaz soldier who had been using the "bathroom" in the tree line nearby saw his comrades go down and immediately knew they were under attack. He released the safety on his rifle and took aim at two of the attackers he saw moving past where his comrades had just been. Then he fired a quick burst from his rifle.

One of the Americans was killed outright when a bullet hit him in the neck and head, another severely injured by several rounds in the chest and right shoulder. The other two operators returned fire, quickly killing the Russian before he even had time to zip up his pants. Unfortunately, the sound of roughly twenty rounds being rapidly fired had alerted the remaining guards and those in the compound that someone was attempting to attack their base.

Delta team, which had been at the edge of the perimeter wall, immediately kicked in the door to the side entrance leading into the compound. In seconds, they were inside the perimeter and had taken out the two guards at the side door to the building. An unlucky Russian soldier was exiting the door as they approached. With a rapid three-round burst, the man dropped immediately to the ground. A second Russian soldier had been right behind him and was also hit by the bullets. He fell backwards into the hallway.

Before any additional soldiers could run through the door, one of the Delta members threw a flash bang into the hallway, which would stun anyone rushing toward the exit with its excessively bright light and irritatingly high-pitched sound. As soon as it burst, several Delta members rushed in and moved down the hallway, throwing fragmentation grenades into each room. These would spray anyone still in those areas with bursts of deadly shrapnel.

Delta's four-man team began to sprint up the stairs, charging forward to the room that was holding the hostages. Just as they approached the entrance to the second floor, several Spetsnaz soldiers opened the door to the stairwell, and they literally ran into each other. Shocked, there was nothing else for either side to do other than to open fire at close range. In seconds, four Spetsnaz soldiers were dead along with two of the Delta members. The other two Delta operators survived the shoot-out and threw several fragmentation grenades down the hallway of the second floor to clear out any remaining hostiles. Then they proceeded to head for the third floor, toward their priority target.

As they reached the entrance to the third floor, one of the members threw a flash bang into the hallway and counted to two. Once the grenade went off, they both entered the hallway and neutralized the guards on the floor. They moved quickly to the room where the Americans were being held and shot the lock off. As they entered the room, they saw the two Americans bound on the floor, bloodied and bruised. They quickly untied their hands and feet and instructed them, "Follow us out of the building!"

Charlie team had just finished clearing the first floor and moved quickly to help Delta. As Charlie moved up to the stairwell, they collected the bodies of their two fallen comrades. Then they assisted Delta team in moving the prisoners to the extraction point.

Major Runyon sent a quick message to headquarters. "Mission completion. Three KIA. Requesting extraction and gunship support."

While the breach team was moving the prisoners and casualties out of the building, Alpha and Bravo teams were heavily engaged outside. Alpha detonated their charges on the SA-19, shooting a bright and loud explosion into the night sky. Soon after, the charges on the other air defense vehicles and armored personnel carriers were ignited as well.

As the snipers of Bravo team continued to pick off enemy soldiers, they spotted several of them sealing themselves into one of the armored personnel carriers. Once inside the vehicle, they immediately began to work the heavy machine gun, pouring 30mm cannon rounds into the American positions near the perimeter wall and the main compound. All the noises from the shooting and explosions had also alerted several of the militia units that were staying in the surrounding area that something was going on. Those forces began to mobilize and head toward the Russian compound to see what all the fuss was about.

The operations team watching the drone feeds sent a series of updates to Major Runyon, letting him know about the additional enemy forces converging on their position. As the Russian armored vehicle continued to discharge showers of heavy machine-gun fire on the Americans, one of the Delta members unslung the AT4 from his backpack, mounted it on his shoulder, took aim at the troop carrier, and fired. In a split second, the rocket fired from the tube and impacted on the side of the vehicle, causing a small explosion. A few seconds later, smoke billowed excessively from its side, and then flames began to grow more and more noticeable.

Runyon yelled into his radio, "Command, this is Striker One. We need air support. Take out those incoming reinforcements and keep them away from our LZ until our gunships arrive. How copy?" As soon as he finished speaking, he raised his rifle to fire another three-round burst in the direction of several enemy soldiers.

"Striker One, this is Command. Good copy. Stand by for air support," the JSOC operators radioed back.

High above the battle going on below, Lightning One received the call to begin dropping ordnance. The F-35 pilot entered the targeting data and double-checked it before arming his JDAMs. In a matter of seconds after receiving the order to engage the ground targets, Lightning One dropped two of his 250 lbs. smart bombs and began to guide them in toward several of the vehicles heading toward the compound.

As the Delta operators moved to the extraction point, the fighting died down until it eventually stopped. The two JDAMs demolished several of the vehicles that had been carrying additional reinforcements toward the Russian compound. The arrival of the two Apache gunships further eviscerated what little resistance remained in the area. As the gunships circled the area, the V-280s landed and picked up the team and began to whisk them away to safety.

Wiping the sweat from his face, Major Runyon sat in the helicopter and began to run through the operation in his head and ruminate on the details of what had transpired. Three of their comrades had been killed, and another four were injured. However, they had recovered the prisoners before they could be transferred to Russia. They had also thoroughly destroyed a Russian Spetsnaz base and killed many separatist rebels.

Chapter 7

Repercussions

Moscow, Russia

Kremlin, Office of the President

"The Americans did *what* this morning?!" the Russian president demanded angrily as he stood up.

"The Americans carried out a raid on our Special Forces base camp early this morning. They recovered the two CIA prisoners, the ones that were scheduled to be transferred to Moscow later this evening," Colonel General Boris Egorkin explained. General Egorkin was the head of the Russian Army, and apparently also the unlucky man charged with bringing the terrible news to President Petrov this morning.

The President pushed his chair back and paced behind his desk, thinking. He looked up at his general and his Secretary of Defense. Indignant, he said, "The Americans believe they can do whatever they want. They believe there are no consequences to their actions. Fine. If they want to play this game, if they want to get directly involved in Ukraine with their military, then so will we."

Squinting at General Egorkin, he demanded, "What forces do we have in Ukraine right now?" The President was extremely angry.

"We've suffered enough humiliation at the hands of the Americans," he thought. He fumed at the idea that those Yankees would believe that they alone could exert their influence on the world. What hubris that they could think they alone were the arbiters of who should remain in control of his country. Enough was enough.

Colonel General Egorkin walked toward the President's desk. Petrov signaled for him to take a seat in one of the golden chairs in the parlor near the fireplace. He knew he needed to calm himself down, so he wanted to move away from his desk and change the scenery up.

The parlor room was the section of his office where he liked to hold discussions with his senior advisors and world leaders when they came to visit. He found that if he changed his immediate setting, he could often change his perspective on a problem, which helped him think more clearly.

Taking his cue from the President as everyone in the room took their seats, General Egorkin began, "We have 100 Spetsnaz soldiers in Ukraine conducting paramilitary training and acting as military advisors. Well…twenty-nine of them were killed this morning during the American raid."

Several angry murmurs and grumbles broke out in the room. He paused a moment to let them get it out of their system, and then he continued, "Mr. President, you asked what forces we have in Ukraine at this time. We have 1,500 soldiers listed in 'unofficial' duty who are engaging the Ukrainian forces with the various militia units. Often, they are the ones leading the ambushes and attacks plaguing the Ukrainians right now. We have another 150 personnel operating the various air defense units throughout the separatist regions, and roughly 400 soldiers operating the various artillery and heavy mortar units." He was reading the figures from a pre-prepared list that he always kept updated just in case the President asked this exact question.

Throughout the last six months, they had increased the number of military members operating in Ukraine, in response to the introduction of NATO personnel. When the Ukrainian PM leased one of their former air bases to NATO, they donated nearly a dozen anti-aircraft systems to the separatists in response. They also increased the number and quality of arms they were supplying to the separatists. Now that the Americans—and to a lesser extent, other NATO member states—were providing military advisors, Russia began to step up the number of advisors in Ukraine as well.

President Petrov paused for a moment, thinking. "I'd hoped we would've been able to use those two prisoners in our next operation, but clearly that is not going to happen," he said. "What the Americans did this morning, however, was a brazen attack on our military. I want to get all the propaganda value we can out of that. I believe this attack, as awful as it was, will give us the pretext we've been looking for to move forward with Red Storm."

The President looked each person in the eye, as if assessing their loyalty or the condition of their soul. Then he turned to his commanding general. "What's the status of Red Storm? Are we ready yet?"

General Egorkin responded, "Our ground forces are ready to begin. So is the air force. We just need the orders to be given."

Sergei Shoygu, the Secretary of Defense, interjected, "Mr. President, the challenge is getting the weapons and personnel into Ukraine without the American and NATO surveillance drones and aircraft detecting them. They are monitoring the border closely and are providing the Ukrainians with a substantial tactical advantage. There's no question that we need to neutralize the drones."

President Petrov sighed. He agreed; the drones were becoming a big problem that needed to be handled. "This needs to be rectified then, before we move forward with backing the referendum and additional troops. Let's consider something else. Why not announce our intention to implement a no-fly zone to bring an end to the bloodshed while the separatists hold their elections?"

Minister Kozlov replied, "I don't think it's advisable to do this."

Petrov turned and barked, "The Americans have instituted a no-fly zone over parts of Syria. I say we institute a no-fly zone over the eastern half of Ukraine. The Ukrainians have made use of their air force against the separatists; the Americans used it this morning against our own forces. So, let's implement our own no-fly zone."

He paused for a second while he looked over the maps again and then placed his finger on an area of the map near the border. "Here, move three of our S-400s to this location here. Let's also deploy two additional S-400s and three S-300s in Belarus as well. I'd also like to have one of our S-500s deployed at this location and guarded by additional S-300s. Finally, let's move several squadrons of Su-34s and Su-35s to our air bases in this sector as well," Petrov ordered.

"Mr. President," Sergei responded, "I agree that what the Americans did this morning is an outrage, and something needs to be done. However, by moving these air defense systems forward like this, and then issuing this ultimatum, it will draw a lot of criticism from NATO and the US. We can walk up to the line with them, but we have to be willing to cross it if we do."

Petrov thought about this for a moment before responding, "This is the pretext we've been waiting for to initiate Red Storm. We need to seize it, especially since we have strong support from the Chinese."

Petrov sat back in his chair. He looked up at the ceiling, admiring the intricate work the designers had carved into the molding. Then he turned his gaze back to the men around him. "I understand the consequence of moving forward with Red Storm. We've been training and rebuilding our military toward this goal for years. We've been in secret talks with the Chinese for nearly as long, and we've finally gained their support. The Americans are at their weakest point politically and militarily in decades. This is the time to act."

Continuing, he added, "At some point, we as a nation have to stand up and defend our interests. At the end of the Cold War, the Americans and NATO agreed that they would not expand NATO's borders closer to our own. Then they accepted the Baltic States, Poland, Hungary and Romania into their fold. They tried to add Georgia, and now they want to add Ukraine. Russia has held up our end of the Cold War deal, it is NATO and the Americans who have not."

Petrov turned to the foreign minister. "Kozlov," he began, "we've been discussing a referendum with the separatist leaders, one that would support them leaving the Ukraine and forming their own country, their own government. Their leader said they are going to announce this shortly. I believe we should move diplomatically to get things rolling with them, get our own allies to support and recognize them as a country once the election is over. I believe it's now time for us to work with these separatist leaders openly and move to have the referendum take place in our no-fly zone."

Looking at his advisors and seeing them nod their heads, Petrov felt a bit more confident in this decision. "Once we institute the no-fly zone, I want us to issue an ultimatum to the Ukrainian government. We'll tell them that they need to withdraw their military from the east so a referendum can be held, and the UN can be brought in to monitor the vote. If the people vote to leave and form their own country, then Ukraine must abide by it. If they vote to remain, then we'll leave eastern Ukraine and withdraw our support from them."

No one seemed to have any objections. There was a moment of silence as Petrov continued to formulate the plan in his mind. Then he asserted, "I also want some of our forces to cross into Ukraine at the appointed time as 'peacekeepers' to protect the civilian population from the fascist government forces. They have killed nearly two thousand civilians in the last few weeks. It's time to send forces in there to help protect them from this illegitimate dictatorship so that a vote can take place."

The President paused for a moment, sitting back in his chair; he looked at some of the pictures on the wall as he thought about what this would all mean. He took a deep breath and slowly exhaled. "I know this action may push us closer to a confrontation with the West. The EU and the Americans need to learn that not every vote goes their way, that sometimes, people do not want to embrace their form of democracy. The EU also needs our natural gas and oil, and this will only become more acute as we get closer to winter. While the Americans may threaten us, I do not believe the EU will follow through on any threat of military force. If they do, we simply turn off their gas and oil and refuse to turn it back on. In the meantime, I want us to begin preparation for a limited war with the West. I hope it doesn't come to that, but I want our military to move to a war footing and begin preparations to deal with the threat," Petrov said, very seriously.

Looking at his Minister of Defense, he ordered, "Begin to have some of our subs and other ships move to shadow the American and NATO warships in the Baltic and Black Seas. Also, have our cyber-hackers prepare their zero-day attacks against Ukraine and Europe. If the Americans do decide they want a fight, then we'll make them realize there is more than one way to fight and win a war," the President said with a sly smile.

The others in the room nodded and smiled as well. They all knew what he meant. The future of warfare was not necessarily going to be through the conventional fight. Russia had spent over a decade building an incredibly talented army of hackers. They had spent years developing a broad portfolio of skilled individuals, testing various countries' cyber defenses. They had even carried out several major cyberattacks, like the time they hit the Georgian government communications system the day that the Russian forces invaded, or when they had successfully taken down a Ukrainian power plant. These attacks proved they could reach out through the digital world and cause damage in the physical realm.

The meeting wound down. There were some clarifying questions on the President's orders, but the overall directives were untouched.

As soon as the official business with Petrov ended, Colonel General Boris Egorkin grabbed a secured line and began to issue mobilization orders to the 1st Tank Army, telling them to begin deploying to various military bases within striking distance of Ukraine. He also began to mobilize the 6th Army, ordering them to prepare to follow the 1st Tank Army into Ukraine if an assault order were to be given.

Foreign Minister Dmitry Kozlov stayed back to talk longer with the President about the timeline of the referendum vote, the issues surrounding getting a UN observer in there, and the deployment of Russian soldiers to remove the Ukrainian forces from east Ukraine so a vote could be held. They also discussed the media campaign and how that would be waged to sway public opinion.

Petrov got an almost nauseated look on his face. "Kozlov, I want you to show unedited footage of all of the dead bodies of our soldiers from the raid the Americans just carried out. Run news articles on the families of the soldiers who were killed—I want it to be clear that the US and NATO are the true aggressors, not Russia. It should be a full-court press to humiliate the Americans and pressure them to leave Ukraine and end their support of this fascist regime in Kiev. We need to paint Prime Minister Groysman for what he is: a monster who is only bent on exacting revenge and killing those who oppose him."

Chapter 8
Red Storm

Moscow, Russia

Chinese Embassy

After going over some of the finer details of Operation Red Storm with the President, it was time for Foreign Minister Dmitry Kozlov to get things rolling with the Chinese. His office phoned ahead and said he needed to speak directly with the ambassador, in person. The officials at the embassy told Kozlov's aide they would be ready for his arrival.

As Minister Kozlov's fancy black Mercedes-Benz pulled up to the embassy, several guards were there to open his door and lead him into the embassy. He quickly made his way up to the ambassador's office, where he saw Ambassador Yin waiting to receive him.

Smiling, Yin offered his hand. "This is a most welcome surprise, Minister Kozlov. To what do I owe this visit?"

While he was quite welcoming, the ambassador had been thrown off by this sudden interruption in his schedule. *"I wonder what has happened to cause this short-notice meeting?*" he wondered. It was certainly not the usual protocol for him to suddenly show up at his office instead of calling first.

Kozlov jumped right into it. "I'm sorry for the short notice, but this couldn't be discussed over the phone. It needed to be done in person. I needed to tell you that it's time to move forward with Red Storm." His voice was quiet, almost hushed.

The ambassador nodded, a slight smile forming on his face. The Chinese had been waiting for this day as well. It was finally time for them to reassert their dominance in Asia as the hegemon, not the US.

"I understand. I'll let Chairman Zhang know Russia is now moving forward," Yin replied as Minister Kozlov got up and made his way out of his office. Nothing more needed to be said; the two countries had been coordinating this plan for years, each slowly implementing their various parts until they were ready to initiate the entire plan. Now, it was time to move forward and begin the final preparations that would change the military and political dimensions of the world.

Chapter 9

Consequences

Kiev, Ukraine

Office of the Prime Minister

Prime Minister Volodymyr Groysman was nervous as he lit his fourth cigarette of the day at the early hour of 11 a.m. He was absolutely incensed that President Petrov had the audacity to declare a no-fly zone over nearly half of his country. As if that weren't enough, Petrov was backing the separatist leaders' call for a referendum vote. As he angrily huffed on his Ziganov, a vein on his forehead pulsated.

"I have no way of stopping this," he bemoaned to himself. Unless the Americans and NATO were willing to intercede, whatever was left of his air force would be grounded.

Despite his negative mood, a glimmer of hope was seated not that far from him. Sitting nearby in the formal meeting room next to his office were the American Secretary of State, Travis Johnson, the Deputy Commander of US European Command or EUCOM, Lieutenant General James Cotton, Ambassador Duncan Rice and his senior defense official, General Luka. There was also a small crowd of aides sitting down at the end of the table with notepads and pens, ready to take notes. The steward poured everyone a cup of coffee and placed a small tray of snacks on the table before he left the room, closing the double oak doors behind him.

Once Groysman saw his trusty steward enter the room, he quickly put out the rest of his cigarette and walked into the room. His military chief of staff, Lieutenant General Serhiv Popko, and two of his aides were already there waiting for him as well.

The prime minister took a deep breath to calm himself before he spoke. "Mr. Secretary, what the Russians have announced is tantamount to war against my country. We are in the middle of a civil war that has lasted for three years because *they* have been supporting and propping up the pro-Russian separatists. Thousands of civilians have died, tens of thousands more have been displaced. What can America do to help us in this crisis?" he implored, looking the Secretary of State in the eyes with an unrelenting stare.

Secretary Johnson was still trying to figure out exactly how far they could push the issue with Russia. In the past three days, the Pryluky Air Base had come under nearly a dozen heavy mortar attacks. Six Americans had been killed and fifteen others had been injured. NATO had also lost eight soldiers in the attacks, with another seventeen wounded. The media were asking a lot of questions about what exactly the US and NATO were doing in Ukraine.

The Secretary glanced toward the Deputy EUCOM Commander before responding in his thick Texas accent, "Mr. Prime Minister, our president understands the tough situation you are in right now. We want to help, but we also want to make sure things do not spiral out of control any further. As you know, the Pryluky Air Base has come under attack multiple times since our Special Forces rescued our two people who had been captured eight days ago. President Gates has affirmed that he wants to provide more support to your government in these trying times. I have been authorized by the President and our congress to provide Ukraine with $1.8 billion in foreign aid to help shore up your economy and put more people in your country back to work."

"I hope there's more," thought Groysman. *"I won't be able to fight off the Russians with a lower unemployment rate."*

Secretary of State Johnson nodded to General Cotton to speak next.

"My command has also been authorized by the Secretary of Defense and the President to provide a significant increase in military aid and assistance. We going to give your military 400 additional MRAP vehicles and 350 Stryker infantry fighting vehicles. We are also going to give your army 90 M1A1 Abrams main battle tanks or MBTs. To assist the integration of your forces with this additional equipment, we are also going to provide 900 military trainers and civilian contractors to help train your forces on the maintenance and servicing of the vehicles." He brought out a stack of folders, which had the details of the military aid that would be provided, and handed them out to the Ukrainians.

Even though the crowd was still rummaging through the folders, General Cotton continued, "This, of course, is not an overnight solution, and it will take time to implement. We can start the shipment of vehicles and equipment to your country tomorrow, but we are still looking at several months before most of this equipment arrives and we can begin to train your forces on it."

Secretary Johnson spoke up again, "We are committed to helping your government gain control of all of Ukraine. We also know it will take time to get your forces trained up to handle this task. Your military has made some great progress these past six weeks, and we know you have suffered heavy losses. We hope this infusion of cash, military equipment, trainers, and additional advisors will help your government succeed in finishing off this pro-Russian separatist movement." He spoke calmly, as if they were talking about a business deal selling computers and not military hardware for the purpose of killing their fellow countrymen.

The prime minister sat back in his chair, digesting what he was just told. While the money and military equipment were greatly needed and would aid them immensely in their struggle, it still didn't address the problem of what to do about the no-fly zone being imposed on their country, or this pending referendum vote.

"Mr. Secretary, my country is grateful for the help and assistance, we truly are. We wouldn't have had the success we've had up to this point without the help and assistance of America and NATO. However, the assistance you are currently offering doesn't address the larger issue of the no-fly zone or this referendum. How are we going to handle this? What's America's solution for dealing with this?" Groysman asked, somewhat annoyed.

"We are not 100% certain that the Russians will actually enforce the no-fly zone. We think they're blustering and hoping that the threat of it will cause you to come to the negotiating table and give in. As to the referendum vote, I'll leave that to Secretary Johnson to answer," General Cotton answered.

Secretary Johnson nodded, adding, "With regard to the vote, we won't recognize the results. We will work with the rest of the NATO members and the EU to deny the authenticity of the results."

The Ukrainian general, Serhiy Popko, interjected, "So is America going to test the no-fly zone with one of your aircraft? We've already lost nearly 40% of our air force in the last six weeks. We can't afford to lose additional aircraft to test your theory," he said, somewhat incensed that the Americans didn't seem to be taking this threat seriously.

Since this was a military question, General Cotton responded, "As a matter of fact, yes, we are planning on using one of our aircraft to test the Russians' resolve. When the no-fly zone goes into effect tomorrow, America, along with NATO, will fly several combat aircraft through it, within Ukrainian airspace."

He paused briefly. Hearing no objections or questions, Cotton continued, "The Germans will be flying two Eurofighters, and we'll have two of our F-16s fly a joint patrol within Ukrainian airspace, along the border. If the Russians do engage our aircraft, then we will respond. The aircraft in question will be carrying antiradar missiles and jamming equipment, just in case."

General Popko leaned back in his chair, smiling proudly. The Americans really were going to honor their word to protect Ukraine and stand up to Vladimir Petrov after all. "I must say, I did not believe you would test their resolve," he said. He was grateful, though a bit concerned about things going south.

Secretary Johnson smiled and let a laugh escape his mouth. "There's a new president in America, and he's not afraid of Petrov or anyone else in the world," he said to the snickering of some of his aides.

Ambassador Rice stayed silent through the two-hour meeting. He couldn't believe what he was hearing. Not only was the President an inexperienced novice at running a government, his Secretary of State was a Texas cowboy as well. They were going to openly test Petrov, forcing him to either lose face or engage them.

"Don't they realize that wars have started over smaller missteps and mistakes than these?" he thought. He shuddered. Nothing good could possibly come of the American and German aircraft crossing that no-fly zone the next day.

Chapter 10

No-Fly Zone

Moscow, Russia

Kremlin, Office of the President

Kozlov and Semenov walked into the parlor room to see President Petrov talking with General Egorkin, General Kuznetsov from the Air Force, and Admiral Petrukhin from the Navy. As they made their way to join them, they noticed the four of them were sipping on some vodka. It was only 9 a.m.—clearly, the President was in a good mood if he was having a drink *this* early with his senior military leaders. They took their seats as a steward brought them a glass of vodka and placed the bottle between them.

Petrov was finishing a story of when he had been the KGB Director in East Germany; he was bemoaning the struggles the Soviet Union had faced back then and the mistakes they'd made in dealing with the West. The President was determined to right some of those wrongs now and create a newer, stronger Russia that was as robust economically as it was militarily.

President Petrov turned to the new arrivals in the room. "General Kuznetsov tells me our air defense systems are operational. We have a multilayered defense, able to defeat anything the Americans throw at them. General Egorkin assures me that our missile defense system protecting our air defense systems are also ready. So, when the no-fly zone goes into effect in forty-seven minutes, I want any US, NATO or Ukrainian aircraft and drones flying over it to be engaged. I want them shot down," the President said resolutely. He raised a glass of vodka to his generals as a salute and downed it with one gulp.

Kozlov felt he should press the President one last time before it was too late to turn back. "Are you sure you want to do this, Mr. President? We have already turned world opinion against the Americans for their attack on our soldiers. We are gaining in global sympathy and moving forward with the referendum vote. I do not want to lose our progress," he said. Although Kozlov was hoping to approach things differently, he too raised his glass of vodka and took a sip. He was hoping he could get by with nursing just the one glass; he wanted to keep his wits about him for what he was sure would be a long day.

"Shoygu, did the Americans shoot down a Syrian helicopter that they said strayed into the no-fly zone they implemented in Syria a few months ago?" asked Petrov.

"Yes, they did shoot down the helicopter, Mr. President. They even threatened to shoot down one of our own before we turned around and went back to base."

The President smiled. "That proves my point. If the Americans can impose a no-fly zone on other countries, then so can Russia. I want all drones, helicopters and aircraft flying over the Ukrainian no-fly zone to be shot down at 10 a.m.," he announced emphatically as he poured himself and the generals another glass of vodka. He motioned for his two senior advisors to join them in a toast.

"Today," Petrov said, "Russia has reasserted itself as a world power."

Chapter 11

Enforcement – The First Steps to War

Kiev, Ukraine

18,000 feet above the ground

Major Jake LaFine, call sign "Frenchy," leveled off his F-16 at 18,000 feet with his wingman, Captain Jorge "Bean" Ramos, as they began to fly toward the self-imposed Russian no-fly zone. They had been briefed on what to do if the Russians fired on them. They were not to hold anything back.

They were each carrying two high-speed anti-radiation missiles, or HARMs. If they were activated, they would search out and destroy the source of nearby radar sites, unless the enemy radar operator turned off their radar before the missiles reached their target. The two German Eurofighters were carrying two HARM missiles each as well. The American aircraft also carried specific electronic warfare pods to help them defeat any potential surface-to-air missiles or SAMs as well.

"Bean, let's get this show on the road and go pay our Russian friends a visit," Frenchy said as he led their little air contingent toward the eastern half of Ukraine.

As they approached the no-fly zone, a Russian voice hailed them over an open international aircraft radio frequency. "NATO aircraft, you are approaching a restricted no-fly zone. If you enter the no-fly zone, you will be fired upon."

They ignored the caller and continued their mission. The voice called out again, "NATO aircraft, once again, you are approaching a no-fly zone. No combat aircraft are allowed to enter the no-fly zone. Turn around before you are fired upon."

****

As Colonel Denis Manturov sat in the command trailer of the S-400 air defense system, or as NATO called them, SA-21 Growlers, he noted the American and German pilots' arrogance and complete disregard of their message. President Petrov was right, the Americans no longer feared them.

"Well, that is about to change," he thought. The SA-21 had never been fired at another nation before, and Manturov was sure the Americans had no idea what they were up against.

As Colonel Manturov looked at the radar screen, he also noticed the Americans had seven drones heading to various positions in the no-fly zone to provide ground support to the government forces. These were the same positions the drones had previously been located at over the past week, providing the eyes and ears for the Ukrainian ground forces attacking the pro-Russian separatists. After the brazen American attack on the Spetsnaz camp two weeks ago, Manturov reveled in being the one to draw first blood for the Motherland.

He turned to the radar operators. "Have the radars lock onto the enemy aircraft and stand by to engage any antiradar missiles the Americans may shoot at us."

The operators simply nodded.

"Send a message to the S-300 battery to have them lock on, and engage the American drones now," Colonel Manturov continued.

After a tense moment of waiting, one of the radar operators said excitedly, "I have radar lock on the four enemy aircraft."

One of the younger soldiers piped up from the radio, "The S-300 battery says they have the American drones locked up as well. Awaiting your order." A trace of excitement could be heard in his voice.

Colonel Manturov looked at the men in the command center; all their eyes were locked on him, waiting for him to deliver the final authorization. At that moment, Denis knew he was about to change the world forever. He took a deep breath, then announced, "Fire! Engage the hostiles and shoot them down."

Within seconds, the S-400 fired eight surface-to-air missiles, two for each of the enemy aircraft. The S-300 battery closest to the Ukrainian border also fired a series of seven surface-to-air missiles at the American drones. In seconds, the Russians made it known to the world that they meant what they said about enforcing a no-fly zone over eastern Ukraine.

Next, Manturov barked a series of orders to help them prepare their systems to engage any American missiles that might be fired at them in response.

****

Major LaFine's warning alarms suddenly blared in a dissonance of obnoxious beeping, alerting him that a Russian air defense radar system had locked onto his aircraft. He silently told himself, *"This is no big deal. They're just trying to scare us."*

His little air contingent continued to ignore the Russian warnings. Though he would never admit it to anyone, he secretly felt terrified by the warning alarm; in the nine years he had been flying, he had never been locked up by an enemy radar system before. Just as he looked to his right to see Bean flying next to him, his alarm system blared a different warning at him—this time telling him that the air defense radar system had just fired two surface-to-air missiles at him. A countdown readout told Frenchy that he had roughly three minutes until the missiles would reach him.

"Bean, we've just been shot at by those Russian SAMs," Frenchy told his friend. "Engage them with your missiles, and then let's try to get out of Dodge as fast as possible."

Frenchy toggled the safety off on his weapon system. In a matter of seconds, he had turned his missiles targeting system on, ensured he had a good lock on the radar system that was tracking him, and fired. In seconds, both of his HARM missiles were on their way to their targets.

Frenchy and his wingman began to take evasive maneuvers, weaving and bobbing, climbing and then plummeting. He had a sickening feeling that his missiles wouldn't hit the enemy radar site before those SAMs reached him. As he turned on his electronic counter-measures, he sent a radio message back to Ground

Command, letting them know that he had just been shot at and that he had two SAMs heading toward him.

The German and American aircraft immediately began to take evasive maneuvers, turning on their electronic counter-measures. The aircrafts' automated self-defense systems began to drop chaff canisters as the missiles began to close in on their targets. Next, the F-16 and Eurofighters began to shoot out flares and additional chaff canisters in an effort to throw off the enemy missiles.

Unbeknownst to the US Air Force and NATO, the Russians had upgraded the tracking software on their missiles, which allowed them to better distinguish between chaff clouds, flare heat signatures, and actual aircraft. The SA-21s could also see through the electronic trickery of the American electronic warfare pods and countermeasures being employed. Within minutes, the SAMs closed the distance on the American and NATO aircraft and collided with all four. As the flaming wreckage began to fall to the earth below, two parachutes could be seen drifting down to the ground. There was one German and one American—the other two pilots were not so lucky.

As the four NATO aircraft were destroyed, the drone pilots watched helplessly as their drones were systematically destroyed by the SA-10s. At first, they had no idea they were being tracked; then they received a flash message that enemy SAMs had been fired at them and they should take evasive maneuvers. The best a drone could do was try to drop as low to the ground as possible and hope they could lose the enemy missiles in the ground clutter. Unfortunately, that did not happen.

The Russians had one A-50 Mainstay airborne early-warning system or AWACS aircraft providing exceptional targeting data for the SA-10s and SA-21 missiles. While the American HARM antiradar missiles began to head toward the Russian radar systems, one of the other S-400 systems that had not engaged the American aircraft fired off a string of missile interceptors. Rather than turning off their radar systems, the Russians wanted to demonstrate the ability of their system to shoot down the American missiles. All four American HARM missiles were destroyed without further incident. The Germans never even got a shot off.

In the blink of an eye, the Russians had enforced the no-fly zone. They had successfully reasserted themselves as a world power, not to be trifled with. They had effectively demonstrated to the US and NATO that they now controlled the skies over eastern Ukraine, and their show of force implied that if they wanted, Russian control could extend to all of Ukraine and the majority of Poland as well.

Chapter 12

The Box

Kiev, Ukraine

US Embassy

Chancellery, Ambassador's Office

Duncan was eating a bagel and cream cheese at his desk as he read the most recent State Department cables from the night before. He was perusing through a message between the Secretary General of NATO and the US Secretary of State discussing the Russian no-fly zone.

"Mr. Secretary, I do not believe the Russians will try to enforce the no-fly zone," wrote the NATO Secretary. "They will bluster and threaten, but in the end, they will blink."

"For all our sakes, I hope they are right," thought Duncan. *"This has the potential to spiral out of control quickly."*

Just as he finished reading the cable and shoved the last bite of his breakfast into his mouth, General Luka barged into his office.

"Ambassador Rice, we have a serious problem," he announced. His face was all red as he towered over Duncan's desk.

The ambassador almost choked as he tried to hurry up and swallow his food, so he could speak without his mouth full. "Please," he said as he grabbed a sip of coffee, "have a seat, General. Tell me what's going on." He had a sick feeling in his stomach.

The general sat down and took a breath before continuing, "They did it. The Russians really did it."

"Did what, exactly?" asked Ambassador Rice, confused.

"I just got confirmation from our people at the airfield. The Russians just shot down two American F-16s and two German Eurofighters that entered the no-fly zone. They also eliminated *all seven* of our drones that we had operating over eastern Ukraine," General Luka explained. He was still almost out of breath and seething with anger.

"*This can't be happening,*" Duncan bemoaned to himself. "*I told them we needed to tread carefully with the Russians.*" Now that they were boxed into a corner, they had no option left but to fight.

"Take a breath, General, please," urged the ambassador. "Let's start from the beginning. You said the

Russians just shot down four Allied aircraft and our drones. Have we recovered the pilots yet? What's their status?"

The general took a deep breath and held it for a second to try and slow his breathing down and regain his composure. "Yes, the search-and-rescue unit recovered two of the pilots—one German and one American. The other two pilots died when their aircraft blew up," he said in a more controlled voice.

The wheels started twirling around inside of Ambassador Rice's head. He'd have to talk to the Secretary of State and the US European Commander. "*Ugh. I'm going to have to be the one to tell Prime Minister Groysman about this incident too,*" he realized, which made him especially unhappy since he'd warned them all this could go south.

Between all the competing thoughts, he realized that he needed all the facts before he talked to anyone. "General Luka, what's being done about this right now? What are the next steps?" He wanted to know if a retaliatory strike was already being planned.

The general, now more composed, responded, "I've alerted the Ukrainian desk at the Pentagon. The commander at the airfield has sent a flash message to NATO headquarters and US European Command headquarters as well—"

Just then, the regional security officer walked into the ambassador's office. Without so much as apologizing for interrupting, the RSO blurted out, "—Sir, we've received an urgent communiqué from Washington. They're requesting that you speak with them down in the Box." He indicated with his arm that they should both follow him down to the basement of the embassy.

Each embassy had a "Box," which is a sensitive compartmented information facility or SCIF. It was typically a small room, big enough to seat maybe eight people, and it was always filled with secret and top-secret communication equipment and computers. It was the one room in the embassy that was truly secured from electronic spying, and typically only a handful of people at an embassy had access to it.

As the group made their way down to the basement, the ambassador saw that the Marine guards had increased their security posture. They were now wearing body armor, and instead of their usual firearms, they were carrying their M4s. Once they all reached the Box, they filed in through the narrow steel door and took their seats at the small conference table.

One of the communications specialists from the National Reconnaissance Office had already gotten the video feed set up. There were several screens: one had been labeled "White House Situation Room," another "Pentagon Operations Center," a third read "SHAPE headquarters," and the final one was labeled "US European Command."

People continued to file into the rooms at the various outstations, until someone came on from the White House Situation Room, indicating the meeting would start shortly. Then, the President of the United States walked into the Situation Room and took his seat at the head of the table.

Gates wasted no time with formalities. "All right," he said, "someone fill me in. What the devil is going on in Ukraine?"

General Wheeler, the Supreme Allied Commander, Europe, who commanded NATO and US European Command, spoke up first. "Mr. President, SACEUR here. Approximately 33 minutes ago, two American F-16s and two German Eurofighters flying under NATO control were shot down by Russian surface-to-air missile systems. They also shot down all seven of our surveillance drones, Mr. President."

Gates turned to his National Security Advisor or NSA, retired general Tom McMillan, and barked, "What the blazes happened, General?! I thought the consensus was that the Russians wouldn't do this. What went wrong?"

The NSA looked at the others in the room briefly, then back to the President. "Sir, it was our assessment that the Russians would not engage our aircraft to enforce their no-fly zone. Clearly, we were wrong, and there is no excuse, Mr. President." McMillan's tone was as apologetic as the retired general could muster—he was never wrong. This was a new concept for him.

Travis Johnson, the Secretary of State, spoke up quickly. "Mr. President, I clearly underestimated the Russians' resolve to enforce this no-fly zone. When I spoke with Foreign Minister Kozlov yesterday, he said that they would enforce it and encouraged us to not test them, but frankly, we believed them to be grandstanding. We thought that they might lock our aircraft up with ground radars, maybe attack one of our drones, but we didn't believe they would attack our fighters," he said in his thick Texas draw.

Tyrone Wilson, the youngest Director of the CIA and a rising star by all accounts, added, "We knew the Russians were moving SA-10s and their more advanced SA-21s into the area, but our analysts believed that this was being done to enforce the idea of the no-fly zone. Our Russia desk has also reported a substantial increase in Russian troop movements toward the border region as well. In light of this recent act of aggression, we have to assume they may be positioning those forces on the border for a potential incursion into eastern Ukraine."

The last statement only muddied the waters for the President. Gates was clearly getting mad; his cheeks were flushed red. However, he didn't break into a tirade or outburst, at least not yet. He simply looked at his senior advisors and asked the obvious next question. "So, what do we do now? How do we recover from this obvious miscalculation in intelligence?"

Tom McMillan spoke up first. "Sir, we need to move our forces in Ukraine and Europe to Threat Condition Delta. They need to be prepared in case the Russians are planning any further military action. Following that, we need to reach out to them diplomatically and get an explanation from them as to why they openly attacked four NATO aircraft. Third, I recommend that we place additional military units in the US on alert in case they need to be rapidly deployed to Europe."

James Castle, the Secretary of Defense, agreed. "I have to concur with the NSA. We should work to solve this diplomatically, but we also need to be ready to respond militarily, if necessary. The Russians just shot down four Allied aircraft. We need to make it clear to them that this kind of aggression will not be tolerated and that their actions will lead to swift repercussions. We should send more military aid to the Ukrainians along with additional military advisors, and then impose additional sanctions on Russia. This way we aren't getting American or NATO troops involved in a direct military confrontation with Russia, but we would also send a strong message that this type of aggression won't be tolerated."

Ambassador Rice couldn't believe what he was hearing. *"Is everyone really so woefully unaware of how all these moves would be viewed by the Kremlin?"* he wondered. Part of him knew he should just stay silent and let the others do the talking, but the other part knew that he had to say something before things spiraled out of control even further.

Clearing his throat rather loudly, he got the attention of everyone on the screens. "Mr. President, this is Ambassador Duncan Rice, the ambassador here in Kiev. If I may, I'd like to say something," he interjected, hoping the President would give him a chance to talk.

The President looked directly at him. "Ambassador Rice, I'm glad you spoke up. You are the man on the ground there—I'd like to know what your opinion is and what you think we should do," Gates said encouragingly.

Duncan couldn't believe that the President was not only going to let him speak but actually wanted to hear his advice. He saw the look on Travis Johnson's face and nearly chuckled aloud. It was obvious that the Secretary of State had no idea what he was about to say and that clearly made him nervous.

Assuming control of the meeting for a brief moment, Ambassador Rice began, "Mr. President, prior to becoming the Ambassador to Ukraine, I worked as the Deputy Chief of Mission to Belarus for four years. Before that, I was the senior political officer at our Moscow embassy. I have a lot of experience dealing with the Russian government and their allies."

The President nodded, appearing impressed with his background so far.

Duncan continued, "The Russians view our involvement in Ukraine as encroaching on their territory and interests, especially when we signed that ten-year lease on the Pryluky Air Base outside of Kiev four months ago. It would be like Russia signing a military lease with Tampico, Mexico, less than fifty-miles from the US border."

Duncan knew he needed to get to his main point, but he also needed to set the context. "Mr. President, at the end of the Cold War, America and NATO agreed that we would not expand the NATO borders closer to Russia. Throughout the late 1990s, and then through the 2000s and 2010s, the US and NATO broke that deal time and time again. We accepted the Baltic States into NATO, then Poland, Hungary, and Romania. We even tried to get the Republic of Georgia to join."

"With Ukraine interested in joining the European Union, if their application were accepted, then joining NATO would be a foregone conclusion. Mr. President, America broke our deal with Russia, and Petrov sees the continued advance of American bases ever closer to their border as a direct threat. I believe that President Petrov has placed a line of no-return over Ukraine. He chose to implement and enforce this no-fly zone *after* our raid on their Special Forces compound. If we push Moscow further, I'm confident the Russians will escalate this conflict, which is something none of us want to see," Duncan said, hoping that he hadn't pushed things too far. He knew he was essentially speaking against what most of the President's advisors were telling him, but he felt he had an obligation to give the President the best advice possible, even if Gates did not like or agree with him.

Tom McMillan jumped right in after Duncan had finished speaking, angrily asserting, "With respect, Mr. Ambassador, whose side are you on?! It sounds like you believe we've brought this upon ourselves and we should just back down and give Petrov what he wants." His voice was dripping with disdain.

Before anyone else could add more to the discussion, the President interrupted to say, "Ambassador Rice, thank you for your candid and frank opinion. I'm still a bit new to the history of Russia and NATO's past dealings, but I can see how the Russians may perceive our new base as a direct threat to them."

McMillan's jaw dropped a bit. *It almost sounds like the President is siding with Duncan*," he thought skeptically. He was sure that Gates would side with the war hawks. "*Maybe I misjudged him*," he considered.

The President continued, "Before we deploy military forces and talk about an appropriate response, I want to know why our intelligence was so faulty as not to know that the Russians would, in fact, shoot our aircraft down. I've been giving the intelligence community a lot of slack since I became president. I've also caught a lot of heat and had to endure endless leaks from them. Now, they colossally screwed up another situation, and because of that failure, people were killed."

The President turned to Mark Jones, the Director for National Intelligence, Wilson, and McMillan, and looked each of them in the eye with an uncomfortably penetrating stare. "I want to know who was in charge of producing these intelligence assessments. I want to know who made the call that the Russians were just blustering, and I want to know *why* they made that assessment. This is a huge mistake, and I want people to be held responsible for it," the President said angrily.

Since the President had been sworn into office, his administration had had to deal with countless leaks from the intelligence community, and even some of his own staffers. From phone conversations between himself and world leaders to questions he had been posing to the community at large, the press had been beating him up for months as inexperienced and incompetent. At the same time, his own intelligence community had been doing their best to undermine him at every turn.

General Wheeler, the SACEUR, tried to change the topic. "Mr. President, if I may—I'd like to order additional fighter aircraft to our base in Poland and Ukraine. I'd also like to begin developing a plan to neutralize the Russian air defense systems, should it become necessary."

The President assessed General Wheeler; he had only met the man once, but he had great respect for him. "Please proceed with making whatever plans you feel are necessary to protect our troops and our allies. I do not want anyone to engage the Russian military or attack their positions, unless I give the order. Until we figure out this crisis within our own intelligence circles, and Travis is able to get a response back from the Russians, I do not want to engage them." Gates wanted to make sure everyone understood that he was not looking to escalate things any further with Russia.

As the meeting broke up, the military went into high gear, alerting various units of a possible deployment to Europe and potential confrontation with Russia. In Europe, General Wheeler had all US and NATO forces go to Threat Condition Delta. Additional F-16s were being scrambled to the US bases in Poland and Ukraine.

Twenty minutes after the assembly concluded, the Secretary of State had a one-on-one call with his ambassador to Ukraine. "Duncan, I want you to assure the Ukrainians that we are still standing behind them, that we are working out this situation. However, please ask them to halt their military operation in eastern Ukraine until we can get things sorted out with the Russians. I don't want them to do anything rash that might escalate the situation further. Also, good job in the meeting. The President needs people to give him good, frank advice. I need that as well from time to time," he said, ending the call.

Chapter 13
Volodymyr

Kiev, Ukraine

Office of the Prime Minister

Prime Minister Volodymyr Groysman was looking over an economic development plan the European Commission on Economic Development had provided to his office on how he could look to improve the farming and logging industry of western Ukraine. In general terms, it recommended massive investments in the infrastructure of the region; paved roads, additional rail lines, and a widening of bridges to enable heavy trucks and additional vehicle traffic. The report also had some excellent ideas on shipping management and ways to bring their crops to the market faster and to more markets outside of Ukraine.

General Popko rushed into the PM's office and immediately interrupted his train of thought. "Mr. Prime Minister, there has been an incident with the Russians," he said with a sense of urgency the PM hadn't often seen from Popko. He could tell something serious must have happened.

The PM stood up slowly. "What kind of incident?" He wasn't sure if he really wanted to know, but he also realized that he had better stay on top of whatever it was.

"About forty-five minutes ago, four NATO planes entered the no-fly zone that the Russians are trying to impose. There were two American and two German aircraft. The Russians hailed them multiple times, warning them to turn back; then they locked the aircraft up with their ground radars and warned them again. When the NATO aircraft continued to ignore the warnings, the Russians fired at them." The general spoke quietly, almost as if he wasn't sure to believe what he was saying himself.

"Did they shoot down the NATO fighters?" the PM asked. Suddenly, his stomach hurt.

The general nodded. "Yes, Sir. They shot down the four NATO aircraft, killing two of the pilots. The other two managed to eject and were recovered by the search-and-rescue teams. The Russians also shot down all seven of the American and NATO surveillance drones." Popko was in a daze himself; he was still trying to come to terms with what this all meant.

Groysman's throat suddenly felt dry. He took a sip of water and then asked, "What about a response? Did the NATO aircraft respond to the attack?"

"Once the Russians had fired on the NATO fighters, Allied forces fired four HARM antiradar missiles toward the Russians in retaliation. Unfortunately, their missile interceptors shot all four missiles down," the general explained. He was clearly angry that the Russians had committed this latest act of aggression.

Volodymyr's thoughts began to race. *"How will the Russians respond to this? How will NATO and the Americans react to this? What do I need to do right now to get things ready in case this escalates?"*

"General, right now we do not know how NATO or Russia is going to act in response to this situation, and unfortunately, we are stuck in the middle. I want you to issue an order to all our units in the field to stand down military operations for the moment. I also want you to raise the alert level of the rest of our military. While I don't want to antagonize the situation any further, we need to be ready in case the Russians respond by invading us or carrying out further attacks. Should NATO decide to attack Russia in response, we should also be ready to support them in that effort."

Chapter 14

JIOC

Stuttgart, Germany

US European Command

Joint Intelligence Operations Center

Lieutenant General James Cotton walked across the cobblestone pathway from the headquarters building to the Joint Intelligence Operations Center or JIOC building on Patch Barracks. He wanted to get the ball rolling on the latest orders from the President and the Pentagon. He had just returned from Kiev less than two weeks ago, so he had a good idea of what things looked like on the ground at the US/NATO air base.

Lieutenant General Cotton had been the Deputy Commander of US European Command for roughly nine months. The DCOM typically ran EUCOM while the actual commander, who also wore the hat of NATO commander, worked out of NATO's headquarters in Mons, Belgium.

General Cotton walked up to the second floor of the JIOC and entered the operations room. It was laid out almost like a college auditorium, in that it had several rows of seats and tables that gradually descended to the first floor which had a small stage and podium. The wall, however, was fixed with nearly a dozen 72" TV monitors, showing various images. One of them displayed a live radar map of Ukraine and Eastern Europe, which was monitoring all of the military aircraft in the region, both Allied and Russian. Another screen was a video conference image between their room and Major General Richard Mueller, the US/NATO ground commander in Ukraine who had just arrived on the scene a couple of days earlier as the US began to beef up their presence in the country. On another monitor, the Commander of US Air Force Europe, who was currently located at the Ramstein Air Force base, was joining in on the video conference. On a fourth monitor, they could see the Pentagon Operation Center, which was a buzz of activity. A fifth monitor was transmitting from the combat information center of the USS *George H.W. Bush* carrier battle group, which had just entered the Mediterranean a couple of days ago. A sixth monitor showed the operations center at Supreme Headquarters Allied Powers, Europe or SHAPE, where the military leaders of NATO were seated.

"Everyone, listen up," barked General Jack Wheeler, trying to get everyone's attention. "I just finished speaking with the President, and he's authorized us to move all US and NATO forces to Threat Condition Delta. He has further directed me to take whatever measures are deemed necessary to protect our forces, short of engaging the Russians. We are authorized to defend ourselves if fired upon, but again, we are not to provoke the Russians."

Wheeler paused for a moment and surveyed the audience; he definitely had everyone's attention. "I'm directing the *Bush* carrier battle group to take up position in the Black Sea. Should the situation calm down, I'll redirect the battle group to the eastern Mediterranean to continue with their previous mission." Should things heat up with the Russians, having the *Bush* carrier group in the Black Sea would provide NATO with not just additional combat aircraft, but several ships capable of launching Tomahawk missiles. The 3,500 Marines accompanying the battle group would also come in handy should they need additional ground forces.

General Wheeler directed his attention to the US Air Force Europe Commander. "I want the Air Force to immediately start flying combat air patrols over our major NATO bases. I want the F-35s armed and on ready alert to go after those SA-10s and SA-21 sites if we are given the go order. I also want our AWACS up and running around the clock—we need those eyes in the sky. Until we're told otherwise, I want our air force to be on a war footing, ready to respond to any further Russian aggression," he directed.

General Wheeler then looked at General Cotton. "I want the 2nd Cavalry Regiment issued alert orders and ready to deploy as a brigade to Kiev within 48 hours. Tell them that if they're given the order, they will have 24 hours to arrive in country and to plan accordingly." Several of the colonels in the JIOC with General Cotton were taking copious notes as they began to dispatch orders to their subordinates to get things moving.

The meeting went on for another hour as General Wheeler continued to issue orders, bringing NATO and US forces to the highest state of readiness since the Cold War. Poland, Germany, and the UK all began to scramble their air forces, providing combat air patrols over critical NATO bases and ports.

Chapter 15
Mobilization

Rostov, Russia

While NATO began to mobilize their forces in response to the shootdown of their aircraft, the Russians moved their own forces to the border of Ukraine in preparation for the next phase of their operations.

Major General Aleksandr Chayko was walking through the marshaling point, viewing the various vehicles of the 137th Reconnaissance Battalion, which would be responsible for leading the way during the next phase of Operation Red Storm. MG Chayko had taken over command of the 4th Guard's elite "Kantemirovskaya" Tank Division roughly seven months ago, at the outset of Operation Red Storm. Since taking over command, he had been given unfettered resources to get his command ready for direct combat against NATO, should the need arise. His division was equipped with 320 T-80U main battle tanks, 600 BMPs and BTRs—Russian infantry fighting vehicles, 130 self-propelled artillery guns and twelve multiple rocket launcher vehicles. As he toured the facilities and saw the various machines, carefully cleaned and maintained by his men, he was proud to be leading this elite armored division. However, he wished they had more of the modern, up-to-date equipment that they would need in order to defeat what everyone thought of as an undefeatable army.

MG Chayko assessed what would make the biggest difference in their fight and then sent a message to his direct superiors, the Commander of the 1st Tank Army and the General of the Army. He requested to replace as many of his T-80s as possible with the newer T-14 Armata MBTs and T-15 IFVs. These were the most powerful tanks and infantry fighting vehicles in the world, and clearly superior to the American Abrams and other NATO tanks. Despite the Russian defense industry moving to full production of the Armata line of vehicles, they had only been able to field roughly 120 of the T-14s and 65 of the T-15s. All of them had been sent to the 4th Guard's Division to be swapped out with the T-80s and BMP-2s. Chayko needed *all* of his divisions to be fortified with the newest equipment available as they readied for war.

One of the new tools his division had was a series of drones that had just been introduced to the Army. The ZALA was a small microdrone used by his reconnaissance units and the infantry; it would provide them with exceptional real-time intelligence as they advanced forward.

However, the crown jewel of the new drones was the Zhukov. It was a rather large drone, with a sleek futuristic design. It looked like something out of a Hollywood movie with its tilt rotors. The Zhukov could perform a multitude of functions, ranging from surveillance to tank hunter, and it could also be used for precision strikes. In addition, it was fast...it could travel up to 190 miles per hour with a range of 320 miles. Because of its tilt-rotor propulsion, it was very maneuverable compared to a traditional drone, though it could still be shot down by a conventional aircraft or air defense system. The Zhukov carried six AT-15 Springer antitank missiles, similar to the American Hellfire missiles. What made the Zhukov so deadly was that in addition to the antitank missiles, it could also be fitted with air-to-air and anti-ship missiles. This made the drone a triple threat against the ground, air and naval forces. His division had nearly two dozen of them available, and he planned on using every one of them when the time came.

Ever since he had taken command and been read in on Operation Red Storm, Chayko had drilled his troops mercilessly. They received increased time at the rifle and tank ranges, and they conducted rigorous training in urban warfare. Some of the best young officers and non-commissioned officers or NCOs across the army had been transferred from other divisions across the army to fill his ranks. He also pushed his men physically, insisting that they become as physically fit as possible in the lead-up to the start of the operation.

Chayko knew his division was going to be the lead division to head into Ukraine, and if there were a confrontation, they would be the first unit to encounter it. Aleksandr thought the plan was bold, but highly risky. Invading Ukraine and capturing territory would not be hard; holding it against a NATO counterattack, should one come, would be the challenge. The entire plan counted on the Americans and NATO agreeing to the new Ukrainian border and not risking a larger war.

As his reconnaissance unit finished their final preparations, he felt excited and anxious. He wished that he could be there with them as they crossed the border, but whether he liked it or not, his place was there at the headquarters unit, managing the battle.

Chapter 16

Pulling the Trigger

Moscow, Russia

Kremlin, Office of the President

As President Petrov surveyed the faces of the advisors seated at the conference table before him, he felt confident in what he was about to say next. "Gentlemen, it's now time to initiate Operation Red Storm," he announced. "Our military is in position, and so are our political operatives throughout eastern Ukraine. Our agitators are going to start their operation in Kiev tomorrow morning."

The men before him were not generally very expressive, but Petrov could see a few smiles. This put him in a good mood as he continued, "I've spoken with our Chinese colleagues, and they have also begun to initiate their own plans. The Americans are about to be blindsided in the Pacific, just as we move to liberate eastern Ukraine from the fascist government in Kiev."

The President gestured toward his foreign minister. "Minister Kozlov will deliver our message to the world during his news conference tonight. Our ambassador to the UN will also present our resolution for a free election in eastern Ukraine for the people to decide whether or not to leave the central government to form their own government. The resolution will be backed by the Chinese UN ambassador, along with five other nations who support us on the Security Council. Once the resolution and ultimatum are delivered, our forces will cross the border as 'peacekeepers' to keep the central government from disrupting the vote. Once the vote is completed, we'll issue our ultimatum to the NATO forces; they will have ten days to withdraw across the Dnieper River, and ten more days to withdraw from Ukraine altogether," Petrov said excitedly. This was the first step in rebuilding Russia as the predominant world power.

His advisors all ate up his words like candy. As the meeting broke up, President Petrov signaled for Minister Kozlov to stay behind. "Sergey—are things really in place and ready with the Chinese?" he asked, looking for reassurance that the Chinese would hold up their end of the arrangement.

Minister Kozlov was resolute in his response. "Yes, Mr. President. The Chinese are in agreement. Once our forces cross into the Ukraine, they are going to start to dump their US Treasury notes and call on the United States to repay its debt. This will cause the US markets to go into a tailspin and force the Americans to deal with their own domestic financial mess. The Chinese will also issue their own declaration, stating their intent to reestablish their Greater China initiative."

Petrov smiled devilishly. Operation Red Storm was a complex operation that had taken years to develop in secrecy. He was excited to see that it was finally starting to fall into place. They had nearly called it off when President Gates had won the election, but the incredible success of the hacking stories and American people's complete fascination with their attempted intrusions had led Petrov and the Chinese to believe they could get away with just about anything.

Chapter 17

No Good Options

Washington, D.C.

White House, Oval Office

President Gates was meeting with Senators Jim McGregor from Arizona, Benjamin Grandy from South Carolina, Levi Leibowitz from New York and Timothy Warbler from Virginia to discuss the latest Russian ultimatum and what to do about it. Senator Timothy Warbler was the first to speak.

"Mr. President, I urge caution when dealing with President Petrov. We don't want to push him into a corner and potentially cause a shooting war with them."

Scoffing at this, the senator from Arizona interjected, "Mr. President, you need to stand strong against Vladimir Petrov. The Russian army can't be allowed to enter Ukraine and impose a referendum on the people there. This is tantamount to war, and we need to stop him."

Before Senator McGregor had even finished, Senator Grandy was chomping at the bit to add his own two cents. "President Petrov is a thug," Grandy asserted. "He's a dictator who needs to be stood up to. We can't let him walk all over us and think he can get away with this. It's bad enough that they shot down four NATO aircraft and we still haven't responded to them. We need to tell the Russians that if they cross the border into Ukraine, they will be met by NATO and American forces," he demanded.

Gates took it all in, not saying much at first. He was letting them do all the talking and giving them the chance to present their case. He wanted to know their concerns, and he did genuinely seek their advice. He turned to Senator Leibowitz. "Levi, what's your take on this? How do you believe we should respond?" the President asked of the Minority Leader.

Senator Leibowitz leaned forward, pausing for a minute before responding. "Mr. President, the Russians interfered in our elections. They've shot down two of our jets, and now they threaten the very survival of another nation. At some point, we have to stand up and say enough is enough. I don't agree with the good senators from Arizona and South Carolina often, but in this instance, I do."

Gates thought about that for a moment. This was a rare moment of true bipartisanship, something he wished he had an opportunity to see more often. "I want to pose a question to everyone. What if the Russians don't back down? Are we willing to go to war over Ukraine?"

He sat back after asking his question, letting it hang there for a minute to see who would answer the question first.

Of course, it was Senator McGregor who responded first. "Yes. Yes, Mr. President. We *should* go to war over Ukraine, if it comes to that. I do not say that lightly, but NATO was attacked. We cannot let that stand. Petrov is a menace; if we don't stop him in Ukraine, he will make a move on Europe. Right now, his military is weak. He doesn't have the capability to project force beyond his border, let alone for any extended period of time. He will bluster, but I say we call his bluff, and if we need to, we hit them hard. That will force them to back down," he said, with full confidence in the US and NATO's ability to stand up to Russia.

Inwardly, the President was shaking his head. *"There was never a country that Senator McGregor hasn't wanted to fight or invade,"* he thought. However, he realized he just might be right about Russia in this case.

"Mr. President, I disagree with my colleague," said the senator from Virginia. "If we push Russia into a corner, they will fight. We need to leave Petrov an out. Perhaps we look to ease sanctions in exchange for them leaving eastern Ukraine. A show of force only works if we're willing to use it, and I do not believe the American people or the rest of Europe would support a war against Russia. Also, we have this burgeoning threat from China in the Pacific that we haven't even begun to discuss." His opinion stood in contrast to the three other senators in the room.

"Senator Warbler brings up a good point concerning China," Gates responded. "While we're so focused on dealing with Russia, are we getting blindsided by the Chinese?"

The room was silent for a moment as everyone stopped to consider all the different angles to the world situation. The quiet lasted long enough that it almost became awkward before the President spoke again. "My greatest concern is that if we do end up in a fight with Russia, our NATO allies may not stand with us. This may turn into a war that we have to fight on our own, or our allies may only reluctantly halfway support us. You've given me a lot to think about, and I value your input. If you'll excuse me now, I have a meeting with the National Security Council shortly to figure out what they believe our next steps should be."

He got up, signaling that the meeting was over.

The senators left the Oval Office feeling that they had made their case to the President and signaled their support should a conflict with Russia ultimately happen.

They knew the President had also met with congressional leaders prior to their meeting, so they would circle back with their colleagues from the House to see how their meeting went.

****

Washington, D.C.
White House

It was nearly 9 p.m. and everyone was tired; it had been a very busy day in Washington. Everyone was reeling from the effects of the Russian foreign minister's statement. He'd certainly caught the world's eye when he had announced that Russia was proposing a resolution to the UN Security Council, calling for the removal of all Ukrainian military forces from eastern Ukraine. Even Senator Leibowitz had been shocked when he'd heard Kozlov call for a secession vote to take place in seven days. Sure, they "welcomed UN election observers" to ensure the election results would be credible, but who could really believe that? The phrase that made all the talking heads in D.C. the most uncomfortable, however, was when Kozlov had stated, "At the invitation of the regional governors, Russia will move forces into eastern Ukraine to end the bloodshed and killing of innocent civilians."

President Petrov went on TV shortly after Kozlov's announcement. "The civil war in Ukraine has gone on long enough," he announced. "Russia is not going to idly sit by and watch as one of its neighbors slaughters civilians, and the fascist central government becomes a puppet of the EU and the Americans."

Speaking like a schoolteacher giving a history lesson, Petrov continued, "At the end of the Cold War, NATO agreed not to encroach its border on Russia. For the past thirty years, America and NATO have broken their word, time and time again. Well—no more. This evening, Russian armed forces will cross into eastern Ukraine at the request of the regional governors to remove the NATO backed government forces and create a 'free zone' where people can once again leave their homes and bunkers and go about their daily lives. One week from today, they will be able to vote and determine once and for all if they want to stay a fascist puppet of the EU or separate from Ukraine and form their own country."

******

President Gates had just finished a late dinner with his senior advisor, Stephen Saunders, and his Chief of Staff,

Ishaan Patel, to go over their meetings with the members of the House and Senate. Although he had spent several hours meeting members of Congress to discuss what to do in Ukraine, nothing was really going to happen until the meeting he was about to have in the Situation Room. The President had given his national security team several hours to gather whatever information and intelligence they could before formulating a series of potential responses he could take. After the past couple weeks' worth of intelligence miscues, the President was growing tired of incompetence. However, he realized that he still needed the national security team he had, at least until he could find better replacements.

When the President walked into the Situation Room and sat down at the head of the table, Tom McMillan started the brief. "Mr. President, the Russians sent us the lines of demarcation: they include the Kharkiv Region, down to the Dnieper River in the Dnipropetrovsk Region, to the Zaporiz'ka Region, which includes the port city of Berdiansk, then to the Donetsk Region, which also includes the critical port city of Mariupol, and the Luhans'ka Region, which hugs Russia's border." He paused for a moment as the image of the demarcation was brought up on a map. Everyone could see that this was a large chunk of Ukraine that would essentially be ripped away from the central government. It also gave the Russians something they had been after for years—a major road and railway to Crimea.

President Gates surveyed the faces of everyone in the room. He could see that several of them wanted to fight; others were hoping they weren't witnessing the opening hours of a new world war. "All right," said Gates, "they've given us their terms. What are our options, and what are your suggestions?"

General Joe Hillman, the Chairman of the Joint Chiefs, spoke up first. "Mr. President, there are several options on the table. Some are military, some are political. I'll go through the military options first and then defer to the Secretary of State to discuss the political options," he said, ever the professional.

The President gestured for Hillman to continue, and the general elaborated. "We can take a stand against the Russians and let them know that if they cross the Ukrainian border, we will defend Ukraine with all of the forces we have in country; we would obviously need to rush additional forces to their aid. That is the most direct military option. Alternatively, we can abide by the terms the Russians have laid out while we work to move sufficient military forces into Ukraine to remove them if they do not leave willingly.

Third, we could stand down. In that scenario, we wouldn't get involved militarily, and we would let the Russians divide up Ukraine." As the general spoke, he scanned the room, looking to see if he could determine where most people appeared to be leaning.

Travis Johnson cleared his throat, indicating he was ready to go over the diplomatic options. The President looked at him and simply nodded. "Mr. President, we vetoed the Russian resolution a couple of hours ago when it was brought up for a vote in the Security Council. That was our first step. Our next step is not to recognize the results of the election next week. We can use several methods to make it clear that we do not view these sham results as legitimate. We can say that the election was rigged, that it was not properly monitored—there's more, but you get the idea."

He then brought up a slide that denoted economic options. "Next, we can impose significantly harsher sanctions on Russia. We can leverage the Treasury Department and tell countries and businesses that if they do business with Russia, then they can't do business with the United States. This would essentially freeze them out of the global economy. Even if they tried to work through other banks, those banks wouldn't be allowed to do business with any bank that works with the US. Very few banks or businesses would be willing to work with the Russians if this happened." Johnson then ran through a number of other economic sanctions options, from mild to extreme, and explained their varying effects on the Russian economy and people.

When Johnson had concluded his presentation, the DNI spoke up. "Mr. President, we have to be cautious with both the economic and military options. President Petrov is posturing right now. He is taking the position that we won't respond either militarily or economically to his provocative actions. While there are consequences to not standing up to him, there's also the potential for severe consequences if he decides to challenge us."

NSA McMillan was the next to speak. "Mr. President, while the diplomatic option may sound like the best course, these types of harsh sanctions will ultimately result in a military confrontation. If we freeze the Russian economy out of the global banking system, that would be like dropping a nuclear weapon on Moscow. It would be foolish not to expect them to respond in kind."

McMillan observed several members of the President's senior circle; they all appeared to be nervous. "Look, we're stuck between a rock and a hard place right now. The DNI is right, we essentially have two options. We can either let the Russians divide up Ukraine like they've wanted to do since the start of this civil war, or we can stand our ground and accept the fact that it's going to lead to a military confrontation."

"There, I said it," McMillan thought. *"No one wanted to say that, but everyone knows it's heading that way."*

The President was not happy with the options being presented, but he didn't see a lot of other possibilities either. He had been so focused on domestic and economic issues that he had left much of the foreign policy to his senior advisors. Clearly, that had been a mistake, but how should he correct it? "If we back down, what will be the consequences across the globe?" Gates asked. "How will this be perceived internationally?"

The NSA answered this question first. "In some circles, it would be viewed as weak, but in others, it would be viewed as prudent. If I had to hazard an estimate, I'd guess that the Europeans will be evenly split. Some of them will be happy that we haven't drawn NATO into a war— mostly the French, Italians and Spanish. The Nordic countries, the UK, Germany, and the Baltic states will side with us, as will Poland, Hungary and Romania. They all view the Russian moves as them trying to reclaim their old empire."

McMillan continued, "China, Iran, and India are the bigger concerns here. They will view this as weakness on our part. Essentially, they will see that if we're threatened with actual military force, we will back down rather than use our military. Remember—the Russians have already shot down four of our aircraft and we haven't responded to that yet. Now they will have essentially invaded a country that we have a military base in, and they would see us do nothing to stop it." He wanted to make sure everyone understood the global repercussions of not responding.

He went on, "If China and Iran believe they can take military action against us or anyone else and face no consequences, then chances are, they will act out. The only thing keeping them in check is the knowledge that we'll use our military force to stop them. If they feel that that's an empty threat, they will proceed, and then we'll be faced with a set of new challenges to deal with."

Everyone in the room stayed silent for a few minutes, ruminating on that heavy scenario. Most of them hadn't really considered how this was being perceived by China and Iran. Essentially, if they did nothing, then they were opening the US up to more hostile military actions by these other countries. Whereas, if America stood fast in Ukraine, they would send a message to the rest of the world that the United States would not back down, even if it meant going to war to enforce America's position and values.

The President responded, "I do not believe America should be the global policeman or the sole enforcer of UN or NATO resolutions. The American people are tired of fighting foreign wars where our country is not being directly threatened. On the other hand, I also know that if we give our word, then we need to honor it. In business, if you issue a threat to a contractor that you will fire them if they do not perform, then you need to follow through and terminate them if they fail to hold up their end of the bargain. America has given our word that we will honor our NATO pledge of mutual defense." The President wanted to reinforce privately what he had said on numerous occasions publicly.

Gates then turned to look at Joe Hillman, the Chairman of the Joint Chiefs. He asked, "General, how prepared are our forces to defend Ukraine right now? Is this even a viable option?"

The general took a deep breath and then exhaled. "Mr. President, right now we are not in a good position. Our Patriot battery at the Pryluky Air Base can shoot down any Russian aircraft that attempt to enter Ukrainian airspace, assuming they don't launch hundreds of aircraft or missiles at it. We can further support our air defense system by sending additional aircraft to our forward bases in Poland and Pryluky. As for ground forces, we have roughly 450 soldiers to defend the air base, and another 780 military advisors. Most of them are Special Forces, but they aren't line units that can stand up to a Russian tank division."

"The Ukrainians have some armored and mechanized forces that can be used; however, they aren't up to strength for stopping a Russian armored division. My military recommendation is this: we should not engage the Russians immediately. If we do, we will be defeated. We should wait until we can get sufficient forces in Ukraine, and then we give them our ultimatum or be forcibly removed. I recommend we immediately deploy the 173rd Airborne Brigade out of Italy to our air base at Pryluky. We should also get the 2nd Cavalry Regiment, stationed at Vilseck, Germany, on the road ASAP. They can be at the air base in roughly 30 hours. I recommend we begin the deployment of the 3rd Infantry Division and the 1st Armored Division as well. It will take time to get them deployed to Europe, so we should act quickly," General Hillman explained.

President Gates turned to Secretary of Defense James Castle. "Jim, I value your advice and opinion on military matters. What do you believe I should do? How would you approach this situation?"

Castle sat forward in his chair. "During the Cold War, the US ran a deployment exercise called Reforger. We essentially role-played a scenario of the Russians invading West Germany and the beginning of a hypothetical World War III, running up a massive mobilization and deployment of our forces from the US to Europe. I recommend that we initiate Reforger now, in real life. If we're able to negotiate a peaceful solution, then great. This will have simply been a tremendous training exercise—one that, I might add, we have not conducted since 1993. If things do turn into a shooting war, then we'll be well on our way to having the forces and equipment either on the way to Europe or already in place."

The President added, "My concern is that all of the preparations of Reforger might lead the Russians to believe that we're planning to attack them first, so they would preemptively initiate the conflict. At the end of the day, gentlemen, our goal is not to go to war. We want to find a way to solve this problem without killing each other."

The Secretary of Defense nodded, not in agreement, but to acknowledge that he had heard. "Mr. President, while I understand your apprehension, these mobilizations take a significant amount of time and resources to accomplish. We can make sure that we effectively handle the PR strategy to cover this as a training exercise, but if we don't do this, then we'll likely be caught with our pants down when a conflict does inevitably begin."

"Hmm...I see what you're saying," the President conceded. "Ok, Castle, you've convinced me. Let's get Reforger up and running. I still have concerns though, gentlemen. What happens if the other NATO members decide that they aren't going to hold up their end of the agreement and send troops to support us if a war does start?"

Secretary Johnson responded, "Mr. President, you bring up a good point. If we *are* going to go to war with Russia, there are a lot of things we need to take into consideration, like the fact that not all NATO members will want to participate. Some members may even openly challenge our effort to get NATO involved. Also, we have to keep in mind that the Iranians and Chinese may see this as an opportunity to go rogue on us, believing that we're too occupied to challenge them. The Chinese have already annexed Mongolia and are even now talking about this 'Greater China' strategy." Johnson went on for another fifteen minutes, discussing the political fallout and ramifications of a potential military confrontation with

Russia. The other men in the room were polite, but most of them were clearly resigned to a world in which conflict was most likely inevitable.

Gates finally butted in. "This is a test for NATO as well. If we do move to a conflict with Russia, and a member of NATO opts not to honor their obligation to the organization, then I want them removed from NATO with a five-year ban on reentry. If NATO is going to stay a relevant organization, then members will either be 100% on board, or they will be out."

The President turned to Castle and Johnson. "I want you both to work the phones and meet with the NATO leaders. I want an agreement from NATO on supporting any military action against Russia. We will need to have consensus to do what needs to be done, or we will not act."

The discussion continued for another hour as everyone went over the various aspects of what needed to happen next. The mobilization of the Army Reserves and activation of key National Guard units was going to raise a lot of red flags and cause a lot of questions to be asked. Everyone needed to work from the same basic talking points and know exactly what to say.

Chapter 18

Peacekeepers and Shots Fired

Rostov, Russia

At 0400 hours, in the twilight hours of the morning, the lead elements of the 137th Reconnaissance Battalion, nicknamed the "Red Foxes," crossed the Russian-Ukrainian border at the small village of Maksimov, which was located along the A280 highway. The critical port city of Mariupol was a mere eight miles away along the same road. As the armored vehicles approached the border, they spotted several Ukrainian border guards and one armored vehicle. The Red Foxes approached the guards and informed them of the recent UN Security Council resolution. "We would also like to reiterate that the governor of your region has requested that Russian peacekeepers come to help observe and protect the referendum vote," they continued. "We respectfully request that you stand down and let us pass."

A tense pause followed, in which no perceptible activity took place. Finally, the Red Foxes issued their ultimatum. "If you do not stand down, you will be fired upon."

The situation had everyone on edge, but ultimately, the border commander ordered his men to stand down. They were clearly outnumbered and outgunned. To have fought would have resulted in certain death for his men, something he was not willing to risk. He did, however, radio ahead to the government forces in the city, letting them know that the Russians were coming. They had managed to delay the Russians for close to an hour before they rolled across the border.

As the armored convoy reached the outskirts of Mariupol, they encountered the first of a series of roadblocks. Several police officers, intermixed with a platoon of Ukrainian soldiers, had formed a makeshift roadblock using three police cars, two army trucks, and two BMP-2s.

As the column of Red Foxes approached the roadblock and came to a stop, a Russian captain got out of his armored vehicle to walk toward the roadblock. He was hoping to talk with the platoon commander and avoid a conflict. As the captain was roughly halfway between the two parties, a shot was fired. It might never be known who fired the first shot; it could have been a nervous police officer, an agitator, or one of the soldiers on either side. At any rate, the bullet hit the young captain who had sought to defuse the situation.

When the captain clutched his chest and fell to the ground, violent chaos ensued. The Russians had the Ukrainians heavily outgunned. In less than a minute, the defenders of the roadblock lay dead in the street, and the vehicles they had been using as cover were completely shredded from the intense gun battle. The T-80s wasted no time in firing their 125mm cannons at the Ukrainian BMPs—they didn't even have time to get off return fire before they were destroyed.

The reverberations of the short exchange of heavy weapons fire and subsequent explosions shook the small city, waking many of the locals from their sleep. The resident Ukrainian battalion commander, Colonel Skopje, was one of the men roused from their slumber. Concerned that his men might be in imminent mortal danger, he threw on his uniform and immediately headed to his office. His battalion had been planning to withdraw behind the demarcation line later in the day, so they had already gathered their vehicles and were ready to move.

Fifteen minutes later, a survivor of the attack was brought to the room and regaled Skopje with the horrors of how the Russians had slaughtered the soldiers at the roadblock. The colonel immediately sent a message to his higher command, telling them that the Russians had slaughtered one of his platoons and were advancing on the city.

Without orders or permission from his superiors, Colonel Skopje issued an order that might very well have been the single act that escalated the conflict to a full-blown war. The colonel commanded his battalion to head for the Russian unit and engage them. He also sent a message to his aviation support unit and requested the two Mi-28 Havoc ground attack helicopters to engage the Russian column. Deep down, Skopje knew his forces couldn't prevent the Russians from capturing the city, but he hoped they could blunt their advance until additional reinforcements arrived— assuming, of course, the central government sent them.

The American advisors he had with him argued against engaging the Russians. One of the men insisted, "You should order your units to leave for the demarcation line immediately. Look to fight another day, when you have sufficient force and support elements."

The colonel wouldn't hear any of it. "I am going to protect my country, even if that means that we are killed in the process," Skopje snapped.

The American major who was the lead advisor for this sector hung his head low. Then he looked up and offered to shake his hand. "I wish you all the best of luck," he said.

Turning to the other advisors who were assigned to this battalion, he ordered, "Let's all get in our own vehicles and head across the demarcation line. I won't have us be a part of this ill-advised and non-sanctioned attack."

****

Captain Nikolai Popov had just woken up when he received word that the Russians had indeed crossed the border in the early hours of the morning. Less than ten minutes later, he found out about the shooting that had happened at the roadblock. Thinking things could get hairy, Captain Popov called out to his lead crew chief, "Get the helicopters fueled and ready to move. I want them equipped with antitank missiles and rocket pods. We may need to fight our way out of this situation."

The group of aviators, mechanics and ordnance technicians began to get the two attack helicopters ready for a potential combat mission. The pilots walked over to the maps and began to orient themselves as to where the enemy formation was currently and where they would most likely move in the immediate future. They also looked at potential egress routes where they could fly once they had expended their ordnance. They decided amongst themselves that if they survived the engagement, they would radio ahead to their support element and find an empty field to settle down into, refuel, and then continue to their original destination, Kryvyi Rih Air Base.

Twenty minutes later, Captain Popov received a request for air support from the army ground commander. He knew an order might come, but he had secretly hoped it would not. He informed the group of the orders anyway. The ground crew was nearly done getting the Havocs loaded with their ordnance. The captain provided some additional guidance to his team. "Fly low and stay between the various buildings. This will provide you with cover. As you spot the enemy tanks and armored vehicles moving through the city, engage them on sight, and keep going until you have expended all your missiles. If all goes well, we will destroy sixteen tanks or armored vehicles and then get out of there as fast as possible."

The other pilot responded, "Yes, Sir," with a wild grin on his face. Then they dutifully climbed into the Havocs and began their preflight checks.

As the rotor blades got up to speed, Captain Popov's helicopter lifted off and began to head toward the city. The sun was fully up at this point. It was a beautiful morning, though as they got closer to the city, they could see black smoke rising from where the Russians had attacked their comrades. Suddenly, Popov spotted the Russian convoy. The Russian armored vehicles were nearly to the downtown and still driving in a single-file column—they hadn't fanned out into the city yet. They were still heading in the direction of the town hall and the airport, which were probably their main objectives. The captain slowed his helicopter down and went into a hover behind a four-story building roughly a mile away. His wingman did the same.

Captain Popov keyed the radio frequency that they were operating on. "OK, here's what we're going to do. I'm going to pop up from behind this building to our front on Nesky Street and fire off my missiles at the lead vehicles. I want you to focus on the tail end of the convoy from that cluster of buildings two blocks north of me."

Captain Popov was feeling confident. "*If the Russians thought they could invade Ukraine and get away with it, they have another thing coming,*" he thought.

As they lifted their helicopters above the buildings and began to paint the armored vehicles with their targeting lasers, the Russian convoy responded. One of the anti-aircraft vehicles, an SA-19 or "Grison," detected the helicopters' presence and immediately moved to engage them. Despite being on tracks, it quickly maneuvered into a better position so that its two 30mm cannons could fire. A barrage of rounds headed toward Popov's wingman, Captain Sirko, who took evasive maneuvers. He swung his helicopter sharply left, then ducked behind another structure while the 30mm rounds peppered the face of the building, throwing chunks of cement and glass to the ground below.

Popov saw this as his opportunity and let loose all eight antitank missiles, making sure that at least one of them was aimed at the Grison. In quick succession, his missiles leapt from his helicopter one after another and raced toward the armored column. The Grison's sensors detected the incoming missiles and immediately switched targets, attempting to shoot down the incoming missiles.

At this point, Captain Sirko's helicopter popped up from behind a different building and fired off his eight missiles as well. While Popov's nose laser continued to guide his missiles toward the armored column, the Grison destroyed four of the incoming missiles as small fireballs appeared in the sky. They had managed to take out the missile that had been directed at them. The Grison aimed its 30mm cannons back at the helicopters. Before Popov could duck back down behind the building he'd been hovering above; the rounds tore through his helicopter's armor, shredding it until the chopper exploded and fell to the ground in a fiery mess.

As Popov met a painful untimely demise, his wingman's eight missiles hit the armored column and destroyed the lone Grison in a blaze of glory. Unfortunately for Sirko, just as he turned his helicopter around to head for safety, a Su-27 Flanker swooped in and obliterated his helicopter with a missile.

The Flanker then climbed back above the city and continued its own reconnaissance mission. As it leveled off around 10,000 feet, it found the Ukrainian armored column it was looking for. The pilot climbed again until he reached 15,000 feet and then began an attack run, swooping down from the direction of the morning sun. He fired off a series of air-to-ground missiles while radioing to his companions that he had found the column. Within minutes, four other Su-27s swooped in and finished off the Ukrainian battalion before they were even able to get in range to attack the Russian advance team.

The attack had not entirely been a one-sided affair. The Ukrainian column also had their own Grison with them, which engaged the Flankers, managing to shoot two of them down and damage a third before it was destroyed.

As the Russian aircraft loitered above the city, smoke rose from the twelve Russian vehicles that had been destroyed by the two Ukrainian helicopters and the nearly three dozen armored Ukrainian vehicles that had been obliterated at the outskirts of the city. The battle for Mariupol was over, but the fight for Ukraine had just begun.

****

Major General Aleksandr Chayko was on his third cigarette of the morning as he watched the various live drone feeds on the monitor in his command center. The first Russian armored vehicles had entered the critical port city of Mariupol, and it was expected that they might encounter some resistance from the Ukrainian army. The drone operator was keeping the drones about 1,000 feet above the convoy, so that the operators manning the various camera feeds could monitor what the convoys were driving into. One camera was focused on everything ahead of the convoy, while the other two cameras were looking to the right and left of the convoy, providing the operations center and the convoy commander with an excellent field of vision.

Shortly after the initial encounter at the roadblock, one of the camera operators spotted movement. Flying between several of the buildings, they spotted two Havoc helicopters moving to attack the convoy. Then, the first Ukrainian helicopter popped out from behind one of the apartment buildings and fired off his missiles at the column. In that moment, his heart sank as it became clear the Ukrainian army was not going to leave the city. They were going to stand and fight, despite knowing they were heavily outnumbered and outgunned. He had hoped to secure the city without bloodshed, but as the missiles streaked in toward his men, he knew that wouldn't happen. The local Ukrainian commander must have decided he wanted combat, rather than to cede the city to him peacefully.

To his surprise, the Russian Grison was able to shoot down four of the eight missiles. Then a second helicopter popped up and fired off eight more, but not before the Grison shredded the first helicopter that had fired on his men. He looked at his air force liaison officer and yelled, "Make sure your fighters take that helicopter out! And find that armored column and destroy it."

"I tried to offer the Ukrainians a chance to live," he thought. They could've seen their families again, but if they wanted to die for their country, then he would oblige them and give them that honor.

He continued to watch as the conflict continued, puffing angrily on his cigarette. Chayko hoped his other columns were having better luck than his group at Mariupol. He walked over to the next group of monitors, which showed another armored column from his division that was advancing on Makiivka, which led to Donetsk. The Ukrainian military had focused a large part of their military operation and forces in this region, and he expected to meet heavy resistance if the government forces planned on fighting. He had been hoping they would take the opportunity to withdraw across the demarcation line before they moved across the border, but after Mariupol, he couldn't take anything for granted.

He had made sure this armored force consisted of additional air defense vehicles and had close air support aircraft overhead, should they be needed. He hated losing soldiers needlessly. He had sworn when he took command that he would do his best to look after them and provide them with whatever support and equipment they needed. This kind of loyalty to his soldiers was not often found in Russian generals, but it had endeared him to his men, and they would fight like angry devils for him.

Chapter 19

Media Madness

For all the political wrangling in Washington about Russian collusion amongst the Gates administration and the 2016 election, the mainstream media seemed oblivious to the fact that a full-scale war between NATO and Russia could be just days away. Meanwhile, nearly 60,000 reservists and national guardsmen had been activated across the country and they all began to arrive at their various reporting stations to draw equipment and prepare to deploy to Europe.

Equipment from the 1st Armored Division began to arrive at the ports on the East Coast of the United States, along with the vehicles and equipment of the 4th Infantry Division. Almost without drawing any attention at all, the 173rd Airborne had already arrived in Ukraine, along with the 2nd Cavalry Regiment out of Vilseck, Germany. While some networks covered this massive increase in military activity in the US and abroad, few if any took the deployments seriously.

It was not until the fourth day of the ceasefire between Ukraine and Russian forces that the media realized something more serious might be happening in the former Soviet republic. At a political rally, the leading presidential candidate for the People's Republic of East Ukraine, Alexander Zakharchenko, was killed when an assailant opened fire on him. The attacker was quickly captured and arrested, and it was soon discovered that the attacker was a pro-Ukrainian nationalist who ten years earlier had run for mayor of Kiev as part of an ultra-rightwing nationalist party.

The death of Zakharchenko caused a slew of antigovernment protests across eastern Ukraine. The attack was viewed by many as a blatant effort by the fascist government in Kiev to interfere with the election. Tensions were high.

Then PM Groysman made a televised speech that was carried on all of the major networks across Europe and the United States. "We will not recognize the results of Saturday's election," he announced. "We are one country, one Ukraine. We won't allow our country to be divided by Russia and their goons. We call on Europe and NATO to help keep Ukraine united as one country, as we always have been."

Once the speech went live, many people suddenly realized the significance of the massive military deployment underway to Europe. The media was caught by surprise with the abrupt awareness that a conflict with Russia could really happen, yet nearly 15,000 US servicemen had already arrived in Europe, with tens of thousands more on the way. Networks suddenly rushed dozens of war correspondents to Kiev in preparation for what might turn into a clash between the world's most modern militaries.

Chapter 20

Planning

Stuttgart, Germany

US European Command Headquarters

Joint Intelligence Operations Center

It had been a busy five days at the JIOC. Military planners were scrambling to get things ready for what everyone believed was an almost certain military confrontation with Russia. Lieutenant General Cotton was getting a situation update from Major General Mueller, the ground force commander at the Pryluky Air Base. "The 2nd Cavalry Regiment's brigade combat team has arrived, and so has the 173rd Airborne brigade combat team," Mueller began. "Most of their equipment is being delivered in a near-constant gravy train of heavy trucks, Air Force C-17 cargo aircraft and C-5s. What was practically an abandoned Ukrainian air base just six months ago has turned into a bustling hub of American military activity."

"I have a concern, General," said Mueller. "I think that my current headquarters element is far too close to the potential frontlines, should hostilities kick off. That puts

15,000 US and NATO members in peril. I'd like to move to the Kiev International Airport at Boryspil."

"I understand the concern, General Mueller," Cotton replied. "Permission granted to move the headquarters element to the Kiev International Airport. How soon until you begin deploying your combat troops to the field?"

Once SACEUR gave the order to deploy, the 2nd Cavalry along with the 173rd would move to designated marshaling points and await further orders on where to move to engage the enemy. This way, the ground forces wouldn't be all bunched up on the bases should the Russians launch a surprise attack.

General Mueller turned and said something to one of his officers just off the screen, then turned back to look at the monitor. "I've given them the warning order. They are retrieving their munitions and ordnance now. The 173rd should have the rest of their equipment arriving later today. Once they've had a chance to get them offloaded and sorted, we'll issue the order. I anticipate the units moving to the field on Friday, 36 hours from now."

"Excellent, keep us apprised of any changes," responded Cotton. "Let's hope the politicians can defuse the situation before it becomes a shooting war. We are still weeks away from having most of the Reforger troops and equipment here." Outwardly, General Cotton sounded confident. Inwardly, he was nervous. He was sure that the US and NATO Air Forces could keep the Russians at bay until additional air assets could be flown in from the States, but he was not as certain about the ground assets.

The Russians had moved several divisions from the 1st Guard's Tank Army into east Ukraine, with the rest of them sitting at the edge of the border. Intelligence also showed that the 6th Army was conducting military exercises in Belarus, which everyone knew was a farce; they had moved so many soldiers and equipment to a border region, just as they were issuing their ultimatum. Cotton and Mueller saw it for what it was, an excuse to deploy them to Belarus and apply additional pressure on NATO. However, between the two Russian Army groups, they had a combined 225,000 troops and tanks, so even if it were a ruse, it couldn't be completely ignored.

Before signing off, General Mueller asked one last thing. "If hostilities do kick off, how long are my forces going to have to hold until additional reinforcements from the US and other member states start to arrive?"

Cotton pondered his response for a moment before he answered, "If hostilities break out, I'm going to need your guys to buy us time. Give ground if you have to, but try and hold the line at Kiev. The SecDef has initiated Operation Reforger. The gravy train of supplies and troops will start to arrive in Europe shortly. I'm sorry, but that's about as much clarity as I can provide you," Cotton replied.

Mueller smiled before responding, "Well, that's about as clear as mud, Sir, but I understand. We'll do our best to hold the line. Just make sure I have plenty of air support, and I'm sure we can make it work."

Chapter 21

Election Fever

Washington, D.C.

White House, Situation Room

That Saturday evening, the people of east Ukraine finished casting their ballots and the polls closed down. The votes began to be counted and certified, all under the scrutiny of UN, EU, and Ukrainian government election monitors. The results were not even close. The people in the region voted overwhelmingly to leave the central government and form their own separate Republic.

Despite a lot of complaints by the Ukrainian government, the EU and UN monitors didn't witness any ballot box stuffing or any other nefarious activity that could have influenced the results of the election. There were Russian soldiers throughout the major cities, but none were within 100 feet of a polling station, which was a stipulation made by the UN to ensure there was no voter intimidation. There was no clear case to be made of corruption in the vote. Apparently, the economic aid package that the Russians had promoted as a gift to a new Eastern Ukraine had been enough of an incentive to entice people to leave what they felt was a fascist pro-EU government in Kiev—well, that and the promised reduced natural gas prices from Russia and the increased security measures that they'd offered.

When the results were announced, President Petrov made a public statement on state-sponsored TV. "Today, I congratulate the people of Eastern Ukraine on their decision to choose freedom from the hold of fascism. All UN election rules were followed in carrying out this vote, so there can be no doubt as to the choice of the people. And now, it is incumbent upon NATO to respect the results of the election and withdraw their forces from Ukraine. This continued buildup of forces is an unnecessary provocation, which, if undeterred, will eventually lead to conflict. I'd like to remind NATO that there are only 48 hours remaining to withdraw all combat forces from the east of the Dnieper River, and seven days to leave Ukraine altogether." President Petrov didn't say what would happen if they didn't leave, but with nearly 65,000 Russian soldiers now in east Ukraine, little was left to the imagination.

****

The President's senior advisors had been meeting for the past hour in advance of Gates's arrival, going over the information that had been pouring into their offices and scrambling to develop a set of recommendations on what to do next. While no one wanted a confrontation with Russia, it appeared they were heading toward one. It was a dangerous game of chicken, waiting to see which nation would blink first.

President Gates walked into the Situation Room and everyone rose to attention. He waved them back down while he took his seat at the head of the table. Gates surveyed the room and saw the tension on everyone's faces. The results of this meeting would change the face of Europe and potentially the world, and everyone knew it.

The President opened the meeting. "Let's just cut right to it. What options do we have right now? What are your recommendations?"

Secretary of State Travis Johnson spoke up first. "Mr. President, I spoke with the Russian ambassador a couple of hours ago, and he simply reiterated to me that with the results of the election, the US and NATO forces must withdraw beyond the Dnieper River within 48 hours and leave Ukraine within seven days. Once those deadlines have passed, he said they will treat our forces as hostile invaders in a sovereign country that they are allied with, and they will respond accordingly."

The room let out a soft murmur at this acknowledgment. Everyone wanted to avoid a conflict with Russia, but it was becoming increasingly unlikely, unless they wanted to walk away from Ukraine.

The President addressed the issue head-on. "So, I want to ask everyone a question. We have deployed troops to Ukraine and are in the process of deploying tens of thousands of troops to Europe. Is standing up to Russia, right now in this situation, worth the lives of American young men and women? Would this war be worth our blood and treasure?"

The President let the question hang there for a minute, wanting to see who would respond. If he was about to commit the lives of American service members to a potential war with Russia, he wanted to know that it was justified.

The Secretary of Defense was the first to answer. "Mr. President, if we do not stand up to the Russians now, then when will we stand up to them? The Russians stole the Crimea from Ukraine under the Obama administration, and the US and Europe stood by and did nothing. We passed some meaningless sanctions that have had a negligible impact on them. The Russians intervened on behalf of Bashar al-Assad in Syria. The rebel army that was going to depose that dictator was systematically destroyed by the Russian Air Force while America and the rest of the world, again, did nothing. The Russians intervened in east Ukraine, fueling a three-year civil war, and now they're about to steal half of the country. If we don't stand up to Vladimir Petrov now, when will we? No, Ukraine is not worth the life of a single American. However, stopping Vladimir Petrov from dividing Europe and the Middle East is."

It was an impassioned statement by the Secretary of Defense and it caused everyone to pause and reflect for a moment. The world was at a turning point. Either they would stop the Russians from dividing up Europe, or they would have to concede defeat.

Tom McMillan leaned forward in his chair. "We need to hold firm, Mr. President…even if it means going to war with Russia. This fight has been a long time coming. Petrov has been bolstering defense spending for nearly fifteen years. He's been building a modern army with one purpose—to rebuild the former Soviet Union. He knows we are at our weakest point militarily in decades. We've been fighting Islamic extremists for sixteen years, which has sapped our strength and spread us thin. The rest of the NATO members are in even worse shape. If ever there were a time to press NATO and America militarily, this is it."

He had a point. The US and NATO were still fighting in Afghanistan, and operations against ISIS in Iraq and Syria had been picking up in pace as Saudi Arabia led an Arab Coalition, with the US continuing to provide intelligence and logistical support. Fortunately, the Russians had withdrawn nearly all their forces from Syria in the past five weeks, probably in anticipation of potential hostilities in Ukraine.

The President listened to other perspectives from his senior advisors for quite some time as they walked through the various options and the consequences for each of them. After several hours of heated discussions, the President felt he had enough information to make a decision. Looking at General Hillman, who had argued for military action, the President said, "General, I've listened to you make your case, and I believe James Castle and Tom McMillan have made a convincing argument for why we need to move forward with a hard line toward Russia as well. This may ultimately lead to a military confrontation with Russia, but as everyone at this table has said, if we do not stand up to the Russians now, then when? While the timing couldn't be worse, I believe we need to be decisive."

Gates took a deep breath and then let it out slowly, almost not sure if he wanted to even utter the words that were about to come out of his mouth. "General, please issue the orders for all US and NATO forces to prepare for hostilities with Russia. Inform them that we are not standing down. If the Russians do not withdraw their military from eastern Ukraine, then we will treat them as hostile and respond appropriately," he said, knowing he was issuing an order that might ultimately trigger the third world war.

The room let out a collective sigh, and then there was a sense of relief. The decision had been made, and now it was time to execute. Everyone put on their game face, and then a flurry of activity began. The various aides grabbed their government-issued smartphones and started making calls to the Pentagon Operations Center and the various other agencies and major commands. As the President changed the DEFCON level from 4 to 2, he essentially placed the country in a de facto state of war, which put into place a whole slew of protocols and actions. Though the US didn't initiate the continuity of government protocol, the leaders of the majority and minority parties were being secretly picked up by the Secret Service and brought to a secured bunker to be briefed and given additional security.

As the meeting broke up, Secretary Castle left the White House and stepped into the up-armored Suburban that was waiting to whisk him back to the Pentagon. Seeing that it was 10:45 p.m., there was little traffic delay. Castle sat in the back of the vehicle and looked out the window, contemplating the events of the meeting.

His perception was that it had been his statement that had shifted the President toward taking military action. *"Did I give the right advice?"* he wondered. The weight of it all hung on his shoulders like a sack of bricks. They were committing the lives of thousands of Americans and Europeans in order to stand up to Russia, and he didn't like bearing this much responsibility for it.

The vehicle pulled up to the side entrance of the Pentagon, which was reserved for the senior officers and the secretary. As he got out of the vehicle, he was met by a number of senior aides. He nodded in acknowledgment to them, and as they walked in the building together, he said, "It's a go. The President has given the order to prepare for hostilities. He has also changed the DEFCON from 4 to 2. Begin to issue the orders and change the country's defense posture immediately."

The group of aides followed their boss as they made their way to the operations center, located in the belly of the building several floors below. As the SecDef walked into the room, everyone stood to attention and waited to be told to resume. Castle walked to the head of the table and announced, "At ease. Everyone, take your seats."

The people in the room all filed into their chairs at the table in a very quick and orderly fashion. "Listen up, everyone," Castle began. The room suddenly became quiet enough to hear a pin drop. All eyes were on the SecDef. "The President has issued the order to prepare for hostilities with Russia. As of this moment, the leaders of the majority and minority parties are being briefed on the decision. We are also moving to DEFCON 2 per presidential directive. I want our nuclear bombers placed on standby and our *Ohio*-class submarines to move to their designated launch points. We are moving forward with the plans for war with Russia. As such, I want our nuclear forces on standby. While we anticipate that this war will be fought conventionally, we need to be prepared in case that nut job Petrov decides to push the envelope."

A few people were taking notes, and because everyone was listening so intently, the sound of their pens on the paper was audible whenever Castle paused. He continued, "I want our carriers on the East Coast to put to sea immediately and head to Europe. I also want all our antisubmarine warfare assets to begin peppering the waters off the East and West Coast with sonar buoys. Get our attack submarines out immediately. Issue a cancelation of all military leave and recall all those currently on leave. I want a full activation order of the Services Reserve branches immediately. Tell the governors that their National Guard units are being placed on alert for federal activation. Then start activating the tier-one National Guard units and get them moving to their deployment centers."

A flurry of activity then took place throughout the operations center as aides, operations officers, and noncommissioned officers began to start drafting the various orders. Keyboards were clicking at a ferocious pace as people cranked out copious emails. The din of chatter slowly grew as more and more people began making the necessary critical phone calls on the secured nets.

It was nearly midnight at the Pentagon as they began to recall everyone back to the office to start work on preparing the nation for war. It was going to be a busy 48 hours; that was all the time they had left on the Russian deadline, and hostilities could begin earlier. No one knew for sure when or if they would.

Chapter 22

A Traitor in Their Midst

Pentagon North Parking Lot

Carl Wiggins walked briskly through the parking lot, casually looking around to make sure no one was paying him any undue attention as he walked to his car, smoking a cigarette. He had arrived at the office an hour ago, and once he had seen the meeting notes from the President's conference in the Situation Room, he knew he had to find an excuse to head to his car and send an emergency message. The best excuse he could come up with was the need for a cigarette break and a java fix. He directed his staff to continue with their duties while he volunteered to grab a bunch of coffees and donuts for everyone to help them get through the long hours. Several people took him up on his offer.

As he walked through the parking lot with his cigarette hanging from the side of his mouth, he observed dozens of cars driving into the parking lot. The spaces began filling up quickly with all the people responding to the midnight recall. It was not often that the Pentagon conducted a 100% recall of military personnel and critical government civilians, but today was not a normal day. It was 0345 in the morning; the sun was still at least a couple of hours away from rising.

Carl slipped his hand in his pants pocket and pulled out the keys to the black 2016 BMW 525i that he had purchased last year. He had been well compensated by various individuals for providing intelligence leaks about the Gates administration. It was almost too easy; everyone was eager to know what was going on, and as one of the communications officers who wrote intelligence summaries of the President's meetings with the National Security Council, he had exceptional placement and access to the inner workings of the administration.

Carl was a deep-cover Russian spy. He had spent nearly his entire adult life working to get into the position he now found himself in. He felt the best way to ensure peace and security in the world was to make sure everyone knew what the other group was thinking. He admired Edward Snowden and Chelsea Manning for their bravery in revealing the illegal intelligence collection that the American government had been perpetrating. Their actions helped to reassure him that what he was doing was truly in the interest of world peace.

He was not Russian by birth or heritage, but during college, where he had been a Russian studies major, he had come to realize that it was the West that was in a constant state of demonizing Russia. The military-industrial complex of America needed a boogeyman—they needed a constant threat and enemy so that they could justify spending over $620 billion a year on defense. It was during this time of self-reflection and searching that he had been recruited by the SVR, part of the Russian FSB, to become a spy.

During his senior year in college, Carl had been encouraged by his new handler to go into military intelligence, obtain a security clearance, and work his way into a government civilian intelligence position at the Pentagon. He'd felt like James Bond during his recruitment phase. After obtaining his commission in the Army, he had been selected for an intelligence career track based on his Russian studies background. While in college, Wiggins had become fluent in the language and had even spent a semester abroad as an exchange student in St. Petersburg; since Russian was such a difficult language to learn, there weren't many people who could fill this need.

During his first four years in the Army, he was stationed at Fort Meade, Maryland, and assigned to the NSA as a Russian specialist on the Russian desk. His handler in the SVR could not have been more thrilled with his posting. He'd intended on staying at his post with NSA for as long as possible—it was a cushy job. Then President Bush had announced the troop surge of 2007, and he'd suddenly found himself deployed.

When President Bush had announced the surge, there had been a critical shortage of intelligence officers deploying with the new combat units. Unfortunately for him, Carl had been selected to join an infantry unit on their deployment to Baghdad as the battalion's S2, or intelligence officer. His Russian handlers had not been happy, but they'd had no choice in the matter, and neither had Wiggins. Besides, filling an S2 billet was a needed requirement for getting selected to major later in his military career.

During his deployment to Iraq, he had been severely injured during a rocket attack on his forward operating base. Shrapnel had torn through his left leg, shredding it to the point that he'd had to have his leg amputated below the knee. Even though he would be able to walk again with the new prosthetic limb he was provided, Carl's injuries meant he was going to be medically discharged once he had recovered. He had been incredibly depressed at the thought of losing his career in the Army and his secret life as a spy. While Wiggins had been recovering from his injuries, his SVR handler approached him again and given him hope. "We want you to try to leverage your war injury to obtain a government civilian position," he'd directed. "After all, you still have your clearances. Maybe this will be a stroke of luck for us after all."

After seven years as a Defense Intelligence Agency civilian employee, serving in a variety of positions, he had obtained a coveted position that was right where his SVR masters wanted him. In his new division, he oversaw the transcripts and development of the daily intelligence summaries of the National Security Council meetings. These meetings included the ones between the President and his staff, advisors, senior military, and intelligence leaders. Once in place, he'd stayed dormant until the situation in Ukraine had begun to grow tense. After nearly three years of civil war in Ukraine, his intelligence had helped the Russians continually stay one step ahead of the US and NATO. Now, with things starting to spiral out of control with President Gates, his intelligence had become critically important.

As he entered his car, he opened the armrest between the two front seats and pulled out his burner phone. He turned it on and began to write a short, but concise text message. "US preparing for war. DEFCON 2, anticipate hostilities within 48 hours," he typed, and then he hit Send.

Once the message had been transmitted, he deleted the message from the phone's history, then took the SIM card and battery out of the phone. He opened the car door and got out, dropping the SIM card to the ground and stomping on it, crushing it and rendering it useless. He then kicked it into the storm drain and began to walk toward the building and back to work. As Carl got closer, he walked over to one of the garbage bins and dropped an empty bag of potato chips inside, along with the phone and the battery. Then he opened the main door, walked in and swiped his card at the security gate before heading to the Dunkin' Donuts to pick up a dozen donuts and some coffee for the others in the office.

Chapter 23

The Day the World Changed

Moscow, Russia

National Defense Control Center

Alexei Semenov, the Minister of Defense, sat down at the conference table, seeing that he was the last to arrive. This was never a good thing, but especially when the meeting was being chaired by President Petrov. Before Alexei could even say anything, Vasily Stepanychev, the director of Russian Foreign Intelligence, announced, "We received an urgent message from our mole in the Pentagon. He informs us that as of seven hours ago, President Gates made the decision that they would not back down from our deadline. He has also issued orders to the military to prepare for hostilities to begin within forty-eight hours. Given the time delay from that decision to right now, that means that they will be ready to start combat operations in thirty-nine hours."

Several of the military and political members at the table began to whisper to each other at the revelation of this information. Ignoring them, Stepanychev continued, "The American president also directed the country to move their armed forces to their defense condition 2, upgraded from 4, which means the Americans have placed their strategic nuclear capabilities on full-alert status. Satellite images show that their nuclear bomber bases have increased their state of readiness in just the past few hours. Our observers at their submarine bases have also reported that several of their nuclear ballistic missile submarines have begun to put to sea."

Alexei saw this as his moment to speak up. "This activity was expected though," he cautioned. "The Americans will want to keep the war conventional, but they will prepare their strategic forces in case we use our nuclear weapons first." Alexei wanted to make sure that his colleagues knew that though this information was alarming, it was not something that should be taken out of context.

President Petrov raised his hand. "Thank you, Alexei, both of you. This is critically important information. We intend to keep this conflict conventional, and we can win a conventional war, so I'm not as concerned about what their nuclear forces are doing. The Americans would never launch a first-strike mission against us, and even if they did, we would still have enough warning to hurt them. Let's put that aside and focus on what we are going to do about the other information the SVR has obtained for us."

The President saw everyone nod their heads and reflected on how the world had changed. Thirty years ago, the thought of considering the avoidance of nuclear weapons against NATO would have been ludicrous. They had always been a part of the Soviet military doctrine. Nowadays, Russia was not looking to gobble up Europe, just Ukraine, creating a buffer zone between them and NATO.

"The Americans are planning for hostilities to start in 39 hours. Minister Kozlov," Petrov said, turning to his foreign minister, "I want you to play a deception game with the Americans. Reach out to them and let them know that we may be softening our position. Tell them that if the Americans would be willing to consider lifting the economic sanctions on us, we would be willing to withdraw our forces from east Ukraine. This will cause them to pause any preemptive military action they might take."

Dmitry Kozlov nodded and smiled at the shrewdness of the idea. He loved ruses. *This will be like the 2016 election all over again,*" he thought. It hadn't even mattered who won that election—after all their rumors of political collusion and corruption, the American people had lost so much of their confidence in the system. They'd begun to question the legitimacy of their leaders. He loved how gullible the Americans were, and the media there just ate up any whiff of conspiracy theories.

While Dmitry was lost in his daydream, Petrov had moved on. "Viktor, is Operation Redworm ready?" he asked.

Viktor Mikhailov was the Chairman of the Government, which meant he essentially ran the administration for Vladimir Petrov. Mikhailov and Petrov were extremely close friends; they had been trading the presidency back and forth, allowing Petrov to remain in power far longer than any politician should legally have been allowed. Mikhailov was also in charge of a very secretive cyber-warfare program that had been established nearly six years ago. The Russians had invested billions of rubles into the program. To complete their stealthy cyberattacks, they had developed the NDMC Supercomputer; it had a speed of 16 petaflops, making it the fastest computer in the world. They had also created a less powerful, but still impressive processor in Belarus, with a capability of 1 petaflop. Both of these devices would be essential for Operation Redworm.

Viktor gave a wry smile and nodded. "We are ready to execute when you give the order."

Petrov smiled and nodded back. He could see the others at the table were curious to know what Redworm was, but now was not the time to tell them. They would learn of it on another day. He turned to his naval commander. "Admiral Petrukhin, are your forces ready to begin?"

Admiral Anatoly Petrukhin cleared his throat before responding. He was nervous; his forces were as ready as they were going to be, but he knew they were no match for the Americans and NATO. The best weapon he had was surprise. He would have exactly one chance to hit the Americans. After that, his force would be hunted down and destroyed, and there was little he could do to stop it. Unlike the air and ground forces, President Petrov had not placed the same sense of urgency on the modernization of the Russian navy.

"We are as ready as we can be. As directed, I have two Akula attack submarines at the entrance to the Black Sea. Both subs are now sitting on the bottom of the sea, waiting for the American carrier battle group to make their way through the Bosphorus. That should happen in about nineteen hours. To throw the Americans off, I have two *Oscar* subs that will be making a lot of noise to distract them from the actual attack. My forces *will* sink the USS *George H.W. Bush* supercarrier," he said with confidence and pride.

Petrov smiled and congratulated him on his well-developed plan to sink one of the American supercarriers.

"If the Americans are really stupid enough to deploy a carrier to the Black Sea, they will pay for that miscalculation," he mused.

"What about the Atlantic Fleet, though?" Petrov asked. "The Americans are sure to deploy the *Dwight D. Eisenhower* carrier group."

Admiral Petrukhin nodded. "The *Truman* is currently on station in the eastern Mediterranean, conducting anti-ISIS operations with the Arab Coalition. The *Eisenhower* set sail two days ago and will head to the North Sea on its way to the Baltic Sea. To counter this, I've deployed six *Kilo* submarines, two *Oscars* and four *Akulas*. NATO and the Americans will be very busy in the North Sea and the Baltic Sea."

The admiral cleared his throat before he continued. "Mr. President, I anticipate that we will lose most of these submarines to American and NATO antisubmarine forces. It's terrible, and there's little I can do about it. Our submarines are just not up to the same standards as those in the West. However, their loss will not be in vain."

President Petrov nodded. He knew the risks.

Petrukhin explained further, "Like playing chess, one has to sacrifice some pawns or even a bishop to get at the queen or king. That is what we are doing. I have the

Severodvinsk, our only *Yasen*-class submarine, lying in wait for the *Bush*. They have taken nearly a week to get on station, and now they are settled on the bottom of the sea, lying in wait for the right time to strike. As the *Bush* battle group moves into the Black Sea, they will strike. I'm not optimistic about their chances of surviving the strike, but the captain assures me he can launch his torpedoes and still get away."

Petrov could see the pain in the admiral's eyes. He was being asked to essentially sacrifice his servicemen for the good of the country. It was hard to commit so many men's lives to a battle plan that would almost certainly result in their deaths, yet that was what needed to happen if they were to succeed. By sinking two of America's supercarriers, they would significantly reduce the number of combat aircraft the Americans could bring to bear in the coming conflict. It would be a huge political win for Russia, and a massive disaster for the Americans.

"Admiral Petrukhin, I know we are asking a lot of your service. But we cannot achieve victory without the sacrifices your men are being asked to make. I make this solemn promise to you—when we are victorious, we will rebuild the Navy and return it back to its former glory," Petrov said reassuringly.

"Gentlemen, this war with the West is going to be won or lost within the first couple of weeks. We must strike fast and hard if we are to win. Unlike wars of the past, this conflict will be fought on many battlefields. I'm counting on each of you to instill in your subordinates a winning attitude. For too long, the West has looked at us as a shell of our former glory. What they do not know is that we are stronger now, more advanced than at any time in our past. For all our past glory, we never had the ability to control so much of the public perception as we do now through social media, or this new ability we've developed to deliver a knockout blow through our cyber-warfare division." He paused to let his words settle in and then casually took a sip of tea.

His military leaders and trusted advisors were hanging on his every word. They had spent the better part of six years working on this plan, and they had poured billions of rubles into designing the computer systems, disinformation programs, and everything else that would be needed to win. They had even employed several American and British authors of war fiction to help them identify weapons of the future and how to employ them. They truly had taken a holistic approach to rebuilding their military.

"Our objective is clear, comrades. We will capture and then hold the Ukraine. Our intent is not to recreate the

Soviet Union. We are not going to bite off more than we can chew, and we are not going to expand the war any more than is necessary. Once we've achieved our objective, we will push for a ceasefire in the UN and call for calmer heads to prevail," Petrov said, convinced that this plan would not fail.

Chapter 24

Opening Salvos

The Russians had given the US and NATO 48 hours to vacate Eastern Ukraine and move back across the Dnieper River. That deadline was still twelve hours away...everyone was tense, unsure of what would happen once it passed.

Sergeant First Class Luke Childers's platoon was the farthest element of the 4th Squadron, known as "The Saber." They were part of the 2nd Cavalry Regiment from Vilseck, Germany, that had arrived in Ukraine to bolster the US and NATO forces already there. The Saber was acting as the eyes and ears for elements of the 1st Armored Division, which was arriving in Ukraine today. They were also the trip wire, in case hostilities did break out. They had been ordered the day before to advance to Kononivka and take up an observation position. The Russians had units stationed throughout the Poltavs'ka Oblast, which placed them within forty miles of the Pryluky Air Base.

A mosquito buzzed by Luke's ear, and he swiftly swung his hand to swat it against the side of his neck. As he looked around their position, he could smell the dirt and tree bark as the sun began to creep over the horizon. The rain had finally tapered off a couple of hours ago, after soaking them for the last sixteen hours. The weather had made the transit to their current position more covert as the sound of the raindrops hid their movement, but it also made identifying their observation post difficult.

"*Six days,*" thought Luke. "*I can't believe we've already been in Ukraine for six days.*" Here they were at the demarcation line, potentially facing off against the Russians who had taken up residence in eastern Ukraine as "peacekeepers." He remembered all those old stories his Dad used to tell him about being stationed along the Fulda Gap during the height of the Cold War, with thousands upon thousands of tanks ready to roll across the border, and he wondered if his old man would be proud to know that forty years later, he was sitting across from a Russian tank unit that might roll across his position.

Sergeant First Class Luke Childers was the platoon sergeant for Second Platoon, Nemesis Troop. He had 46 soldiers he was responsible for, and one Second Lieutenant to mentor into hopefully becoming a great officer and military leader. His father *would* have been proud to see his son serving his country, if he hadn't passed away in his fifties from a heart attack.

Nemesis Troop advanced to a small copse of trees, not far from the main highway where they also had a good commanding view of the E40 highway, which led to Kiev. If the Russians were going to launch an attack toward Kiev, they would have to pass through this area.

Once they had arrived, the platoon immediately began to get their positions ready. They dug several fighting positions, set up camouflage netting for the vehicles, and posted two listening posts on the far sides of each flank. In addition to the antitank missiles on the Strykers, they also had four Javelin launcher positions set up in the tree line. Their battalion commander had also assigned four soldiers from the forward support troop, which provided them with direct access to the regiment's Paladin self-propelled 155mm artillery battalion. The forward observers immediately began to plot several pre-positioned artillery plots so if the Russians did show up, all they had to do was radio in the predetermined positions, which was significantly faster than trying to plot the enemy positions while under fire.

As the fog began to clear with the rising of the sun, Sergeant Childers thought he heard a soft sound of engines starting up in the distance. Suddenly, the birds in the trees down in the valley below them took to the air. *"The noise came from a thicket about two kilometers in front of our position,"* thought Luke. *"Something scared those birds."*

Childers turned to look at the soldiers to his right and his left. The soldiers in his platoon had their faces covered in camouflage to help them blend in with their surroundings, which had the added benefit of helping to keep some of the mosquitoes at bay. He lifted his right hand to his face, signaling to the others around that they might have possible movement to their front. Everyone settled down a little deeper against their hastily dug positions. Water from the rainfall not fully absorbed into the soil yet, so crouching down was covering their legs in mud and water.

Childers lifted his hand slightly and depressed his radio transmitter. He spoke in a soft voice so as not to draw any attention to his position. "Warhorse, this is Nemesis Two-Two. We have possible contact, two kilometers to our front. Please advise on enemy activity in the area, over."

Luke placed his rifle down in front of him and pulled out his micro-binoculars from a pouch on his individual body armor or IBA. He slowly scanned the area in the direction of the possible contact. *"Maybe I can catch a glimpse of something,"* he thought.

Their battalion commander responded to Luke's radio message. "Nemesis Two-Two, this is Warhorse actual. Intelligence reports possible motorized Russian battalion in the area. What do you see? Over."

As the morning fog continued to clear, they began to see more movement below in the valley. A second later, Second Lieutenant Jack Taylor squatted down next to him. "What do you see Sergeant?" he asked, leaning on his platoon sergeant for the expertise he lacked as a junior officer.

Turning slightly, Childers replied quietly, "In that wooded area, about two kilometers in front of us, we have movement near the village of Oleksiivka, just on the other side of the demarcation zone. You can see the soldiers at the checkpoint." He pointed. "There appears to be a lot of activity of some sort just outside our view."

Luke handed Jack the radio. "Why don't you tell HQ what we're observing and let them figure out what they want us to do about it?"

Taylor nodded, then depressed the talk button on the radio. "Warhorse, this is Nemesis Two-Two. We have probable enemy vehicles to our front, two kilometers. Primary objective is still covered in mist, possible enemy activity. How copy?" he asked, hoping they would instruct him to just sit tight and wait for the sun to do its work and burn the mist away.

The men scattered in the tree line were wound tight, apprehensive about what might be waiting down in the valley below as the sun slowly dispersed the morning fog. It would not be long before they would discover if hostilities with the Russians really were going to happen.

"Nemesis Two-Two, this is Warhorse. Can you send your Raven up? We need eyes on that village, over." The Raven was a small handheld infantry drone that had recently been issued to their unit a couple of months ago. It was a small drone, but it could provide real-time video to the ground operators.

Childers nodded to Taylor, who responded, "Copy that, Warhorse. Will advise shortly." They both knew the Raven was a good way to get eyes on the village, but they were concerned the Russians would spot it. The Russians, unlike the Taliban or ISIS, had the ability to track electronic signatures and radio traffic.

"*The Russians are a* real *army*," thought Childers. "*They could do a lot more damage than the Islamic extremists I've spent most of my military career fighting.*" This was going to be new territory for Sergeant Childers; almost all his experience in combat had been in the Middle East, where the enemy was disorganized and, while very scrappy, completely lacking in technique.

He turned slightly and signaled for two of his soldiers to come toward him. "Specialist Tiller, Private Black, I want you to deploy the Raven. Get it up over the village. Let's see what you can spot," he directed.

Specialist Tiller was one of his best younger troopers. The kid was extremely bright. He was already into flying civilian drones, so when they offered him the opportunity to be responsible for the troop's Raven, he jumped at it. They only had three soldiers in the troop that had been officially trained on how to operate the Raven; however, Tiller had taken it upon himself to train several others in his squad and platoon on how to operate it. He even volunteered his own personal drone to help teach others how they worked and how to fly them.

Specialist Tiller took his backpack off and unzipped it into two halves. He pulled the small Raven out of the carrying case and quickly attached the camera to the body of the drone and then unfolded the wings. His partner, Private First-Class Ernest Black, got the wireless controller ready, turned it on and did a quick check to see that the camera was transmitting to the small monitor on the controller and the Toughbook that they had with them.

A minute later, Private Black took the drone from Specialist Tiller, arched his right arm back and gave the drone a quick throw into the air. Specialist Tiller immediately gave the little drone a bit of power and it quickly gained altitude. Within a minute, the drone had risen to nearly 500 feet above their position as it headed down the valley toward the sound of the vehicles in the village.

Lieutenant Taylor and Sergeant Childers gathered around the Toughbook, looking at the images being transmitted by the drone. "Private Black, is the drone synced with headquarters? I want to make sure they're seeing what we are seeing," Taylor said, hoping the private had made sure this was taken care of before they had launched the drone.

Private Black looked at the lieutenant with one of those looks that said, "I know what I'm doing," and just nodded. "I synced it with the comms from your vehicle before we sent it up. They should be seeing what we're seeing," he explained, much to the relief of his lieutenant.

Lieutenant Jack Taylor had only been with the squadron for three months prior to their deployment. He had just completed his officer advance school and airborne school a few months prior to being assigned to Nemesis Troop.

Before Taylor left for this mission, his squadron commander had sat him down. "I just want you to know, in no uncertain terms, that you should listen to Sergeant First Class Childers. He was an Army Ranger, with eight deployments before he got injured. Not only is he an experienced and outstanding NCO, he will help you grow as a leader. There's a reason he's up for master sergeant—the guy is a wealth of information." Jack had taken the conversation to heart.

As the drone made its way toward the checkpoint, the four men nervously watched the screen of the Toughbook. The drone flew about eight hundred feet above the copse of trees, and then it passed the checkpoint and started to fly over the village. Their stomachs sank. The video feed showed them twelve T-80 MBTs lining up, along with a slew of other armored vehicles. Soldiers were quickly swarming around the vehicles, affixing various tree branches and foliage to the armor. It looked like the tanks were also covered in reactive armor, which meant they were geared up for combat.

"Oh, wow, are those BMP-3s?" asked Lieutenant Taylor.

"Yeah, it looks like they have sixteen of them, if my count is right," answered Sergeant Childers. The BMP-3 was an amphibious vehicle that ran on a pair of tracks like a tank. Each one had either a 100mm or a 30mm cannon as its main armament and carried seven soldiers inside its armored compartment. Even though they had come out in the 1980s, they were still feared on the battlefield.

As they panned the camera to the other side of the village, they saw a small column of twenty-five BTR-80s. They were 8x8 wheeled amphibious armored personnel carriers that each carried seven soldiers and had 14.5mm heavy machine guns. The BMP-3s and the BTR-80s were very similar to the American Strykers and Bradleys.

"Specialist Tiller, zoom in on that section over there, near the edge of those woods," directed Lieutenant Taylor, pointing. "I think those are additional tanks."

Childers was impressed. The LT had spotted the barrels of tank cannons sticking out through edges of the trees. As Specialist Tiller zoomed in, they could make out what appeared to be eight T-14 Armata tanks. These were the Russians' newest tanks. Each one had a 125mm main gun with a new antitank round. It was rumored that these tanks could outmatch the American M1A2s and the German Leopard tanks that were deployed in Ukraine.

Sergeant Childers told Lieutenant Taylor, "This isn't good, Sir. This is a large armored force we are facing. Something beyond what we can handle."

The lieutenant nodded. He tapped Tiller on the shoulder. "Head over toward that other field behind the village, over there. I think there are helicopters spooling up."

Although he was already feeling the weight of the situation, he had to know what was waiting for them back there.

As the drone expanded its camera view, Tiller moved the drone back toward a large empty field. Sure enough, there sat six Mi-24D Hind helicopters, which were being fueled. They were getting close to moving out, too, because their rotors were already beginning to spin.

Sergeant Childers turned to the lieutenant. "Sir, you better call this in. They will want an exact count of what we are seeing."

Childers wanted to give the lieutenant a chance to shine for his superiors. *"It's time he starts to take the lead, while I'm here to help make sure he doesn't screw things up too badly,"* he thought, half humorously. The lieutenant was still really green, but he wanted to see him succeed.

Lieutenant Taylor nodded and lowered his head toward the speaker on the radio. "Warhorse, this is Nemesis Two-Two. We have eyes on the village. Are you seeing what we are seeing?" he asked, wanting to know if he should relay what they discovered or just wait for further orders.

Nearly thirty seconds went by with no response. Then a voice suddenly buzzed through. "Nemesis Two-Two, this is Warhorse. We copy. We want you to continue to monitor the units' movements as best you can without being spotted. If they cross the demarcation line, then they are declared hostiles and I want you to engage them as best you can. I've alerted our artillery support. They will give you full priority."

"Good, copy. We'll engage them if they cross. Nemesis Two-Two out," Lieutenant Taylor responded. He flashed a look at his platoon sergeant that seemed to ask for some reassurance that he had done everything correctly.

Smiling, Sergeant Childers said, "Good job, LT. We made sure they knew what we were seeing. I'm a bit concerned about those T-14s, though. That's a lot of tanks across the way, and six attack helicopters on top of it. This could get real dicey very quick."

****

Lieutenant Colonel Bradley Porter had just taken over command of the 4th Squadron, known as "The Saber," eight weeks ago. He was new to the 2nd Cavalry, but definitely not new to the cavalry. He had still been learning the capabilities of his various troops, noncommissioned officers, and officers, when suddenly they were all placed on alert status and subsequently deployed practically overnight to Kiev, Ukraine. They had quickly headed to the Pryluky

Air Base, ninety miles east of Kiev and forty-two miles from the current demarcation zone, where the Russian units were.

In the span of a few days, his squadron had become one of the most forward American elements in Ukraine charged with supporting the 2nd Armored Brigade Combat Team and the 1st Armored Division, which was still half a day away. The armored units had been moving most of the night from Poland, heading toward their frontline positions. This left Lieutenant Colonel Porter's squadron rather exposed, but also gave the armored units the eyes they needed to know where to deploy their forces, should they need to repel a Russian invasion.

Major Light, the Squadron S3, or operations officer, confronted Colonel Porter. "Sir, it looks like that Russian unit is getting ready to pull out of their position. Shouldn't we order the platoon back? Their firepower won't be enough to stop them."

Porter replied, "No, I want them to stay in position. We need them to keep an eye on that unit now that they have been found. Besides, they have Stinger missiles, TOWs, and Javelins with them. We may need them to set an ambush for the armor units," he said, confident that he had made the right decision.

"What Ukrainian units do we have in the area?" Porter inquired, hoping they could get some additional armor support from them until that armored brigade arrived.

Major Light walked over to the map board hanging on one of the tent poles. "Part of the 17th Tank Brigade is in the area," he said as he pulled down a clipboard near the map and looked at some of the units written on it. "Yes, right here," he asserted as he pointed to a spot on the map.

"About twelve kilometers away is the 25th Armored Battalion," he continued. "We have two American LNOs attached to it—call sign Echo Twelve. You want me to reach out to them and see if we can get them to reinforce Nemesis Troop?" the major asked, hoping he could send some additional reinforcements.

As Colonel Porter walked over to the map board, he placed a red X on the village Major Light had just pointed out. He looked at the location of his other units near the Russian armored unit and the location of the Ukrainian troops. If he could get the Ukrainian armored units to cooperate, perhaps they could help provide some additional support to his battalion until additional American units arrived.

"Contact the American LNOs that are imbedded with that Ukrainian unit," directed Colonel Porter. "Tell them what we're facing and see if they will move to reinforce our troops at the demarcation line. Then, make sure 2nd Armor knows what we're seeing and where those tanks are. Also, make sure they know we spotted T-14 Armatas and six Hinds. Find out if they're ready to assist if we need them," he added.

They still had twelve hours until the end of the Russian deadline. The S3 turned and began to make several radio calls to the other units operating in their area. 2nd Armor had an advance unit, a battalion of tanks, and an aviation unit that arrived at Pryluky a couple of hours ago, ahead of the main body. As the men and women of the operations center began to coordinate their operations with the next higher command and other units in the area, the realization that a confrontation with Russia could be hours away set in. No one wanted a shooting war with Russia, but everyone had a job to do and was determined to do it to the best of their ability.

****

Colonel General Igor Nikolaev was the Commander of the Western Military District, and though he didn't agree with the decisions his superiors were making, he executed his orders without fail. He kept many thoughts to himself, which kept him out of trouble.

"We are playing with fire by testing the Americans' resolve," he reasoned. He had seen how the Americans had risen to their challenges so far. He tried to look at the bright side. At least he wouldn't have to answer any more questions from his subordinate commanders about when they were going to engage the Americans in Ukraine—that decision had finally been made.

Kersschh. General Nikolaev heard a sound emanating from his radio. He grabbed the device and smacked it down on the counter to "fix" it—surprisingly, his harsh methods worked.

On the other end, he heard the voice of Lieutenant General Mikhail Chayko, the Commander of the 1st Tank Army and the Ground Force Commander for Russian Forces in the Ukraine. "General Nikolaev, my forces stand ready to execute Red Storm," he announced excitedly. "We will remind the Americans and NATO that Russia is not to be pushed around."

"Acknowledged, General Chayko." Nikolaev felt that the excitement was a bit misplaced; he was not convinced that Russia would come out ahead. However, he dared not utter even a syllable of dissent.

Chayko's voice suddenly dropped lower and became much more serious. "Please ensure we have the required air support so that my armor units have a chance," he requested.

"Understood, General Chayko. We will do what we can to support your troops," General Nikolaev replied. He liked Chayko. He was probably their most capable military commander, which was why Nikolaev had promoted him to take over command of the 1st Tank Army and all ground units in Ukraine.

As he concluded his conversation with Chayko, Nikolaev reflected on the situation. "*Well, the US and NATO did bring this on themselves,*" he reasoned. They'd promised at the end of the Cold War not to expand their borders further east, and now they were walking all the way up to the Russian border. They'd routinely flown surveillance flights along the border, as if they had the right to interfere in Russian affairs. As he thought about the gall that the US would demand that they withdraw from Eastern Ukraine, despite the election results, he felt that it was time for the Americans to be taught a lesson. After all, the Russian bear still had teeth and claws.

"*Do they realize that Petrov won't back down this time?*" he wondered. The orders from up top were to hit the Americans hard and fast; Petrov wanted the Russians to bloody the Yankees quickly and then force them to withdraw from Ukraine. If their mission succeeded, then the only ceasefire the Americans would achieve would be with Moscow had secured all of Ukraine as compensation.

****

Colonel Alexei Semenov, the ground force commander of the Pyriatyn region, had arrived the night before with the new Armatas. So far, he was impressed with what he saw. The unit commanders had their men and equipment ready for war. All they needed was to be given the order to attack, and he had finally received the directive to strike the NATO positions.

He found his executive officer and took him aside. "Comrade, our glorious leader has given us the order. We are to attack immediately."

Colonel Semenov felt a certain satisfaction as the words came out of his mouth. *"There, I've done it. I've just issued the first combat order of what should be a short and victorious war,"* he thought.

A sergeant walked into the house that was being used as a command post; he made a beeline for Major Lavra and whispered something into his ear. A moment later, Major Lavra was getting the attention of Colonel Semenov.

"Sir," he said, "we've just received word that one of our scouts spotted a Ukrainian armored unit moving toward the demarcation line."

He pointed to a location on the map board that was about twenty or so miles from their current location.

Colonel Semenov studied the map board, trying to determine whether or not they could destroy the enemy by the end of the day. Then he grunted and turned to Major Lavra. "Have you spoken with our air force liaison officer yet about our air cover?"

Major Lavra nodded. "I just spoke with the air force LNO, and he said they are initiating their air attack shortly."

Lavra put his hand up as if he had suddenly just remembered something important. "Also, I just received word that some of our soldiers spotted a small reconnaissance drone flying over our area, maybe twenty minutes ago. Some of the soldiers are doing their best to follow the drone back to wherever it originated from. It was a small infantry-style scout drone, which means there must be an American or NATO unit operating very close to our position right now." Major Lavra might have delayed telling Semenov about this unfortunate bit of news because he was concerned that they might have been discovered before they could launch their own operation.

Colonel Semenov just nodded with a slight smile. "Get our helicopters heading toward that Ukrainian armor unit. I also want you to dispatch one of the companies to track that American unit down and destroy them. We must assume that the Americans know we are here, and now they know how many tanks and troops we have. We must move quickly now, before they can react to us." He was frustrated that the Americans might already know his intentions before he had a chance to act, but if they moved quickly, he might still catch them unprepared.

****

In the fall of 2016, a group of Russian hackers operating out of Belarus, code name Marten, had tested out a botnet attack on network connected devices. Modern technology had brought many marvels, such as turning on lighting from a cell phone, starting cars remotely, or monitoring closed-circuit security footage 24/7, but each of these network-enabled items created a potential opening for the hackers to exploit. Marten found a back door to utilize this weakness and hit a French-based hosting provider named OVH with a record-breaking distributed-denial-of-service or DDoS attack, flooding the network with over one terabit of data per second. The botnet attack was more successful than they had hoped, shutting down large portions of the internet for a short time. The plans for a more formalized Operation Redworm had been born.

A year later, on a quiet Sunday morning in September, the head of Marten had received a message from the Kremlin. He'd alerted all of his team members, bellowing, "Operation Redworm is a go! This is not a drill. It's time to sow as much chaos as possible. Get to work!"

The clicking of keys in the room immediately drowned out all other noise. They began scanning the web for unsecured IoT devices and quickly hit pay dirt. The internet was covered with a plethora of IoT devices— printers, heating and cooling systems, vehicle dashboard systems, household appliances, etc.—that hadn't received regular patch updates to their security. Marten began indiscriminately taking control of these devices. Within 24 hours, they had collected a botnet army of nearly 18 million devices. One of the members had broken the botnets down into smaller attack groups, so that they could create a series of attack waves. This would make it significantly harder for the US and NATO to respond when they eventually figured out what was happening to their IT infrastructure.

With their botnet army ready, Marten launched the first series of attacks. The first attack hit a group of internet service providers in the EU, UK, and US with an IoT botnet DDoS attack that was nearly 1 Tbps strong. The bandwidth that was syphoned away through this attack reached unheard-of levels, degrading the performance of the internet in those regions to the point of making it unusable. Next, they infiltrated individual service providers' servers, summarily locking them out using a crypto-locker tool they had developed.

With phases one and two of Operation Redworm complete, Marten turned to an assault on the power grids in Poland, Ukraine, and Germany. The goal of that particular attack was not to destroy these power grids to the point of creating an unrecoverable blackout situation; rather, they simply wanted to take them offline for the first few hours of armed conflict, throwing the US and NATO forces into chaos just as they were trying to organize a resistance.

While the attacks against the internet service providers and power grids were underway, a separate assault was launched against the US and NATO satellite systems. They attacked the control systems within hundreds of GPS satellites, causing them to burn out. Within minutes, the Russians had effectively destroyed the globe's entire GPS satellite system—or at least, any GPS that was being accessed by the enemies of Russia.

In Europe, there was an immediate effect of chaos as large-scale blackouts and internet outages prevailed. The US as a nation would not fully realize what had happened until later; it was still nighttime in America, and most of its citizens were blissfully sleeping, unaware of the attack that had just occurred.

While skirmishes had taken place up to this point in isolation, historians would later argue that Operation Redworm was Russia's opening act of war.

Chapter 25
Geben Sie Ihren Zweck

Geilenkirchen, Germany
NATO Air Base

Since they had finally received their attack order, Major Victor Schepin's Spetsnaz team was anxious to get things going. It was just about time for them to execute an attack plan that had initially been drawn up during the height of the Cold War. The men of his unit were spread out in three vans, and each van had four members armed to the teeth, ready to carry out their mission. They were going to hit the NATO base at Geilenkirchen, which was responsible for providing the bulk of NATO's E-3 Sentries, commonly known as AWACS; this would be a critical base to incapacitate in the early hours of the war.

Despite the Cold War having ended, the Russians still maintained a small contingent of Spetsnaz units operating in Germany, Belgium, and the Netherlands. They even had a team that was still operating in the UK. At the height of the Cold War, there had been over thirty individual teams operating behind enemy lines, ready to be activated and carry out their mission at a minute's notice; now that number was closer to twelve.

Major Schepin checked his watch and saw that they had only a minute left. He signaled for the driver to proceed to the gate. While there had been no official declaration of war between NATO and Russia yet, the guards at the NATO base were on alert and had been augmented by additional security. Instead of the standard three guards at the gate, there were now six of them. Beyond the guards, Major Schepin could see the runway and the aircraft hangars. Two of the E-3s were on the tarmac, with a ground crew around them getting them ready to fly.

As their repair van approached the gate, they rounded some cement vehicle barricades that had been placed there to force vehicles to slow down in order to navigate around them. As they neared the guard shack, they readied their weapons. They would have to be quick and neutralize the guards before they could sound the alarm and alert the rest of the base security.

Dieter depressed the button on his driver side window, lowering it as he approached the guard. "*Papieren. Geben Sie ihren Zweck*," barked the guard, asking for their identification papers and the purpose for their visit.

Dieter smiled at the guard innocently enough, then, instead of reaching down to pull his papers out, he pulled out a pistol outfitted with a silencer from the center console and shot the guard right between the eyes. As the guard's body collapsed to the ground, Major Schepin opened the front passenger-side door, bringing his silenced MP-5 to his shoulder and firing a quick three-round burst. He successfully hit the guard nearest him in the upper chest, dropping the man immediately.

The cargo door behind the driver opened and two additional Spetsnaz soldiers leaped from the van, their silenced MP-5s at the ready. Each man fired several quick bursts at the guards in the guard shack before they could even react to what was unfolding. Dieter, the driver, fired several quick shots, hitting the final guard in the back as he ran to hit the alarm button on the side of the guard shack. In less than thirty seconds, all six guards had been killed before they could alert anyone else on base or prevent Major Schepin's team from gaining access to Geilenkirchen. One of Schepin's men ran up to the guard shack and opened the gates so that the other vehicles in their group could follow them onto the base as well.

Their next goal was to drive toward the flight line and destroy all seven NATO E-3 aircraft. The remaining eight aircraft of the squadron were deployed at other bases and would be handled by other Spetsnaz teams. One of the vehicles in Schepin's crew headed toward the flight line to destroy the aircraft. The second vehicle headed toward the building where the crew were usually located. The final vehicle headed toward the fuel depot, where they would place explosive charges to destroy the airport's fuel farms. The operation went off without a hitch.

******

Near Castlegate

Captain Hermann Wulf pulled out another cigarette and lit it, pulling in a long drag, letting the smoke fill his lungs as his body absorbed the nicotine it so desperately longed for. As he exhaled the smoke through his nose, one of his staff sergeants walked up to him, signaling he wanted a smoke as well.

Captain Wulf tossed his pack to the sergeant and retrieved his lighter for him. "Many thanks, Captain," the sergeant said as he handed him back his pack of cigarettes.

"Are the troops ready?" Hauptmann Wulf asked. Their unit had been placed on alert twenty-four hours ago as the Russian NATO deadline neared. They didn't know if the

Russians would try to attack Castlegate, but the German government and SACEUR were not going to take any chances. They had moved Captain Wulf's company to a position near the NATO facility to help beef up the security.

Just as the sergeant was about to respond, the radio in their vehicle crackled to life. "We see a suspicious-looking vehicle from the right tower," said one of the scouts, observing the only entrance to Castlegate.

Wulf didn't want his unit to draw undue attention or give themselves away, so he had placed a couple of soldiers in hidden positions, covering the various approaches to the facility. He also kept his armored vehicle hidden, only a couple of blocks away.

Just as Captain Wulf reached for the radio to inquire what the scouts were seeing, they heard an explosion and then the unmistakable sound of automatic machine-gun fire.

Without thinking, the sergeant yelled out to the soldiers outside their vehicle, "Mount up!"

Captain Wulf grabbed the radio and yelled, "All vehicles, converge on Castlegate!"

He also made a quick call to their headquarters, letting them know, "The facility is under attack!"

The GTX Boxer armored vehicle lurched forward as the driver headed toward the NATO facility. The rest of

Wulf's command quickly followed in their vehicles and raced to assist the soldiers, who appeared to be under some sort of attack. It took less than three minutes for their vehicle to reach the facility, and when they arrived, they could see four utility vans parked awkwardly near the road leading to the facility. As they moved past the utility vehicles, a barrage of bullets hit the armored shell of their vehicle, bouncing off harmlessly.

The Boxer armored vehicle was unique in that it was equipped with a remote-controlled turret operated by a gunner within the vehicle. When the vehicle started to take fire, the gunner immediately looked for where the bullets were coming from and returned fire with his 12.7mm automatic heavy machine gun.

As the vehicle came to a stop, Captain Wulf ordered the back hatch lowered, and eight soldiers immediately rushed out. The first soldier that exited the vehicle turned to the right of the vehicle and ran forward, charging the attackers. He only managed to travel four steps before he was hit multiple times in the chest, collapsing to the ground, dead.

Captain Wulf was the last man out of the vehicle. He could see that several of his soldiers were pinned down by nearly a dozen attackers, who had turned their attention to focus on his force. The other attackers had continued to try and fight their way into the NATO facility. As the rest of Captain Wulf's unit arrived, the attackers quickly became outnumbered and overwhelmed. Before long, the Russians were all either killed or captured.

The attack on Castlegate lasted less than ten minutes. It was a vicious attack that resulted in fourteen NATO soldiers killed and twenty-three injured. The four attackers that were captured turned out to be Russian Spetsnaz soldiers; another 43 had died during the incursion. The Russians never penetrated the facility, though they were able to substantially damage the external communications ability of Castlegate, which temporarily shut it down as an alternate command facility.

****

Ukraine

High above the skies of Myronivka, not far from the Dnieper River, an American Northrop Grumman RQ-4 "Global Hawk" surveillance drone was loitering 10,000 feet above the countryside when it detected the movement of multiple Russian ground units heading toward the various American armored and infantry units along the demarcation line. The information was immediately relayed to the various ground commands, alerting them to the Russian advance.

Major General Mueller, the American ground commander, immediately sent a flash message to NATO and US European Command headquarters, warning them of the hostile Russian movement and relaying to HQ that he was ordering his units to engage them. He realized that the Russians were clearly moving to attack his forces.

"Well, I'm not about to be caught flat-footed, waiting for the Russians to fire the first shot," he thought. He planned to have his units engage those Reds as soon as they were within range.

MG Mueller yelled out to whoever was within earshot in the headquarters building, "Everyone, get on your IBA and helmets! We need to get ready. The Russians are on the move!"

"Yes, Sir!" came the refrain, and the men and women around him quickly scurried around to put on their body armor and then pass the word along to everyone else.

The army engineers, realizing that hostilities were likely imminent, placed blast barriers around the buildings on the military portion of the Kiev International Airport airfield. While their forces would not be safe from a direct hit from a Russian bomb, these blast barriers would provide protection from flying shrapnel.

The advance party of the 2nd Armored Division had just arrived and was in the process of offloading their Abrams M1A2 main battle tanks. They had twenty-four of them, along with a complement of sixteen Bradley fighting vehicles for support. General Mueller saw what was happening and grabbed one of his officers. "Hey, I need you to run down to the battalion commander and tell him to get his tanks on the road to Pryluky Air Base ASAP. 2nd Cavalry has spotted a heavy formation of T-90s, T-80s and T-14s gearing up to cross the demarcation line, and they'll need immediate armor support. I know it'll take them close to two hours to get there, so time is of the essence."

"Yes, Sir!" replied the officer, and he ran off to notify 2nd Armored Division of their new orders.

****

While the Global Hawk was notifying NATO forces of the changes in the ground troops moving toward the demarcation line, a French-operated NATO E-3 Sentry AWACS was operating over west Ukraine to monitor changes in air capabilities. Suddenly, it detected the takeoff of 32 Su-34 "Fullbacks," twin-seat, all-weather supersonic medium-range fighter bombers. The Su-34s were notorious and feared in the military world; they were large aircraft that carried a substantial amount of air-to-ground ordnance, perfect for providing air support under heavy enemy fire. The E-3 also detected the takeoff of twenty-three MiG-31MB "Foxhound" interceptors, all heading toward Ukrainian airspace at supersonic speeds in a standard Russian attack formation.

In addition to the attack aircraft, the E-3 spotted eight Tu-160 "Blackjack" bombers, coming in swiftly at low altitudes across Belarus toward Polish airspace. When the radar operator saw the Blackjacks, his stomach sank; they were more frightening to him than the fighters. They were a supersonic aircraft, intended to swoop in fast and low and deliver devastating conventional or nuclear attacks. NATO considered them to be a first-strike weapon, like the B-1 Lancer bombers.

While the group of radar operators began to identify and track all the inbound aircraft, one of the operators announced, "A new group of aircraft has just appeared."

The air battle manager, Major Brian Nicodemus, walked over to the young officer and looked at his screen. He immediately saw one, then two, then a total of four groups of twenty Tu-22M "Backfire" bombers about a hundred miles behind the fighters, moving quickly toward Ukraine. The Backfire was a supersonic long-range strategic and maritime strike bomber, similar to the Blackjack. It also carried a large number of conventional bombs, or up to ten cruise missiles.

Major Nicodemus balked at the new information. The Russians were clearly launching a full-out air attack against NATO forces. *"They've caught us completely unprepared,"* he realized.

Brian immediately began to alert the aircraft that were flying combat air patrol over Ukraine. There were four American F-15s armed with air-to-air missiles and six German Eurofighters that were flying a combat patrol near the Poland, Belarus and Ukraine border. The E-3 immediately began to vector the American fighters toward the group of Fullbacks, since they were closest to them. The German Eurofighters were vectored to engage the group of Blackjacks that were streaking in quickly from Belarus.

The French commander on the E-3 also issued an alert to the two NATO air bases in Ukraine, along with the bases in Poland and Germany. The US had four F-22 Raptors on a five-minute ready alert in the vicinity of Krakow, along with six F-15s at the Pryluky Air Base and another six Eurofighters at the Kiev International Airport. In the next five minutes, NATO would have another sixteen aircraft in the air to meet the Russians.

For their part, the Ukrainian air force also scrambled their own MiGs and Su-27s to join the NATO aircraft. In short order, twelve Ukrainian aircraft would be in the air to help defend their country from what was now clearly a Russian invasion. Fortunately, the Ukrainians had also deployed nearly a dozen SA-10 air defense missile systems around their air bases and the capital of Kiev. These systems immediately engaged the incoming Russian aircraft with support from the E-3s.

The key to air combat in the 21st century was the ability of an air force to leverage the immense capability of an AWACS system, like the E-3s. Operating an AWACS allowed the fighters to operate with their search radars off, meaning they emitted no radar emissions, which normally would have given their positions away. The AWACS could use their powerful search radars and vector the fighters toward the enemy aircraft, essentially sharing their radar screens with the fighters so they could see what the AWACS were seeing.

What the E-3 did not detect, at least not right away, was the six Sukhoi Su-57 stealth fighters that had taken off thirty minutes earlier from deeper within Russia. These aircraft immediately headed toward the NATO and American E-3s that were operating in the area. Their objective was to blind NATO and prevent them from coordinating a proper air defense while their Su-34s attacked the American ground forces and the Ukrainian air defense units. The Backfires and Blackjacks were going for the NATO air bases in Poland and Germany, hoping to completely eliminate NATO's air power, which was their most potent defense.

As the French E-3 alerted additional NATO fighters and vectored in the ones already aloft, one of the radar operators saw a brief blip of an aircraft no less than six miles from their position. His eyes grew wide as saucers as he realized that the aircraft that had appeared out of nowhere had just fired two air-to-air missiles at them. There was no time to react, or even to try to evade the missiles.

As the enemy missiles closed the distance to the E-3, the pilot immediately fired off flares and deployed multiple chaff canisters in hopes of spoofing the inbound missiles. In less than forty seconds, the two R-73M Archer missiles got within 40 feet of the E-3's engines and exploded, spraying the area with shrapnel. This metal cloud ripped apart two of the airplanes' engines and tore chunks from the wings and fuselage. The fires from the explosion quickly found the fuel bladders in the wings, which exploded, causing both wings to snap off and forcing the aircraft into a steep dive as it spun out of control.

As the first NATO E-3 went down, the second E-3, operated by the American Air Force, immediately took over control of the air battle. A third E-3 was scrambled out of Ramstein Air Base, along with additional fighters.

Four minutes after the first E-3 went down, the US Air Force operator who had assumed control of the battle, Major Tony Giovani, saw a similar blip on their radar screen. Just as the blip disappeared, four R-37M Arrow missiles appeared out of nowhere, about 62 miles away from their position.

Major Giovani immediately took evasive maneuvers, steering the aircraft to a lower altitude to try and lose the missiles in the ground clutter. Tony knew at once what must have fired those missiles—a Sukhoi Su-57, the Russian version of the American F-22 Raptor. Even while he had his aircraft in a hard pull, he grabbed his radio and contacted his superiors. "Ground Command, Ground Command, this is Watch Tower Two. There's a Sukhoi Su-57 in the air here. They've just launched a set of missiles at me. Performing evasive maneuvers. You need to get the Raptors and the F-

15s airborne quickly. Send to my coordinates to engage the Su-57, over!"

"Watch Tower Two, this is Ground Command. Acknowledged. Currently scrambling additional aircraft to your location," came the reply.

"*I don't know that we have much chance of surviving this encounter*," thought Tony, "*but maybe I just increased our odds.*"

As he continued to maneuver his E-3 rapidly, the air battle managers in the back of the aircraft also detected three Beriev A-100 Russian-built AWACS, which had suddenly turned on their powerful search radars now that the air war had officially started. They would search for the NATO aircraft and then guide the Russian fighters toward them.

"*Lord, help us. I don't want to die right now,*" Major Giovani prayed. If the last NATO E-3 went down, then the NATO fighters would have to either fly blind or turn on their own search radars, which would give away their positions to the swarm of enemy aircraft now heading toward them.

Following Major Giovani's coordinates, the American F-15s had successfully taken off and gotten within missile range of the MiG-31s. The F-15 pilots had wanted to go after the Fullbacks, but the MiGs had raced ahead to intercept them.

The lead F-15 pilot directed his team, "Fire your AMRAAM missiles at the MiGs from maximum range!"

As sixteen projectiles streaked across the sky toward the MiGs, they left ribbons of smoke and steam behind them. The Russian aircraft immediately took evasive action, but not before firing off their own air-to-air missiles at the Americans. Each MiG discharged three missiles at the F-15s.

Both Russian and American aircraft popped flares and chaff canisters to try to spoof each other's missiles and do their best to evade them. While the F-15s succeeded in shooting down eleven of the sixteen MiGs that they had engaged, all four F-15s were shot down.

****

As the battle in the sky started, a group of Germans in a radar truck were continually adjusting the paths of a Patriot missile battery situated on the military side of the Kiev International Airport, attempting to keep aim on the numerous enemy aircraft heading toward them.

Once they finally received confirmation of hostile intent, the officer on watch, Captain Isaac Krüger, hurriedly ran over to the radar operator. "Hey, Alice, we have authorization to fire," he blurted out. "I want you to prioritize and engage the enemy aircraft. The most pressing threat at the moment is the Su-34s. I count twenty-four of those Fullbacks—if we are lucky, we will take them all down."

Alice Weber quickly moved to activate one of the four-missile battery pods and launched all four missiles at the incoming Fullbacks. She then moved to the next battery of missiles and launched the next batch of four Patriot II missiles. As she activated the third battery, the other radar operator, Bucky, announced, "The Backfires just fired off a wave of cruise missiles at us!"

Captain Krüger immediately instructed them, "OK, stop targeting the Fullbacks now. Engage the incoming cruise missiles with *all* our remaining missiles. We still have sixteen left, so we should be fine."

The mood remained calm; they felt confident in shooting down the incoming fire with their own missiles…until a second wave of cruise missiles appeared on their radar screen.

Krüger felt nauseous. He knew in that moment that they wouldn't be able to take all the incoming cruise missiles down. He had technicians at the first two batteries, doing their best to get the next set of missile pods reloaded, but even under the best training exercise, they hadn't been able to get them up and ready in less than ten minutes. There just wasn't time.

Isaac calculated the situation mentally. The targeting computer now had control of all twenty-four missiles, and it would guide the missiles to the Su-34s and cruise missiles they had already locked them on. *"Well...there's no reason for us to stay in these vehicles any more, since we are clearly going to be targeted ourselves,"* he realized.

Captain Krüger yelled, "Everyone, out! Run to the closest bomb bunker and pray you survive!"

While his men ran for protection, Isaac chose to stay behind and make sure the missiles functioned as they should. It was the last time his men saw him. The radar and control vehicle was demolished as soon as the second wave of cruise missiles began to pulverize the airport.

****

In less than twenty minutes, all the NATO fighter aircraft flying over Ukraine were destroyed. The Russian Backfires began to focus their attack runs against the Ukrainian air defenses and air bases, especially the Kiev International Airport, where the rest of the NATO alert fighters were stationed and still in the process of taking off. They fired off two waves of twenty missiles each. As the first wave of cruise missiles streaked across the skies to the runways, the missiles dispersed their cluster munitions. As those exploded on the runways, large craters were formed, making it impossible for any aircraft to take off or land there. They also managed to destroy several German Eurofighters that had been in the process of taking off.

Just as the Russians were beginning to feel cocky, six of the NATO Patriot missiles got into range of the Fullbacks they had been locked on. As the proximity sensors on the missiles were activated, a cloud of shrapnel was released right into the path of the Su-34s, ripping the hulls of those aircraft apart. Debris from the Fullbacks rained down from the sky. The larger chunks of the wings and tails flew toward the ground at high speeds, impacting violently.

Two fortunate Fullback pilots had managed to perform evasive maneuvers and escape the path of the incoming Patriot missiles. They pulled their aircraft hard enough that the proximity sensors on the incoming projectiles were never activated. Those missiles streaked right past the Fullbacks, eventually exploding in mini-fireballs and harmlessly releasing small clouds of shrapnel.

Just before the cruise missiles arrived, two Eurofighters had succeeded in taking off. Their luck was short-lived though; they were quickly shot down while they desperately tried to gain altitude and get into the fight. Even if another helicopter or plane had attempted to use the cratered runway, the MiGs had the airport blanketed in air cover at that point, preventing any additional aircraft or helicopters from getting airborne.

Of the sixteen Patriot missiles that had been aimed at the cruise missiles, twelve met their marks. Each time one of the cruise missiles came into range of one of the Patriot missiles, a scattered shotgun-like blast erupted from the Patriot, throwing chunks of metal into the path of the cruise missile. The cruise missiles were ripped apart, creating explosions that were almost beautiful, reminiscent of fireworks.

Twenty-eight cruise missiles continued unhindered toward the Kiev International Airport. As each one impacted, the sound wave from the blast created a mini earthquake. Clouds of dust and debris rose quickly into the air like the tumultuous edge of a thunderstorm. There wasn't an aircraft hangar left after that attack.

Following the two waves of cruise missiles, pairs of Su-34s began to drop the Russian version of 1,000 lbs. JDAMs on the fuel farms, and the dozens of NATO fighters that had been getting ready to fly. NATO engineers had erected dozens of blast walls separating the aircraft, which prevented a single bomb from causing damage to other nearby aircraft. However, the Russians knew this, so they used their guided smart bombs to destroy the remaining NATO aircraft.

The Fullbacks also targeted the US/NATO command center and communications equipment. They hit the temporary lodging facilities, and other military vehicles and positions as they found them. In the span of fifteen minutes, the Kiev International Airport was completely wrecked. Nearly every NATO aircraft and helicopter had been destroyed or severely damaged. Major General Mueller and his deputy, a German brigadier general, had both been killed along with most of their staff during the attack. Nine hundred US and NATO soldiers had been killed, and nearly three times that number had been wounded.

In addition to the military loss of life, nearly a thousand civilians had been killed at the airport. Although the Russians had focused on the military side of the airport, several large commercial aircraft were destroyed during the cruise missile attack, causing further death and destruction.
****

While the attack on the international airport was taking place, a small group of MiGs headed toward the Polish border to protect the flight of twenty Backfires as they moved to get in range of two other Polish air bases being used by NATO. Their goal was to damage the Polish airfields where additional NATO aircraft were stationed. This would further inhibit the US/NATO ability to respond to the Russian invasion, and if they were lucky, would disable or destroy additional fighter aircraft. The Su-34s wouldn't be following the Backfire attack like they had in Kiev and Pryluky, so the cruise missiles had to accomplish the job on their own.

Staff Sergeant Noah Troy was on watch in the radar vehicle of the Patriot battery at Pryluky when the Russian air attack started. He watched nervously as his radar tracked dozens of MiGs and other attack aircraft while they took off from their bases in Russia and headed toward Ukrainian airspace. *"Holy cow, this must be the attack they warned us about,"* he thought.

Noah had a sick feeling in his stomach. He turned to one of the soldiers next to him and ordered, "Go get the lieutenant. She needs to see this now."

1st Lieutenant Nichole Mattie was standing not far from the radar vehicle, talking with one of her soldiers who was having a problem with his girlfriend back home. *"One of the many duties of being an officer—listening to your soldiers' life drama,"* she thought.

While Nichole was in the middle of telling this young kid that there were plenty of fish in the sea, she looked up and saw one of her soldiers exit the radar truck, frantically waving to get her attention.

"LT! Sergeant Troy needs you in the truck ASAP!" the soldier yelled with a distraught look on his face.

"*Ugh, what the heck is wrong now?*" she wondered.

"I'm on my way," she responded, ending her conversation with the other soldier and walking swiftly back to the radar truck.

"What do you have, Sergeant Troy?" Lieutenant Mattie asked as she closed the door behind her.

Troy looked up nervously as the lieutenant walked in. "Ma'am, I think the Russians are about to attack. If you look here, see? We're tracking over forty aircraft heading in our direction and a lot more heading toward Kiev. I think we should sound the base alarm," he said, hoping someone else would agree with his assessment.

Lieutenant Mattie saw the radar display and the color drained from her face. This was the most Russian aircraft she had ever seen at one time, and she knew it meant only one thing. "Yes, I agree with you. Hit the base alarm and get the missile pods spun up to engage those aircraft once they cross into Ukrainian airspace. I'll be back shortly. I'm going to run over to the operations center and let them know what's going on." She left Troy to get the battery ready to respond to the threat.

Sergeant Troy sighed in relief, then reached over and hit the red button that would sound an air raid alarm across the base. Once the siren began to wail, he immediately activated the missile pods and turned them in the direction of the incoming enemy aircraft. *"Man, we've only been here four days—and now the Russians decide they want to attack?"* he thought.

The specialist who had been sitting next to him interjected, "Sergeant, the Russian aircraft are about to cross into Ukrainian airspace—are we cleared to engage?"

Sergeant Troy paused for a second and looked at Specialist Matthews, who appeared to be moments away from completely freaking out. "Listen up. When those Russians cross the border, we're going to engage them with our missiles. If they launch any cruise missiles, then we're going to switch targets and go after those instead. Remember your training, and just do what we've practiced a million times. There are alert fighters being scrambled right now and other fighters above us. We do our part and let them do their part, OK?" he said, trying to calm his fellow soldier's nerves down and keep him focused.

A minute later, the Russian aircraft began to cross into Ukrainian airspace, heading right for them. Trevor nodded toward Specialist Matthews, who lifted the cover off the firing button and discharged the first pod's worth of missiles. In seconds, the pod fired off its volley of surface-to-air missiles at the incoming Russian aircraft. They switched to the second pod of missiles and locked on to additional aircraft; then they fired off that pod's worth of missiles as well.

All of a sudden, they spotted a volley of cruise missiles being fired from the Russian bombers.

"Oh crap—that's a lot of cruise missiles," Sergeant Troy thought. *"We don't have enough missiles to stop them all."*

Noah immediately blurted out, "We're changing targets. Let's go after those incoming cruise missiles. Hopefully we can thin them out a bit." He was not feeling at all confident in their chances. Even under the best training circumstances, they couldn't get the spent missile pods reloaded in enough time to reengage the incoming missiles and aircraft.

Just as they began to switch targets and go after the incoming cruise missiles, they felt the concussion of a massive explosion rock their vehicle. Overwhelming noise from the blast soon followed. Then, the roof of their vehicle imploded, and their worlds went black as a mortar round scored a direct hit on their radar truck.

Lieutenant Mattie had just walked out of the operations center when the radar truck exploded. She was shoved to the ground by the shockwave from the blast, right before her ears were overpowered by the boom from the mortar. As she lay there on the ground, stunned for a second, she caught her breath and then heard the C-RAM's 20mm cannon open fire on additional incoming mortars, too late to save her soldiers in the radar vehicle. Several additional explosions could be heard from rounds that were still getting through the C-RAM. She pulled herself up to see soldiers running to different fighting positions and protective bunkers. It was controlled chaos as the base began to respond to the attack.

****

Colonel Joe Jenkinson had arrived at Pryluky Air Base twenty-four hours ago as part of the advance party for elements of the 82nd Airborne. The Division had started to arrive in country to help reinforce the 2nd Cavalry Regiment and the 173rd Airborne, which had already deployed to the field. Colonel Jenkinson had just walked into the operations center to meet with the base commander when the air raid sirens began to wail. He looked around and saw that the highest-ranking officer in the operations center was an Air Force major. The base commander must still have been on the way.

"Major Dusty, we have incoming Russian aircraft!" yelled a young female lieutenant as she walked into the operations center. All eyes turned to face her, not sure what to make of what she just said.

Major Dusty was the base's operations officer. This was his second month in Ukraine, so he had gone through this type of drill many times. He knew the next few minutes were going to be critically important to the survival of the base if this was the main attack they thought might happen. He turned to one of the NCOs from flight operations. "Order the alert fighters to scramble immediately. Flush the rest of the fighters from the base right away and get our helicopters airborne!" he barked.

As orders were being issued to the various groups throughout the base, the C-RAM system engaged an unseen target. Then, a loud explosion shook the building. A tense moment went by before another powerful blast shook the building, only this time, they heard shrapnel hitting the outer walls and what must have been debris raining down on the ceiling above them.

"Everyone, get your IBA on. We're under attack!" Major Dusty yelled.

Colonel Jenkinson moved quickly to the major, grabbing hold of his arm to get his attention. "Get me a radio to the QRF now!" he said. The major just nodded and pointed to one of the soldiers manning a bank of SINCGAR radios.

The colonel walked over to the soldier. "Hey, I need the radio to the helicopters," he said.

The soldier nodded, then handed him one of the handsets he had just used. "This one is set up to talk to the Apaches right now," he responded.

Colonel Jenkinson picked up the radio and let them know to head to a specific area not far from the base and look for the enemy mortar team. One of the first things Colonel Jenkinson had done when he had arrived at the base was to look for where the Russians would most likely set up their mortars or launch attacks. Once the rest of his unit arrived, he had planned on placing several listening posts in those areas to watch them. Unfortunately, the rest of his unit wasn't going to arrive for a couple more days.

****

Major Igor Yelson's men were ready to attack the Americans. They had moved into position less than an hour ago, as soon as they had been given the attack orders. He had had his men split up into several teams. He had two mortar teams that would attack the American air defense systems, while one of his ground teams would pour a ton of heavy machine-gun fire at the perimeter in hopes of drawing the American soldiers out in the open once the cruise missiles started to hit.

Major Yelson's main concern was the Apache helicopters that his scouts had identified. They would need to take those choppers out quickly or they would shred his force. To counter the Apaches, he had six of his soldiers ready, equipped with the newest MANPADs available, the SA-25 "Willow." Yelson knew the American helicopters would come for his mortar teams, so he had the MANPADs positioned just right to take them out.

"It's time," Major Yelson announced. "Start hitting the base with the mortars," he ordered one of his lieutenants.

The lieutenant nodded, lifted a radio to his mouth, and spoke a single word.

In seconds, they heard the first *thump, thump, thump* of the mortars being fired. Then, they heard a noise they were not expecting. It sounded like a piece of linen being torn or ripped apart. Then they saw two strings of tracer fire emanating from the base into the sky where their mortars had just fired.

An explosion could be heard as the first couple of mortars hit. There was a pause, and then a secondary blast could be heard as the next group of mortars hit.

"*Those blasted Americans*," thought Igor. "*They must have set up an anti-mortar-rocket system.*"

At least some of the mortars were still getting through though, because they were still hearing additional explosions within the base. Then, the unmistakable sound of chopper blades slapping rhythmically rose above the din. Major Yelson squinted as he looked off in the distance of the runway and saw an Apache helicopter take off and head in their direction. He also observed a pair of fighters hit their afterburners as they raced down the runway to get airborne.

As the first Apache approached their positions, it let loose a slew of antipersonnel rockets at one of his mortar positions. In that instant, he thought, "*This is it. My mortar team is doomed.*"

Then, Major Yelson saw the first of his MANPADs fire from the tree line toward the helicopter, then a second. The helicopter moved incredibly quickly and somehow evaded the first missile but was hit by the second one. Igor thought the helicopter would have blown up or crashed, but it resumed its attack on his men. In seconds, it was nearly on top of his second mortar team, when another MANPAD reached out and nailed it. The helicopter spewed smoke and flames and quickly turned to head back to the base. It only stayed aloft for a few more minutes before it made a hard-crash landing at the edge of the perimeter.

Just then, the cruise missiles started to hit the NATO base, exploding across the runways and then the rest of the base buildings. Major Yelson smiled, knowing that his unit had done their part; they had helped to eliminate the Patriot missile battery, the only real threat to the air raid now destroying the base.

He picked up his radio and ordered, "Disengage. Return to our rally point. We need to regroup, rearm, and get ready for our next mission."

****

Captain Ian Hawk had been getting his Apache ready for a routine flight when the base alarm went off. They received an alert, letting them know of a possible Russian air raid and telling them to get airborne as quickly as possible.

Captain Hawk closed the window to the cockpit and brought the helicopter to full power. In less than a minute, he began to steer out of their revetment toward the taxiway while continuing to gain power. Then he saw the C-RAM system fire at an unseen target toward the opposite side of the base. A voice came over the radio and told them to head toward a specific grid to see if the mortar team was near there.

Ian applied power to the helicopter and began to fly toward the coordinates he was given. He got the attention of his gunner, at the front of the chopper. "Hey, Tom, if you spot that mortar team before I do, engage them with the rockets and take them out. We can't let them walk those rounds in on the runway." Captain Hawk was concerned about the pair of F-15s that were heading toward the end of the runway to take off.

Suddenly, he spotted a projectile flying from a small clearing near some wooded areas, roughly two kilometers from the base perimeter. "Over there! Hit them with the rockets quick!" Hawk yelled to his gunner, who proceeded to let loose a number of their antipersonnel rockets. As Tom was firing the rockets, Hawk increased speed and raced toward the position, betting there were additional enemy soldiers in that area.

As he moved closer to the Russian positions, his air defense alarms began to growl in his ears, and then a blaring alarm overpowered him. Before he could even react, the helicopter's automated defense spat out flares and it jerked hard to one side, just in time for him to watch an enemy missile fly right past them. Then, they felt a sudden jolt and heard the explosion. All kinds of alarms sounded in the cockpit.

Tom stayed focused on engaging the ground soldiers, who were now shooting at them. Hawk regained control of the helicopter, hitting the fire extinguisher on the engine that was damaged. He pulled the helicopter into a hard-right turn as he looked to gain some altitude and pull them away from the ground fire. Then, several more missiles raced toward their position. Captain Hawk fired off more flares and jinked hard from side to side, trying to evade the new missiles.

Suddenly, the glass canopy above him exploded. As soon as he stopped shielding his face from the falling shards of glass, Ian realized that his left arm didn't work. His right leg was on fire, and there was smoke pouring into the cockpit from the engine intake above him. Hawk turned the helicopter back toward the base, trying to get them back to safety. He attempted to use his left hand to reach for the fire extinguisher, but it still wouldn't work. He looked down and saw his left hand had been severed and was squirting blood. As he tried to bring the helicopter in for an emergency landing, he lost too much blood, and lost consciousness.

****

Several of the F-15s fought to gain altitude and engage the enemy fighters just as the first wave of cruise missiles arrived. The C-RAM switched from engaging the mortars to the cruise missiles and threw a sheer wall of 20mm rounds at the incoming missiles, destroying dozens of them.

However, while the C-RAM was occupied with the incoming missiles, several pairs of Su-34s released a series of JDAMs on the airfield. They specifically targeted the C-RAM system, the base communication systems, power generation, command and control buildings, and the dozens of US and NATO aircraft and helicopters that were trying to get into the air and join the battle.

As the air base's defenses went down, the waves of enemy cruise missiles and JDAMs began to systematically destroy the base and hammer units of the 2nd Cavalry Regiment and 173rd Airborne that were not already dispersed at their marshaling points away from the base.

While the base was under air and ground attack, two Russian surveillance drones loitered not far away, providing exceptional video coverage of the attack. The recordings from these drones would be used by the Russian psychological operation groups and Russian media to produce graphic and gripping descriptions of the battle. This, of course, would be promulgated across social media to the entire world.

While the initial air battle was over, NATO's two Patriot batteries had successfully shot down sixteen Russian aircraft and fourteen cruise missiles; however, they were still destroyed. NATO's most potent air defense system had been destroyed in the first thirteen minutes of the war. The Ukrainian air defense systems had fared slightly better, shooting down seventeen Russian aircraft before they were taken offline. Still, the defeat was demoralizing.

Chapter 26

30,000 Leagues Under the Sea

Northwestern Turkey

Bosphorus Strait

Admiral James Munch was extremely nervous as his carrier strike group exited the Bosporus into the Black Sea. They were entering the Russians' pond, and he had a bad feeling the Russians had a nasty surprise waiting for them. Several of his destroyers had reported the presence of multiple submarine contacts, and so did the two attack submarines that were escorting his strike group. Although he had thirteen cruisers, destroyers, and submarines in his strike group, all the intelligence leading up to today indicated that war with Russia was imminent, and no amount of force was ever "enough" when beginning a conflict.

Captain John Miller, the captain of the USS *Bush*, found the admiral in the combat information center or CIC and handed him a message. "Sir, the *O'Bannon* has positive contact on four *Kilo* submarines and two *Akulas*. They had contact with an *Oscar* but lost it about five minutes ago. The subs are keeping their distance, but they are not shy about making their presence known," the captain said nervously.

"The strike group may be the responsibility of the Admiral," thought Captain Miller, *"but the carrier is mine, and I don't like the way this looks..."*

The admiral seemed to agree with Miller's unspoken thoughts. "I don't like this, John—not one bit. I almost feel like we're walking into some sort of trap." He looked around the room. Everyone was busy trying to digest all the potential threats to the strike group and what they all meant. "How many more ships still need to exit the straits before we can get some maneuver room?" he asked.

The captain walked over to one of the computer screens being manned by a petty officer first class. After analyzing what he saw for a moment, he answered, "Just two—both destroyers. What are you thinking, sir?"

The admiral asked, "If you were going to lay a trap for a carrier strike group exiting the Bosporus, when would you spring it?"

Several of the officers and sailors stopped what they were doing and turned to the captain to see what he would say. The admiral had asked a good question. While the captain was formulating a response, one of the communications officers interrupted everyone's thoughts with an urgent message.

"Captain, you need to see this," announced Petty Officer King, who had been manning one of the communications terminals.

Just then, Archie Martin, another petty officer who had been monitoring the navigation and map of the strike group, stood up and blurted out, "We just lost our GPS signals!"

The admiral walked toward Petty Officer Martin. "What do you mean, 'we just lost our GPS signal'? Is it a problem on our end?" he asked, hoping it was just a glitch.

"It's not a computer malfunction," explained Petty Officer King. "We just lost our satellite link with NAVEUR and the rest of the fleet. I've switched us over to standard radio communications, but it'll degrade the volume of data that can be sent between the fleet and fleet headquarters," he said to the horror of everyone in the room.

If the fleet had lost access to the GPS and communication satellites, that meant they could not properly coordinate their defenses or communicate with higher headquarters as quickly or securely as they had just a few minutes ago. The admiral knew immediately what this meant—the Russians had just taken down America's satellite capabilities in preparation for an attack. It's what he would have done if the roles had been reversed.

In that instant, Admiral Munch took control of the situation and began to issue orders to the fleet. "Sound general quarters. Bring the fleet to Condition One and order the DDs and ASW assets to engage and destroy the Russian submarines now!" he shouted.

Then he turned to the captain. "Get this ship moving to flank speed immediately, and prepare for a Russian attack," Munch said in an urgent and commanding voice.

Just as the captain was about to say that perhaps they should try to raise NAVEUR to see if they were experiencing the same problem, one of the officers manning the carrier's defense systems shouted, "Vampires! Vampires! We have inbound cruise missiles coming from heading zero-one-eight. I count four missiles. Fifty seconds to impact!"

Everyone's eyes simultaneously turned toward the officer who had just shouted, and then to the threat monitor on one of the walls.

Another voice shouted, "Torpedoes in the water! I count one—no, four torpedoes heading toward us. Make that *thirteen* torpedoes now. They appear to be targeting several of the ships in the fleet!"

Chapter 27

The Other Side

The Black Sea

Captain Rubin Malahit had settled his submarine, the *Severodvinsk*, on the bottom of the ocean floor, not far from the exit of the Bosporus, just as he had been instructed to do. He did not like his orders one bit. He had been in the Navy for nearly twenty years, and in all that time, he never thought he would be sent on a suicide mission until now. Attacking an American carrier group was a pipe dream—something the admirals talked about and submariners joked about, but the reality of pulling it off and surviving to tell the tale was something completely different. Yet those were his orders.

Of course, he had the support of several *Kilo*, *Akula*, and *Oscar* submarines to distract the Americans, but he was the one who had to get close enough to the American carrier to launch his torpedoes. They had been monitoring the movement of the carrier strike group as they entered the Black Sea, waiting for their primary target to head their way. The *Kilos* and *Akulas* had two of the other avenues well covered, and their presence would help to guide the Americans in his direction.

After a stressful two hours of monitoring the American strike group as it exited the Bosporus, the Americans began to slowly head in his direction, and so did their prized primary target, the carrier, which was finally moving within striking distance. Captain Malahit looked at the clock; they were running late. The American satellites were supposed to go down in the next forty minutes and his submarine was still not in position yet.

Malahit turned to his pilot. "Navigator, raise us up off the bottom of the ocean, slowly, so as to make as little noise as possible. I want to settle about a hundred feet above the floor of the ocean."

"Aye, Captain," came the response. The sub moved gradually; when it stopped, they were still nearly 1,200 feet below the surface.

Once they reached the desired depth, Malahit ordered, "Approach the American aircraft carrier at three knots."

"That should be slow enough," he thought. *"It's barely a crawl…hopefully they won't detect us before we are in place."*

All around them, the other submarines of his attack group were making noise—far more noise than they should have, but that was all part of the plan. They were there to attract the Americans' attention and keep them focused elsewhere while the *Severodvinsk* snuck up on the carrier. The closer they were to the carrier when they fired their torpedoes, the less time the Yankees would have to respond to his torpedoes, and the higher the likelihood of sinking the carrier.

Thirty-nine minutes had gone by; one more minute until it was showtime. They were now within five miles of the carrier, having slipped past her destroyer escorts roughly thirty minutes earlier. As the seconds ticked by, the captain looked at the faces of the sailors around him. Beads of sweat were forming on many of their faces…the stress had reached a boiling point. They were about to sink an American aircraft carrier. It was exciting but also terrifying, since the chances of them surviving were low. However, they would certainly try.

Finally, the appointed time arrived. The Americans should just be realizing they had lost access to their GPS satellites and communications systems. He turned his head to look at the sonar operators. One of them was lifting his headset. "The *Akulas* and *Kilos* have begun their attack runs," he announced. "We are now reporting multiple torpedoes in the water, some heading for the carrier, and others heading toward the destroyers and guided missile cruisers."

Then another sonar operator reported, "The *Oscar* is launching his anti-ship missiles." That was their signal. It was time for the *Severodvinsk* to launch its torpedoes.

The Americans above them would be far too occupied with the numerous torpedoes in the water and cruise missiles heading toward them to realize that his submarine had breached their defensive perimeter and was now practically on top of their prized possession. The carrier had gone to flank speed and so had the rest of the fleet, meaning their ability to listen for his submarine had greatly diminished.

The captain looked at his weapons officer and uttered the words the crew had been waiting to hear for the past several days. "Fire all torpedoes!"

With that simple order, the submarine shuddered as one after another of her eight 650mm torpedoes was ejected from the submarine and began to race quickly toward the USS *George H.W. Bush*. In less than five minutes, the torpedoes would impact against their target.

As soon as all cylinders had fired, Malahit immediately ordered, "Bring the sub back down to a depth of 1,000 feet and turn 56 degrees to port. Vacate the area at five knots!" The captain hoped that moving at such a slow pace would allow them to make a "silent crawl" to their escape.

****

"Captain Miller! One of the torpedoes appears be going for the *Nixie*, but the others are going to impact us in less than a minute!" yelled one of the antisubmarine warfare officers, breaking through the chorus of voices vying for the captain's attention.

"Alert damage control that we're about to take some hits, and brace for impact!" shouted the captain.

Someone yelled over the ship's PA system, "Prepare for impact from a torpedo!" The warning came mere seconds before the first "fish in the water" hit.

The first torpedo battered the rear of the ship near the engineering room, detonating underneath the keel. The explosion from the warhead created an enormous overpressure of the water around the keel, causing the hull to collapse and throwing its explosive force into the engineering room and the lower decks. As the explosion dissipated, the back of the carrier fell into the newly created hole of water, causing further strain on the rest of the keel of the ship.

Then the second and the third detonated underneath the center of the carrier, lifting the 97,000 ton ship several feet upwards before it crashed back down into the waterless hole left by the explosion. These twin blasts blew two large holes through the bottom of the ship, filling the lower deck with an immediate flash explosion, then enveloping the lower decks in water. One of the two torpedoes exploded near the ship's aircraft fuel tank, which ignited, causing an enormous secondary explosion that ripped through numerous decks of the ship until it reached the hangar deck, where a series of aircraft were in the process of being armed with anti-ship missiles.

Those anti-ship missiles ignited, creating a massive explosion of their own. Men and women in the hangar decks ran to grab their fire suppression equipment, but unfortunately, some of their shipmates were simply engulfed in the flames.

Captain Smith had been thrown to the ground by the explosion on the hangar deck. Alarms were showing red all across the damage control board as he tried to pick himself off the floor. He saw that others in the CIC had been injured and were helping each other as best they could. He turned to find Admiral Munch, only to see him bleeding on the floor with a cut to his forehead. One of the petty officers nearby was tending to him. Pushing aside his concern for the admiral, he began to focus on trying to save his ship and ensuring he was not going to be the first captain in naval history to lose a nuclear-powered aircraft carrier.

****

Commander Matt Walsh watched in horror as the scene of chaos continued to unfold below them while they flew above it all in their E-2D Hawkeye, the newest and most advanced carrier-capable tactical airborne early-warning aircraft. They were the eyes of the strike group, providing continuous radar coverage of the area for hundreds of miles surrounding the carrier. If a missile launch was detected, the radar images that they sent to the carrier's CIC would aid the targeting computers' AI in identifying and destroying the incoming threats.

Commander Walsh knew something was wrong when they suddenly lost access to the GPS navigation satellites. They could fly without them, but the GPS gave them a much more precise picture of their location, and that made their information a lot more accurate. Then, they received a flash message from the admiral, setting the fleet to Condition One and moving everyone to battle stations. Below them, Walsh saw the ships of the fleet suddenly pick up speed. Some of them looked to be taking evasive maneuvers.

One of the radar operators came over the headset. "We have inbound cruise missiles heading toward the fleet!" he warned.

"How many missiles are you tracking?" asked Commander Walsh.

"I'm tracking four—no, it just jumped to a dozen inbound cruise missiles," responded the radar operator. "Some of them have originated from that Russian-guided missile ship, and at least four appear to have been submarine-launched." The radar operator's voice had a hint of excitement in it, which might have seemed odd to an outsider, but Commander Walsh understood that he was feeling the adrenaline of doing what he had trained for his entire life.

"*If it's only a dozen missiles, then chances are, the fleet defenses will easily handle them,*" thought Walsh. Their aircraft were already streaming the data to the carrier's CIC, and the targeting AI was undoubtedly tracking them all.

A few seconds later, he saw several of the destroyers who were screening for the carrier group fire off a series of Standard Missile 2s at the incoming missiles.

A second radar operator interrupted everyone's thoughts as he announced, "Sir, I just received a flash message from the carrier. They have multiple inbound torpedoes heading toward them. They aren't confident they can evade them. They are doing their best to launch as many aircraft as they can."

Just then, the Commander, Air Group or CAG hailed them. "Ghost One, this is Henhouse. If the carrier goes down, I need you to guide the rest of the airwing to the nearest friendly air base. Do you understand?" His voice sounded much calmer than Commander Walsh thought humanly possible, considering the situation.

"Yes Sir, we'll make sure everyone gets to safety. Good luck, and see you on the other side," Walsh replied, signing off for what might be the last time with his group commander.

"What in the blazes is going on, Sir?!" bellowed one of the frustrated radar operators over the crew communication net.

Walsh looked down at the fleet below them. He saw several of the incoming missiles explode violently on the carrier. A couple more were knocked down by the point defense systems. One of the frigates took a direct hit from one of the cruise missiles. He knew he needed to respond to his radar operator, but he didn't know what to say. So, he said the only thing that came to mind.

"It would appear World War III has just started," Walsh replied. "Listen up. We are professionals. We trained for this, and we have a job to do. I want you guys to keep a close eye out for enemy air activity. Also, what's the status of the enemy fleet?" Commander Walsh asked, wanting to get his crew's attention focused back on the task at hand.

"Regardless of what happens to the carrier, we still have to provide support to the fleet and the fighters circling above with us," he thought.

As Commander Walsh and his copilot continued to loiter over the strike group, they watched helplessly as the battle below them played out. Their radar operators continued to relay critical targeting data and information to the fleet, but there was little else they could do other than watch.

The cruisers in the battlegroup fired off a series of anti-ship missiles at the Russians, ensuring that they had their revenge and got some payback. Off to their right, Matt saw one of the destroyers rise slightly out of the water, then an enormous explosion nearly ripped the ship in half.

"It must have been hit by a torpedo," he thought in shock. *"How many men and women just died on that ship?"*

He tried to push the image out of his mind and focus on flying.

It was hard to concentrate when the other crew members of his command were still down on the carrier. His copilot let out a short yelp and pointed to the left, where the carrier was. Commander Walsh angled the aircraft in the direction of the carrier. He wanted to see the situation for himself. Sure enough, the carrier had been hit by a torpedo...from the looks of it, multiple torpedoes. He watched aghast as plumes of black smoke came from under the flight deck. There were a couple of minor explosions, then a large blast that seemed to have caused significant damage. The ship began to list slightly to the left as it took on more water.

Now it was a race against time. Matt wondered if they could possibly seal off enough parts of the ship to keep it from sinking, and if they could get the fires under control.

Then, one of the fighter pilots came over the radio. "Ghost One, this is Eagle Leader. It doesn't look like any of us are going to be setting back down on the carrier. Do you have a new landing site for us? Most of us don't have a lot of fuel to hang out for a long time," he urged.

Commander Walsh asked his radar operators if they had found a suitable site yet.

"Eagle Leader, Ghost One. The closest airport is Istanbul Atatürk Airport, twenty-five miles away. We've sent an emergency message over to them, letting them know that we have twenty-three combat aircraft needing to make an emergency landing. They weren't happy, but they've given us clearance to land," he explained.

Taking control of the situation, Walsh directed, "I want your flight and the others to form up around us as we collectively head toward Atatürk. I want the F/A-18s to land first, since you guys have the least amount of fuel. The remaining aircraft will follow, and we'll bring up the rear. Is that understood?"

It was now Commander Walsh's job to shepherd the remnants of Carrier Air Wing 3 back to safety. Hopefully, the higher-ups would be able to get them back into the fight soon. For now, it looked like their participation in the war had ended, without them even firing a single shot.

Chapter 28

No Plan Survives First Contact

Eastern Ukraine, Demarcation Line

As Sergeant Childers watched the Russian attack helicopters take off from the field with the drone, he heard numerous sonic booms from high-flying aircraft. His eyes raced across the sky, searching for the source of the noise. He saw what appeared to be some missile tracks in the air...then, after a couple of minutes, he saw several explosions. Clearly, a skirmish was taking place in the sky above him, but he had no idea which side was winning.

Childers looked at the LT. "This doesn't look good, Sir. I'm not sure what's going on, but my money says those are Russian and American aircraft shooting at each other up there."

Lieutenant Taylor responded cautiously. "I think you're right, Sergeant. Tell everyone to get ready to engage those Russian vehicles should they head our direction," he said nervously, his eyes searching the woods around their position.

"I hope the armor unit that is supporting us is getting close," thought Taylor. *"If those Russian tanks move toward us, we're going to be in real trouble."*

Childers just nodded. The LT was right; they needed to stay frosty now and be ready for anything. Speaking into his headset, Childers announced, "Everyone listen up. It looks like there's some sort of air battle going on above us. That means hostilities have probably started. We knew this was a possibility, and we've trained for this. Everyone knows what to do. We have enough firepower with us to kick the teeth out of those Russians in that village. If and when they do cross the demarcation line and head toward us, I want you all to start calling out your targets. Make sure you're not shooting at the same vehicles!" He was trying to fire the platoon up.

"From what we're seeing from the drone feed, it looks like we'll probably have about a company, maybe a battalion-sized element heading our way, if those other units follow this one," Childers continued. "The rest of those tanks and armored vehicles are heading further up north....So, here's what we're going to do. TOW gunners, make sure to focus on the tanks. Javelin crews, focus on the BMPs and BTRs. My Stinger operators, be ready in case those helicopters head our way. Most importantly, remember your training. We'll get through this together, and we'll kick the crap out of these guys! Hooah!" he yelled.

"Hooah!" came the reply. Everyone in the platoon was filled with adrenaline as they shouted the Army slogan together.

The soldiers in the platoon readied their crew. They all hoped that the Russians hadn't spotted them in this thicket of trees yet. The Raven scout drone spotted the BMPs, BTRs and tanks heading toward the village and the demarcation line. It wouldn't be long now until they were in range of their antitank missiles.

Ten nervous minutes passed before the first Russian vehicle crossed the demarcation line at the edge of a small village named Pyriatyn. They let the vehicles continue to pass and get closer to their position. They wanted as much of the column out of the village as possible before they called in the artillery strike and began to engage them with their TOWs.

Lieutenant Taylor was getting antsy; he wanted to launch the attack right then. Childers reminded him, "We need the vehicles to move a bit closer, so that they're in range of our TOWs. The enemy needs to get within 2,000 meters of us."

Slowly, painfully, they waited and watched. Then, when the middle of the column reached 2,000 meters away, Childers turned to Taylor and nodded. "It's time," he affirmed.

LT Taylor depressed his talk button. "TOW gunners, engage the tanks now," he ordered. In a mere second, a loud popping noise could be heard, then a *whoosh* as four TOWs rushed out of the midst of the thicket of trees they had been hiding in. They streaked quickly toward their intended targets, four T-90 main battle tanks.

Sergeant Childers signaled to his artillery forward observers. "Start raining death on the enemy."

The forward observers called in multiple artillery strikes to their battalion of self-propelled 155mm Paladins. One of the sergeants gave him a quick thumbs-up to let him know the mission had been received. *"It won't be long now until the rounds start to land and really plaster the Russians,"* Sergeant Childers thought.

Just after the TOWs left the tree line, the four Javelin crews fired off their missiles at the lead group of BMPs and BTR infantry fighting vehicles.

The Russians reacted quickly. Within a few seconds of the TOWs being fired, several of their tanks turned their turrets toward the tree line to engage the Strykers. Just as they were about to fire, the TOWs began to hit them, blowing several turrets right off the chasses of the vehicles. Then the Javelins found their marks, and three BMPs and one BTR blew up in a blaze of flaming glory.

The crews of the Stryker vehicles reloaded the TOW launchers as fast as they could, and so did the Javelin crews. One of the T-90s that had not been destroyed fired at the tree line, hitting one of the Stryker vehicles. It promptly exploded, throwing one of the crew members from the vehicle several feet away. Several of the BMPs then raked the tree line with 30mm and 100mm cannon rounds from their main guns. Tree limbs, branches, and bushes simply burst, throwing bark and chunks of trees in every direction at the soldiers below and around them.

One of the Stryker vehicles had its TOW launcher reloaded and fired off both missiles almost immediately. The missiles streaked across the field toward two more of the Russian tanks, which were now racing toward the tree line, firing their main guns. One of the light armored tactical vehicles or LATVs took a direct hit, exploding and throwing shrapnel everywhere. One of the Javelin missile crews hit another BMP, just as the gunner of the same BMP killed them with a fiery blast from their 100mm gun.

Then Childers heard the artillery come flying over their head, impacting all around the remaining Russian tanks and infantry fighting vehicles. The artillery guys were yelling in their handsets, "Hey, Gun Bunnies—keep it coming!"

"We are plastering the Russians," thought Luke.

As the artillery continued to land, the remaining Russian force fell back to the village they had just left to get away from the artillery. The forward observers continued to walk the artillery in toward the village, making sure the Russians found no safety, even in falling back to a populated village.

Lieutenant Taylor yelled over the radio, "Cease fire! Stop firing on that village. There could be civilians in there!" The forward observers who were with the platoon radioed back for the battalion to check fire, which is how the artillerymen say cease fire. It took a few minutes for all the soldiers to stop shooting and for the artillery barrage to end. Once it had, and the smoke began to clear, they saw the absolute carnage their platoon had just inflicted on the Russians. They had nearly wiped out what was probably a company-sized armored unit, along with their support vehicles and troops. When they looked further back at the village, they saw that most of the little township was a smoking ruin.

Several additional armored vehicles and tanks were burning in the village, strung across the various roads and side streets. They all felt a little better about plastering the village once they saw that they had also killed a lot of Russians. Sergeant Childers put his binoculars back in his pocket. He had seen enough.

"Listen up, everyone!" he yelled. "Grab our dead and wounded and get back in the vehicles. We are getting out of here *now*!" He picked himself up off the ground and ran up to the various positions where his soldiers were dug in, encouraging them to grab their gear and get in the vehicles.

Lieutenant Taylor walked up to Sergeant Childers and put his hand on his shoulder to grab his attention. "Hey, we just stopped them. Why are we falling back now?" he asked, not fully understanding the logic in his platoon sergeant's decision or the urgency in trying to get everyone loaded up, along with their wounded and their equipment.

Childers paused for a second, like a father trying to have patience as he answers a question from his teenage son. "Sir, we just plastered the Russians. They're either going to call in artillery on our position or an airstrike. In either case, we can't stay here. We need to fall back to our secondary position and see if headquarters wants us to link up with the rest of the troop or what they want us to do."

The lieutenant had that look on his face like he realized that he should have known that. He was thankful that Sergeant Childers had talked just loud enough so that only he could hear him, and not the rest of the platoon.

"Come on, LT, I'll lead the platoon to the next position," offered Childers. "You get on the radio with headquarters and find out what they want us to do next. Good?" he asked, hoping the lieutenant fully grasped the situation now. He needed him to step up and handle the radio call while he focused on getting them out of there alive.

Taylor nodded, and they both got back to work.

The vehicles were in the process of backing out of their position when several artillery rounds started to land where they had just been. They had made it out less than two minutes before their old positions were plastered by enemy artillery fire. As they fully cleared the copse of trees, they turned around and sped away as fast as they could toward their next position.

The lieutenant tried raising their higher headquarters multiple times but just got static. He tried raising several of the other troop leaders to see if they were available. He managed to get in touch with two of them. They were also falling back to link up with a battalion of heavy tanks from the 1st Armored Division. He got their coordinates and agreed to fall back and link up with them. He advised them of his wounded and asked if they had any. They all replied that they hadn't run into any Russian units yet but had seen a lot of attack helicopters and aircraft heading toward the NATO base further north.

"It's really odd that none of the other platoons have engaged any of the Russian units yet," he thought. *"Our sector can't have been the only one that the Russians tried to breach."*

Twenty-five minutes later, they found the battalion of M1A2s and the rest of 4th Squadron, their parent unit. Their captain, a man by the name of Len Richards, walked up to them all smiles. "That was one heck of an engagement you guys had. Well done on stopping that Russian armored column," he said, shaking the lieutenant's hand.

Sergeant Childers looked confused. "You saw the engagement?" he asked.

Amused at their confusion, Captain Richards replied, "Yes, we saw it. You still had your scout drone loitering over the area, sending back the video. You guys did a bang-up job."

He looked down briefly, as if paying respects. "I'm also sorry for your losses. They were good men. I'm going to make sure everyone is put in for some medals for that action. Your platoon temporarily stopped the Russian advance in this area, which is giving us the time we need to reorganize after headquarters was wiped out at the air base," the captain said, full of pride about what one of his platoons had managed to accomplish on their own.

Several of the medics from the other troops had run over to their vehicles and helped to unload Nemesis Troop's wounded as they began to provide them aid.

Breaking the train of thought, Lieutenant Taylor suddenly announced, "Sir, we need ammo. My vehicles and men are short on just about everything. Also, what about air support? Those Hinds are still out there and it's only a matter of time before they, or those aircraft up there, find us and start dropping bombs and missiles on us."

The captain smiled, glad his lieutenant was thinking of the broader picture. He motioned with his arm. "Walk with me back to the command track. I need to show you what's happening," Captain Richards said. He led the three of them through the wooded area to where the Command Stryker vehicle was tucked away. As they walked through the trees, Lieutenant Taylor and Sergeant Childers saw dozens of Abrams battle tanks geared up to fight.

As they approached the command post, they also saw a major and a lieutenant colonel talking with a command sergeant major. The captain waited for a break in the conversation before he introduced them. "Colonel Munch, Sergeant Major Fields, this is the platoon commander and sergeant from my second platoon. They're the ones who stopped that Russian column down the road." Captain Richards was beaming with pride.

The lieutenant colonel and the sergeant major smiled warmly at them. The colonel was the first to greet the newcomers. "Good work out there. You guys probably bought us at least an hour before they try that again." The colonel paused and looked down. "My condolences on the loss of your men. They did an amazing job, and as I'm sure your captain already told you, we're going to make sure everyone gets recognized for their heroic acts." The colonel's facial expressions somehow simultaneously conveyed genuine concern and pride. He came across as a leader who cared about his men and the sacrifices they were making.

Lieutenant Colonel Munch continued, "We need to bring you guys up to speed before we push off and go hunting for Russians. Pryluky Air Base has been hit hard. Headquarters is offline. They also hit Kiev International Airport at Boryspil relentlessly as well. Word has it that MG Mueller and most of his staff were killed in the attack. So right now, that leaves us with no idea of who's in charge or what in the world we're supposed to do beyond our initial orders." He spoke with the smugness you'd expect from a senior officer who had probably seen a lot of combat and liked to make things up as he went.

Smiling at the colonel's comments, Sergeant Childers commented, "Well, I was taught in the Rangers that in the absence of orders—attack without mercy." The command sergeant major smiled a wicked grin at the mention of Ranger School. Like Childers, he also sported a Ranger tab on his shoulder. Childers, however, also had a 75th Ranger Regiment Combat patch, so he'd actually been a Ranger, not just gone through the school.

The colonel, who also had a Ranger tab, smiled and said, "Oh, I'm going to like you, Sergeant Childers. That is exactly what we're going to do. I've got five Avenger air defense vehicles with us too, so we have some air defense should those fighters up there, or those Hinds you reported, decide to get frisky."

"How did you manage to get five Avengers?" Captain Richards asked, surprised. Typically, a unit might have one, maybe two of them. Not five.

"Let's say I saw a lost air defense unit that was looking for an escort to the Pryluky Air Base," Colonel Munch replied with a smirk. "By the time we got halfway to the air base, we heard it had been thoroughly hammered and we were being redirected to this location to link up with you guys. As we were headed along in our little gaggle, some Russian Su-34s saw us moving along and thought that we might make nice sitting ducks to attack. That was a stupid move on their part though, because the Avengers we had with us managed to shoot down two of the Su-34s before they even managed to cause us any damage. After that, the Russians diverted course, and we all decided to stick together as we hauled tail out of there." The command sergeant major had a wry smile on his face as he spat a stream of chewing tobacco on the ground.

"Enough chatting—it's time to get down to business," the colonel said as he walked over to the map. "Here's what we're going to do..."

Chapter 29

Hardly a Vacation

Near Krakow, Poland
NATO Air Base

Major Dale Young, call sign "Honey Badger," had been stationed at Spangdahlem Air Base for the past two years. His wife, who had been his college sweetheart, loved living in Germany. They were a young couple with no children, and for the time being, they were just enjoying being childless and living in Europe. They had planned on traveling to Sorrento, Italy, for a weeklong vacation along the Amalfi coast when his leave was canceled, and his squadron was sent to Krakow and placed on ready alert for possible military action against Russia.

Dale wasn't too upset over the change in plans, although his wife certainly was. This was what he had signed up for—to be a fighter pilot and face down America's enemies. His squadron, the 480th, had a long and proud lineage that dated back to World War II, when they'd fought against the Nazis. The squadron had recently gone through the transition from being an F-16 squadron to flying F-22s. Dale had been an F-22 pilot at the beginning, so he had been helping the other pilots through the transition and qualification process since he'd arrived two years ago.

Being stationed in Germany and flying an F-22 Raptor meant he was certain to see action should the Russians decide to test NATO's resolve and not leave eastern Ukraine. However, after sitting in his cockpit with the canopy open for the last two hours, he was starting to get tired and bored; he still had another hour left on his alert status before he would be relieved. Since arriving in Poland a few days ago, they had been scrambled twice to respond to Russian aircraft, but each time they had returned to base without incident.

Just as he got to the good part of the book he'd been reading, an urgent message came across the radio, scrambling all alert fighters. In that instant, Dale shoved his book into one of the pockets on his flight suit and lowered the canopy. As the cover closed, he powered up his engines and headed toward the runway. In less than two minutes, he was at the edge of the runway, lighting his afterburners to get airborne as quickly as possible. While he was working to gain altitude along with his wingman, he heard the air battle manager come over the radio, informing them of possible Russian Su-57 fighters in the area. The E-3 also relayed the number of enemy aircraft in the air and where they were all heading.

As Major Young looked at his radar display, he was shocked by the droves of enemy aircraft that he saw heading in their direction. It looked like the entire Russian Air Force was attacking Ukraine.

As Dale listened to the voices over the radio, he couldn't believe what he was hearing. One of the E-3s had just been shot down. A couple of minutes later, the American F-15s that had been flying CAP over Ukraine were destroyed. Just as he thought things couldn't get any worse for them, the E-3 reported that the German Eurofighters that had just taken off from Kiev were immediately blown out of the sky.

"What in the blazes is going on?!" he thought. *"How did the Russians manage to shoot down ten NATO aircraft in the first five minutes of whatever this fight is?"*

"Raptor 66, proceed with all speed toward Sector Six and engage all hostile aircraft," the air battle manager ordered. A couple of minutes later, the second NATO E-3 was shot down, leaving the NATO aircraft with no air battle managers or airborne radars operational to guide them to the enemy aircraft. Fortunately, the Patriot air defense system at the Kiev International Airport was still operational. They made quick contact with them and were immediately linked up with their radar feed.

For the time being, the Raptors would leverage the ground radar to guide them to the enemy fighters. Another E-3 was just lifting off from Ramstein Air Base, but it would be at least five minutes before they were at an operational altitude for their radar to be of much assistance. Their distance from the front line meant their signal was not going to be nearly as strong as would be needed if the Russians started to employ a lot of jamming.

As his aircraft continued to gain altitude, Major Young looked to his right and saw his wingman, "Iceman," flying Raptor 67 next to him. "Iceman, I'm not sure we're going to find those Su-57s without AWACS support, so we need to go after those Fullbacks before they can destroy our airfields," Major Young said. He tried to maintain a calm and reassuring voice while talking to his younger wingman.

Iceman, or Captain Jorge Montoya, was a junior captain who had just joined his squadron two weeks prior, fresh from F-22 school, so this was only the second time Major Young had flown with him. The other two F-22 pilots in his flight were seasoned captains who had been flying Raptors for several years like he had.

In all, there were sixteen F-22s in Poland; twelve other Raptors were quickly being scrambled to get airborne and deal with the Backfire bombers that were heading toward Poland. As their F-22s continued to gain altitude, they headed toward the Kiev International Airport at nearly full speed, trying to intercept the Russian ground attack aircraft before they destroyed the airport. NATO would need that airfield in Kiev.

As they moved closer to the Ukrainian border, Major Young spotted dozens of Russian aircraft flying over the international airport at varying altitudes, all carrying out a variety of attacks against ground targets. He was in shock as he saw aircraft swooping down, dropping cluster bombs. Clouds of smoke and debris were billowing up. Cruise missiles streaked through the sky; so many were flying, that it created what would have been a beautiful spider web in the air if it hadn't been so deadly.

Then the Patriots' radar went offline, indicating that they had probably been destroyed. Despite their best efforts to get there ahead of the Russians, they had too much ground to cover and not enough time.

There were only four F-22s to engage what looked to be about 33 enemy aircraft. Major Young quickly spotted the MiGs being vectored toward them and identified them as the first aircraft they would engage. Although they were heavily outnumbered, Dale maintained some optimism. The targeting computer on the Raptor helped to make it very deadly. Besides being able to track and engage dozens of targets simultaneously, it could also sync with the other fighters in its group to ensure that none of the pilots fired missiles at the same aircraft unless it was planned.

Their squadron commander, Lieutenant Colonel Lesley Philips, call sign "Gold Digger," had just gotten airborne, along with the rest of their squadron. He affirmed Young's assumptions when he got on the radio and ordered, "Engage the enemy MiGs over Kiev. The rest of the squadron will focus on going after the Backfire bombers."

As they closed to within sixty-five miles of the enemy MiGs, Major Young and the rest of the Raptors began to fire off their missiles. Each aircraft launched their complement of six over-the-horizon air-to-air missiles before turning to rush off to the safe airspace of Poland to reload and get back into the fight. As Dale turned to head back home, he saw the MiGs begin to fire off their own missiles. His heart beat quickly in his chest, pounding with adrenaline. Seconds later, his onboard sensors calmed him down again by confirming that none of the enemy missiles had achieved lock. Once the F-22s had closed the weapon bays that dispensed their missiles, their stealth technology once again made them invisible to the enemy radar; Major Young felt like he had cheated death.

Meanwhile, the twenty-four air-to-air missiles the Raptors had fired destroyed seventeen of the attacking MiGs. Unfortunately for the Americans, some of the MiGs had managed to evade the remaining missiles.

****

In the opening hours of the air battle over Ukraine, the Russians lost 49 of 247 aircraft. However, they had succeeded in shooting down sixteen Ukrainian aircraft and twelve NATO aircraft, including both of their E-3 AWACS aircraft. The NATO Patriot air defense systems had also met their demise. The Russians had also succeeded in destroying the runways at the Kiev International Airport and four other Ukrainian military air bases.

The Fullbacks had destroyed the fuel bunkers at the Kiev Airport, which would further hurt the operational capability of the airport once NATO had repaired the runways. The most disastrous attack came from the eight supersonic Blackjack bombers and the 80 Backfire bombers.

Two of the supersonic Blackjack bombers headed toward the NATO military headquarters building at Mons,

Belgium. Once they got within range of their cruise missiles, they rose in altitude and proceeded to release their twelve AS-15 Kent cruise missiles. The projectiles streaked through the air, reaching their cruising speed of Mach .75 and dropping down to a mere 300 feet above the ground as they raced toward their target.

The missiles flew for nearly an hour, until they reached the NATO headquarters, where they began to pummel the Allied Command Operations Building, along with several other support buildings. Within minutes, the NATO command facility had been pulverized, killing hundreds of member state military representatives.

The remaining bombers headed toward the American air bases at Spangdahlem and Ramstein, releasing their 72 cruise missiles. Those cruise missiles were specifically targeting the aircraft hangars, parking ramps, fuel dumps, and communication centers. They avoided cratering the runways, since those could be quickly repaired. The lost aircraft, however, could not be replaced quickly, and for a short period, this would leave the US and NATO with very few fighter aircraft to stop the Russian ground forces from securing their initial objectives.

The 80 Backfire bombers split off into eight attack groups of ten, each carrying a total of ten AS-16 "Kickback" air-to-surface missiles. These missiles had a much smaller range of only 300 kilometers, so they were sent in during the second wave of the attack, after the Blackjacks and other fighters had already cleared the air of NATO fighters. These bomber groups hit two Ukrainian air bases, three Polish air bases, and three German air bases. Within the first couple hours of the Russian attack, they had effectively neutralized the NATO air forces for at least a full day—maybe two or three—before new aircraft could be flown in from other NATO members and the US.

The attack caught the US, Poland and Germany completely by surprise. Until then, they had believed that while Russia was posturing more forcefully than before, they would ultimately back down and not follow through on their threat of force. The assault also proved how woefully unprepared the NATO members were for a potential conflict with Russia.

Chapter 30
Regrouping

Stuttgart, Germany
US European Command Headquarters
Joint Intelligence Operations Center

As Lieutenant General Cotton walked into the JIOC, he realized that things were starting to come unglued very quickly. He had just come from a secured video teleconference with General Wheeler, the Supreme Allied Commander or SACEUR. Things were a complete mess up there from the cruise missile attack, and for the time being, the headquarters had been taken offline. They were transferring operations to one of the alternate locations. For all of NATO's preparedness, the Russians had still managed to catch them with their pants down.

From what General Cotton could tell during the video conference call and what he was seeing in the JIOC right now, this was turning into a Class A screw-up of epic proportions. As he walked down to the front of the room, all eyes turned to look at the general. He took up a post behind the lectern and prepared to address the group.

"Listen up, everyone. I don't know how, and right now, I don't care about the why, but somehow, the Russians managed to launch a sneak attack on us and we were caught completely flat-footed. I can assure you that before long, heads will roll. However, right now, we need to focus on how we're going to get past what just happened. I want blood for blood, people!" he blared at the group.

A million cuss words swirled around in General Cotton's mind, but as he took a deep breath, he realized that yelling a bunch of expletives at his group was not necessarily the way to get them to work better. As he surveyed the group before him, he saw in their eyes and faces that they were doing their best…it just wasn't good enough.

"Listen, it's been a rough few hours. Right now, we have US and NATO soldiers fighting and dying in eastern Ukraine, not to mention what just happened to the Navy and our forces at Ramstein and Spangdahlem. Let's start to run through the various situations and then start executing orders." He gestured to his first target in the room. "Colonel George, bring us up to speed on the attacks on our bases in Germany."

As Colonel George came forward, General Cotton walked back to his traditional seat at the top of the auditorium. He hoped it wouldn't *all* be bad news.

Colonel Philip George was the JIOC Commander who oversaw all the operations happening in the European jurisdiction. Originally an Air Force flyer, he had graduated to desk duty as he was being groomed for general. Perhaps General Cotton had picked him to go first because he had the most hope in Colonel George.

As soon as he reached the podium, the colonel began to answer the question. "Sir, the Russians hit our bases in Germany with their Blackjack bombers, the Tu-160s. They swept in across Belarus and Poland at speeds of roughly Mach 2.3—they flew in at near tree-level, which made them difficult to track at first. When they got within range of their cruise missiles, they rose up to 1,000 feet and unleashed a series of missiles at each of the bases and the NATO headquarters building before ducking back down to treetop level and returning home."

Colonel George brought up an image of the Blackjack, which was strikingly similar to the American B1 Lancer bomber. Additional slides showed the flight path, and launch points of the cruise missiles, as well as the types of cruise missiles that were launched. Next, he brought up images of the damage to the two American air bases, which was substantial. "A lot of these images were taken less than an hour ago," he explained. "Fortunately, these were conventional cruise missiles and not nuclear. They hit us with the A-Triple Five Kents, which carry an 880-pound high-explosive warhead. They targeted our aircraft hangars, fuel farms, radar, and control tower and several other high-value targets. The runways were left untouched. It appears they wanted to hit our ability to respond more than our ability to launch or receive aircraft."

Colonel George continued to walk through the damage assessment, the timelines to get things repaired, and the casualty figures. General Cotton was fuming inside. With the loss of so many aircraft and fuel farms, it would be difficult for them to provide any credible ground support to their ground support units under attack in Ukraine.

"Shoot, at this point, we'll be lucky if we can prevent the Russians from launching a second attack," he thought.

The general pressed for more information. "OK, I can see the damage is bad. How soon until we can get things operational at the bases and get fighters back in the skies providing CAP?"

"Right now, the bases are already operational. We lost 68 fighters, fourteen transports, six midair re-fuelers and one E-3. It's a hard loss, but we still have aircraft that weren't damaged or destroyed. We have twenty-two fighters flying CAP right now over our bases. The Germans also have 52 fighters flying over their country to ward off any further intrusions. The Polish, on the other hand, were hit hard. They received the brunt of the cruise missile attacks by the Backfires, along with a series of short-range ballistic missiles, which really hit them hard. Most of their airfields have been taken offline for the time being. The last situation report we received said that it'll be at least a full day before the runways are serviceable, and longer still until they have fuel and other services back up and running."

Colonel George continued, "The Polish and the Germans now have 42 aircraft in the air, but they are also engaging Russian fighters fairly frequently at their borders—"

"—Putting all that aside," General Cotton interrupted before he could go any further, "what air defense systems do we have operational right now to prevent the Russians from launching a second strike with their Blackjacks? Second, what defenses do we have to protect us here at Patch Barracks and the other facilities around Stuttgart? Third, I thought we had air defenses operational here in Germany. Why did they not respond to this attack?"

Colonel George nodded. He had anticipated these questions. "Sir, nearly a dozen Spetsnaz teams carried out attacks against a number of the air defense sites that we had operational. They also hit the NATO E-3 sentry base at Geilenkirchen and several communication, command and control centers." He gestured to the army major who had been manning the air defense desk. "I believe the Army has some additional air defense systems that just came online…"

Major Anderson stood up where he was sitting instead of spending the time walking to the front. "Sir, the THAAD missile system is now operational at Ramstein, Kaiserslautern, and the Stuttgart Army Air Field. The one at SHAPE should be operational in a couple of hours, as well as the two systems in the UK. We have two more being set up as we speak in Poland, one in Hungary and two in Romania. We also have a dozen Patriot systems, both American and German, now active as well," he explained.

The Terminal High-Altitude Area Defense was a significantly more advanced version of the Patriot missile system. THAAD had the capability of shooting down ballistic missiles in space and was incredibly effective at hitting cruise and ballistic missiles. Unlike the Patriot, which retained its primary air-defense mission against aircraft, the THAAD was designed purely to engage missiles. It should have prevented the American and NATO bases from being hammered by the Russian bombers.

"Why was the THAAD not operational *earlier* and able to knock down those missiles?" General Cotton pressed, which made the major squirm a bit.

Major Anderson cleared his throat before answering, "Sir, as you know, the Russians launched a massive cyberattack a couple of hours before they began their physical assault. The cyberattack crippled our GPS satellites and took down our communication systems as well. Unfortunately, the THAAD relies heavily on this technology to guide the missiles to their targets."

Anderson hesitated. He shifted from one foot to the other, thinking of what to say next. He looked very uncomfortable. "Sir, there was also an incident at the Ramstein and Spangdahlem locations. The situation is still under investigation, so I wasn't comfortable with sharing it as I don't have all the information yet."

This caught everyone by surprise; no one had heard about any incident involving the THAAD. "Please share with us what you have, Major. I will determine if it is important," Cotton directed. He was a little perturbed that apparently General Wheeler either didn't know about this or hadn't briefed him on it either.

"Yes, Sir," the major replied, sweat visibly forming on his forehead. "Well, as you know, in the launch vehicles, there are two radar/missile operators, which are NCOs or soldiers, and then there's a launch officer. In this case, there was a captain in each of the launch vehicles as the launch officer. Both of the captains that were on duty at the time of the Russian attack…well…they slit the throats of the launch crew." Audible gasps could be heard in the room, along with a few swear words. "That's why none of our THAADs engaged the enemy cruise missiles. They'd been sabotaged before they could get a single missile off."

General Cotton sat there stunned for a minute, not sure if this was some sort of cruel joke. "Major, this is not the time for gags. What in the blazes really happened?!" he yelled, on the verge of completely losing it.

"Sir, this isn't a joke. This is why I wanted to hold off on saying anything until I had more information. The military police and CID are still investigating this," Anderson responded, wishing he was anywhere but there at that moment.

"So, what the hell happened to the two launch officers? Did they just disappear? Tell me you have them in custody, Major!" The general's face was flushed with anger, and he felt his pulse beginning to race.

"No, Sir. We do not have them in custody," Anderson answered quietly, barely getting the words out.

"This appears to have been a preplanned effort on the part of the Russians. The two captains that were in charge at the time, we believe had been deep-cover GRU operatives or SVR. In either case, they are traitors, and cost the lives of thousands of people. I feel terrible about this, Sir. It was my battalion's job to operate those THAADs and to protect our bases. I know all the soldiers that were killed personally. We completely screwed things up, and thousands of people are dead," the major said as he began to lose control of his emotions and sank back into his chair, fighting to hold back tears.

The major had been assigned to the JIOC once the THAADs went online, to act as the liaison between them and the JIOC. He had known the two captains and the men of those crews. The loss of so many lives because of his battalion's failure was becoming too much.

General Cotton saw that Anderson was trying his best. He couldn't hold the major responsible for the actions of these two traitors. Clearly this entire sneak attack—from the cyberattacks, to the disabling of the THAADs—was planned months, if not years, in advance.

"Major, I am sorry for your loss. I truly am. This is critically important information. Thank you for sharing it. This explains so much of why we were caught off guard by the Russians. I'm sure their actions aren't the only ones we'll hear about today. During the Cold War, it was believed the Russians would employ a lot of these types of tactics."

Some of the color returned to Anderson's face as he realized that General Cotton was showing him a bit of mercy.

Cotton tapped the desk in front of him, thinking. "OK. What I want you to do now is sit down and write out all the details and information you have. We need to get that sent to SHAPE and to the other bases, so they know to watch for saboteurs, especially since some apparently have already struck."

"Yes, Sir," Major Anderson replied. He immediately began to scribble out notes on the pad of paper in front of him.

The general motioned back to the front of the room. "Colonel George, please continue."

Colonel George was a bit shocked by what they had just heard, but he rallied himself mentally to go on. "Sir, we'll move over to the Navy. As you know, the *George Bush* Carrier Strike Group suffered a huge loss. While they were exiting the Bosporus, nearly a dozen Russian submarines and eight Russian surface warships sprang a trap on the strike group. While the fleet was heavily engaged, a submarine had been lying in wait at the bottom of the ocean, roughly 1,300 feet below the surface. That sub launched six torpedoes at the USS *Bush*. Because of the close proximity of the sub to the carrier, the torpedoes didn't have far to travel."

He showed images of the battle taken by the E-2D Hawkeye that had been loitering above the fleet. "One of the torpedoes went for the *Nixie*, the device the carrier can trail to mimic their own signature in an attempt to lure the torpedoes away from the carrier. The other three torpedoes struck the carrier." Colonel George sighed, then continued, "While we were discussing the THAAD issue, we received word that after nearly three hours of trying to save the carrier, the captain ordered it to be abandoned. They just couldn't control the fires and flooding."

As Colonel George finished the recap of the battle, everyone in the room felt even more shock, but also anger. The Russians had really done a number on them, and they wanted revenge. They wanted to fight back.

General Cotton rubbed his head. He was starting to get a migraine with all the bad information that was being relayed. When he'd been on the secure video call to SHAPE, they'd been discussing the damage the carrier had taken, but it had been thought that the ship could be saved. Things had obviously changed in the last hour and a half.

"How many casualties from the *Bush*?" he asked, not sure if he wanted the answer.

"They're still in the process of accounting for everyone. As of right now, there are 480 unaccounted for, 963 dead, and nearly twice that number wounded. The rest were able to evacuate from the ship. Those are just the figures from the carrier though. I still need to brief you on the rest of the fleet," George explained, to the dismay of everyone in the room.

"Between our subs and ASW units, we sank eleven Russian submarines and all eight Russian surface ships. However, this came at tremendous cost. The American fleet was traveling with six destroyers, three guided missile cruisers, and two submarines. Of those, one destroyer was sunk, one destroyer was damaged—the other two are fine— and one of the guided missile cruisers suffered minor damage. Fortunately, the other two guided missile cruisers are fine. However…both of our submarines were lost. We're still getting the final count, but we lost well over 2,500 sailors, and at least that many more were injured."

A collective groan filled the room. Colonel George pressed on though. "The rest of the strike group is heading to the NATO naval base in Romania to regroup with the rest of the NATO fleet. Turkey, Romania and Bulgaria have sent their warships to join the remainder of the strike group and will continue to hunt and destroy the rest of the Russian subs in the Black Sea. Admiral Munch, the Strike Group Commander, has transferred his flag to the guided missile cruiser, *Gettysburg*. He's asked for permission to hit the Russian naval base in Crimea. He also wants to know if the ground forces need any of his cruise missiles. He said he has 244 Tomahawks on the cruisers that need a mission." Colonel George managed a small smile on his face with that last statement. *"We are going to need those cruise missiles,"* he thought.

General Cotton grunted. "Shoot, tell him to plaster that Russian naval base. Also, provide him with the grids of the Russian air bases that are being used to launch all those bombers and fighters. I want him to take them offline immediately." The general was happy to finally be able to issue some real retaliatory orders.

The briefing went on for some time while General Cotton continued to issue additional orders to get more US forces into the fight. "Sixty-Two F-35s have just arrived from the US after an arduous transatlantic flight. I know the pilots are exhausted, but I want you to give them some uppers and throw them right back into the fight. For the sake of the ground forces still alive in Ukraine, the US needs to get air superiority as quickly as possible. Understood?"

"Yes, Sir," came the response.

"Good," said the general. "We've got 35 additional F-22s, 180 F-16s and twenty F-15s in the process of flying across the Atlantic right now. When they arrive, I want you to give them some coffee and throw them into the fight, just like the F-35s."

"Now, what many of you may not know is that several B-2 stealth bombers arrived last night at Lajos airfield in the Azores. In the coming hours, they will fly their first combat mission into Russia. Their first mission is to hit the Russian command and control centers, including the grand prize, the brand new National Defense Control Center in the heart of Moscow."

A few people gasped. This was a daring plan.

Ignoring the reactions, General Cotton continued, "They will also hit the FSB headquarters, which is still located at Lubyanka Square, the original heart of the KGB. While the B-2s are busy with that, the B-1 Lancers will be going after the various rail, road, and bridge networks that are vital to keeping the Russian war machine going. The Russians may have numbers, but those 'numbers' chew through a lot of fuel, munitions and food. Destroying their logistical capability to fight is the surest way to cripple their army fast."

General Cotton then turned to his senior National Security Agency liaison officer and asked, "What's the NSA doing to reestablish our GPS and satellite communication systems, and what are we doing to go after the Russian systems?"

All eyes turned to the NSA LNO, who had been relatively silent during the briefing thus far. Mr. Justin Lake was the Senior Executive Service or SES representative to EUCOM and NATO from the NSA, and while he had a small staff of people that worked for him in Stuttgart, he was just a forward contact for the agency at the command.

He cleared his throat before replying, "I spoke with several of my colleagues before coming to this briefing. I was told roughly half of our GPS satellites will need to be replaced. The industrial control systems were burnt out, rendering the satellites useless. I have it on good authority that we will have close to 25% of these satellites replaced in the next few days."

He continued, "Now, the larger issue is the communications and surveillance satellites. Not everyone knows this, but we maintain a certain stockpile of these satellites, which we have kept ready to launch in case of a situation like this. When the Russians launched their DDoS and cyberattack, they effectively crippled 70% of the world's GPS satellites and nearly all the US military's surveillance and communication satellites. Fortunately, they didn't go after the private sector's satellites, and we've temporarily commandeered many of them until we can get our replacement satellites in place."

Mr. Lake then turned to specifically address General Cotton. "As to what we're doing in response, most of that is classified beyond what the folks in this room have clearance for. However, I can assure you that we've launched a massive cyberattack against the Russians' logistics and transportation sector. Shortly, their communications infrastructure will be attacked, along with their banking sector. There are certain unspoken thresholds that both the US and Russia have unofficially agreed not to touch, like the power grid. They won't look to turn the lights out permanently in the US, and neither will we in Russia. Suffice it to say, a cyberattack is well underway against Russia, with the specific intent of going after their ability to wage and sustain a war." As he finished speaking, he reached over and took a drink of water from a bottle he had brought with him.

Nodding in approval, General Cotton was pleased with the response. He knew he wouldn't get any more details unless he went to another secured room to talk privately with Mr. Lake or cleared the briefing room. For the moment, he was content to know the NSA was on top of it and they had it handled.

At the end of the meeting, the people in the room felt like General Cotton was the modern version of General Patton. Despite the losses, he had a way of making everyone feel like things were under control.

Chapter 31

The Crossroads

Berezan & Baryshivka, Ukraine
55 Miles East of Kiev

Lieutenant Colonel Brian Munch of the 1st Armored Division, 1st Battalion, 37th Armored Regiment, was the only operational commander in the area. He had ordered the remnants of 2nd Cavalry Troops to form up with his battalion, along with their field artillery squadron, aptly named the "Artillery Hell," to take up positions in the strategic towns of Berezan and Baryshivka. The two municipalities sat on the P03 highway and the E40, which led straight to Kiev and passed by the Boryspil International Airport.

Sergeant Childers looked over at Lieutenant Taylor. "So, what do you think of our position?" he asked, wanting to know if the lieutenant was thinking the same thing he was about this plan.

Taylor thought for a minute before responding, "I think we have our Strykers and LATVs placed well. They have fallback positions and alternative firing positions, just like the tanks do. Overall, though, I'm concerned about our placement near these two towns. While we're in an excellent blocking position, we're also sitting right in the way of what is probably a very large Russian force that's headed our direction. With no air cover, and no idea if we'll have reinforcements, I think we should fall back to Kiev. Unfortunately, Captain Richards and Colonel Munch want to make a stand."

Childers nodded in approval. The lieutenant was finally learning, putting together the bigger picture and then figuring out how his platoon fit into it. While it wasn't the sergeant's job to handle the big picture stuff, a good sergeant would understand it so that he could help guide his lieutenant or captain to best utilize their unit's strengths.

"I agree, LT," responded Sergeant Childers. "Now that we both have the same understanding of the situation, our goal should be to make sure our guys come out of this alive—and that we can bloody up as many Russians as possible in the process. I'm going to walk the line and make sure the Javelin crews are ready and know what to do. Perhaps you can check on the vehicles and make sure the TOW gunners are ready, Sir."

Once Lieutenant Taylor nodded in agreement, Luke turned away to go walk the line where the infantry soldiers were still digging their foxholes and other fighting positions.

Jack had always been a smart young man, scoring well on academic tests and making good grades. That kind of book smarts didn't always translate into real-world intelligence though. He was grateful for the guidance of Sergeant Childers; having a sounding board to bounce his thoughts off of was really helping to boost his confidence. Surviving their first encounter with the Russians had also increased his poise and self-assurance. He still had fear, but it was healthy fear—respect for the force of the enemy.

He put his head down and put one foot in front of the other. The best thing he could do now was to make sure that his soldiers were as ready as they could be to meet the Russian force that would undoubtedly head their way.

****

Donetsk, East Ukraine

Lieutenant General Mikhail Chayko, the Commander of the 1st Tank Army, had moved his field headquarters from Rostov, Russia, to Donetsk, the new capital of Eastern Ukraine, just as soon as it had been secured a few days ago. As he sat in an underground bunker, he looked over the digital map of Ukraine and the various units on it.

He smiled like a child seeing a video game for the first time. These new maps that the technology sector had developed were amazing. The large one-meter by one-meter touchscreen was fully interactive, and several of the operations staff kept it updated with the exact real-time location and disposition of the various Russian and East Ukrainian militia units as they advanced across the demarcation line. In addition, the map displayed each friendly or enemy artillery strike as it was happening, as well as showing each enemy aircraft as it entered the area of the map. Most of that information was being delivered via a series of Russian and commercial satellites, as well as Russian ground and airborne radar and surveillance platforms. The end product was incredibly detailed and allowed the mission planners to direct or redirect military units to where they were truly needed most.

Chayko smiled and thought, *"The Americans aren't the only ones who know how to integrate technology into battle management and combat operations."*

As he continued to examine the map, General Chayko's smile disappeared completely. What caught his eye at that exact moment was the stall in the advancement of the 12th Guard's Tank Regiment. They had apparently run into a well-organized American unit that had somehow managed to nearly destroy a battalion's worth of tanks and infantry fighting vehicles. The map showed that the unit had lost twelve main battle tanks and nineteen BMPs and BTRs—that was a lot of men and material lost, with very few Americans killed in return. It appeared they had only destroyed two of the Americans' new HUMVEE replacement vehicles and one Stryker vehicle. They had captured two wounded Americans and found five other dead bodies.

"I'll bet the Americans tried to collect their wounded and dead before they left," he thought. *"There's no way that's all they lost from that engagement."*

The other lines of attack were showing great progress. The 6th Tank Brigade and the 27th Guard's Motor Rifle Brigade had passed Mykolaiv along the coast and would be at Odessa by tomorrow. Once they reached Odessa, they would continue to drive west and push through southern Moldova and the coastal area of Ukraine. His biggest concern now was making sure the Allied air forces were not able to slow down or destroy his tank regiments before they had met their objectives. The goal was not to invade further NATO countries, but to make them believe that invasion was a real threat, forcing them to the negotiation table.

As he re-centered the map over Pryluky, General Chayko suddenly felt angry. He turned to the army group's operation officer, who had been examining the map with him. "Colonel Sokolov, why is there a delay in capturing the NATO air base at Pryluky? It should have been in our hands by now."

Sokolov swallowed hard. "Sir, I spoke with the division commander, and they are moving to take it now. We have several Su-34s assigned to provide them air support. He says they should have the base by tomorrow morning," the colonel responded, knowing that was not the answer the general was looking for.

Looking at the map and the division's location, General Chayko could see that his men were only 50 miles away from Pryluky. That division should be able to have that base under his control by dark, not the following morning.

"*I may have to replace him if he doesn't get a move on,*" he thought.

****

Sergeant First Class Childers and Second Lieutenant Taylor sat in their fighting position along a narrow tree line, overlooking the E40 highway. It was the first time since the fighting had started nearly ten hours ago that they had a chance to just sit, drink some water, and eat an MRE. Today's meal-ready-to-eat consisted of beef steak, but it came with a special prize, the jalapeño cheese sauce—the most-prized condiment in any MRE. It was the most-often traded item and was treated like pure gold by those who regularly ate MREs. Childers looked briefly at his watch as he squeezed some cheese on his crackers. "It'll be dark soon. We have maybe another hour of light," he said.

"You think the Russians are going to hit us at night?" asked Lieutenant Taylor. He wasn't sure if that would be a good thing or a bad thing for them, since all the American soldiers in their unit had night vision goggles, and most of the Russian soldiers would likely not be equipped with them.

Childers paused for a moment, calculating. "Probably," he answered. "I would. If you want to rush through an area, what better time to do it than at night? They know we're tired, and they know we're a small group of Strykers and tanks....we'll make them pay for it though." As he finished speaking, he patted the pouch that held night vision goggles.

Luke wanted to change the subject and take his mind off the war, if only for a few minutes. "Why did you join the Army, LT?" he asked.

"Hmm, that's a good question, Sergeant, and it's a long story. Not sure we have time for it right now," he replied with a wry laugh.

Snickering himself, Childers responded, "Well, we have a few minutes until the Russians decide to do something. Besides, it'll help take my mind off our situation here. So, why did you join?"

"OK, OK," Taylor said, putting his hands in the air in surrender.

"Well, believe it or not, I was accepted and went to college at Yale. I originally wanted to be a lawyer, so going to Yale made sense. I figured I'd go to another Ivy League school afterwards and go to work for some fancy law firm in New York and make the big bucks. During my junior year, I got an internship for a law firm in New York over the summer—it was a prestigious firm, the kind that pays you high salaries right out of college. They had me working 100-hour work weeks, which was brutal. I talked with a few of the first-year lawyers and they told me they also worked more than 100 hours every week. Most of them did their first two or three years, until they got promoted to associate lawyer. Then their schedule dropped down to sixty to eighty hours."

Pulling out his wallet, the LT handed Childers a picture of a very beautiful woman. "Then I met her over the summer of my senior year—Cindy. She was going to school for accounting. We dated, and by the time the fall semester of my senior year was over, I was completely head-over-heels in love. She got pregnant unexpectedly, and I realized that I couldn't live a moment of my life without her and asked her to marry me." He began to rub his wedding ring and looked like he might get emotional.

"With a new fiancée and a baby on the way, I suddenly realized that I couldn't be a lawyer. My father was a workaholic, and I never saw him much. We had a nice house, nice cars, and fancy clothes growing up. I mean, I never wanted for anything...except time with my dad. He never made it to any of my sporting events at school, or anything else that really mattered to me. Now that I was going to be a father, I vowed I wouldn't be like my dad. My entire perspective changed, and I knew I needed to change my path. So, what was I supposed to do? I was about to graduate Yale with $82,000 in student debt, and I was no longer going on to law school to get one of those high-paying lawyer jobs in New York to pay it all off."

"As fate would have it, I ran into an Army recruiter during finals' week. He asked me if I'd given any thought to how I was going to pay off my student loans. Well, that got me to stop and talk with him. He told me if I joined as an infantry officer, he could get me a $10,000 signing bonus, and the Army would pay off all $82,000 of my student loans over a six-year enlistment. After that, I was free to stay in the Army or leave."

"I talked it over with my fiancée and we agreed that I should join and get my student loans wiped out. She was going to have a degree in accounting, so she could get a job anywhere the Army sent us, except here in Germany. But, then again, our son is only a few months old, so she'll just plan on being a stay-at-home mom until we return to the States. So, that's how I ended up in the Army. How about you? How did you end up here, Sergeant Childers?" Taylor asked.

Just as Childers was about to go into his story of how he ended up joining the military, they heard a missile streak over their position toward a target just over the horizon. Seconds later, they heard a *bang*! Then a Russian Hind helicopter emerged in the distance, flying straight for their position. The Hind was emitting some smoke but still appeared to be combat-effective as it continued to head toward them. Then, another missile streaked over their position and hit the Hind just below the rotor blades, exploding directly into the engine. The chopper wasn't flying that far off the ground, so when this second Stinger missile hit it, it didn't have very far to fall before it blew up.

A loud whistling noise overwhelmed their ears, which meant either artillery or bombs falling. Explosions rocked the area all around their positions. The Russians hit the American positions with 152mm artillery rounds, softening them up before their tanks and infantry fighting vehicles began their attack. The artillery barrage lasted for about five minutes; then, as soon as it ended, they heard the unmistakable sound of tanks.

Sergeant Childers poked his head above their foxhole and saw numerous Russian tanks spread out in a wide attack pattern, supported by dozens of BMPs and BTR infantry assault vehicles. They raced toward the American positions, trying to get within knife range and limit the ability of the American tanks to use their primary advantage, their long reach. Following behind the armored vehicles was the infantry—and not a small number of soldiers, but a whole regiment's worth.

"It looks like it's time for us to earn our pay again," Childers said with a wicked grin on his face as he raised his rifle and took aim at the advancing Russian infantry.
****

Lieutenant Colonel Brian Munch was sitting in his Stryker command vehicle, scarfing down an MRE before the next round of fighting started. As tough and macho as he acted in front of his men, he was nervous. He knew they were outnumbered, and he knew the smart move would have been to fall back to the international airport or even Kiev. However, he also knew that they needed to buy NATO time to get more forces into Ukraine and to the front lines. The rest of their division was less than a day away. If they could hold this position until morning, the rest of the division might reach Kiev and even be able to relieve them.

He was also concerned about his oldest brother, who he knew had been commanding the carrier, USS *Bush*, in the Black Sea. He was aware that the ship had been sunk, but so far, he had no updates on the whether or not his brother had survived the attack. The Munch family was a military family, through and through. Of course, Brian was the only one to join the Army. The rest of the family was all a part of the Navy; his father had retired as a three-star admiral, James was the two-star admiral in charge of the carrier, and his other brother, Adam, was a submarine commander. Even though his brothers often gave him a hard time about bucking the family trend and going Army instead, he really hoped that everyone would come out of this OK and they would all see each other at Christmas.

A warning came over the radio, interrupting his thoughts. One of the Avenger crews announced, "We've detected two Russian Hind helicopters heading toward our position. We are currently engaging the choppers. Chances are, there will be tanks behind these helicopters."

"Copy that," answered Lieutenant Colonel Brian Munch.

He switched frequencies on the radio to address his battalion. "Listen up, everyone. Our air defense guys are going to engage some enemy helicopters. Be ready for a possible bum rush by some enemy tanks," he announced, wanting to make sure everyone was as ready as they could be.

Then Munch turned to his drone operator. "Specialist Lee, move the scout drone toward where that Hind is coming in from. I want to see if there's anything else that may be following the helicopters," he directed.

"Yes, Sir," responded the specialist, and he dutifully redirected the drone.

As Brian was watched the drone feed and reexamined the electronic map with the disposition of his forces, he felt confident in their position.

A voice from one of the cavalry troops interrupted everyone's thoughts. "This is Outlaw One-One. We have tanks three kilometers to our front. T-80s, it looks like." The voice sounded like it was filled with adrenaline and anticipation.

Then another troop reported tanks to their front, and a third troop reported BMPs and BTRs coming from a different direction. As Colonel Munch looked over the various troop locations on the map, he could see that the Russians were coming at them from three different directions.

Colonel Munch snapped his fingers and waved his hand to get the attention of his fire support team LNO; the FIST coordinated artillery missions between the armor units and the battalion of self-propelled 155mm Paladins.

Captain Charlie Prim had been on the radio with his squadron, letting them know that they should be ready for a fire mission and that several of the cavalry troops had spotted enemy tanks. He saw Colonel Munch was trying to get his attention, so he placed the hand receiver down and looked up. "You have a fire mission, Sir?" he asked.

Munch just nodded and signaled for Captain Prim to scoot over to the map table. "It's nearly dark right now. The scouts are reporting enemy tanks here and here, and BMPs moving in from this direction. I'd like your guns to throw some illumination rounds in these areas. We need to make sure we don't have additional enemy troops or vehicles trying to slip through under the cover of night. Also, make sure they know to keep the flares constantly coming throughout the night, all right?"

"I understand, Sir. We'll keep the illumination rounds coming. I've let the squadron know to expect fire missions at any time. They are ready, Sir," he said confidently.

Then, just as they were starting to gather more information and get themselves ready for the pending Russian assault, they heard the unmistakable sound of incoming artillery. Dozens of 152mm artillery rounds began to land among the various clusters of trees and among the buildings of the two villages where the Americans had taken cover.

"Get in your vehicles and move out!" shouted Colonel Munch, trying to make his voice heard over the din of the explosions nearby. Everyone rushed to their armored IFVs and raced off. As his tires peeled out, Munch grabbed his radio and told the others to fall back. He didn't want everyone to stay there like sitting ducks, waiting to be hit from above.

The artillery fire was ferocious as the Russian tank and infantry fighting vehicles continued to maneuver to get in place for their attack. Once the artillery fire started to taper off, the Russians launched an all-out attack. Nearly 130 Russian T-80s and T-14 Armatas began to race toward the American positions from multiple different directions, followed quickly by waves of BTRs, BMPs, and T-15 heavy infantry fighting vehicles.

****

Alpha Five was commanded by Sergeant First Class Joe Dukes, "JD" to his friends and tank companions. His M1A2 Abrams was positioned to the side of a house that had an overview of the E40 highway. The home also had a lot of trees and overgrown bushes surrounding it, which made it about as good of a tank hiding place as he was going to find. He had identified a couple of firing positions they could use, all nearby and easily accessible. When the scouts began to report spotting tanks, JD had his driver inch the vehicle forward, so they could see the highway.

JD and his gunner, Smokey, switched their sights to thermals as the sunlight began to disappear; they quickly spotted the Russian tanks from their heat signatures. Sergeant Jay Smokes had been Joe's gunner for the past year, and the two of them got along well. They were both from Texas, so their families and upbringing had been very similar. It certainly didn't hurt anything.

"Smokey, I'm going to start calling targets. I want you to get them locked up with the gun and then start taking them out," JD announced, making sure his gunner knew what the plan was.

"Roger that," Smokey replied.

Next, he turned to his loader, Specialist Eric Jones. "Jones, make sure you have the Sabot rounds ready. We're going to focus on the tanks and let the scouts use their TOWs on the BMPs, OK?" JD asked, again looking to clarify his expectations.

"Roger that, Sergeant. Sabot. All day. Got it," Jones said with a wry grin. He had joined the team about eight months ago. He was a sharp young guy who had been in the Army for two years. He was also their unofficial tech guy, since he seemed to have a knack for anything electronic.

Then JD addressed his driver. "Specialist Miller, be ready to move us to our other firing positions when I give the order. We are going to be moving a lot once the shooting starts, OK?"

"Roger that, Sergeant," Miller replied.

JD went back to looking through his commander's scope and started to identify targets. "Crap, that's a T-14. I didn't think they had any of those ready for combat," he said to the crew. The others looked up at him, not sure what to say.

"T-14s burn just as easily as a T-80 or T-90. It's just a tank, JD—let's kill it," Smokey said nonchalantly.

JD just smiled and laughed. "I don't think you know anything about that tank. But you're right, let's kill it. Target, T-14, three o'clock. Twenty-five hundred meters, Sabot," he said as they got into their rhythm of calling targets, just like in training.

"Sabot up," said Jones as he stood to the side of the gun, waiting for it to recoil from being fired.

"Fire!" yelled JD.

"Round away," announced Smokey, pulling the trigger on his targeting control. The whole tank rocketed back on its track as the gun fired its round.

JD watched as the Sabot round flew directly for the T-14. Then, to his utter shock, he saw the tank's defense system fire some kind of small explosive device that threw the Sabot round off course just slightly, causing the depleted uranium dart to hit the tank at the wrong angle. The round ricocheted off the tank and flew harmlessly into the sky. "My

God…the round missed. That tank has some sort of defense mechanism. Give me another Sabot round!" he yelled out.

Smokey had seen the round fly off the tank as well, and he couldn't believe it either. This time, he aimed the round a little lower and toward the rear of the tank. He was going to try and nail the engine.

"Sabot up!" yelled Jones.

"Fire!" shouted JD, and the tank rocketed back on its track from the recoil. This time the round flew a little lower and slammed directly into the side of the engine compartment. In seconds, the engine blew out flames and smoke. The T-14 suddenly stopped moving forward. The engine compartment became a burning cauldron as the fuel tank exploded. The top hatch of the tank flew open as the crew rushed to try and bail out.

Smokey switched from the main gun control to the coax gun and fired a quick burst of the M2 .50 as the crew tried to get out of the burning tank. He managed to cut down two of the three crew members. The third guy rolled off the tank and out of Smokey's sights.

"T-80, two o'clock, twelve hundred meters," JD directed as he identified the next tank. "Sabot."

"T-80, twelve hundred meters identified," Smokey replied.

"Sabot up," Jones answered.

"Fire!" yelled JD to his gunner.

"Firing. Reload Sabot," Smokey said as he tracked the round to the tank. Seconds later, the Sabot slammed into the side of the turret and the chassis of the body. It blew the turret right off the tank, killing the crew instantly.

This went on for a while; they lost track of time as they got into the zone. It was spot, aim, load, fire, and repeat. Then, the tank near them was blown up by Russian fire, and JD yelled to his driver, "It's time to change locations!"

As they moved on to the next spot, JD breathed a sigh of relief. He had gotten so zeroed in on blowing the enemy up that he had put his men at risk. He felt very lucky that they were all alive and vowed not to make the same mistake again.

****

Sergeant First Class Lance Peeler was lying on the roof of a two-story house in the village, overlooking the E40 highway. There were a few three-story buildings, but Peeler stayed away from them since those would likely be the first ones destroyed by the Russians. Sergeant Peeler was a new addition to the 2nd Cavalry field artillery squadron. He had joined the unit eight weeks ago, after spending two years as an instructor at the Army's Artillery School at Fort Sill in Oklahoma. He had two young soldiers with him, and ironically enough, they had been students of his not that long ago.

They had lugged their AN/PED-1 lightweight laser designator rangefinder up on the roof with them, along with their own scout drone and Toughbook to watch the real-time video from it. The LLDR was a great new tool. It had been in service for roughly ten years, but the newest version was a huge improvement over previous models. It was lighter, smaller, and more accurate. This tool definitely helped them to identify specific targets much more accurately, and it could also be used to lase for guided munitions.

Sergeant Peeler turned to one of the young soldiers with him. "Hey, I need you to get the scout drone up," he instructed. "It's nearly dusk and the enemy will most likely launch their attack soon."

Not long after the drone got airborne, they heard the unmistakable scream of incoming artillery. The Russians were known to flatten an area with artillery rounds before sending in their troops or armored vehicles, so Peeler had expected an incoming barrage, but no one could ever really be prepared for the experience. Explosions were going off all around, and there wasn't anything they could do, except lie in wait on the roof and pray that a round didn't land on top of them.

Fortunately, the specialist had managed to get the drone up to around a thousand feet and guide it over to the village of Borschiv, roughly 3000 meters away, before the artillery started to hit. At the far end of the village, they spotted the Russian armored units, all fanned out in a combat formation, waiting for their artillery support to stop; then they would launch their own attack.

"Private, you see those armored vehicles? They're getting ready to move. Hand me the radio, will you?" Peeler asked the private first-class who was lying on the roof next to him.

"Yes, Sir," he responded over the racket of the constant blasts.

With the radio in hand, Sergeant Peeler called back to get the first fire mission going. "Hellraisers, this is Foxtrot Three. Fire mission. Regimental-size element of Russian armor. Requesting fire-for-effect, three rounds WP, 300-foot airburst, grid...Second fire mission. Same grid, fire-for-effect, eight rounds HE, ground burst. How copy?"

The two young soldiers sitting on the roof with him looked at him in awe of how easily he had just called in what was a very complex fire mission. They felt bad for the enemy that was about to have death and destruction unleashed on them.

A few seconds went by, then the radio crackled to life, "Foxtrot Three. This is Hellraisers. Good copy. Stand by for fire mission."

In the Russian Army, armored vehicle commanders typically drove into an attack while standing in the hatch of their turret. This provided the commander with the best possible field of vision and allowed him to take in the scene of the battle far better than he could while looking through the observation slits in the turret. Since the Russian tanks didn't incorporate nearly as much targeting technology as the American tanks did, it meant the tank commander had to be a lot more observant and rely on seeing the enemy.

To take advantage of this tactical difference, Sergeant Peeler had called for a fire-for-effect of three rounds of WP, which stood for white phosphorus. "Willie Pete," as it was called by the gun bunnies, was an incredibly hot-burning chemical. Calling the rounds as a 300-foot airburst meant it would essentially rain twenty-four WP canisters down on top of the entire enemy position, creating a chemically-induced burning gas cloud that would force the tank commanders to get back into their vehicles and move out of the area.

The second fire-for-effect mission would send 64 high-explosive rounds at the enemy. Due to the number of rounds being requested, the blasts would probably be distributed across the squadron rather than just one battery. If everything played out in their favor, the Americans would destroy more than a few dozen enemy armored vehicles between these two attacks.

The radio came to life again when the fire direction command or FDC who was coordinating the artillery fire announced, "Rounds shot."

Ten seconds later, the voice came back over the radio saying, "Splash," indicating the rounds should begin to impact in five seconds.

"Splash out," Sergeant Peeler responded, letting the FDC know that he had received the message.

While the Russian artillery bombardment continued, Peeler and his two young soldiers watched the scout drone's footage of their own artillery rounds starting to land amongst the Russian armored vehicles. As the WP rounds began to air-burst, sure enough, the tank commanders dropped back into their tanks, closing their hatches to escape the chemical cloud. The entire column started their engines and tried to get out of the area. Just as most of the vehicles were beginning to move, the 64 high-explosive rounds landed across their positions, killing dozens of soldiers who hadn't returned to their vehicles yet. Several tanks also took direct hits, exploding in place.

Moments later, the Russian bombardment of their positions ended, and the ground attack began, utilizing whatever forces had survived the American artillery attack.

Sergeant Peeler told the two soldiers with him, "Start calling out targets as they enter the previously designated zones." They had pre-arranged fire missions with the battalion FDC to hit certain zones around the American positions as the enemy started to enter them. This would save an enormous amount of time and provide for faster, more accurate fire support. Considering they had no air support, the artillery battalion's support was going to be worth its weight in gold.

****

As the bombardment ended, Sergeant Childers poked his head above his hastily dug foxhole to see who else from the troop was still alive. The scream of wounded soldiers could be heard all around, sending a chill down his spine. Childers climbed out of his hole and moved down the line, checking on his soldiers.

He approached the foxhole next to his and saw the two soldiers sitting in the bottom of it, shaken but OK. "Hey, stay frosty guys," he said. "The ground attack is most likely going to come next." Then he proceeded to the next foxhole.

While moving forward, he heard some crying to his left, near a thicket of bushes. He moved toward the noise and saw one of his soldiers had crawled over to the greenery for cover. The man had been hit by shrapnel in multiple places; his right leg was nearly torn off and bleeding steadily. He had jimmied his own tourniquet and tried his best to stop the bleeding on his own. "Hang on, soldier. I'm here," said Luke calmly.

He moved to the injured man's side and began to apply an additional bandage. "Medic! I need a medic over here!" he shouted to the soldiers around them.

A second later, one of the medics called back, "I'm on the way!"

Another nearby soldier heard Childer's cry for help and ran over to assist as well. Within moments, the medic had arrived at their position. He placed his aid bag on the ground next to the wounded soldier, opening it swiftly and deftly searching for the exact supplies he needed. The medic immediately poured a clotting powder on the wounded man's leg, then made sure the tourniquet was on tight. He gave the soldier a quick shot of morphine and began to establish an IV bag.

Once the initial life-saving measures were complete, Childers knew he would have to move on. He addressed the medic, "Specialist Jenkins, try to get him stabilized and back to the aid station. I'm not sure if or when we'll be able to get any additional medical help, so do your best, son."

Jenkins nodded, and the other soldier stayed with them to help move their injured comrade.

Sergeant Childers grabbed his rifle and walked further into the woods, checking the rest of the firing positions as he went. He needed to make sure the platoon was ready for the next attack.

He found Lieutenant Taylor helping one of the soldiers get their heavy machine gun repositioned. A large tree branch had fallen and pinned the weapon to the ground until they were able to wrestle it out and get it set up in a new position. "Everyone OK here, LT?" he asked, hoping no one had been killed or injured.

Looking up, he saw Childers, covered in dirt and sweat, and a little bit of blood trickling down from a small cut on the side of his right cheek. "You look like crap, Sergeant. Are you OK?" he asked in reply.

Chuckling, Childers answered, "Yeah, I'm OK. We had a couple of guys wounded down by my section of the line. The medics are getting them back to the aid station. We got lucky the Russians didn't focus that barrage on our position like they did the armor guys," he said, looking off toward where the tanks were hiding. He saw a couple columns of smoke, which meant a few of them must have been hit.

Suddenly, the percussion of tank cannon rounds, mortars, and heavy machine guns broke the conversation. "It appears the ground attack's about to start. Sergeant, get the rest of the platoon ready while I help get this gun operational again," the LT said as he turned back to the gun.

Sergeant Childers smiled and ran toward the next line. *"I'm glad to see the LT is starting to take ownership of the platoon. We'll make an infantry officer out of him yet,"* he thought.

Luke saw that the next group of three soldiers was ready. They had the M240 mounted on a tripod with the spare barrel and glove nearby, ready to be swapped out. "You guys have enough ammo for that thing?" he asked.

One of the soldiers, who couldn't have been much older than eighteen, looked up. "Yes, Sergeant. We have fourteen belts."

Childers nodded and then moved down to the next foxhole. He saw only one soldier where there should have been two or three, so he jumped in. "Where are your battle buddies?" he asked, genuinely concerned.

"They both got injured during the artillery barrage. I'm here alone," he answered, clearly still in a bit of shock.

Childers reached out, putting his hand on the young soldier's shoulder. "Hey, it's OK. They will be fine and so will you. I'll stay here with you. You'll be my battle buddy now, OK?" His kindness brought a smile to the soldier's face.

"Thank you, Sergeant Childers. You're a good sergeant," the young soldier said.

Snap...Zip...Crack! Dozens of bullets flew over their heads, hitting the tree branches and other objects they were using for cover in front of their fighting position.

"Private Torres, remember to aim each shot. Find your target, then gently squeeze the trigger and move to the next target. Don't stay up for more than a few seconds before ducking back down, OK?" Childers felt the need to try to convey some of his experience to the youngster.

"Man, we have a lot of young soldiers in this platoon," Childers realized.

PV2 Jesus Torres looked over the top of his fighting position with his M4 at the enemy soldiers, heading toward their position. He did just as Sergeant Childers told him; he found a Russian soldier that was bounding from one covered position to another, stopping every few minutes to fire his AK-74 at their positions. He placed the red dot on the soldier's center mass, just as he had been taught in basic combat training at Fort Benning, and gently squeezed the trigger. He felt his rifle bark once and recoil. The enemy soldier clutched his chest and fell to the ground. He had hit him.

PV2 Torres then slid down the side of his fighting position, his heart and mind racing.

He looked at Childers. "Sergeant, I did it. I got one of them!" he yelled over the now-continuous popping of the platoon's weapons.

Looking at the young soldier, Luke responded, "Great job, Torres! I told you that you could do it. Now, keep going. We have to stop these guys, and the platoon is depending on you!"

Sergeant Childers spotted what appeared to be a Russian officer. He was the only guy he saw yelling at the soldiers, pointing them to various parts of the American lines where they would direct machine-gun fire. Childers took careful aim and gently squeezed the trigger, just as he had done so many times throughout his military career. He released a three-round burst, which hit the Russian officer in the chest. The officer dropped to the ground, dead. The soldiers near the officer suddenly looked up and pointed directly at Childers. Childers and Torres then found their position being heavily raked over with enemy gunfire. Dirt, grass, and tree leaves were all kicked up around them as the enemy lit up their position.

Childers put his hand on Torres' shoulder, indicating for him to stay down a bit longer. "Let the enemy fire at us for a while. Once they believe they got us, they'll move on to the next position. Then we can get up and start shooting at them again, OK?"

After what felt like an eternity, but was probably no more than thirty seconds, Childers popped back up and brought his rifle to bear. He sighted in a group of Russian soldiers moving toward their position. They were being smart about it. Two of them would run while the other three would lay down covering fire. One of the soldiers had an RPG-7 and would stop from time to time to fire a rocket at the American lines. Childers looked down at Torres and signaled for him to get up.

"See that group of soldiers over there to our ten o'clock? Try and take out the guy with the RPG. I'm going to try and take out the other guys around him, OK?"

Torres just nodded, still rattled from all the gunfire happening around them. Childers took aim at one of the attackers. He had stopped shooting to change out magazines when Childers placed the red dot on him and squeezed the trigger. The Russian soldier fell backwards. His buddy to the left looked right at Childers just as he squeezed the trigger a second time, hitting the soldier in the face.

It was practically dark now. The Americans had moved to using their night vision goggles. Roughly half the Russian soldiers had them. The other half didn't; they were just running and attacking in the direction they were told. As night descended on the battle, it turned into complete chaos. Red and green tracer fire crisscrossed back and forth across the battle lines while soldiers and armored vehicles attempted to race between them. Explosions could be heard everywhere. Bullets whipped through the air, striking tree trunks, branches, vehicles and human flesh. The sickening cacophony of war continued unabated, both sides relentlessly trying to kill each other.

The ground attack lasted nearly two hours before the Russians broke off their attack. They hadn't penetrated the

American positions, but they'd bloodied the Americans up pretty well. For the moment, the Americans had delayed a significantly larger enemy force from moving on to capture the international airport and the capital—at least for several hours, maybe more.

Chapter 32

Disunity at the Top

Washington, D.C.

White House, Situation Room

The Secret Service was still requesting to move the President to a more secured command bunker. "Mr. President," pressed one of the agents. "This is a shooting war with Russia, a nation that has nuclear capability and submarines potentially off the East Coast. Our concern is for your safety."

The President waved them off. "I respect your opinion, but I need to stay in the White House and project strength and calm until the situation changes," he responded calmly. He felt confident in his assessment that Russia had no more desire to make this a nuclear war than he did.

As to the broader picture, however, the President had admitted privately to his closest advisors that he didn't have any serious military experience or understanding of how these things worked. He was relying heavily on their experience and knowledge. Right now, it appeared to him they had completely underestimated the Russians' resolve to stand their ground, and their ability to strike at the US and

NATO. The only person he had spoken to in the last few days who had signaled any sort of warning was that ambassador in Ukraine.

"I'll have to speak with him more—he seems to know what he's talking about," the President thought.

The room was abuzz with activity. Generals and colonels studied various digital maps, some of Ukraine, some of Europe. President Gates had been sitting in the Situation Room, absorbing the information being thrown at him for the past two and a half hours during this second emergency session of the day. Finally, the President cleared his throat and stood up.

"Enough!" he exclaimed. "Everyone, take a seat and shut up. There's too much chaos and yelling going on right now, and nothing productive is going to come from it. I need each of you to provide me with the situation update as of right now, and then tell me what our options are."

The room suddenly calmed down. Everyone walked back to their chairs and sat down. General Hillman, the Chairman of the Joint Chiefs, replied, "You're right, Mr. President. Please accept my apology for our behavior. We're trying to talk through our options and the situation right now. Not all of us agree on what to do next. We normally hash this out before you join the meeting. You are kind of seeing us as we brainstorm and work through the problems." The other officers and generals nodded in agreement, realizing that this was not the time or place to have such a disagreement.

NSA Tom McMillan stood up and walked over to the digital map of Ukraine. "Mr. President, what we're trying to figure out right now is what to do about this American unit that is positioned right here," he said, pointing to a section on the map that then zoomed in. "It's roughly 40 miles from Kiev, and 53 miles or so from our base at Pryluky here," he explained, zooming in again on the base.

The President interrupted to ask, "Isn't that our base that the Russians essentially destroyed during the sneak attack?"

"Yes, Mr. President. The Russians hit the base with both an airstrike and a cruise missile attack. The base also fought off a Spetsnaz ground attack. There are still 2,800 soldiers at the base, getting it ready for another Russian ground and air attack." McMillan pulled up a side screen, which listed some of the units that were still at the base.

Another general, the deputy to the Army's Chief of Staff, spoke up to add, "We've moved nearly 400 wounded soldiers from the base back to Kiev. We still have a lot of seriously wounded soldiers there that are presently stranded and need to be evacuated from Ukraine."

The President's Chief of Staff, Ishaan Patel, interjected to ask, "What are we doing to evacuate our wounded soldiers, General Sparks?"

Sparks grunted and shrugged a little, exasperated. "Right now, we aren't doing anything. Two of our medevac helicopters have been shot down by Russian aircraft. We've lost eleven helicopters in the past three hours in that area right now. Until the Air Force can get some air cover to our choppers, they aren't going to keep flying into that base." He was clearly angry that his soldiers could not get the medical support they desperately needed.

Gates looked to his Air Force General, Dustin LaSalle. "What are we doing to get air support to our troops and to cover Spark's medical helicopters?"

The Air Force General felt all eyes turn toward him. "A wing of F-35s just arrived at Ramstein Air Base. They're being readied to carry out operations in Ukraine and just across the Russian border, which should start to help alleviate our ground forces."

Gates raised his hand to stop the general. "LaSalle, talk plain English to me. What exactly does that mean?"

"Sorry, Sir. The F-35s that just arrived in Germany are going after the Russian air defense systems—the SA-10 and SA-21 missile batteries, their SAMs. As those systems are taken offline, our F-15s, F-16s, and A-10s will be able to provide ground support to our troops. We have 41 F-22s in Germany and twelve in Poland. They're going to start flying round-the-clock air operations over Ukraine now that we have additional E-3 aircraft from the UK to help provide air battle management support. These efforts are going to result in us regaining air superiority over the next couple of days," General LaSalle explained.

Gates nodded in approval. "Thank you, General, for explaining that. When will our B-2 stealth bombers and B-1s begin their attacks against Moscow?" he asked. Secretly, he was hoping that somehow, some way, they might get lucky and even kill Petrov.

"The B-2 strike will happen in two more hours. The bombers are just now penetrating Russian airspace," one of the Air Force colonels said from his spot against the back wall.

"What about the Navy? How's that front going?" asked the President. The last update he had received was a few hours ago, when it had been reported that the Supercarrier *George H.W. Bush* had to be abandoned. When part of the carrier's air wing had to land at the Atatürk Airport in Istanbul, it had created a bit of an issue with the Turks, despite them being a part of NATO. They were not happy. They complained that it made the international airport a legitimate military target while those military aircraft were there. However, the air wing was being refueled and would fly on to the US Air Force base at Aviano, Italy. The President was hoping to avoid further issues with his NATO partners.

Admiral William Richardson, the Chief of Naval Operations, took the question. "Mr. President, the remaining ships of Strike Group Two have linked up with the Bulgarian and Romanian navy. They just launched cruise missile strikes against the Russian naval base at Sevastopol in Crimea, and also against the two Russian airfields there. Strike Group Two will move toward Crimea and finish off the rest of the Russian Black Sea Fleet, then provide air defense support over as much of Ukraine as possible."

The admiral continued the briefing on the naval situation. "We held back on sending the *Eisenhower* into the Baltic Sea until it can be properly secured. The strike group has been engaging numerous Russian submarines since the start of hostilities. So far, no submarines have gotten close enough to launch any torpedoes at her, but one of the destroyer escorts was sunk in the North Sea."

"I've also ordered the *Truman* Carrier Strike Group to withdraw from the eastern Mediterranean Sea and start heading to the Black Sea. We'll need the carrier's air wing and strike package as we continue to hit the Russians. Plus, the 3,500 Marines they have traveling with them, along with the 3,500 Marines from the *Bush* Strike Group, will give us a solid ground force we can use against the Russians," Admiral Richardson concluded.

President Gates nodded in acknowledgment. "Thank you, Admiral. I appreciate your taking extra precautions with the *Eisenhower* carrier group and getting the *Truman* into position. I like the idea of having 7,000 angry Marines we can deploy in the Black Sea."

"The Russians are obviously hitting us with a lot of cyberattacks. Are we going to have these attacks under control? And are we taking appropriate attacks of our own against them?" asked Gates. Prior to coming into the meeting, he had seen a news bulletin from one of the networks talking about a series of cyberattacks taking place across the country; he didn't want to leave any stone unturned.

The Director of the NSA spoke up as this was his primary lane. "Mr. President, certain parts of the economy are being attacked with a series of DDoS attacks and other malicious cyberattacks. We have our best people working on countering this, along with the private sector, to restore service and to prevent these types of events from happening again. Our country, unlike most, has been the target of vicious cyberattacks for more than a decade. As a result, we are far more prepared to deal with them than our European counterparts. Our agency is currently carrying out a myriad of cyberattacks against parts of the Russian government and economy that support their military and forces in Ukraine."

The President nodded, knowing this was a complex issue. He felt good that his people were on top of it for the time being. He'd have to check back with them over the next few days to verify their progress.

Then he turned to face the broader group. "I don't believe we addressed the initial problem McMillan brought up—that small pocket of American troops southeast of Kiev. How many soldiers do we have there?" asked Gates.

General Hillman took back over, standing up next to the map. "It's kind of a hodgepodge of units. It's being led right now by a lieutenant colonel, Brian Munch, the battalion commander from the 37th Armored Regiment. They're the first armored regiment from the 1st Armored Division that arrived in Europe three days ago. They hauled butt to get to Kiev and then ran straight to the front lines when hostilities started. The other unit is about half of the 2nd Cavalry Regiment's brigade combat team. All in all, they have roughly 1,900 troops: about 64 Abram battle tanks, 46 Stryker vehicles, and 32 Bradley fighting vehicles. The 2nd Cavalry also had a battalion of Paladin self-propelled artillery guns. That unit has been providing them with the bulk of their fire support."

"They've positioned themselves in such a way as to block the bulk of the Russian forces from capturing Pryluky or Kiev quickly. The Russians must either push through them or find a way around them. The Russians already attempted to launch an attack against them, but after two hours, they were beaten back. Although our guys managed to stop them, we know that the Russians will hit them again—either with more forces or, most likely, they will go around them, leaving them completely cut off. While I'd like to leave them in place as they are buying us more time, we have virtually no way to resupply them or relieve them. We have roughly 8,000 soldiers in and around Kiev, but roughly 3,800 of them are combat arms. The rest are support units: supply, air defense, engineers, etc."

Tracing his finger along the highways in Poland leading into Ukraine, General Hillman went on, "We have 12,000 combat troops traveling down these three highways, heading into Ukraine right now. They're at least twelve hours away from reaching Kiev, and that's if they don't come under heavy air attack. The Polish are reluctant to release any of their combat units right now, with the Russian 4th Army currently sitting in Belarus. It's not clear what the intentions of the 4th Army are, but they're in excellent position to invade Poland if they want to. Mr. President, it's my recommendation that we order Colonel Munch to have his forces fall back to Kiev and attempt to hold the city for the next twenty-four hours while additional combat forces arrive from Germany."

Looking at his other generals, Gates asked, "Does everyone else agree with this assessment? Should we have them fall back?"

Several of the generals looked around at each other and then all nodded. It was sound advice. No one wanted to give ground, especially if it looked like they might be able to win, but it was the prudent move to try to hold Kiev rather than this road junction.

The President was still unsure. "One last question, General. How many Russian forces are those guys blocking right now?" Gates wasn't sure if they could potentially hold out.

General Hillman frowned slightly at this question. "They're standing in the way of a Russian tank division and a motorized rifle division, so roughly 48,000 soldiers. They're punching way above their weight class right now, but when the Russians throw the full weight of those divisions at them, they will be wiped out."

The President nodded, more to himself than to anyone in the room. "OK, I understand now. If that's the recommendation of my military advisors, then have them pull back to Kiev. I want them to hold the city. No more falling back. The Russians never should have gotten the jump on us like this," Gates said as he looked at his intelligence directors. "I can't totally fault the military for this one, gentlemen. It's your organizations' job to provide the generals and myself the needed information to prevent things like this from happening. We can't have your organizations fumbling the football—not at a critical time like this."

The President had been chastising his intelligence agencies since taking office. They had been one gigantic leak center. From classified conversations with world leaders to notes from key meetings, it had been a major source of frustration for the President. Gates felt like they had failed the country in a major way by not foreseeing that the Russians would launch this sneak attack. Something needed to be done, that was for sure.

Chapter 33

Midnight in Moscow

32,000 feet above Moscow, Russia

Lieutenant Colonel Rob Fortney, "Pappi," was hoping that the Russian air defense systems over Moscow didn't detect them when they went in for their bomb run. They were less than ten minutes away as they crossed over into what their briefers had said was the most highly guarded airspace in Russia. This was not a comforting thought as he began the arming process of the two bombs he was carrying today.

"*What am I doing here?*" he wondered.

After twenty-five years in the Air Force, he was set to retire in five months and join the ranks of United Airlines as a commercial airline pilot. However, instead of a cushy Boeing 747, that night he found himself flying a B-2 stealth bomber, the *Spirit of America*, into the heart of the Russian empire on a very dangerous mission—a mission his aircraft had specifically been built to conduct nearly thirty years ago.

In the 1980s, the B-2 had been designed to be a deep-penetration stealth bomber that could rain nuclear missiles or bombs across the Soviet Union. Years after the Cold War had ended, Pappi was carrying two 30,000-pound bunker-busting bombs with 5,000-pound warheads in his aircraft, fulfilling the plane's original purpose; the Pentagon hoped this would be a decapitation strike. Decapitation strikes were always dangerous. They required use of new and sometimes untested ordnance, and the pilots would have to fly directly into the heart of enemy territory.

His bomber, along with another B-2 from his squadron, would be dropping the relatively new GBU-57B massive ordnance penetrator or MOP on the National Defense Control Center in hopes of killing President Petrov and crippling the Russian military leadership. These MOPs they were carrying could penetrate some of the deepest bunkers known to man. However, the B-2 could only carry two of these massive explosives, so a second bomber needed to accompany him on this dangerous mission.

The rest of the squadron had already fired off their AGM-158 joint air-to-surface standoff missiles at the Russian air defense systems around Moscow and near the Ukrainian battlefront. Lieutenant Colonel Fortney hoped that these long-range cruise missiles, each packing a 1,000-pound warhead, would have taken out enough of the Russian surface-to-air missile systems and anti-aircraft guns that he could survive this mission.

Colonel Fortney looked at his co-pilot, Major Richard "Ricky" James. "So…you think one of these bombs is going to kill that megalomaniac Petrov?" he asked his friend.

Ricky just grunted. "I don't know. Maybe. Then again, who cares? The war will still continue on without him, and right now, I just want to drop our bombs and get the heck out of here." Ricky wasn't much of a talker. He was working on getting his master's in aeronautical engineering and fluid dynamics, so he spent most of his time—including when they were flying—with his head in a book or writing a paper. Fortney didn't fault the young guy for it. He had just made major, and everyone knew if you wanted to make the next grade, you had to get your master's degree done. A lot of guys started this process when they were captains, but not Ricky.

Ricky had been living the wild life as a young hotshot Air Force bomber pilot, spending his time chasing women and boozing it up. Then he'd met his wife and they'd had a daughter, and his whole world had changed. He had begun to realize that he needed to take care of a family and had become a lot more career-focused. He almost hadn't been selected for major because he hadn't pursued his master's degree, but being a B-2 pilot almost made it a certainty. Had he been a fighter pilot, or the pilot of some other airframe, he might have been passed over.

Suddenly, Ricky put his flash cards back in his pocket. "Pappi, you think their air defense systems may pick us up when we open the bomb bay doors?" It was a thought they both had been having, and neither of them felt really happy about the response they'd received from their superiors before they left for the mission.

"Well, they say we won't be visible, but frankly, I'm not confident about that," remarked Pappi. "Fortunately, we're only dropping two bombs, so we won't have to have the doors open that long. If their radars do get a lock on us, they should lose it once we close the doors again," Colonel Fortney reassured his young compatriot. Deep down, though, he had his doubts…but he would keep those to himself. It was incumbent upon him, not just as the aircraft commander, but also as the 13th Bomb Squadron Commander, to lead by example and show no fear.

As they approached the drop point, they readied the bombs, arming them and making sure the coordinates were locked in. The United States' GPS satellites were still down, but the NSA had managed to hack into the Russians' own GPS satellites without them realizing it. It would be a Russian GPS satellite guiding this bomb down on the

National Defense Control Center, the irony of which wasn't lost on the pilots.

Looking down below, the pilots could see that Moscow was still lit up. This wasn't like World War II, where all the cities' lights had been off at night to prevent them from guiding bombers to their targets. In today's modern world, with GPS and satellite imagery, you didn't need lights to direct you to your target.

"Bombs are ready, Pappi," Ricky said nervously. This was Ricky's first combat bombing mission. He had been in training when the B-2s were last used in Iraq and Afghanistan, so this was the first time he had flown over enemy territory.

Nodding, Pappi ordered, "Open bomb bays."

"Bomb bay doors open," Ricky replied, hoping fiercely that they could get the bombs out before they were detected.

Pappi lifted the weapons lock cover and depressed the button, arming the bombs for release. He then moved his hand back to the red-and-yellow button that would release the bombs and depressed it. In a second, he felt the aircraft lift slightly as the weight of the two 30,000-pound bombs fell free of his aircraft. Without waiting to be told, Ricky closed the bomb doors once their deadly cargo had finally been released.

Pappi immediately turned the aircraft for home. Just as he was about to breathe a sigh of relief, their warning systems came on, letting them know they had just been acquired by a Russian surface-to-air missile system.

Pappi chided himself, "*Ugh! I shouldn't have turned the aircraft so soon.*" He knew he should have waited to make sure the bomb doors were fully closed first. There must've been a sliver of the doors open and it gave away just enough surface area for the SAM to acquire a lock.

"*Crap!*" he thought.

****

In the less than 60 seconds it took for Lieutenant Colonel Fortney's B-2 to open its bomb bay doors and release the two MOPs, a Russian S-500 anti-ballistic-missile system detected both his aircraft and the two bombs it had just released. The S-500 acquired an immediate lock on the bombs and fired off missiles to intercept them. A nearby SA-21 fired off two missiles at the B-2 before it disappeared from their radar screen.

The S-500 then detected the two bombs dropped by the *Spirit of Indiana*, the second B-2 on this bombing mission. The SA-21 was not able to acquire the bomber before it closed its bomb bay door, slipping away.

The men manning the S-500 then had four falling objects and one enemy bomber that it was engaging. The operators immediately launched a series of missiles at the bombs and two missiles toward the B-2. The missiles raced out of their launchers, accelerating to Mach 4. Within ten seconds of launch, the two missiles heading toward the B-2 lost acquisition of their target, although they continued to fly toward what the targeting computer estimated the B-2's position to be when it reached the same altitude.

This was the first time the Russians would be using the new Lenovo targeting system, which, if successful, might finally be the key to defeating the American stealth systems. The Lenovo looked at the acquired target's speed, altitude, and current flight path and then calculated the path the missile should travel to intercept it. It had a proximity sensor built in, so when it detected an object consisting of metal, polymers or other aircraft-type materials, it would cause the warhead to explode. While this specific technology was not new, what was new was the aero displacement reader. When an object flies, it displaces air, just as water is displaced when something travels through it—the Lenovo continually looked for the displacement of air caused by high-speed objects, like an aircraft, missile, or bomb, and then guided the missile toward the source. When the object came within its roughly 2,500-meter detonation radius, it would explode.

While the two missiles targeted at the B-2 lost the radar acquisition, they continued to head toward the B-2's projected path. As the missile sped away after the B-2, the other missiles headed straight toward the four bombs. Unlike most guided munitions, the GBU-57B also had a rocket motor to assist the bomb in generating the necessary speed to be able to punch through earth and concrete to get at the bunkers deep below. While the Russian missile interceptors were racing at Mach 4 toward the bombs, the GBU-57Bs themselves were racing toward the earth below at speeds of nearly Mach 3.

As one of the missiles came within a few hundred feet of one of the GBU-57B, it detonated its warhead, hitting the bomb with enough shrapnel that it caused the warhead to go off. The detonation of 5,000 pounds of high explosives made for a thunderous bang in the night sky, briefly lighting it up for anyone who happened to be looking in that direction. The second missile also intercepted its mark and destroyed the bomb as well. The third bomb was thrown slightly off course but was otherwise undamaged, although it would miss its primary target and land nearby. The fourth bomb, however, was able to evade the air defense system and pulverize its way through floor after floor of the National Defense Control Center building's east tower.

The bomb drove through the building's twelve floors and three basement levels before it detonated its 5,000-pound warhead, throwing flames and destruction up through the hole it had just created. As designed, once the GBU-57B sensed that it had impacted something, the tail end released a heavy fuel-air mist until the bomb came to a complete stop. The volatile mixture ignited, causing even more devastation. A 100-foot radius around the initial entry hole burst into a blazing inferno, causing significant structural damage to the building. Fires spread throughout the east side of the building. As the flames found their way to the gas lines that ran throughout the building, numerous secondary explosions erupted.

The bomb that had gone off course plowed into a dense area of residential buildings, not far from the Kremlin and Red Square, causing significant civilian casualties. The bunker-busting bomb not only plowed through the fifteen-story apartment building, it buried itself near several Metro lines before detonating. The GBU-57 collapsed three different Metro line tubes, killing and trapping hundreds of people. It also ignited numerous underground gas lines, which subsequently destroyed several other buildings. In all, this bomb resulted in the deaths of roughly 1,763 civilians, and close to double that number were injured. In addition, thousands of people were left without a home.

****

"What do we do now, Pappi? That missile seems to have lost our lock, but it's still tracking toward us," Ricky said nervously as he strained himself trying to look below and behind them for the missile.

As thoughts raced through his head, Pappi kept going back to his training. If the missile lost lock on your aircraft, then it would estimate the most likely position your aircraft would travel to and then detonate, hoping you were in range of its blast. With that thought in mind, Pappi increased airspeed, turned the B-2 eight degrees to their right, and began to climb. He wanted to add a few thousand feet of altitude and veer off course. Hopefully, that would be enough to evade the missile.

"Hang on, Ricky, I'm getting us some more altitude and changing course. This should throw the missile off our trail," Pappi said, hoping he sounded more confident than he felt.

The missile continued to track toward where they would have been. However, as the missile got within eight kilometers, it suddenly changed course and began to head right for them.

"Oh my God, the missile just turned...it's following us!" Ricky shouted over the intercom, suddenly realizing it might actually hit them.

"How in the hell did that missile know where we were?" Pappi thought. *"How could it have redirected like that?"*

Pappi had no good answers for any of his own questions, but he didn't have time to get bogged down with trying to figure it all out. He simply increased the throttle to the max, climbed and angled his aircraft harder to the right, hoping his stealth ability would again aid him in evading the enemy missile.

To both of their horror, the missile continued to close in on them like it knew where they were. Then, it exploded, spraying shrapnel everywhere. The aircraft shook hard, alarm bells blaring in their ears, letting them know the aircraft had been damaged. The bomber shook violently and pulled to the left. Pappi saw that they were losing hydraulic pressure. Shrapnel must have hit some of the lines. He hit a few buttons, switching over to their auxiliary system and hoping it would work.

Ricky called out the problems on the dashboard. "We're hit! I'm showing a fire in engine two, loss of oil pressure in engine two, and hydraulic pressure loss on the left side of the aircraft."

"Turn engine two off and hit the fire suppression system. We need to get that under control. I'm switching over to auxiliary hydraulics now," Pappi directed. Then, realizing there was a real possibility they might have to abandon the aircraft, he ordered, "Do a quick check of our location, Ricky. What are we near? How far away from Latvia are we?"

As the two of them struggled with getting the aircraft under control and addressing the problems as best as one can at 34,000 feet, the SAM alarm came on again. Two more missiles had been launched at them from another SA-21 system and began streaking in the sky toward them.

"We are roughly 109 miles west of Moscow, and several hundred miles away from Latvia. Those SA-21s missiles are still at least four minutes away. What are your thoughts, Pappi?" Ricky asked, voice trembling. He knew the plane wasn't going to make it. He just wasn't sure when and how they needed to bail out.

"We're going to have to eject. The bomber is too badly damaged, and we've lost our stealth ability. I'm angling us toward Toropets. There are several forest preserves in that area. Try to steer your parachute toward this section here," he said, pointing to a green area on the map. "Let's try to meet up at this spot, near Lake Yassy."

Pappi paused for a second, then, seeing that the enemy missiles were now less than 60 seconds away from impact, he offered one final word of encouragement. "You can do this, Ricky. Just remember your training, and you'll get through this."

Then, without another thought, he hit both of their ejection buttons, sending them flying into the air, away from their crippled bomber. As he bolted through the air, wind whipping past his face as he waited for his parachute to open, he managed to see that Ricky's chute had just opened up. He was grateful that he looked to be OK. Seconds later, his own chute opened as well, making a snapping sound as it jerked him like a ragdoll.

"Dear God, did that hurt," he thought.

Once he got his bearings again, Pappi looked up and saw his B-2 still heading toward Latvia, trailing smoke as it flew. The two Russian missiles were still streaking toward it. They both abruptly impacted against the bomber, ripping it into a million little pieces.

As chunks of his bomber rained down to the ground below, he thought, "*Well, this is a rather inglorious way to end my Air Force career.*"

He'd flown dozens of combat missions and never lost an aircraft, but now in his last few months in the Air Force he had managed to lose a $2 billion bomber. While he continued to drift down toward the earth, he hoped that he wouldn't be captured and that maybe, just maybe, he could hold out long enough for a search-and-rescue team to recover him.

Chapter 34

Bunker Down

Moscow, Russia

National Defense Control Center

President Vladimir Petrov had been sitting in the Central Command Room, going over the progress of the war with his generals and senior advisors for the past hour. On the one hand, they had lost a lot of fighter aircraft throughout the day, which was troubling, considering these were some of their tier-one frontline aircraft. On the other hand, they had also shot down three NATO E-3 aircraft and seriously damaged a number American and NATO air bases. One analyst reported that over 160 fighter aircraft were destroyed on the ground alone.

The admirals were still upset over the loss of so many submarines and surface ships. They had effectively lost nearly 50% of the entire Russian navy in the opening day of the war. On the bright side, they had sunk the Supercarrier *George H.W. Bush* and several other critically important surface ships. The Americans didn't have as large a fleet as they had during the Cold War. Back then, they could absorb losses in carriers and other vessels. However, that was simply not the case in the budget-constrained environment the US found itself in now.

One of the Air Force officers was droning on about the effectiveness of the new S-400 and S-500 defensive systems. "We intercepted 98 cruise missiles throughout the day, preventing the Americans from causing crippling damage to our critical infrastructure and air bases. With the new Lenovo targeting computers, even the S-300 is seeing a significant improvement in effectiveness."

Petrov was glad to have the good news, but he was also getting bored listening to one officer after the other blather on. Then, as they were discussing tomorrow's objectives, an alarm blared inside the building. Everyone looked up at the ceiling, as if somehow a bomb was about to drop through it.

An officer walked up to the group. "Mr. President, we need to evacuate to the bunker immediately. Our radar just detected a B-2 bomber over Moscow," he explained hastily. Everyone stood up and walked briskly toward one of the stairways to head down to the bunker.

As they were all moving down the halls, the bomb hit the building. It knocked everyone to the ground, some falling down the stairs, others able to catch themselves by grasping at the railing. The entire building shook, and they heard a loud explosion. The lights flickered off, then back on before turning off again. The emergency lights kicked in, and everyone began to regain their composure, trying to figure out what to do next.

One of the guards in Petrov's protective detail helped the world leader off the floor. "We need to keep going this direction," he said as he pointed toward one of the doors back up on the ground floor level. They ran as a group up the stairs and through that door. The guard continued to lead them to a side entrance that would bring them to one of the underground tunnels connecting to the Kremlin.

The guards then separated the leaders into two groups. Following their continuation-of-government plan, the President and the military leaders were ushered in one direction and the other political figureheads were whisked off another way. Petrov and the military men were soon racing through the tunnels underneath the city. Within five minutes, they had made their way to a command bunker that was somewhere between the two buildings, roughly 300 feet underground.

As President Petrov walked into the alternative command bunker, he saw officers and other specialists getting the room up and running, turning computers and monitors on and making sure all the systems were operational. Until they could determine that the President was safe, they would operate out of this bunker, which could run the war, if necessary.

President Petrov walked up to one of the military officers. "I want to know what in the world just hit our building. Is the threat over?!"

Petrov's cheeks were red, and a vein on the side of his neck was visibly pulsating. Here these guys had just been bragging to him about how effective the new air defense system had been, and then the building alarms started going off. *"The officers better not be lying to me about how effective the system is, or someone is going to be shot,"* he thought.

An Army officer dared to take the question. "The defense building has been hit with what appears to have been a bunker-busting bomb. It hit the east tower, causing substantial damage. Preliminary reports show that the Central Command Center, where we had all been meeting, was not damaged in the blast. However, until the fires can be brought under control, I highly recommend that we continue to operate out of this command bunker for the time being."

Everyone seemed pleased that only part of the building had been hit, and not the critical command center in the center of the structure. Had that room been hit, it could have killed them all, along with a lot of the mission-critical personnel currently on duty.

Another Army officer spoke up. "Mr. President, I have a report from the Moscow aircraft defense command on what happened."

Petrov signaled for everyone to take a seat, so the officer could bring them up to speed on what had happened.

Clearing his throat, the Army colonel began, "The S-500 commander identified a B-2 stealth bomber and engaged it with two missiles. The radar system also identified a total of four guided bombs that we've now determined to be bunker-busting bombs. These were most likely the American GBU-57B, which is a 30,000-pound bomb with roughly a 5,000-pound warhead."

The room was silent as they all realized how close to death they had just been.

The colonel continued, "The S-500 was able to intercept two of the bombs, destroying them over the city. A third bomb hit the defense building, and the fourth bomb was apparently thrown off course and landed in a residential area, a couple of blocks away from Red Square. We are still assessing the damage to the residential area, but we expect casualties to be high."

Petrov interrupted, "—What about the B-2? Did we shoot it down?"

The colonel nodded. "Yes, Mr. President. The bomber was damaged by the first missile from the S-500 battery. The bomber's stealth system had nearly defeated our traditional targeting systems, but the Lenovo targeting computer was able to get the missile within range of the bomber, causing significant damage to it. This destroyed the bomber's stealth capabilities and a S-400 battery roughly 100 kilometers away was able to reacquire the B-2 as a target. They fired two missiles, which successfully destroyed the bomber. The two pilots bailed out of the aircraft, and we currently have search parties out looking for them."

Everyone in the room was excited by this news. They had successfully shot down an American B-2 over Russia and intercepted three of the four bombs dropped on their beloved city. The new Lenovo targeting computer really was living up to the hype of its creator. The missile still had to have an initial lock on an aircraft to work, but this was promising.

Petrov smiled, letting everyone in the room know that he was pleased with the success of the shootdown of the B-2 and the S-500's performance. If this was the best the Americans could throw at him, then he was confident Russia would win this conflict. If the Americans thought his country was reeling now, he couldn't wait to see how they were going to respond to the next phase of operations.

Chapter 35

Once in a Movie

Toropets, Russia

400 Kilometers West of Moscow

As Lieutenant Colonel Rob Fortney descended below 7,000 feet, he started to get a good picture of the landmarks below. At 2200 hours, it was dark, but it he could still make out some of the fast-approaching landscape by the light of the full moon. He saw Lake Yassy, which he had pointed out to Ricky, and he knew exactly where he needed to go to meet up with his copilot. From the darkness below, he also saw the lights from several buildings and houses. His main concern now was making sure he steered himself toward an acceptable landing spot and did not injure himself.

With the ground quickly getting closer and closer, he bent his knees slightly, just as he had been taught. As the terrain rushed up toward him, he landed and rolled to the side, just as they had been told a million times. The technique worked; he spun and then quickly detached his parachute, rolling it up. Once he had it gathered in his arms, he ran toward the forested area, where he stashed it in some bushes. In the daylight it would be found, but at least he had hidden it from plain sight. Now he needed to make his way through the forest, toward the edge of the lake they had identified as their rally point. Then he could wait for his partner to arrive.

After trudging through the woods in the relative dark for about thirty minutes, he came to the area of the lake he believed to be roughly where they were supposed to meet and waited. After nearly twenty minutes, he decided to try to use his emergency radio. He was reluctant, since the signal could be triangulated and give away his position if the Russians were listening for it. However, seeing that they were in the middle of nowhere, he thought the chances of that happening were relatively small.

Pappi made a couple of attempts to establish radio contact with Ricky but received no reply. Finally, he heard something faintly, but then the sound grew louder. Dogs…they were barking loudly, and then he heard men's voices yelling something in Russian. He wished he could understand what they were saying. It was at that moment that Pappi decided he needed to get moving, even if it meant leaving his copilot behind. He couldn't sit there waiting while those dogs and enemy soldiers got closer.

As Pappi made his way through the woods, he came across a small stream. Rather than trying to ford the stream and continue to move through the woods in the direction of Belarus or Latvia, he waded in and proceeded to move with the water. He hoped that by walking through the stream, it would throw the dogs off his scent. After a mile or so of walking in the stream, he planned to return to dry land and resume his overland trek to freedom.

"I saw it in a movie once, so it has to work, right?" he thought. Although it had been nearly two decades since he had been through the ultra-intensive SERE school, which prepares pilots and Special Forces to escape and evade capture behind enemy lines, he thought he vaguely remembered them telling him to do something like this as well.

Three hours went by. His feet were killing him. The sound of the dogs began to drift further away until he no longer heard them. Looking at his watch, he knew it would be dawn in a few more hours. He needed to find a place to rest for a while; he wanted to continue, but after five hours since ejecting from his bomber, he was exhausted. He had been in the air flying for nearly seven hours before he was shot down and had been awake for nearly that long before his flight. The stress and the long hours he had been working these past several weeks was starting to overtake him. He also knew if he were captured, his ordeal would only be beginning, which was why he needed to find a good hiding spot to set himself up and rest.

Chapter 36

Breaking News

"This is Brett Mitchel, coming to you live from Moscow's Red Square, where less than ten minutes ago, the National Defense Control Center just a few blocks away was hit by an American bomb or missile of some sort. A projectile also appears to have hit a nearby residential building, killing hundreds, perhaps even thousands of civilians in their homes. As you can see, there are fires in several sections of Moscow from what we are being told was an American bombing raid on the capital. The images we are seeing are just horrific. Hundreds of building have been evacuated, and smoke continues to billow out of the subway lines here. Stay tuned to RT News, where we'll continue to keep you updated on the latest developments as we get them."

Images of the bombing attack were spreading across the various news outlets and social media sites. They kept showing the part of the National Defense Control Center where the bomb had penetrated the building. The flames and destruction made for good viewer ratings. The apartment building was probably shown even more frequently; there were a lot of clips of rescue workers pulling body after body out of the wreckage of a giant smoldering ruin. As the saying goes in the news, "If it bleeds, it leads." This was especially true when the victims included children and the elderly.

Chapter 37
Retreat

Ukraine

Villages of Voloshynivka and Baryshivka

It was 0200 as the last soldiers of Second Platoon, Nemesis Troop, loaded into their remaining vehicles. They were under a tight timeline to get out of the area and fall back to Kiev. The order had finally come down to get out of Dodge—it couldn't have come at a better time. The Russians had pulled back after a brutally failed attack. Childers, for one, was glad someone had finally ordered them to retreat. He had been concerned that Lieutenant Colonel Munch would have had them fight on until they were either surrounded or completely overrun.

Second Lieutenant Taylor hopped into the LATV and signaled for the driver to start driving. Childers looked over at the LT. "So, what did you learn from the colonel?" he asked, hoping to see if he had a better picture of what was going on with the war. It had been a rough 24 hours, and they still had no idea what was going on in the world. All they really knew was they were at war with Russia. They were as starved for information as they were for sleep.

"I wasn't able to learn much. What had been passed down to him was that all NATO forces were being pulled back to Kiev, where we've been ordered to make our stand. He did say that the rest of his division should be in Kiev in the next few hours," explained Taylor. He sighed deeply. "If it's all right with you, Sergeant, I'm going to try and catch a little bit of sleep. I don't think I can keep my eyes open any longer." He leaned his head against the side of the vehicle, falling asleep in mere seconds.

"What I wouldn't give to know what in the world is going on right now," remarked Sergeant Childers out of frustration, speaking to no one in particular. The private who was driving the vehicle just nodded and grunted in agreement. Childers let out an enormous yawn. He just wanted to get to Kiev in one piece, and hopefully find a quiet place to sleep.

****

Lieutenant Colonel Brian Munch rubbed his eyes. His ragtag command had finally arrived in Kiev a little after 0420 in the morning, exhausted and beaten up. The Russians had only tried to attack them once by air. A group of Su-27s had swooped in and taken out several of his tanks and Stryker vehicles. He'd also lost two of his Avenger air defense vehicles, but not before they'd shot down two Su-27s. He felt lucky the Russian armored forces hadn't pressed home the attack. If he were the Russian commander in charge, he certainly would have, but he was glad they had given him a bit of a reprieve.

Once they entered the outskirts of the city, the first thing Lieutenant Colonel Munch ordered the units to do was to find out where the other NATO forces were. He wanted to know if his forces were needed elsewhere before they could get settled in and finally get some rest.

When they entered Boryspil, Munch saw the devastation of the international terminal and the NATO side of the airport. He also observed that a German armored brigade was well-entrenched and ready to meet the Russians when they showed up. He also saw the remnants of the American units, mostly the 82nd Airborne's 2nd Brigade Combat Team, which had arrived the day before hostilities started. The 173rd Airborne Brigade Combat Team, was still held up at the Pryluky Air Base.

As they passed through the German/American positions, Colonel Munch ran into a US brigadier general, Matt Fenzol, the Deputy Commander of the 82nd Airborne. "I want to commend you on your gallant effort in stopping the Russians the day before. I want your soldiers to take up a position in the forested area around Prolisky and get some rest as soon as possible. That's an order. I'll be holding a leadership meeting at 1300 hours, so I want you and your officers to be present, but not before you get at least four hours of sleep. I must insist that you all get some sleep…otherwise, you'll all be useless."

Colonel Munch didn't fight General Fenzol at all. Most of his ragtag group had been awake and in combat for nearly 48 hours. He needed them rested and ready to meet the Russian force that would probably hit their positions sometime this evening.

****

Sergeant Childers made sure the rest of Second Platoon had their vehicle camouflage netting up and their vehicles hidden from any potential air attacks. Once that was done and the bulk of his troops were getting some much-needed rest, he found a quiet spot where he could also get a few hours of shut-eye. He crawled underneath the LATV he had been sitting in for most of the evening and morning and quickly fell asleep.

Several hours later, he was jolted awake by the violent shaking of the earth by a bomb that went off nearby. As his senses came back to him, he heard the unmistakable sound of an explosion and someone yelling that they were under an air attack. Luke grabbed his rifle off the ground next to him, searched for one of the slit trenches that the engineers had hastily dug a few hours ago, and swiftly dove in. As he lay there in anticipation, he could hear multiple jets overhead, several heavy-caliber machine guns firing away, and the unmistakable sound of more bombs falling toward them.

Boom, boom, crump! Bang!

Flame, dirt and shrapnel were flying in all directions, cutting off radio antennas on the vehicles, ripping flesh from bone, and damaging everything in the camp. The attack didn't last long, but it accomplished its goal of damaging the American positions and killing more soldiers.

Once the explosions ended, Childers got out of the trench. A couple of his soldiers were pointing upward, and he followed their line-of-sight to see a Russian pilot slowly drifting to the ground on a parachute. Apparently, his plane had been shot down during the attack. As he drifted into the woods, several of the soldiers in his platoon ran after him.

"Come on, Sergeant Childers, we need to capture him!" shouted one of the soldiers as he took off running toward the woods.

Luke knew he'd better go with these young soldiers and supervise the capture of this Russian aviator before his soldiers beat him to death. As he ran after them, he came to the clearing. Sure enough, he saw four of his soldiers kicking and stomping on the Russian pilot as he tried to curl up in a ball to protect himself. "Enough!" he yelled. "All of you, back off right now before I write you up and strip you of your rank!" Sergeant Childers yelled as he pulled one of the soldiers back and threw another one to the ground.

One of his soldiers yelled back at him, "He just attacked us! Why are you protecting him, Luke?"

Now Luke was truly incensed. His vision turned red as his blood boiled over. He signaled for the Russian pilot to stay on the ground for a second while the other soldiers around him looked like they wanted to go right back to beating him. "First off, don't ever address me by my first name! It's either Sergeant or Sergeant First Class! Do you understand?!" he yelled at the young man in an effort to snap his brain back into being a soldier and not some vengeance-driven animal.

The soldier lowered his head, realizing he had screwed up. "Yes, Sergeant. I'm sorry. I do not know what came over me," he said.

"I know you're all angry. I understand and respect that—but we are American soldiers. As such, you will not beat a prisoner. This pilot—," he said, pointing down at the Russian, "is just doing his job, just like you and me. He's not some raghead terrorist. He's a professional soldier like the rest of us, and you will afford him the same courtesies you would hope to receive as a prisoner. Do you all understand?" Sergeant Childers lectured, making a point of drilling this fact into their heads.

"This is not how American soldiers should act," he thought. *"I certainly won't let it happen under my watch."*

"Now, let's get this guy back to the tactical operations center and let the intelligence guys see what they can get from him," he said, extending his hand to the Russian pilot to lift him to his feet. The soldiers nodded in agreement, grabbed their weapons and escorted the pilot back to their area with Sergeant Childers in the lead.

****

Brigadier General Matt Fenzol was furious. His soldiers had been attacked by Russian aircraft for the better part of thirty-six hours. The last three hours had seen a dramatic increase in air attacks, and he had little in the way of air defense capabilities to stop them. One of the captains in his operations center had told him that one of the Avenger vehicles had just shot down a Su-25 ground attack aircraft a few minutes ago.

The Su-25 Frogfoot was designed to provide close air support, similar to the American A-10 Warthog. These planes carried several antipersonnel rocket pods, antitank missiles, and 500 lbs. bombs. It was also an armored plane like the A-10, so it could take a lot of damage without being shot down. With near air supremacy, the Russians began using a lot more Su-25 and Su-24 ground attack aircraft against the German and American positions. They had greater quantities of these aircraft, and if they lost a few, it wouldn't hurt them nearly as bad as tier-one aircraft losses would. Those were being saved for the more dangerous missions and dog fighting against the growing presence of NATO fighters.

As BG Fenzol looked around his temporary command center, he was outraged. He had been promised greater air support several hours ago by those bureaucrats back at EUCOM, and here he was, still getting attacked. "Where the hell is my air cover?!" he yelled at one of his operations officers.

The major who was running the operations group spoke up. "I just got off the horn with one of the air battle managers in the E-3s. He told me that they have a flight of F-22s that's just now coming on station near Kiev. They should be in orbit now for the next several hours, or until their ordnance is expended." As he answered, Major Woods couldn't hide his own disgust that they were not on station an hour ago like they'd said they would be.

Major Tyrone Woods hated working for General Fenzol. Being a Mormon, he disliked working for a commander who often used curse words and belittled those around him. Everyone in the operations group was doing their best. Three days ago, when they'd first arrived in Kiev, Colonel Jelanski had been the S3, but he had been killed during one of the many Russian air attacks, along with his deputy and the next person below him. That left Major Woods as the only senior officer left from the S3 office, forcing him to be General Fenzol's S3 until a higher-ranked guy showed up.

Fenzol didn't particularly care for his new S3 either, but they had to work together, at least for a while. "*I'm not sure our joint US/German command will stand up to the Russian divisions that are amassing less than twenty miles away*," he worried. The Russians had been hitting them hard with airpower all night and into the morning; it was only a matter of time until they launched their main attack.

"Major Woods, what's the status on Second and Third Brigade Combat Teams from the 1st Armored Division? Are they in Kiev yet?"

"Yes, Sir. We made contact with the Third BCT's S3. They just finished offloading their tanks on the west side of the city. Lieutenant Colonel Wightman said they were going to get underway and head for our position within the hour. He gave us an ETA of 1300 hours," Woods said, hoping this might appease his hot-headed commander.

BG Fenzol nodded in approval. "Good job, Major Woods. Stay in contact with them and see what the ETA of the Second BCT is as well. Let them know that the Russians are most likely going to launch their attack shortly. We desperately need their tanks if we're going to hold this position," he explained.

Brigadier General Matt Fenzol knew he had a reputation as a tough nut, but this was the 82nd Airborne. They were paratroopers. If people got their feelings hurt or bent out of shape by his hard-charging attitude, then they just weren't cut out for the Airborne. He turned to his command sergeant major and asked, "What's the status on the ammunition front?"

In the Army, the three major functions a first sergeant and sergeant major were responsible for were "beans, bullets, and soldiers." At that exact moment, ammunition was a bigger concern than food. They had been expending a lot of it lately, and the NATO supply lines hadn't exactly been established yet.

"We're OK for the moment, General, but we'll need a resupply if the enemy does launch any sort of major attack. We blew through a lot of Stinger and heavy weapons' ammo trying to shoot down these Russian helicopters and attack planes," the command sergeant major explained as he spat out a stream of tobacco juice on the dirt floor of their command center.

"Stay on it, Sergeant Major. Make sure Supply is getting us what we need," the general responded, knowing that if anyone could make things happen, it was his sergeant major.

It was time for his officer's call. He could hear the officers talking and gathering outside the command tent. He needed to get out there and get these guys their orders and make sure everyone knew what they were supposed to be doing before the Russians launched their attack. It was going to be another long, rough day.

He lifted the flap to the command tent and walked out to a small gaggle of probably 40 officers. These were the troop and company commanders of the various infantry, armor and scout units that made up his temporary ragtag force of roughly 11,000 US and German soldiers. When the officers returned to their units, they would disseminate the information to the officers and NCOs who weren't able to attend. Someone had to man the shop and keep the soldiers in line.

"Listen up. I know everyone is starved for news of what's going on in the world and with the war in general. I don't have a lot of news, but I'll pass on what I do have after we go over today's plans. The S2 says there are roughly three Russian divisions less than twenty miles from our position, and we anticipate them launching their attack anytime. I want your men to be ready for it. We've also received word, thanks to Major Woods, that 1st Armor's Third BCT should arrive in our lines within the next hour."

The officers were all smiles at this news. A couple even clapped jokingly. "Calm down, guys," barked the general. "We have more information to push out. Listen, we've been ordered to hold our position while the rest of our NATO allies continue to rush more troops to Kiev. 1st Armor's Second BCT should arrive in our lines by the end of the evening, along with the British 12th Armored Infantry Brigade. That will bring our manpower up to roughly 23,300 soldiers. However, things are going to get rough and nasty before they get better."

One of the captains from the Second Cavalry Troop that had folded into his ragtag command raised his hand, signaling that he had a question to ask.

"Go ahead, Captain," said the general.

"Sir, my unit's been slugging it out with the Russians since they crossed the demarcation line. I've lost nearly half of my soldiers, vehicles, and equipment, and we have absolutely no idea what in the world is going on, other than a crap ton of Russians are trying to kill us. Can you give us any insight I can pass along to my soldiers? My guys have tried using their smartphones to get information from the mainstream media, Twitter, and Facebook, but as you know, the cell towers have been taken offline since the start of hostilities," he said, dejected, exhausted, and frustrated.

The general hung his head down for a second, collecting his own thoughts. "We were passed along an intelligence summary from EUCOM a couple of hours ago. I'll go ahead and read off some of it for you guys. Some of this is still highly classified, so no one write anything down. Just pass things on verbally." He then opened his notepad and began to read aloud to them.

"Classified SECRET: Carrier *George H.W. Bush* sunk by Russian submarines at the entrance to the Black Sea. US Carrier Strike Group sank eleven Russian submarines and nine Russian surface warfare ships. Navy casualties are listed as high."

Audible gasps and swearing could be heard by most of the soldiers and officers present. It took a minute for things to quiet down before BG Fenzol continued.

"Classified TOP SECRET/SCI: Russian saboteurs temporarily disabled Europe THAAD missile systems during opening hours of conflict.

"Classified SECRET: US Air Force Base Ramstein hit by Russian cruise missile attack. One hundred and forty US aircraft destroyed on the ground.

"Classified SECRET: US Air Force Base Spangdahlem hit by Russian cruise missile attack. Ninety US aircraft destroyed on the ground.

"Classified CONFIDENTIAL: US Air Force stealth bombers bombed Russian National Defense Control Center in Moscow.

"Classified CONFIDENTIAL: US Air Force bombs numerous Russia air bases across Western Russia.

"Classified CONFIDENTIAL: US Navy destroys Russian Black Sea Fleet base and headquarters.

"Classified SECRET: US Navy sinks thirteen Russian submarines in the North Sea.

"Classified SECRET: Russian submarines sink five US Navy transports in the Atlantic, ferrying equipment from the US to NATO bases in Europe.

"Unclassified: US media reports US government caught completely by surprise by Russian sneak attack."

More gasps, cursing and grumbling could be heard from the NCOs and officers. It was a bit of a shock to hear how bad the war was starting out. Most of the men and women present had spent their entire careers fighting Islamic extremists, terrorists, and the Taliban. The Department of Defense had not done a very good job of keeping the force ready and trained to fight a conventional war against a regular well-equipped and determined army. They were paying the price for it now.

"OK, that's roughly the gist of the report and what's important. I know it's not a lot to go on, but it's the best I can give you guys for the time being. I know it doesn't sound good, but remember, we're in the first three days of this war. America's just getting started, and we are going to kick the crap out of these Russian bastards. Now, get back to your units and give 'em hell." As he dismissed his officers, he could see from the looks on their faces that the news had shaken some of them. It was a lot to take in. He understood; he still couldn't believe the Navy had lost a supercarrier.

Chapter 38
Fake News-ageddon

Minsk, Belarus
Minsk State Linguistic University

In the subbasement of the Linguistic University, a group of fifty hackers were hard at work on their computer terminals. Each hacker was piped into one of the fastest mainframe supercomputer systems in the world, maximizing their productivity with dual 32-inch computer screens. The supercomputer had been built in secret over the past twelve months and had only just come online two weeks ago in preparation for Operation Redworm.

Thirty of these hackers were spending close to eighteen hours a day creating and then promoting thousands upon thousands of fake news articles across Twitter, Instagram, Snapchat, and Facebook, in what was perhaps the first 21st century information warfare campaign against NATO.

As Nestor Petyaev, one of the chief hacking supervisors, walked into the room, he felt a sense of pride when he saw the headlines splashed across the screens all around him. "Russia Invades Norway and Poland" sure made for good news—that one had received a lot of clicks. "Fascist German Forces Bomb Ukraine" had not been quite as successful but was still making headway.

There were two stories that were taking on a life of their own. Nestor walked over to one of his hackers and saw several different versions of the headline "Turkey Withdraws from NATO." He patted his comrade on the back.

"Ivan, I thought you would like to know that your story is having an impact on the real world."

"Oh?" asked Ivan with a smile.

"Yes, there are demonstrations popping up all over Turkey. Some of the citizens are marching, demanding that the government not get involved in the war, and counterdemonstrations are urging the government to honor its treaty obligation. Perhaps you can incorporate some of the coverage of the antiwar marches in with your stories?" suggested Nestor.

"Ok, I'll get right on that," answered Ivan, eagerly.

Nestor walked over to another colleague, who was working on a story about the Iranians closing the Straits of Hormuz.

"Igor, did you know that you are actually writing a true story?" Nestor asked jovially.

"What do you mean, Boss?" wondered Igor.

"Well, in response to the press that we have been pushing, the Iranians are actually moving more of their warships to the sea. Our gossip is becoming truth." Nestor smirked.

"This is great news. I will incorporate some of the real reporting in my next set of articles," Igor explained proudly.

The group was also busy posting propaganda videos. They had pieced the footage together from clips given to them from helmet cameras from Spetsnaz raids, frontline soldiers, fighter combat cameras—anything that showed the Russian military winning a battle or air strike against NATO. They also began promoting any videos of the apartment building and subway stations that had been accidentally destroyed by the American bunker-busting bomb the night before.

President Petrov had visited the hospitals to meet with the victims and made several appearances on TV, pleading for the Americans and NATO to keep the war conventional and not kill innocent civilians. Those videos were gaining a lot of traction around the world, so they began to run a lot of info pieces on the victims. Their entire goal with pushing this narrative was to show the Americans and

NATO as the aggressors and the Russians as the victims. The images of the casualties from the now famous "Moscow Massacre" were compelling.

The video of the US Supercarrier *George H.W. Bush* sinking was a particularly potent video that had gone viral the second it was posted. The sight of hundreds of sailors being rescued amongst a sea of floating dead bodies was truly horrifying to the American public.

While the media arm continued to propagate their material, a separate group of hackers was breaking into the French, German, Italian, and Spanish transportation systems. They were interfering with train schedules, communications, and traffic signals—anything that would cause chaos and confusion in the Allied nations. Most of their attacks were being carried out through the use of botnets, which would capture network-connected devices and then slave those devices to act as a collective botnet army in order to accomplish DDoS attacks. When combined, these attacks were causing the electronic infrastructure of the Allies to grind to a halt.

Several of the more gifted hackers in this division were given the particularly hard task of coopting the companies' industrial control systems. In one case, they had successfully taken control of a train engine on an extremely vital German rail line, causing the engine to burn out while it was in transit. Then they'd disabled the switching station so that the engineers in the control rooms couldn't remotely divert trains around the affected track. This had caused a series of delays.

In the US, the hackers had taken control of the Astoria Gas Generating Station in New York State and forced the generator to spin out of control until it blew up and destroyed the plant. Ten workers had been killed, nineteen others injured. The loss of 1,296 megawatts of power was a huge hit to the city of New York and to the state as a whole. The hackers had also hit four other power generators, which had caused a series of rolling blackouts across much of the East Coast and parts of the Midwest. Power companies were scrambling to get old turbines turned on to pick up the slack and restore power.

While the hackers were sowing chaos on the internet against the NATO members, the disinformation campaign was having the desired effect amongst the population. Public opinion against the war was soaring in Europe, and the US media couldn't help themselves in trying to pin all the failings of the allies on President Gates.

To make matters worse, two Spetsnaz teams carried out a devastating attack against two liquid natural gas terminals—the Dominion Cove Point LNG depot in Maryland, and the Cheniere's Sabine Pass LNG station in Louisiana. The Spetsnaz members shot their way through the perimeter security of both facilities and then blew the terminals up using C-4 explosives that they detonated remotely. Following the attack, the two attack teams blended right back into the population and disappeared, at least until the FBI could hunt them down.

The destruction of these two terminals cut the US's ability to export liquid natural gas to Europe by 68%. This was a huge loss, especially considering Europe had been cut off from importing additional liquid natural gas from Russia once the hostilities had officially begun. The Continent would now be thrown into a widespread gas shortage.

Chapter 39
Old Friend

Donetsk, East Ukraine

Lieutenant General Mikhail Chayko was not happy with the progress of his forward units. They had been stopped from securing Kiev twice in the last twenty-four hours, and now the Americans and British had rushed in two armored brigades. Securing the city just became a lot more challenging…not impossible, but certainly a lot more difficult.

He sent a second message to the 4th Guard's Tank Division, the 2nd Guard's Motor Rifle Division and the 6th Tank Brigade. "We have to secure Kiev by morning tomorrow," he directed. "It's imperative that we drive out the Americans now, before they hurry any additional combat forces into Europe."

Lieutenant General Chayko wasn't sure that all his comrades were pulling their weight, but his Air Force counterpart had tried to reassure his fears. "A major air operation is well underway," he asserted. "Your armored units will have continuous air support for the next twenty-four hours while you secure Kiev."

He tried to remain optimistic about their chances. As Mikhail sat there looking at the various maps, an old friend walked in. His face lit up, and he immediately passed his comrade a flask of vodka. "Admiral Ivan Vitko, it's good to see you. I feared you had been killed the other day when your base had been hit by the Americans."

Admiral Vitko took the flask and downed several large gulps before handing it back and taking a seat opposite his friend. "Thank you, comrade. It has been a long couple of days. The Americans will have to try harder if they want to kill me," he said, snickering.

After only a moment, his face suddenly turned very serious again. "General Chayko, I wanted to talk with you about something of great urgency," he said, lowering his voice as if discussing a secret.

Chayko sighed. "*Ugh...I'm already under a lot of pressure from Moscow,*" he thought. He suddenly had the feeling that Vitko was about to drop another problem in his lap, and he didn't have time for that.

"As you can imagine, Admiral, I'm dealing with my own problems. What's so urgent that you traveled all the way here to meet me in person?" he asked tentatively, not sure he really wanted the answer.

Vitko pulled out a map and placed it on the table between them. "This is where the NATO fleet is currently located. As you know, most of my fleet has been sunk. I still have two *Oscar* submarines and a couple of *Kilos* trying to stay alive right now. This here is the problem," he said, pointing to the map.

"The Americans have moved a second Marine expeditionary unit to the Black Sea. It will give them close to 7,000 Marines. I believe the Marines are going to try and launch a seaborne invasion along the coast of Ukraine. This could present a massive problem for you, my friend," Vitko said as he pulled his own flask of vodka out and took a large drink from it.

"If I'd known he had his own vodka, I wouldn't have offered him some of mine," Chayko thought, rather annoyed.

"This could certainly be a problem," he responded aloud. "Thank you for bringing this to my attention. How do you propose we handle this, if you have no fleet and I have to keep my forces focused on capturing Kiev?" he asked hoping he had a solution.

Smiling, Vitko pulled out another piece of paper. "This. This is how I propose we solve the problem. That, and of course, I need some of your air power," he said. What he had been pointing to was a dossier on the new drone that the

Russian Air Force was going to unveil shortly against NATO, the Zhukov. They were being held as a surprise, which was why they hadn't been used yet, but there would certainly be merits for using them now.

The new Russian drone system was very similar to the American Reaper. It was designed to be a standoff missile platform with three hard points on each wing for missiles. It could be used in an antitank role or anti-air role.

"Comrade, we need to defeat this American battlegroup in the Black Sea before they land their Marines and the Americans send in more ships," said the admiral. "They already have a second aircraft carrier on the way. What I'd like to propose is to hit the Americans with a missile swarm attack—but of course, I would need your aircraft for that." He took another pull of vodka from his flask.

Chayko rubbed his stubbled chin, thinking about this. While he wanted to keep his aircraft focused on ground support and maintaining air superiority, he also recognized the importance of keeping the American Navy out of the Black Sea.

"Tell me, Comrade, how would this missile swarm attack work?" he asked, wanting more details.

"I'd need you to commit your fighters to head toward the NATO forces in Romania and engage them. While they are fighting in the air, your Backfire bombers would be equipped with anti-ship missiles and once in range, would release them all at once. Your bombers would never be in any real danger because their missiles can be fired beyond the range of the American naval surface-to-air missile systems."

The admiral continued, "Following in behind the cruise missiles, your Su-27s and Su-34s would then move into range of their smaller, yet still dangerous anti-ship missiles and release them as well, further adding to the swarm of missiles that would be headed to the American fleet. The overarching goal is to overwhelm their defenses and sink them."

"You mentioned my Zhukovs. How did you envision using them?"

Smiling, Admiral Vitko answered, "Yes, this would be the big surprise. We would have them fly low, right at ground level, beneath the air battle taking place between your fighters and the NATO fighters. Once they've maneuvered behind them, we turn them around, raise them up about 100 meters, and then fire off their air-to-air missiles. The NATO aircraft will be so focused on dealing with your fighters, they will never suspect that drones had been flown in behind them. They should easily shoot down a number of additional NATO aircraft, which again, should help aid in your efforts to secure air supremacy over Ukraine." The corners of his lips curled up in a devilish smile.

Chayko thought about the plans as he looked at the map across from where they were seated. It was a risky move committing so many of his aircraft and bombers to one battle, but if he won, it could be a decisive victory and help end the war sooner.

"All right, Comrade. You've sold me on this little plan of yours. Let's work together now to iron out the details and make it happen," he said, raising his own flask in salute.

Chapter 40

Vampires, Vampires, Vampires

Fifteen Miles off the Coast of Constanța, Romania

Admiral James Munch had moved his command from the carrier *George H.W. Bush* to the *Gettysburg* within hours after his flagship had sunk. The *Gettysburg* was a Ticonderoga-class guided missile cruiser, carrying 122 Tomahawk cruise missiles, which packed some serious firepower. It was a formidable warship. Together with the *Arleigh Burke* destroyers traveling with them, it had an incredible air defense capability. Despite the tremendous losses he had just endured, Admiral Munch was feeling hopeful about their position, especially given that the Truman Carrier Strike Group was in the process of transitioning to the Bosporus Strait and would join them tomorrow.

The Romanians, for their part, had sent their three frigates to join his fleet, along with a couple of corvettes. None of their ships packed any sort of serious firepower, though they could perform picket duty at the outskirts of the fleet, which is where he had them positioned. Everything seemed to be well-prepared...

At roughly 0122 in the morning, an American E-3 that was on station loitering over Bucharest, Romania, suddenly detected 60 Russian Backfire bombers lifting off from several bases deep inside Russia. The radar operator, who had been feeling rather sleepy, was jolted into a very alert state. As he continued to scan the air, he spotted 30 Su-34s and 35 Su-27s heading toward the direction of the naval fleet.

What the radar operator didn't see was the twelve Russian Zhukov drones, which were flying at less than 100 feet above the ground. Each one was carrying six air-to-air missiles to surprise the American fighters.

As the enemy air armada began to amass near the Russian border, the air battle manager aboard the E-3 vectored in two squadrons of F-15s and a squadron of F/A-18s that had been flying combat air patrol over Romania and the fleet. While the American fighters were headed toward the Russian bombers, three squadrons of Russian MiG-31s and a squadron of the new MiG-35s that no one in the US military knew were operational also headed in the same direction, ready to join the melee. Then, completely undetected, a squadron of Su-57 stealth fighters were also guided to the battle by two Russian AWACS aircraft, ready to silently swoop in and snipe at the Americans.

The air battle in the night sky was shaping up to be one of the largest air battles in modern warfare. While the NATO and Russian fighters began to engage each other, each of the Backfire bombers fired off all three of their anti-ship cruise missiles from their maximum range, and then quickly turned around to head back to base. Altogether, the 60 bombers let loose a combined 180 anti-ship missiles at the American fleet.

In response to the massive wave of missiles streaming through the air, the Aegis-equipped destroyers and Ticonderoga cruisers began to fire off their missile interceptors. Meanwhile, the Russian Su-27s and Su-34s dove in at max speed to try and attack the American fleet. As they approached the ships, nearly a third of the Russian fighter bombers were shot down by the American fighters; fireballs lit up the night sky. However, the ones that got through fired off their anti-ship missiles. This added another 260 missiles for the American fleet to try and stop.

As the USS *Gettysburg* launched its last missile interceptors, Admiral James Munch had a stark moment of realization. *"My God...the remnants of my carrier strike group are most likely going to be sunk."* He saw himself going down in naval history as the only US admiral to have lost an entire strike group during combat. It wouldn't even matter how courageously they fought at this point—they simply didn't have enough missile interceptors or point defense weapons to shoot down all of the incoming missiles.

Every naval analysis group had warned that this was a serious vulnerability. In an age of cheap anti-ship missiles and cheaper throw-away missile platforms, the more technologically superior weapon systems could simply be overwhelmed by a missile swarm.

Hundreds of missiles could be seen exploding in the air as they approached the fleet from various angles and heights. Then, as if in slow motion, the missiles began to impact against their targets. In the span of seven minutes, the remaining anti-ship missiles, which still numbered in excess of two hundred, began to find their marks. At first, it was the outer picket ships that were hit, exploding in spectacular fashion as the missiles ripped through the bulkheads of the ships. Then, the missiles started to strike the larger more important ships, the Ticonderoga guided missile cruisers and the Marine amphibious assault ships. Most of the ships were hit on their sides, some so many times that they burst apart, blowing chunks of debris into the air. The others had so much damage to the superstructure of the ships that they simply had no hope of staying above water.

In minutes, the vaunted ships of the *George H.W. Bush* Strike Group slipped beneath the waves with thousands of crew members, never to see the dawn of a new day. It was the single worst naval loss since World War II.

While the American fleet was being overrun by cruise missile explosions, the twelve Zhukov drones slipped past the American fighters, dancing in aerial combat nearby. The drones proceeded to fire off their six air-to-air missiles, throwing the allied formations into chaos. The sudden appearance of seventy-two missiles from behind the NATO aircraft caught them off guard, resulting in the expedient shootdown of 48 additional NATO fighters that might otherwise have lived to fight another day.

By the end of the multi-hour air and naval battle, the Russians had lost 92 aircraft in all. However, NATO had lost 103 aircraft, along with the remaining American warships in the Black Sea. The various amphibious assault ships carrying the 22nd Marine Expeditionary Unit or MEU had also been sunk during the missile swarm attack.

Fortunately, roughly half of the Marines had been able to get to their amphibious vehicles and landing craft and managed to evacuate the ships before they went down. While they were unable to grab most of their equipment, they did manage to escape with their lives. Despite their valiant effort, of the roughly 3,500 Marines in the MEU, 921 of them still lost their lives during the attack. The survivors made best speed in their vehicles for the Romanian coast.

The *Truman* Carrier Battle Group had not yet entered the Bosporus Strait. After the battle, they halted their forward progress. The 6th Fleet Commander would have to reassess whether or not the Black Sea should continue to be contested. They might have to cede it to Russia.

Chapter 41

The Last Straw

Washington, D.C.

White House, Situation Room

The President was starting to think his generals and senior advisors either didn't know what was going on in Europe or were just incompetent. On top of everything else, things were heating up in Iran with the Straits of Hormuz now. Moreover, the Chinese were making waves about bringing Taiwan back into the fold and were posturing toward Vietnam and Myanmar. The world situation was feeling very volatile.

Europe, however, was the immediate problem. President Gates knew he needed to think of solutions to the problems, but he couldn't help but get lost in a sea of thoughts about how America had gotten into this situation to begin with.

"I should have never gone against my own gut," he bemoaned. He couldn't believe how many voices there had been, talking in his ear, telling him that this was a good idea. The intelligence agencies, his senior military advisors, congressional leaders—they'd all thought that if the US

stood up to Russia, Vladimir Petrov would back down. Then again, he realized that some of them, like Senators McGregor and Grandy, had made their entire careers advocating for military intervention against one country or another.

"I should've paid better attention in history class," thought Gates. He remembered that Eisenhower did warn that the military industrial complex craves for war. *"I wonder if this is somehow what the hawks in my party wanted all along,"* he contemplated.

As the President listened to his advisors brief him on the situation up to this point, it all washed together as one sea of awfulness. The Navy had lost a supercarrier, the Air Force had lost nearly 208 combat aircraft, and a stealth bomber had been shot down outside of Moscow after one of its bombs had gone off course, killing nearly 2,000 civilians. They had already used up or lost nearly $120 billion in military equipment, 8,000 service members had sacrificed their lives already, and nearly twice that number had been wounded.

"Ugh...is there any good news?" wondered the President.

Instead, the advisors moved from the military situation to the international scene. The President had to control himself from audibly groaning. He already knew about the issue with Turkey; they had announced that they were going to remain neutral in the fight with Russia, and they had withdrawn their warships from the NATO fleet in the Black Sea just before the Russian missile swarm attack. Further, Turkey declared that it would no longer allow NATO to use its military bases, in fear that the Russians might launch a strike against them. A few hours ago, the Turkish ambassador to the United States had even suggested to the Secretary of State that they might close off the Bosporus Strait to NATO military traffic.

President Gates had already partially responded to that last issue prior to this meeting. He had personally called President Yavuz. Among other things, he told him, "In no uncertain terms, if you close the Bosporus Strait, I will use all available military force to keep them open, even if I need to destroy the Turkish Air Force and Navy. Do you understand?"

President Yavuz had cursed and hurled numerous accusations at President Gates, but ultimately, he had backed down.

Then there was Chancellor Schneider. The German armored brigade that was fighting alongside the Americans in Kiev had taken horrific combat losses. Casualties were so high that Schneider was reluctant to send additional forces. The Russians had also attacked a German air base near Berlin, causing considerable damage. This assault so close to the German capital had shaken the government to the core and caused them to become hesitant when they needed to be resolute.

Germany wasn't the only country reluctant to send reinforcements to NATO. France and Spain were also hesitant to put more troops in harm's way. Poland was holding the bulk of their army in reserve along the Belarus border as the Russian 4th Army continued to stay deployed not far away from their border. At least the Netherlands, Belgium and Denmark were rushing whatever available forces they could to Ukraine. However, without that additional support from their other allies, it placed an enormous strain on the remaining US forces in Ukraine as they tried to hold out against a significantly larger Russian force. Though he was horrified by the situation, President Gates couldn't help but admire President Petrov; he sure knew where to squeeze the Europeans to get the results he wanted.

As Gates watched his military advisors argue amongst themselves, he turned and watched two of the TV monitors. They created a split screen between CNN and Fox

News. It was amazing to watch them side by side like this and see the almost night-and-day difference in the coverage. CNN had gone from their nonstop coverage of how he was a puppet of Vladimir Petrov to pounding the drum that he had led America into a war it couldn't win against Russia. Fox News seemed to be trying to rally the country around him; they kept talking about how the US was responding to an unprovoked attack by Russia.

Disgusted by the indecisiveness and bickering, the President got up and walked out of the room. He was repulsed by the whole lot of them. American soldiers were fighting and dying in a war they had pushed for, and now they couldn't figure out how to win it. The Russians had suckered-punched them hard. If NATO had been able to hit the Russians on their timeframe, things would have turned out differently, but here they were.

Gates walked back to the Oval Office and sat down in the chair behind his desk. His Chief of Staff, Ishaan Patel, came in right after him.

"Sir, why did you leave the meeting?" he asked, visibly concerned. "We still need to make a number of big decisions…I think you should come back to the Situation Room."

The President looked at his Chief of Staff, who was a good man by all accounts. Then he hung his head down and turned his chair to face the window. As soon as he looked outside, he saw crowds of protesters outside the fence.

"It just doesn't even seem to matter what I do," he lamented. Every decision he made was ridiculed, every action attacked. *"Why did I give up my life to do this?"* he wondered. *"I was so crazy to think that somehow I could fix this country."*

After not saying anything for a moment, he turned around and looked his Chief of Staff in the eye. "Ishaan, I've lost confidence in them. The generals have been wrong from the beginning, and so were Leibowitz, McGregor and Grandy. I trusted these men's judgment. I believed them when they said NATO would hold together. I had confidence in the DIA, CIA, and NSA when they said Russia didn't have the capability to attack us and push our forces out of Ukraine. They were all wrong."

The President let out a long sigh before continuing, "They either lied to us, or they're just incompetent. In either case, Ishaan, I just don't trust their judgment anymore."

Ishaan sat down at the chair in front of his boss's desk. This was a very serious thing that the President had just said. "Sir…I can't say that I'm completely surprised to hear you say this. I feel like we've been misled by some of them as well. However, right now, we're in the middle of a war, and lives are on the line. We need to figure out what we are going to do, and then we can focus on righting the ship."

There was silence as the two men thought. Ishaan decided on a different approach. "Mr. President, if I may, I recommend that Steve and Jonathan come in and we discuss this. We need to get this resolved now, so we can move forward. If we need to fire some people and get new ones in place, then that needs to happen ASAP. We have soldiers dying, and we need to make sure we are doing our best to help them."

The President nodded in agreement. "Make it happen, Ishaan. Tell the generals in the Situation Room to continue with their existing plans for now, fighting the war with the current strategy and orders in place. We will have a meeting tomorrow morning at 0700 to discuss the next steps."

****

An hour later, Stephen Saunders and Jonathan Rosenblatt walked into the Oval Office with Ishaan Patel to discuss a major military shake-up.

The President opened the meeting by saying, "As Ishaan has most likely hinted, I've lost confidence in a number of our military leaders, along with the broader intelligence community. We must replace some of them immediately and get the situation in Europe under control. What I need to know from you three is, who do you think should absolutely stay in place?"

Stephen nodded. He'd been arguing to clean house for a while now. *"It's too bad I met so much resistance from Ishaan and other administration members,"* he thought. They'd told him that he shouldn't shake the system too hard or else it might break. Well, now that they had this horrible military disaster in Europe, at least they could finally make some changes.

"Mr. President," he began, "the men I believe we should leave in place are the National Security Advisor, the Secretary of Defense, and the Secretary of State. For reasons I'll explain later, I do think it's time to let go of the Director of the NSA, though."

Gates shifted in his chair. He wanted to know what that last sentence meant, but he decided not to interrupt.

"Sir, for now, we should leave in place the Director of the CIA and Director of National Intelligence. Even though the intelligence community as a whole has failed you,

435

these leaders are our new appointees and need to be in place to help us right the ship. This may sound severe, but honestly, we need to completely wipe the slate clean when it comes to the vast majority of the intelligence appointees at the SES and GS-15 level. This is the level where the bureaucracy has been truly hamstringing us, setting us up for failure from day one. Our secretaries have done as well as they can with the people the Senate has been appointing, but the continual delay in confirmations has left us operating with far too many holdovers from the previous administration. The red tape, and the failure of the system as a whole, have allowed the poor performers to float to the top, and the country is paying for it in a bad way right now," Stephen said emphatically.

The President nodded. He had heard the saying floating around the government, "failing upwards." Because it was nearly impossible to fire a government civilian, most organizations would promote the poor performers out of their organization. This would get rid of the person and made them someone else's problem. Unfortunately, this often meant that the worst government employees ended up becoming some of the most senior leaders in the government civilian ranks.

"Does everyone else agree with Stephen's assessment?" asked the President.

Ishaan nodded his head. "I've been against a complete house cleaning until we had more of our folks in place, but obviously, with the military catastrophe that is unfolding in Europe, something needs to change. I would add that I recommend we fire most of the generals in charge as well. They supremely misled us, and our soldiers, sailors, and airmen have been paying the price for it." His tone was very solemn, as if speaking at a funeral.

The President's advisor nodded his head in agreement. "The intelligence community has continued to provide us with intelligence that is either false or misleading since the day you were sworn into office. They insisted that Russia didn't have the military ability to effectively attack NATO. We were told time and time again that the Russians' military was old and outdated. Yet, we all sat in that briefing detailing the 1st Armored Division's engagement against those T-14 Armatas. How in the world did the CIA and DIA not know about the tanks' defensive systems? Our antitank missiles aren't even hitting the tanks, and the rounds that do hit bounce off. This is a complete disaster, and thousands of Americans are dead because of it. I agree with Stephen. We need to completely start over when it comes to the upper-level intelligence appointees," he said.

The President took in a deep breath and then let it out. "OK, here is what we are going to do. Tomorrow, we are going to fire the Chairman of the Joint Chiefs, the EUCOM Commander, the Director of the NSA, the Chief of Naval Operations, the Chief of Staff for both the Army and Air Force, along with the Navy Europe Commander. If the Commander of the *Bush* Carrier Group hadn't been killed in that last naval engagement, I would've fired him as well. How was his battle group not ready to deal with a possible submarine attack and then subsequent air attack? I mean, he should have at least put his marines ashore in Romania until we figured out what to do with them. Now most of them are dead." The President felt horrible about how many sailors and marines had died in this war so far. It was appalling, and the public was rightfully outraged and in mourning.

Looking at his Chief of Staff, the President continued, "I want the base commanders at Ramstein and Spangdahlem both fired for allowing their bases to be hit." He paused for a second, weighing the gravity of what he was about to say. "I know that it won't be popular, but I want every appointee from the previous administration who is still in the government to be fired. I want all these people replaced with their deputies for the time being, until we either find a replacement or determine if the deputy should stay in charge." Ishaan was frantically writing everything down. It was going to be a long night crafting all these letters. They would have to bring the press secretary into the loop and make sure she was ready for the morning brief. The media was going to have a field day.

Saunders signaled that he wanted to add something. "Mr. President, as you know, I've been working on laying a trap inside the intelligence community to figure out who has been leaking classified intelligence to the media and potentially to our enemies. This has been an ongoing effort for the past five months, while I've had those three FBI agents working for me down in the basement. We've identified several leakers. Since we're cleaning house tomorrow, I believe it would be a great time to announce who the leakers are and have them publicly arrested and charged with treason."

Everyone turned to Steve in a bit of shock. They knew he had been working on identifying who the leakers were, but they didn't realize he had suspects yet. "How many leakers do we have?" asked the President, his left eyebrow raised.

"On the one hand, I feel some vindication that I might actually get some justice in this whole situation...but why in the world am I just now hearing about this?" wondered the President.

"Sir, just to back up a little—I had planned on telling you during our next one-on-one meeting, now that we have the evidence we need to charge them. I wanted to make sure the FBI agents had everything they would need to make an arrest. We also brought one DOJ lawyer into the mix to make sure she had everything she needed to secure a conviction. She informed me earlier this morning that she does, so we can make the arrests whenever we are ready. Now, as to the leakers—there are twelve leakers at the CIA, eight at the NSA, three inside the DIA, sixteen inside the DoD, eighteen inside the DOJ and nine at the FBI," he said casually. Their mouths dropped.

Ishaan was the first to speak. "Please tell me you have rock-solid evidence on them. Not conjecture, but rock-solid evidence."

"As I said, I've had my FBI team working with a DOJ lawyer to make sure everything is airtight on this one," Steve replied, sounded almost irritated at being questioned. "We also have email, text and phone conversations of each one of them passing classified intelligence to a reporter or foreign intelligence agent. In the dragnet we set up, we also ensnared one Democratic senator, two Democratic congressmen, and one Republican congressman." He had a very smug and satisfied smile on his face.

Jonathan let out a soft whistle. "The question now is, do we charge the congressional members? If we do, do we have enough evidence to make it all stick?" he asked rhetorically.

Saunders replied, "We've them caught dead to rights. I don't see why we would *not* charge them with treason. The American people are sick and tired of politicians being held above the law and getting away with shady stuff like this. We should make an example of them all and perp-walk them in front of the cameras."

Saunders continued before anyone else could jump in and add anything further, "There's one other major concern; one of the folks we identified as a leaker is currently working inside the Pentagon. We believe he's actually a deep-cover SVR operative. We caught a text message that he sent to a known FSB agent operating in New York. The text gave the gist of the national security meeting where you decided that we would forcefully evict the Russians from Ukraine if they didn't withdraw. It was later that same day that the Russians launched their preemptive attack on us."

The President and his other advisers were shocked at the news.

"*This would explain why we were caught off guard,*" thought the President. However, the military should have been able to handle the Russians' attacks. He wondered why the Director of the NSA didn't bring this to his attention right away? Why was he hearing about it several days later from Saunders instead? Something just didn't seem right with the intelligence community that they couldn't identify high value information and get it to his office. "*No wonder Stephen wanted to fire the director,*" he mused.

Ishaan spoke up next. "This is incredible, Steve. I'm still not sure why the NSA didn't bring this to us, but we'll have to find out when we question the director about it tomorrow. In the meantime, Mr. President, I think we should move forward with the arrests of the congressional members who've betrayed our country. We can't have them operating in their positions of power and influence while at the same time disclosing classified intelligence that's now being used against us by our enemies. People are dying because of their actions."

Gates smiled at the thought of having them walked in front of the press while they were formally charged with treason. "OK, then here's what we're going to do. I want the traitors arrested first thing in the morning. We need to stop them from leaking information, especially that Russian agent. Then on Friday, I want the four congressional leaders arrested and charged. At the same time, I want all the firings of the government employees to take place across the spectrum. That will ensure the entire coverage over the weekend will be of the traitors within the government being arrested."

Gates continued, "On Saturday, we'll announce who will be taking over as the new commanders of the positions we just relieved and publicize our new approach to the war in Europe."

Ishaan jumped into the conversation, almost cutting the President off. "Mr. President, we do have one major thing that needs to be taken into consideration. While I agree with the firings, we are in the middle of a ground war with Russia. We still have important decisions that have to be made on what we're going to do next."

Gates nodded. "I agree. I'm not about to lose more soldiers to incompetence. After the SACEUR is fired, I want to speak with the Deputy EUCOM Commander immediately. I want to know from him what the strategy is, along with his recommendations on what we should do next. I want him brought up to speed on what has transpired, and more importantly, I want his advice on what we should do in Europe to right the ship."

The meeting continued for another hour as they dissected the various positions that would need to be backfilled quickly, and which ones could wait a few days or a week. It was going to be the largest shake-up of the government in history, but one that was much needed.

Chapter 42

The Shake-Up

Washington, D.C.

It had been a rough morning, and the day had only started. The Press Secretary, Linda Wagner, had gotten the call late last night to come in extra early because there was going to be a major military shake-up of the situation unfolding in Europe.

When she got off the phone, her husband rolled over and asked, "Do you think America could lose the war with the Russians?"

It caught her off guard. *"If my own husband, who knows more than the average American, thinks that the US could possibly lose the war, then what's the average person thinking?"* she wondered.

She arrived at the office two hours early, to get ready for a staff briefing at 0500. Thank goodness the kitchen crew had brought in some strong coffee and breakfast foods. She hadn't had a chance to eat yet.

As Ishaan went over what had transpired last night, her mouth almost dropped to the floor. She knew there had been military failures. Anyone with eyes had to see all the footage that the media was showing of the frontlines on a continuous loop. People were starting to lose their minds over how badly things were going. The military shake-up didn't seem like that big of a surprise. However, then they moved to the firings, and the congressional members who had been caught leaking classified intelligence to the media.

"*My God...there really were a lot of government civilians leaking classified intelligence,*" she gasped. "*And now there was a spy in the Pentagon?*" It was a lot to take in.

Her mind began to race. "*How do I present this information in a rational manner and try to control the narrative here?*"

She thought back to Roosevelt, and how he had made big changes after Pearl Harbor. It seemed like the right direction to take this. She began to contemplate bullet points that went along with that theme. "*The President is providing decisive leadership in a time of crisis. He is a strong-minded Commander-in-Chief who sees that people have been dying and wants to right the ship before our nation reaches a tipping point,*" she thought.

When the meeting finished, Linda gathered her team and brought everyone up to speed. She began to draft talking points for surrogates to use and for her own staff. This was explosive information that was about to be released, and it was going to cause a lot of alarm across the country. They all needed to have their story straight and spread a united narrative of strong and decisive leadership running at full steam.

An hour later, the Press Secretary walked into the press room and took her place at the podium. For the first time in a while, the press had no idea what was coming, and she relished the fact that they had, at long last, identified the leakers. The two individuals in the White House who had also been identified had been arrested a couple of hours ago, when they'd arrived for work. They were still being held in detention in the basement of the White House until after the briefing was done. There could be no chances taken that the media would spot their two moles being walked out in cuffs—not until after the briefing.

Looking at the wolves before her, she began. "Good morning, America. The President would like to make a brief statement, then I will answer your questions." She took a step back, and then the President walked in through the side entrance and took his place at the podium. The reporters in the room grew restless. They wanted to jump out of their seats to pound the President with questions, but they knew they had to let him speak first.

The President cleared his throat as he pulled out a paper with his notes written on it. He then looked up at the anxious faces before him. "The war in Europe with Russia has been an unmitigated disaster."

The room let out a collective gasp. They couldn't believe President Gates would say such a thing while US forces were still fighting and dying in Europe. They began to scribble quickly, several of them tweeting and sending text messages.

Gates ignored the rapid clicking of keys and continued, "We as Americans look to our military to protect us, to understand the threats that face us and have a plan to deal with them. Likewise, we also look to our political leaders to protect us, to understand the threats and ensure our military has the right resources, leaders, and equipment needed to fight and win America's wars. Sadly, that has not happened, and it is for this reason that I have asked for, and received, the resignation of the Chairman of the Joint Chiefs, the entire staff of the Joint Chiefs, the General of the Army, Air Force, Chief of Naval Operations, and the Commandant of the Marine Corps. I have also relieved the NATO Commander, who is also the commander at US European Command, the Naval Commander Europe, the Commander of US Air Force Europe, and US Army Europe."

More audible gasps could be heard as the press continued to become more and more restless. They were chomping at the bit to yell out questions, but he was not done delivering the news.

"Everyone has seen the numerous videos on the internet and media of the fighting in Europe. A change in leadership was needed, and as president, it is my responsibility to protect our country. To that effect, as the Commander-in-Chief of the Armed Forces, I've taken decisive action and relieved the commanders responsible for both failing our nation, and more importantly, failing the soldiers, sailors, airmen and Marines they are responsible for leading."

"In the aftermath of the Japanese sneak attack at Pearl Harbor, President Roosevelt fired and demoted the military commanders responsible for the defense of Hawaii and the Pacific Fleet. Roosevelt took decisive action and rallied the nation to defeat the Japanese and Adolf Hitler's Germany. Today, I ask for that same support for our armed forces and for the country, to rally together as one nation, so that we can effectively meet this threat imposed upon us by Russia."

"The recent cyberattacks against our power grid and the brazen assault on two of our natural gas export terminals by Russian Special Forces show that they are determined to defeat us, not just on the battlefield, but in cyberspace, the media, and economically. Let me remind you of that attack on our natural gas terminals last night. Those were Russian Special Forces operating on American soil that carried out that attack. Russian soldiers…on American soil." Gates let that sink in for a moment and could see the wheels spinning in the various reporters' heads.

"I have charged the FBI and DHS with finding these saboteurs. In the meantime, I've authorized National Guard units across the country to augment the security around many of our critical infrastructure elements: power plants, bridges, water treatment facilities, and so on. Do not be alarmed if you see soldiers guarding these crucial places. If you see something suspicious, then say something. Report it. Do not wait for another attack to happen."

As he continued to speak, the President could see a sense of bewilderment and then anger in their eyes as the realization of what he was saying was finally sinking in. America had been attacked at home—a foreign army was operating Special Forces on American soil, and that was not sitting well with them. Now he needed to hammer home his message of unity.

"We need to unite as a country and stand together against this threat. Today and tomorrow are going to be days of reckoning for those who have sought to undermine our country and placed us in the danger in which we now find ourselves. I want to assure the American people that your government is going to win this war. We will not surrender or accept defeat at the hands of Vladimir Petrov. I will now leave you with Linda to answer some of your questions. I'll be making another statement this afternoon, so please stay tuned for further information," the President announced.

As he turned to leave the room, the President tilted his head down toward Linda. "You can do this, Linda. I trust you," he encouraged. Then he walked off the stage through the side door, headed back to the West Wing.

Nearly all the reporters jumped to their feet, shouting questions at the President as he slipped away into the hallway. Once Gates had left the room, they all turned to the Press Secretary and immediately began to shout out their questions, hoping she would choose their question to answer.

One of the CNN reporters shouted, "Linda, how can the administration simply fire the heads of all the branches of the military and Joint Chiefs of Staff overnight while the country is in the midst of a military disaster unfolding in Europe?!"

Linda raised her hand to try to calm the roaring lions, so she could start to answer their many questions. She pointed at the CNN reporter who had just shouted at her. "Monica, I believe you just answered your own question," she began. "The situation in Europe is dire. These military commanders were responsible for ensuring our forces were prepared to meet this challenge, and they were not. The President wants to turn things around, and that means replacing those who have failed with others who can do the job," Linda explained. She spoke cautiously but confidently, knowing that the press was currently snapping like a bunch of sharks that had located a source of blood.

The questioning continued for another hour while the major networks continued to report on the massive firings taking place across the military leadership. Several former generals who were employed by the various news agencies were sounding off. Some were calling this a much-needed move and a sign of decisive leadership. Others called it reckless and said it was dangerous to replace so much of the command structure in the middle of a war. Meanwhile, the real conflict continued, both on the battlefield and in cyberspace.

Chapter 43
Traitors

Arlington, Virginia
Pentagon City

Carl Wiggins was nearly done getting ready for work when he saw the breaking news on the TV. "*More news about the war in Ukraine,*" he groaned to himself. He couldn't help but think he'd screwed up, giving the Russians a heads-up on their intentions in Ukraine. They'd told him they were going to use the information to confront President Gates and get him to back down, not use it to launch a preemptive attack. "*What a mess,*" he thought.

As he finished tying his shoes and was just about to grab his sport coat, he heard a knock on the door. Not sure who would be knocking at his door at this hour of the morning, he walked over and opened it to find several men wearing FBI jackets holding their badges in his face as they pushed their way into his apartment.

"Hey, what's the meaning of this?" Carl demanded. "I didn't give you permission to enter my house. I insist that you leave immediately!"

As he spoke, one of the FBI agents grabbed him firmly by arm and guiding him to the living room.

"You are Carl Wiggins, correct?" the agent asked in a forceful tone.

"Yes. I'm Carl Wiggins, and I demand to know what in the world is going on right now!" Carl replied angrily. People were crawling all over his apartment. One agent had a box and was cataloging and then collecting all his electronic devices.

"I'm Special Agent Walt Wittman from the FBI. We have a search warrant to search your home and seize any electronic devices. We also have a warrant for your arrest," he said proudly, as if he had just arrested the most important person of his career.

Carl did a double take before responding. "Arrest? Arrested for what?!" he yelled as Wittman turned him around and began to place his handcuffs on his hands.

"Mr. Wiggins, you're under arrest for espionage and treason. We caught you providing classified intelligence to the Russians," he replied calmly as he began to guide Carl through the doorway and into the hallway of his apartment building. "I advise you to remain silent and not say anything further, Mr. Wiggins."

Carl couldn't believe it. He had been so careful. How could the FBI have found out he was providing intelligence to the Russians? As they placed Carl into the back of a government car, the reality of the situation began to sink in.

"*I'm in serious trouble if they're charging me with treason,*" he thought. That could carry the death penalty…if he wanted to save his own skin, he was going to have to cut a deal.

Chapter 44

Ambush Alley

Prolisky, Ukraine

Sergeant Childers's platoon had taken up residency in the small but strategically positioned village of Prolisky. It was located between the international airport and the city of Kiev, and on one of three major routes the Russian army would have to travel to capture the city. The Russians had hit the British, German, and American armor units near the Boryspil Airport throughout the entire day with both air and ground forces, causing significant casualties despite the arrival of the two BCTs from the 1st Armored Division. The Russians were throwing their best tanks and aircraft into this fight, and the NATO forces were getting hammered. By midafternoon, the bulk of NATO forces had fallen back to the surrounding villages and suburbs around Kiev and would look to make this a street fight unless ordered otherwise.

Lieutenant Taylor walked up to Captain Jordan, the new troop commander, to get some final instructions for his platoon. Both men were physically and mentally exhausted from near-constant fighting.

"Sir, Sergeant Childers and the rest of my platoon are getting the rest of the artillery shells and Claymores ready for the ambush. Once we light it off, my guys are supposed to abandon our positions and run to this point here," he said, pointing to the map. "Then you want them to get ready for the next ambush?" he asked.

Captain Jordan had been the executive officer of Nemesis Troop for the past year. However, earlier in the morning, their captain had been killed during one of the many Russian air attacks. He was then given battlefield promotion to captain and told to take over by their squadron commander. Now he had the job of trying to carry out a series of ambushes designed to delay the Russian advance on Kiev.

"Yes, exactly," Captain Jordan answered. "I have First Platoon here," he explained, showing Taylor a point on the map. "They have another series of artillery shells ready along this stretch of the highway. Once your platoon falls back, they will need to get this position here and get ready for the third and final ambush. If all goes well, we'll get three shots at hitting the Russians along this highway before we fall back to this section of the NATO lines. I was told that the Second BCT from 1st Armor that passed through our lines a couple of hours ago will be positioned here. We'll function as their infantry support until told otherwise."

Their meeting broke up and Second Lieutenant Taylor and the other second lieutenant from First Platoon ran back to their respective platoons to get their men ready for the coming fight. Third and Fourth Platoons had already been consolidated into First and Second Platoons earlier in the morning, when they arrived in the village. The troop had taken more than forty percent casualties since the start of the war, and there was no need to keep four significantly weakened platoons and spread their diminished supply of officers and NCOs across four platoons.

While Lieutenant Taylor had been coordinating the ambush with the rest of the company, Sergeant Childers was having the soldiers string up their Claymore antipersonnel mines and 152mm artillery shells along the highway for the ambush.

"Peterson, you unscrew the fuse cap on the artillery round like this," Childers explained as he demonstrated to a couple of the soldiers in his little group.

"Once you have the fuse cap removed, you take the blasting cap and place it inside the fuse well, and then seal it up like this." After Childers had demonstrated what to do, he took the back of a phone apart and attached a small copper wire from the phone's circuit to another wire attached to the blasting cap.

"As you can see, we need to be careful when we wire this up. Once it's done, each one of these rounds is going to be an independent IED that can be set off by sending a SMS text from this phone. To make sure they all go off at the same time, I've created a group text that will send the message to all of the phones attached to the IEDs simultaneously."

One of the soldiers asked, "How did you learn all this?"

The question broke Childers's concentration for a second and brought a smile to his face. "I learned how to make these things back in 2003 in Iraq, during the invasion. I was with the Rangers, and we had captured a couple of Saddam Fedayeen soldiers who had been building these types of IEDs to use against us. When we raided the building and captured those guys, they had a couple dozen of these things laying around. We had a few of the explosive ordnance disposal guys with us, so they set out disarming them. Later that evening, when we got back to base, I talked with some of the explosive ordnance disposal guys and they walked me through the process of how these guys were building them. As we started to encounter these types of IED ambushes in Iraq and Afghanistan more often, we *all* started to learn a lot more about them—how to build them and how to disarm them."

The soldiers listened to his story intently. They looked at him with a bit more awe and respect. Childers smiled and began to work with the IEDs again, turning their attention back to the task at hand.

"Ok, so look here. Once this is done, be careful as these IEDs are now live. We only have five of the blasting caps, so we have to use these IEDs carefully. I want them placed inside these five buildings lining the street here," he said, pointing to three buildings on the right and two buildings on the left in the center of the village.

"We're going to use these IEDs for our secondary attack. Now, the rest of these 152mm artillery rounds are going to be placed in these vehicles lining the highway here, and along these four street gutters," Childers explained as he showed them where he wanted the remaining artillery rounds placed.

One of the soldiers interrupted to ask, "—Sergeant Childers, if we don't have any additional blasting caps, how are we going to remote-detonate these other IEDs?"

Smiling at the question, Childers reached down and pulled out a roll of detonation cord. "We're going to use some det-cord for these. The ragheads in Iraq used to do this to us. It was pretty effective, but pay attention—this is also dangerous and can kill you if you screw it up. Just like with the blasting cap, you place some of it down into the fuse well, then you wrap it around the round. We are going to daisy-chain the remaining artillery rounds along the side of the highway in these abandoned vehicles here." He pointed down the road.

"In this case, we'll have to trigger this manually. We'll run the trigger wire back to this building here, which I'll be in. I will personally trigger this IED when the Russians enter the kill zone." The blaring percussion of battle down the road at the airport was growing in intensity. It wouldn't be long before the Russians pushed their way through their ambush.

"Now listen up," he said to the soldiers, "I want two of our M240s set up on the right side of the road in these buildings here."

"Then I want the other two M240s placed here, on the left side of the road. This will create a cross fire for our machine guns. Now, we only have two AT4s—I want one on each side of the road, so we have good covering fire. When the Russians move through the ambush, I will detonate the first string of IEDs. If the Russians follow their standard doctrine, which they have thus far, they will dismount their troops from the BMPs and BTRs."

"Those troops are going to fan out and move forward to clear the village," Childers continued. "That's when I want you M240 gunners to let 'em have it. They'll charge the ambush just like we would, only this next time around, they're going to charge right into our second ambush." His face lit up with a devilish grin, almost like he relished the destruction he was about to unleash on the enemy.

"When the Claymores go off, they'll send additional tanks and armored vehicles forward to push through the ambush. You M240 gunners need to get the hell out of Dodge and head to the rally point once you hear the explosions. If you stay too long, I guarantee one of those Russian tanks is going to put a high-explosive round into your position." Childers paused to look at the M240 crews to make sure they understood what he was telling them. He wanted them to stick around long enough to hit the infantry, but they needed to get out of there once the tanks started to move forward again or they would get blown up.

The men all nodded.

Luke pressed on. "Once you guys break contact, I'll send the SMS to the IEDs, and hopefully they will destroy the second group of tanks and armored vehicles."

He sighed loudly, then looked back at his young soldiers and added, "Look, this is going to be tough. It's going to be bloody, and it's going to happen fast. The key to this ambush is going to be speed. So, once it's time to get out of here, you need to run to the rally point like your life depends on it. Don't try to be heroes. Just do your jobs, remember your training, and let's try to get out of this alive, all right?"

The soldiers all nodded in agreement, and responded with, "Yes, Sergeant." Then they went back to work, getting everything set up.

Once Lieutenant Taylor got back to the cluster of houses that sat along the highway, he briefed his men on what the other platoons were going to do and what their plan of action was once they carried out this ambush. They would hit the Russians hard once they walked into their trap and then quickly race to the next ambush point and try to repeat the process. He showed them on the map the second point and where the additional artillery shells had been placed so they could find them when they arrived. He also showed them where they would rendezvous with their unit once they crossed back into the new NATO lines.

Several Ukrainian army units streamed past their positions at this point. They looked ragged and beaten up.

Most of the vehicles had scars cut into them from bullets and shrapnel. The soldiers looked dirty and exhausted—many of them had bandages covering bloody wounds.

Childers had to give the Ukrainian Army credit; they'd fought fiercely against the Russians, despite being heavily outnumbered. Most of the units were simply outmatched by the Russians. It was also hard to integrate them into the fight with NATO, since their unit's communications and digital equipment wasn't interoperable with that used by the US or NATO. The electronic jamming the Russians were using heavily was becoming a problem in keeping the multinational units communicating. However, for some unknown reason, the Russians were not actively jamming cellular service—of course, this was also a lot easier for them to eavesdrop on.

Most of the US Special Forces who had been working with the Ukrainians as military advisors were essentially stuck with those same units, acting as liaison officers and coordinators between US and NATO forces. The interoperability problem was something that had to be overcome, but until additional communications equipment could be integrated into the Ukrainian Army, the SF soldiers and their equipment would have to be the stopgap solution. While this was not ideal, it did mean the Ukrainian units had seasoned combat veterans to help advise them during some of the heaviest fighting.

The next three hours went by with a near-constant stream of Russian ground attack aircraft and helicopters flying all over the place, attacking anything that moved below. As the platoon sat waiting in the village for the final allied troops to withdraw past them, they saw a pair of Su-25s dive down on what was most likely the remaining Ukrainian forces. These fighters were armored like the American A-10s, and they carried dozens of bombs, rocket pods, missiles and a 30mm autocannon.

Thump, thump, BOOM, BOOM. As the black smoke and fire rose in the distance from the latest Su-25 bombing run, Childers thought, "*I wish we could shoot them down.*" However, they had run out of Stinger missiles the day before, and there was no more to be had.

From time to time, they would see a massive aerial battle, but it was hard to tell who was winning and losing. Very seldom did they see an F-16 swoop down and plaster some Russian armor. When they did, they were quickly shot at by multiple air defense vehicles.

"Look at that, Sergeant Childers," one of the soldiers near him said, pointing to the sky.

A single F-16 flew in low over the trees and, in a spectacular display of bravery, headed right for the Russian tanks with his afterburner lit. It released a pair of cluster munitions as it flew over them, only to explode into a million pieces seconds later. A missile that seemed to have come out of nowhere must have hit it.

"Ugh, I was hoping that guy was going to make it," Sergeant Childers said, speaking to no one in particular.

"Hey, here come two more fighters—I think those are Germans," Specialist Cross said excitedly.

The two German Eurofighters tried to provide their countrymen with some close air support, both releasing a pair of 500 lbs. bombs. However, as the two aircraft peeled off to the right and gained altitude, a pair of MiGs came out of nowhere and blotted them both from the sky.

Childers churned through conflicting thoughts. "*It's so unbelievably frustrating to see our air support being shot down like this,*" he groaned to himself. Still, it was encouraging to know that the Air Force was doing their best to support them despite the incredible danger the pilots were placing themselves in.

As the air battle continued and the remaining allied units passed through their ambush back to the new NATO lines, they began to hear the creaking and cracking of metal tracks. It was the unmistakable sound of tanks and other armored vehicles advancing toward them.

One of their scouts radioed in to Lieutenant Taylor and Sergeant Childers, "Nemesis Two-Two, this is Nemesis Two-Four. We have a column of T-90s approaching the village now. Count twelve enemy tanks. We also count eighteen BTRs and at least half a dozen BMPs. Stand by for contact, out."

"Crap. They're bringing in T-90s now instead of T-80s," thought Taylor. He wasn't sure the artillery shells were going to penetrate their armor.

With the scouts at the edge of the town reporting the enemy tanks, it was only a matter of minutes now until they saw the lead vehicles entering their kill zone.

Lieutenant Taylor looked through the window of the building that his squad was in to see if he could spot Sergeant Childers and his crew. They were fairly well hidden, but he thought he could still see them. He looked slightly to his right, not wanting to give away his position as he glanced outside the window. The Russian tanks were well within the kill zone. It looked like Childers was waiting for some of the BMPs and BTRs to get within the box as well.

"A little closer...now I have you guys," Sergeant Childers said to himself as he detonated the daisy-chained artillery rounds.

BOOM, BOOM, BOOM, BOOM. The cars and storm drains the IEDs had been placed in erupted in orange balls of flames as thousands of chunks of scalding-hot metal were thrown into the lead Russian infantry fighting vehicles and the tanks caught in the ambush. The force of the explosion was so great that several of the armored vehicles were thrown over on their sides.

"Now, Cross," Childers said over the platoon net.

Specialist Cross was on the roof of the building next to them. He quickly popped up above the lip of the flat room and aimed his AT4 at the first tank he saw, a T-90. Cross depressed the fire button, igniting the rocket motor. In a split second, the rocket shot out of the tube and slammed into the left rear side of the tank, causing a small explosion. The tank jerked to a stop and the engine area burst into flame.

As Specialist Cross was firing his rocket, a second soldier also popped up and fired off his AT4. Like Cross's rocket, his rocket flew right for the T-90 he had aimed at, only this time, the tank's anti-rocket defense system activated, deflecting the rocket just as it was about to hit the tank. It flew into the dirt and exploded harmlessly.

While this was happening, the Russian soldiers who had been riding inside the infantry fighting vehicles and troop carriers disgorged from their vehicles and fanned out, moving toward the American positions. The Russians poured heavy machine-gun fire toward the roofs of the nearby buildings, trying to kill any soldiers who might be hiding up there with additional antitank weapons.

"Now!" Sergeant Childers yelled over the radio.

The rest of the platoon opened fire on the Russian soldiers, causing most of them to drop to the ground for cover. The M240 gunners raked the Russian positions, crisscrossing the highway with heavy machine-gun fire, killing dozens of enemy soldiers before they even knew what happened.

Lieutenant Taylor saw the building one of his M240 crews was set up in suddenly explode as a tank fired an HE round right into it. In a split second, he watched in horror as the upper torso of Private First-Class Torino got ejected from the building, still holding on to the ammunition belt he had been feeding into the machine gun.

"*Dear God, he's still alive*," Taylor thought to himself as he briefly saw Torino try to crawl to cover, only to get hit by a bullet in the head.

As more explosions rocked the buildings they were hiding in, a massive wave of Russian soldiers began to bumrush their positions, just as the Americans would have done in a similar ambush.

"Where the hell are those Claymores, Sergeant Childers?!" the lieutenant shouted inside his own head. Taylor dropped his 30-round magazine and slapped another one in place, hitting the bolt release. He took aim at the enemy soldiers no more than 50 yards away.

BAM, BAM, BAM, BAM! The entire front half of the wave of enemy soldiers disappeared into a bright red mist of blood, torn uniforms and body parts as the ten Claymore mines detonated, throwing thousands of steel ball bearings into the charging enemy.

"Everyone, get out of here now!" Childers screamed over the radio, hoping to be heard above the cacophony of small-arms fire, explosions, and the screaming of soldiers on both sides.

"These blasted Russians and their doctrine, if they're not predictable," Childers dismayed as he saw several T-90s run over half a dozen screaming wounded soldiers in an attempt to try and push their way through the ambush. Several BMPs and BTRs were quickly trying to

follow the tanks through the village to get out of the kill zone as well.

"Blow it, Sergeant Childers! What are you waiting for?!" Lieutenant Taylor yelled over the platoon net. Childers looked down at the cell phone and hit Send on the text message. In a fraction of a second, the additional IEDs went off, disabling one of the two T-90s and destroying two other infantry fighting vehicles. He then grabbed his M4 and ran out the back of the building, down the alleyway, heading straight for the wooded area not far from the ambush point.

Childers caught up to some of his soldiers, who were panting hard as they were lugging the M240 and extra ammo. As they ran, he heard the whistling sound of incoming artillery rounds and yelled, "Hit the ground!"

Luke and the soldiers near him collectively dove forward and landed hard, skidding briefly on the ground before rolling to a stop. The earth beneath them shook violently as artillery rounds began to strike nearby, throwing enormous amounts of dirt and debris from the surrounding buildings into the area. Craning his neck back to look at the village they had just left, he saw several additional artillery rounds plaster the remaining buildings, leveling everything.

"Come on, guys, we need to get the heck out of here," Childers said as he helped to lift several of his soldiers to their feet and they began to run to their next rally point.

"That attack ought to slow them up a bit while they deal with their wounded," Luke thought.

As Lieutenant Taylor was running through the woods with several of his soldiers he hoped Sergeant Childers and his group made it out all right. As he ran though, he couldn't shake the images he had just seen. His mind raced, filled with the unmistakable yelling and screaming of wounded soldiers, men howling in agony. He saw that young soldier picking up his own severed arm off the side of the road. Taylor's mind could not turn off.

While Nemesis Troop was carrying out their ambushes along the E40 highway, the other troops of the 2nd Cavalry carried out their own traps on the other highways. While none of these ensnarements would stop the Russian advance altogether, it was slowing them down while NATO continued to rush additional forces to Kiev.

Chapter 45

New Commander, New Strategy

Mons, Belgium

Supreme Headquarters Allied Powers Europe

General James Cotton had just arrived in Mons and was viewing the damage to the building from the Russian cruise missile attack that had hit SHAPE at the outset of the war. It was practically a total loss. What few people knew about—and thankfully the Russians had not destroyed—was the newly developed alternate command post built at the opposite end of the military base, which had been cleverly designed as a museum. About fifty feet below the building, was an underground command post that had been built to be used during a time of war. The bunker had been completed in 2014, so it was significantly more modern than the actual command center.

"As you can see, General, we have a Patriot missile battery set up now, and the THAADs are operational again. This type of attack should not happen again," a Belgian colonel said as he finished showing the new SACEUR the damage.

Shaking his head in disgust at how poorly things had gone so far with the war, he resolved to fix the situation and get things back under control. The past 24 hours had been a whirlwind of activity; the President had fired his boss, General Wheeler, and then a host of other generals and admirals to include all the service chiefs. Then he'd fired nearly 300 Senior Executive Service government civilians, along with dozens of deputy and assistant secretaries across the CIA, FBI, DIA, and NSA, because of their colossal failure to understand the true military threat posed by Russia. However, the biggest shake-up to happen—and the one that directly affected his position—was the deep-cover SVR agent who had been recently arrested. This spy had been passing numerous high-level meeting transcripts between the President and his military commanders to the Russians, which would explain why they appeared to always be a step ahead of their moves or lying in ambush of NATO forces.

General Cotton still couldn't believe how many people had been involved in leaking classified intelligence to the media. *"And how in the heck did the SVR get a mole who had access to the National Security Council meeting notes?"* he wondered. These traitors had cost the lives of thousands of military members.

Following a review of the damage, the military escorts led General Cotton to the elevator that would lead them to the underground command center for his morning brief. They needed to get him up to speed on the situation on the ground.

As General Cotton walked into the hallway that led to the operations center, he was impressed with how modern and high-tech the operations center looked. There were dozens of large-screen computer monitors on one of the walls, with various maps and images on them. On a different wall were several different news channels from the various member states. They were all reporting on various aspects of the war.

His escort led him past the operations center, promising him a more thorough tour of the bunker following the meeting. There was a lot that needed to be taken care of, since he had just assumed command of NATO.

Taking his seat at the center of the table at the back of the room, General Cotton said, "All right, let's get down to business. What's the situation in the air right now? Do we have air supremacy yet, or anything close to it?"

His NATO Air Commander, a British air marshal, cleared his throat before proceeding. "General Cotton, we presently do not have air supremacy over the battlefield. We do have control of the skies near the Polish border and the western portion of Ukraine. However, the central and eastern part of the country are in Russian hands. We've attempted to secure the skies over Kiev and the current frontline on numerous occasions over the last twenty-four hours; in each instance, our fighters were either heavily engaged by Russian Su-57 stealth fighters, Su-35s and MiG-31s, or an inordinate amount of SAMs. It's a hot mess right now Sir," the air marshal explained, summarizing the situation.

General Cotton was upset. *"We are going to have to get the air situation sorted out soon,"* he worried. *"This is ridiculous that we haven't been able to secure the air yet."* General Cotton looked around the room, and everyone seemed to be satisfied with the air marshal's response, as if the lack of air superiority over the battlefield was acceptable given the circumstances.

"Please excuse me if I get anyone's names or ranks wrong—I haven't been at NATO long enough to know all your titles and the various ranks structures of your nations' services. For the moment, I will plan on addressing everyone as General, Marshal, Admiral or Colonel, as I would speak to my own country's military members, just for sake of clarity." He saw some people were kind of put off by his lack of wanting to learn their proper military ranks, but frankly he didn't have time. These officers had so fouled up the war unfolding in Ukraine that he didn't care if he offended their sensibilities.

General Cotton continued, "Marshal Pierce, I do not accept that report or that outcome. I want to know why we're five days into this conflict and NATO still doesn't have even 50% air supremacy over the battlefield yet. NATO has spent decades developing plans to handle the Russian Air Force and air defense capabilities. Britain, France, Germany, and others have exceptionally capable air assets to handle the Russian threat. Please explain to me what the problem is, so we can work to address it."

Marshal Pierce looked like a hurt puppy at the comment. He lowered his head and sighed softly before replying, "General, we do not have air superiority because we've sustained heavy aircraft losses, and several member nations haven't committed additional air assets to the campaign yet. Until we get additional squadrons that can be brought to bear, there's only so much we can do. We also do not have the vast array of satellites that we used to. We rely so heavily on them to track and locate the now hundreds of Russians SAMs across Ukraine, and that ability has been seriously degraded." As he spoke, he stared daggers at the

Spanish, French, and Italian officers, who were the biggest offenders in terms of breaking air support promises.

The French Air Force General shot back, "Marshal Pierce, I know this looks bad, and believe me, I wish there was more we could do. We are being held back by our president. He has not authorized the release of additional squadrons to NATO control." He spoke angrily to the British air marshal, as if he personally was holding out on them.

General Cotton knew there had been a lot of consternation between the military members of NATO and their political counterparts. The NATO military generals wanted to beat back the Russians, but the lack of resources being released by the political leaders of these member states was greatly affecting their ability to adequately respond to the Russian invasion of Ukraine. He knew President Gates was working on this, but he sure hoped it got resolved quickly.

"Nothing like fighting a battle with both arms tied behind your back," he thought.

"I understand everyone here wants to get in the fight. I know there's a lot of pressure being placed on you all by your elected officials right now, and they are the ones holding up the release of the requested forces. President Gates and Ambassador Wilkins, our new ambassador to

NATO, are currently working that issue with your leaders right now. What I need from all of you is a plan that will be ready to execute as we get more forces released. We need anti-SAM missions drawn up, we need air superiority missions drawn up, we need our supply lines to start flowing, and men and material moved to the battlefield as quickly as possible. There's a tremendous amount of work that needs to happen while we let the politicians sort things out," General Cotton explained, trying to light a fire under everyone. NATO had vast war supplies across the various member states. It was time to start getting them opened and on the move to the frontlines.

Just then, a Turkish officer walked in and whispered something to General Mehmet Yamut, handing him a note. General Yamut was the Turkish military representative, responsible for coordinating Turkey's efforts in the war against Russia. He turned his head slightly and then did a double take at the officer who just brought him the note. He whispered something back, and the officer nodded, then quickly left the room.

At first, no one responded. Then all eyes turned to General Cotton and then to General Yamut, who raised his hand to signal that he needed to address the group. Cotton nodded for him to go ahead. "Colleagues, I want you to know that I do not agree with this decision," Yamut began. "Most of the general officers within the military will be unhappy as well, but our president has directed that no Turkish military forces will participate in this war against Russia. Our nation conducts a large percentage of our international trade with Russia, and our president doesn't wish to upset that relationship—even if it means not honoring our agreement with NATO," he explained as he squirmed in his chair. He was clearly not comfortable with providing this statement in front of the other NATO member states.

General Cotton already knew the Turkish government was not going to support NATO in the current war with Russia. He also knew what he had to do, as uncomfortable as it might be.

"I understand your position, General. I also understand that this is a political decision being made by your government and not something the military agrees with. However, if Turkey is not going to honor its military commitment when the organization was clearly attacked, then Turkey can no longer be a part of the planning of the war or take part in any of the war updates. My understanding is that Ambassador Wilkins, at the direction of our president, will move to have Turkey removed from the alliance for its failure to live up to its obligation."

A collective gasp filled the room.

General Cotton continued, "While this is a political decision, as the SACEUR responsible for the defense of Europe and the lives of hundreds of thousands of soldiers, I cannot allow you to remain privy to the war plans being developed or implemented by NATO." He took a deep breath before he dropped the final hammer. "I kindly ask that you excuse yourself from the room while we continue to discuss the war."

Many of the generals in the room had their mouths wide open in surprise. No one had ever asked another member state to leave before, and no one had ever told a member state they could no longer participate in any further military discussions, planning, or updates either.

General Yamut nodded. He was upset to be asked to leave, but he understood. He gathered his things and walked out of the room while everyone watched in silence.

With the uncomfortable tension still hanging in the air, General Cotton addressed the rest of the representatives at the table. "Before we continue with the war update, are there any other member states who are not going to honor their military agreements?"

Silence filled the room as everyone stared down all their counterparts. Then, to everyone's shock and horror, first the Hungarian general and then the Spanish general both stood up and walked out.

"*What in the world is going on?*" thought General Cotton. However, there was no time to dwell on it. There was only time to move forward.

Chapter 46
Before You Leave

Kiev, Ukraine

Sergeant Childers counted to two, then leaned slightly out the window and dropped the grenade he had been holding into the gaggle of soldiers stacking up against the wall of the ground floor below him. The Russians immediately dove for cover as the grenade went off, killing and injuring many in the group that had been piling up to breach their building. As Childers quickly ducked his head and arm back inside the building, the windowsill exploded into splinters and shards. The soldiers below him and outside the building opened up on where he had just been. Lying on his belly, he crawled quickly out of the room and into the hallway before getting up and running quickly to the back of the building and into the next room. One of his soldiers was waiting for him as he arrived and waved him through the hole they had cut out in the wall that allowed them to pass from one building to another.

"You sure stirred up a hornet's nest out there, Sergeant," the private said with a wicked grin.

"You could say that," Luke responded, snickering. Then his facial expression quickly turned serious. "Hey, they're going to breach the first floor shortly. Get the charge set and let's get out of here. We need to get to the next building before they arrive."

Childers stopped a minute to catch his breath as the other soldier finished tying the tripwire to the Claymore mine. When the Russians saw the hole between the two buildings, they would rush through it in hopes of following the Americans. If they did, they would hit the tripwire, causing the Claymore to go off. Hopefully, it would take several more of them out.

The Russians had finally punched through the NATO lines at the outskirts of the city ten hours ago, and it had been a mad melee of house-to-house fighting ever since. The German brigade was supposed to fall back in an orderly manner and allow time for the new lines to form, but the Russians had gotten to them before they reorganized, and the brigade collapsed. A group of Su-25s dove on the Germans and took out a good chunk of their tanks. The Russians saw a weak spot and fully exploited it, resulting in the breakdown of part of the city's defenses. Once they had a hole in the lines, they rammed as many units as possible through it, crumpling much of the NATO lines.

Nemesis Troop was forced to take cover in a block of buildings not far from Patona Bridge. British engineers had dropped the Darnyts'kyi Bridge when the breach in the lines had occurred but had been unable to successfully destroy the Patona Bridge before it was captured. A company of American tanks tried to recapture the bridge with support from a British infantry unit, but was summarily beaten back by waves of precision guided antitank missiles. At first, no one knew where the missiles were coming from, since there were no Su-25s in the area. Then a British soldier spotted them off in the distance—drones. The Russians had brought forward nearly a dozen of their newest antitank infantry support drones for this battle, the now-infamous Zhukovs.

Each one of the drones carried six antitank missiles, which quickly wiped out the American tanks attempting to re-secure the bridge, or at least get in position to destroy it. It was a blessing and a curse when those drones finally left— a blessing because they had run out of missiles, a curse because everyone knew they would be back and wreak further havoc.

The remnants of Sergeant Childers's platoon was now held up in a building several blocks away from the bridge, doing their best to slow the Russians up and find a way out of the city themselves. Word had come down from the higher-ups that NATO was going to abandon the city and that the Allied forces should begin conducting a fighting retreat. This made a lot of sense. However, the problem was, a lot of Allied units had been lost or cut off in various parts of the city from the other main elements, leaving thousands of soldiers in a bad spot. Unless the area commander could figure out where the pockets of Allied soldiers were all taking cover and find a way to break some of them out, a lot of soldiers were going to end up being captured as they ran out of ammo.

Chapter 47
Taking Flight

Warsaw, Poland
US Embassy

Ambassador Duncan Rice could not believe how badly things were playing out in Ukraine. He had tried to warn the President and his national security team of the grave consequences if they backed Russia into a corner, and now everyone was paying the price for it. As he sat in the Chancellery, reading the latest intelligence summary, he thought he might be sick. NATO had really underestimated the Russians' capability to wage war and overestimated their ability to defeat them.

It had only been 24 hours since his own embassy in Kiev had to be evacuated to Warsaw. Ten hours later, the Ukrainian government fled to the city of Lviv in western Ukraine when it became clear NATO was not going to be able to hold Kiev. There were reports now of numerous US, German, and British units trapped in various parts of Kiev as the Russians continued to envelop the city, attempting to capture as much of the NATO army as possible.

Just then, Duncan's phone rang. Looking at his secured smartphone, he saw the caller ID. It was the Beijing embassy, and he knew it was his old friend Vincent Jones, one of the senior political officers at the embassy. They had gone through their diplomatic training together many years ago and had stayed in touch ever since.

"Hello, Vincent. How are you doing, my friend?" he asked jovially.

"I'm doing good, Duncan. This was the first chance I've had to call and see how *you're* doing. I heard they had to evacuate the embassy yesterday," he said with genuine concern in his voice.

"Yes, the Russian army was advancing quickly on Kiev. It's believed they will capture it sometime today," Ambassador Rice responded sadly.

"That's terrible," replied Vincent. "From what we're following, it looks like the war isn't going well for our side. Is there anything Jennifer and I can do for you and your family?"

"No, we're fine. My wife and the kids flew back to the States two weeks ago, so they are safe. I'm just trying to do what I can to help mediate things and see if we can work out a ceasefire, but I'm not hopeful," Duncan said candidly.

"You are probably too busy right now, but things are starting to take a turn here in China as well. The Chinese see the US in a weak position with how the war is shaping up in Ukraine. Our Defense Attaché's Office and others at the embassy had a briefing with the ambassador, showing a significant troop increase all along China's southern and southwestern borders. We are not sure what's going on yet, but they may be looking to take advantage of the situation and expand their own borders, knowing that the US has little in the way of stopping them."

Duncan thought for a moment. This was troubling. Petrov had practically staged this entire event to turn out the way he wanted. Now things were starting to heat up with Iran in the Straits of Hormuz, and China was moving soldiers to their borders. *"Could this possibly be a well-orchestrated global event?"* he wondered. It certainly would make sense, given how fractured politically America had become at home.

"This is rather disturbing, my friend," Duncan said aloud. "I need to let you go. I have to talk with someone about something. Some pieces are finally starting to fit together. Please stay safe, and we'll talk again soon."

As he ended the call, he leaned back in his chair thinking for a minute. *"What could all this mean? Could it really be a global conspiracy?"* he wondered. It seemed a bit crazy that he was contemplating whether or not there was a plot to taint the US 2016 elections, cause scandal after scandal, and then orchestrate a military expansion in Europe and Asia while America was distracted.

Duncan had to shove those thoughts aside for the moment. He had a briefing with the embassy staff in a few hours, and he needed to get caught up on the latest happenings in the war. The ambassador in Poland was going to reach out to the Russian ambassador here and see if they couldn't find a way to end the fighting.

Ten minutes into reading the various intelligence summaries, it became clear that as bad as the military front was, the diplomatic front was in even worse shape. Due to the sustained disinformation campaign being played out by the Russians, the general population in each of the NATO member states was increasingly against their country joining the war. Yesterday evening, President Yavuz had announced that Turkey would not participate in any armed conflict against Russia. That announcement was quickly followed by Hungary and Spain also signaling that they wouldn't participate in the war.

As Ambassador Duncan read on, there were at least some glimmers of hope in the responses of the world leaders.

The British prime minister had called this a blatant act of sabotage to the NATO alliance and publicly chastised the heads of Turkey, Hungary, and Spain. The presidents of Italy and France, along with the Chancellor of Germany, announced their support of the alliance and, at long last, released their armed forces to the command of SACEUR and NATO high command. President Gates, along with the leaders of France, Germany, and the UK, had called for the removal of Turkey, Spain, and Hungary from NATO for their failure to honor their military obligation.

Several other NATO members said this was too rash of a move to make while in the midst of a war, while others said any member not willing to honor its agreement should lose its membership.

While the politics of NATO was quickly becoming a mess, President Gates had announced the deployment of 250,000 US soldiers to Europe and called on all able-bodied men and women in America to answer the nation's call to arms and join the military, attempting to rally the nation to unite against Russia. Had the Russians not carried out a domestic attack against America's energy export industry, his call for unity might have failed. As it was, Gates was able to fully capitalize on this supreme political miscalculation by Moscow. The people of the US were hot for revenge.

Then the President asked for a formal declaration of war by the US Congress, even though a state of war had essentially existed for several days. He also asked Congress to double the size of the current armed forces and announced the activation of the entire Reserve and National Guard Forces. This war was spiraling out of control fast. If someone didn't get things under control in Washington and in Europe, this could turn nuclear.

Just as Duncan's thoughts were turning dark, his phone buzzed. He looked at it and saw on the caller ID it was from the White House. He picked up and said, "Hello, this is Ambassador Rice."

"Hello, Ambassador Rice, please hold for the President," he heard the voice of the White House operator say. Duncan was in shock.

A minute went by and then he heard the President pick up. "Ambassador Rice, I think you and I should talk some more. I'm in need of some clear, level-headed advice on this unfolding disaster in Ukraine, and I believe you may be able to help provide that. Can I count on you to travel back to Washington and give us some insight?" asked the President.

Duncan didn't know what to say at first. This was exactly what he had wanted, and now the opportunity had presented itself. This was a real chance to help right this situation before it could spiral any further out of control. He knew there was only one answer he could give. "I'll be on the next flight to Washington, Mr. President. Thank you for thinking of me," he replied, and then the President hung up.

****

Less than twenty-four hours later, Ambassador Rice was standing under the covered entrance to the JW Marriott hotel in Washington, D.C. His chartered flight from Warsaw had arrived nine hours ago, which meant he had only had enough time to catch a couple of hours of sleep, talk briefly to his family and get dressed for his meeting with the President. As he stood under the covered entrance, looking out at the city, everyone was rushing around doing their normal activities as if it was just any ordinary day. Being there, it was as if there wasn't a major war with Russia going on, and there were no men and women dying in a foreign land.

Just as he was about to get lost in his thoughts, a black Chevy Suburban pulled up. As it came to a halt, the front passenger door opened, and a solidly built African-American man with a black suit, sunglasses, and an earpiece stepped out and walked up to him.

"Are you Ambassador Duncan Rice?" he asked in a very serious tone as he surveyed the surrounding area.

Duncan hadn't been expecting the Secret Service to pick him up for this meeting; he'd thought a regular State Department vehicle would collect him. Duncan nodded and replied, "Yes, I'm Ambassador Rice."

The agent then walked toward the rear passenger-side door and held it opened for Duncan. As he walked over to the door and began to get in, he saw Secretary of State Johnson sitting in the other seat.

"Mr. Secretary, I wasn't expecting you. Good morning," he said as he got into the vehicle. The Secret Service agent closed the door and the vehicle began to move the short distance to the White House.

"I wanted to personally greet you, Duncan, and welcome you home. You were placed in a tough position in Ukraine. I wanted to let you know you've done a good job trying to defuse the situation and prevent this war from happening."

Rice snorted slightly before responding. "It doesn't seem like any of that did any good at preventing this war from starting, though. I fear things are now going to spiral out of control, and I'm not sure what can be done to stop that from happening," Duncan replied, clearly dismayed.

Johnson sat there for a minute, not saying anything as he looked out the window. They were approaching the vehicle entrance at the back of the White House. The driver flashed his ID and so did his partner. The vehicle was quickly waved through and directed over to the area for further inspection before being allowed to drive up to the building.

Secretary Johnson turned and looked at Duncan. "I know you're frustrated, and you have every right to be. Right now, it's our job to provide the President with the best possible counsel and advice we can to help bring an end to this war, or at least ensure it stays conventional. Do you think you can work with me and the President on doing that, Duncan?"

As Duncan thought about what his boss had just said, the phrase "keep it conventional" sent shivers down his spine. Russia was a nuclear power, and it was not out of the question that they could potentially use those horrible weapons to achieve the political and military outcome they were looking for.

He turned and faced the secretary. "I will do my utmost to help end this conflict, Sir."

Before either man could say anything further, their doors were opened, and they exited the vehicle. They followed their escorts into the building and through security to the corridor that would take them to the West Wing. The last time Duncan had been to the White House was during the last administration, when he had been officially appointed as ambassador to Ukraine. It had been the crowning achievement of his diplomatic career, to be officially recognized as an ambassador on behalf of the United States.

As the two men entered the Oval Office, they saw the President get up and walk toward them. He greeted Johnson with a warm smile and a firm handshake. Then he turned to Duncan. "Ambassador, thank you for traveling here to meet with me today. We have much to talk about." He gestured for them to take a seat at the couches near the fireplace.

A couple of stewards brought everyone some coffee, and they got down to business. The President looked at Duncan and began, "Ambassador, whether we like it or not, we now find ourselves in a shooting war with Russia. What I need from you is some frank and honest assessments on the political environment in Ukraine and Russia. I need to have a better understanding of what Petrov's goals may be and see if there's a way to end this war before more blood is shed."

Duncan thought about that for a minute before responding, then he steeled himself and gave his assessment.

"Mr. President, Petrov believes the US and NATO have been closing in on him. He's angry over the inclusion of nearly every former Warsaw Pact nation into NATO. The sanctions against his country's economic and political leaders are viewed internally as America's way of removing him, and the oligarchs who control much of Russia, from power. They view the US's actions over the last seventeen years as a preemptive move toward regime change," he explained, trying to clarify how they had gotten to this point.

The President sat there listening intently to what Ambassador Rice had to say. Then he posed his own question. "You believe Ukraine's move to join the EU was the last straw—his red line that we, along with the Ukrainian government, crossed?"

Duncan nodded before replying, "Yes, Mr. President. With acceptance into the EU, membership in NATO was a foregone conclusion. When the US signed the lease to establish a military ground and air base in Ukraine, it brought Petrov's worst fear to fruition. Russia was officially surrounded by US and NATO military bases, and it would only be a matter of time before we destabilized his government and removed him from power. It was at that moment that he had nothing left to lose and everything to gain by attacking NATO."

"Petrov had to know the US and NATO would fight back. Why would he risk a full-scale war?" the President probed, trying to better understand Petrov's reasoning.

Duncan let out a short sigh. "Petrov knows he would lose a long war with America, so he has no intentions of fighting a long war. His objective, which I'm sure your military advisors have told you, is to remove NATO from Ukraine and then negotiate a peace agreement. Petrov knows he can win a short war. He knows it will take months for the US to mobilize for war, and even longer for the Europeans. If he can succeed in pushing NATO out of Ukraine, he can then move to create a peace deal through the UN and the people of our country. The NATO member countries would clamor for us to agree to whatever terms he gives if it means ending the war. This is what he's fighting toward," Duncan explained, feeling better now that he had put into words what he knew Petrov was going to do. It was a relief to be able to say it directly to the one person who mattered, the President of the United States.

Gates sat back on the couch and looked up briefly, thinking to himself. He then looked directly at Duncan and asked, "Do you think we should give in to him, or fight him tooth and nail?"

Duncan was a bit taken aback by the question. He wasn't sure how to respond. "Sir, that's not my decision to make. I am only an ambassador. Only you and the secretary here can answer that question," he finally replied.

The President smiled slightly at the answer, then nodded. "You've given me a lot to think about, Ambassador Rice. I'd like you to stay in D.C. for the time being and work with Johnson here on trying to negotiate an end to this conflict. Arrange a time to meet with the Russian ambassador to the US and start to see what their ideal end-state might look like. I'm not saying we are going to agree to their terms, but I'd like to know what they're thinking so that we can plan around them."

Duncan nodded his agreement, and the President concluded the meeting.

As Ambassador Rice got up, he shook the President's hand one last time and then left the Oval. He was escorted out of the building and offered a ride to the State Department. He accepted the offer and was driven to the headquarters building where he was met by the Russian desk team. Then they led him to a temporary office and he began to work on arranging a meeting with the Russian ambassador.

Chapter 48

Techno-Communism Convention

Novosibirsk, Siberia

Marins Park Hotel

The flight to Siberia had been long but uneventful. It was probably the last time that President Xi and Chairman Zhang would travel together before their part of the global plot to remove the US and NATO as world powers went into full swing. This would also be the final time the two men would meet with President Petrov and his two closest advisors, Alexander Bortnikov and Foreign Minister Lavrov.

It had been risky for Petrov to leave Moscow; NATO had been carrying out several deep strikes within Russia. They had nearly killed Petrov during the first couple days of the war, when the Americans had bombed the military headquarters building. After that close call, his security service was now moving Petrov to a different location every couple of days.

President Xi looked out the window as his vehicle sped through the old Russian city. It was beautiful seeing the old Byzantine architecture and the blending of both Asian and European cultures. Then he watched in disgust as they drove by signs for McDonald's and Coca Cola.

Xi bemoaned that the morally corrupt Western culture had permeated the fiber of every nation. *"Well, that's about to change,"* he thought. Soon, it would be the Chinese and Russian influences that would permeate the world.

The Kortezh limousine slowed down and began to pull into the Marins Park Hotel, and several security personnel immediately fanned out to protect the approach of the vehicle. While they pulled up to the covered front entrance, one of the security guards moved forward to open the door for the leaders of China and proceeded to guide them into the building. As Chairman Zhang stepped outside, the crisp cool air of a Siberian autumn hit his face, causing him to momentarily shiver.

Once the group entered the hotel, they proceeded to walk down a hallway until they reached a conference room that was flanked by additional security personnel. It was very dangerous for President Petrov to be anywhere outside of a bunker. If NATO knew of his presence, they would most likely try to assassinate him with a cruise missile or one of their fancy stealth bombers.

As the leaders of China entered the conference room, President Petrov smiled and walked up to them, shaking their hands. "It's good to see you both. I'm sorry we aren't able to hold a formal state dinner for you. However, as you know, NATO is very intent on trying to kill me if they get the chance," he said with a smile and a slight chuckle.

The men laughed at the craziness of political assassination during a war. Not since World War II had another world power tried so hard to kill the other warring party's leader—as if a war ended with the death of the leader. After a few pleasantries were exchanged, the men began to take their seats.

Knowing their time together was limited, President Xi opened the discussion. "I'll admit, I was skeptical that your plan to seize Ukraine would work. However, it seems that your forces caught NATO by surprise. As a matter of fact, we didn't believe the American technology to be nearly as far behind as your forces have demonstrated."

Xi continued, "The speed with which your forces were able to remove NATO from eastern Ukraine was incredible. We are also impressed with the S-400 air defense weapon and the S-500 ballistic missile defense system. I'm exceedingly happy that we purchased so many of these defensive systems from Russia the past few years. The Americans seem to be impotent in stopping them."

President Petrov smiled at the compliment, and then responded, "While the Americans have spent nearly a trillion dollars on a stealth fighter program, we've spent a fraction of that on building systems that can defeat it. The new Lenovo targeting software is absolutely incredible at being able to examine both the heat and air displacement of a stealth aircraft—it's as if they have no stealth system at all."

Petrov lifted his cup of tea to his lips and took a small sip, savoring the flavor before swallowing. "Defeating America and NATO, while challenging, is not insurmountable. Look at America now. We have so thoroughly distorted their media and news agencies that the public no longer believes anything they say. Our social media groups have taken the term 'fake news' to a new level, dividing the public in the NATO member states and America to the breaking point. Instead of being unified against us in this war, nearly half of the American people are sympathetic to Russia."

The Russian president leaned forward to make his next point. "Xi, this is our time. America and the Europeans have never been weaker—both economically and militarily, than they are right now. Now is the time to strike."

President Xi nodded. He didn't need any further convincing. A mischievous smile curled at the corners of his mouth. "When we return to Beijing, we'll issue the orders to start our part of Operation Red Storm. The Americans and Europeans will never know what hit them when we annex Southeast Asia and the Korean Peninsula is once again united."

It was time to introduce the world to techno-communism. They would spend hours discussing the details, but the cogs had already been set in motion. The men behind Red Storm would soon be the only true leaders of superpowers in the world.

From the Authors

Miranda and I sincerely hope you have enjoyed this book. We just finished up writing the last book in the Red Storm series, and now we are currently working on a modern civil war series. In the meantime, we do have several audiobooks coming out. *Battlefield Ukraine*, *Battlefield Korea*, and *Battlefield Taiwan* have all been released in audiobook and the rest of the books in the Red Storm Series are currently in production. The first three books of the World War III series are available on audiobook now, and the final book should be released by the end of the year.

If you would like to stay up to date on new releases and receive emails about any special pricing deals we may make available, please sign up for our email distribution list. Simply go to http://www.author-james-rosone.com and scroll to the bottom of the page.

As independent authors, reviews are very important to us and make a huge difference to other prospective readers. If you enjoyed this book, we humbly ask you to write up a positive review on Amazon and Goodreads. We sincerely appreciate each person that takes the time to write one.

We have really valued connecting with our readers via social media, especially on our Facebook page https://www.facebook.com/RosoneandWatson/. Sometimes we ask for help from our readers as we write future books—we love to draw upon all your different areas of expertise. We also have a group of beta readers who get to look at the books before they are officially published and help us fine-tune last-minute adjustments. If you would like to be a part of this team, please go to our author website: http://www.author-james-rosone.com, and send us a message through the "Contact" tab. You can also follow us on Twitter: @jamesrosone and @AuthorMirandaW. We look forward to hearing from you.

You may also enjoy some of our other works. A full list can be found below:

World War III Series
Prelude to World War III: The Rise of the Islamic Republic and the Rebirth of America
Operation Red Dragon and the Unthinkable
Operation Red Dawn and the Invasion of America
Cyber Warfare and the New World Order

Michael Stone Series
Traitors Within

The Red Storm Series

Battlefield Ukraine

Battlefield Korea

Battlefield Taiwan

Battlefield Pacific

Battlefield Russia

Battlefield China

For the Veterans

I have been pretty open with our fans about the fact that PTSD has had a tremendous direct impact on our lives; it affected my relationship with my wife, job opportunities, finances, parenting—everything. It is also no secret that for me, the help from the VA was not the most ideal form of treatment. Although I am still on this journey, I did find one organization that did assist the healing process for me, and I would like to share that information.

Welcome Home Initiative is a ministry of By His Wounds Ministry, and they run seminars for veterans and their spouses for free. The weekends are a combination of prayer and more traditional counseling and left us with resources to aid in moving forward. The entire cost of the retreat—hotel costs, food, and sessions, are completely free from the moment the veteran and their spouse arrive at the location.

If you feel that you or someone you love might benefit from one of Welcome Home Initiative's sessions, please visit their website to learn more: https://welcomehomeinitiative.org/

We have decided to donate a portion of our profits to this organization, because it made such an impact in our lives and we believe in what they are doing. If you would also like to donate to Welcome Home Initiative and help to keep these weekend retreats going, you can do so by visiting the following link: https://welcomehomeinitiative.org/donate/

Acronym Key

ASAP	As soon as possible
ASW	Anti-Submarine Warfare
ATU	Anti-Terrorism Unit
AWACS	Airborne Warning and Control System
BCT	Brigade Combat Team
BG	Brigadier General
BMP	Boyevaya Mashina Pekhoty (Russian infantry fighting vehicle)
BTR	Bronetransportyor (Russian armored personnel carrier)
CAG	Commander, Air Group
CAP	Combat Air Patrol
CIA	Central Intelligence Agency
CIC	Combat Information Center
CID	Criminal Investigation Division
DCOM	Deputy Commander of US European Command
DDoS	Distributed Denial of Service
DIA	Defense Intelligence Agency
DNI	Director of National Intelligence
DoD	Department of Defense
DOJ	Department of Justice

EU	European Union
EUCOM	European Command
FBI	Federal Bureau of Investigations
FDC	Fire Direction Command
FIST	Fire Support Team
FSB	Federalnaya Sluzhba Bezopasnosti (Russian intelligence agency that came after the KGB)
GRU	Glavnoye Razvedyvatel'noye Upravleniye (Russian military intelligence)
HARM	High-Speed Anti-Radiation Missile
IBA	Individual Body Armor
IED	Improvised Explosive Device
IFV	Infantry Fighting Vehicle
IoT	Internet of Things (all devices that are network-enabled, including thermostats, cars, printers, etc.)
JDAM	Joint Direct Attack Munition
JIOC	Joint Intelligence Operations Center
JSOC	Joint Special Operations Command
LATV	Light Armored Tactical Vehicle
LLDR	Lightweight Laser Designator Rangefinder
LNG	Liquid Natural Gas
LNO	Liaison Officer

LT	Lieutenant
MANPADS	Man-Portable Air Defense System
MBT	Main Battle Tank
MEU	Marine Expeditionary Unit
MG	Major General
MOP	Massive Ordnance Penetrator
MRAP	Mine-Resistant Ambush Protected
MRE	Meal-Ready-to-Eat
NATO	North Atlantic Treaty Organization
NCO	Noncommissioned Officer
NSA	National Security Advisor *or* National Security Agency
PM	Prime Minister
PR	Public Relations
PRC	People's Republic of China
PV2	Private 2
QRF	Quick Reaction Force
RPG	Rocket Propelled Grenade
RSO	Regional Security Officer
S2	Intelligence Officer
S3	Operations Officer
SACEUR	Supreme Allied Command, Europe
SAD	Special Activities Division
SAM	Surface-to-Air Missile

SAR	Search and Rescue
SCIF	Sensitive Compartmented Information Facility
SDO	Senior Defense Officer
SecDef	Secretary of Defense
SES	Senior Executive Service
SHAPE	Supreme Headquarters Allied Powers, Europe
SINCGAR	Single Channel Ground and Airborne Radio System
SVR	Sluzhba Vneshney Razvedki (Russia's external intelligence agency, mainly for civilian affairs)
Tbps	Terabit per second
THAAD	Terminal High-Altitude Area Directory
TOW	Tube-launched, Optically Tracked, Wire-guided or Wireless
WP	White Phosphorus

Made in the USA
Monee, IL
26 June 2021

72338707R10282